ONE MORE *Time*

NIK ROBBINS

Content Warnings

Alcohol Consumption
Assault
Attempted murder
Blood
Bullying
Cheating
Other Woman
Other Man Chemical Drugging
Child Endangerment
Death Of A Character
Degradation (With A Praise)
Depression
Divorce
Defense Of Narcissistic Behavior
Dom/Sub Interaction
Explicit Sex Scenes
Gaslighting
Grief and Loss
Gun Violence
Hostages
Humiliation
Hooker Is A Term Of Endearment
Kidnapping
Parental Neglect (Not By MC)
Photos Without Consent
Photos Of Deceased Animals
Physical Abuse Of Spouse

Revenge
Self-Depreciation: Thoughts, Verbal
Slight Bongade/BDSM
Slut Shaming
Stalking
Manipulation Of Child For Parental Gain
Mental & Verbal Abuse On Spouse & Child
Mentioning Of The Devil/Hell
Mentioning Of Death Of A Child (Not MC's)
Mention Of Miscarriage
Mentioning Of Religious Trauma/Cult
Mentioning Of Terminal Illness (In Passing)
Murder
Murder Of Aquatic Pets
Narcissistic Behavior
Trauma Responses: Anxiety Attack, Shutting Down, Over Apologizing, Violence
Questioning A Victim
Vomiting

Disclaimer:

This is book one in a duet, the duet will end with an HEA. But, first. They must suffer as I have suffered.

If you or anyone you know is contemplating suicide or the victim of domestic violence, please use the resources below. I see you, I hear you, I love you and I'm glad that you're here.
Suicide Prevention Lifeline 1-800-273-TALK (8255)
National Domestic Hotline 24/7 availability 1-800-799-7233
SMS: Text START to 88788

Prologue

Kye

"Hey fucker, get me another beer while I piss won't ya?" Tommy yells at me over the roar in the bar.

Venturing in downtown Salt Lake City on one of the coldest nights of the year wasn't part of my plan. A bottle of bourbon awaits me back at my apartment. Drinking the pain of *her* refusal away and licking my wounds alone sounds pretty fucking good right about now. Instead, I'm elbow to elbow inside this crowded sports bar with one of the most misogynistic assholes on this forsaken planet.

Warm beer washes down the honey hot wings Tommy had me order while I try to catch the last MMA fight of the night. The TV screen flashes brightly as the announcers hype up the crowd ringside. It's the perfect excuse to ignore the bartender, whose advances are painfully obvious.

After exhaling a sigh of relief for my moment of peace, I take another swig of beer. My patience growing thinner with each sarcastic remark from Tommy about needing to get my dick wet has worn on me. Do I consider him a friend? I mull over the question for a bit. I haven't trusted anyone since that catastrophic cluster fuck in Phoenix. No, we're not friends, more like drinking partners. He's a safe spotter at the gym where we met but wouldn't be my first choice to call for a conversation or financial advice. As long as he doesn't talk too much, we can share a few beers.

The bartender is an entirely different story. I *could* take her in the back and give her a quick fuck. Use her body to find my own release before walking away. The option is clearly there.

Her tits have been in my face since I sat down, and she's sporting one of those come fuck me pouts. I'm accustomed to receiving this kind of attention after laying down my black card. Ignorance is not something I suffer from. Between the money and my looks, women come to me willingly, and often. I don't judge them or their actions. *Hey, fucking get it ladies. You do you.*

She's a beautiful woman, just not the one for me. Mine has hair so brilliant in its depth of darkness, that it's often mistaken for black. I'm sure the woman popping tabs off beer bottles behind the bar is a wonderful human being. I just won't be able to *not* compare her bleached hair and heavily outlined eyes to the perfection of the one that got away.

There's no woman on God's green earth that can compete with my girl's golden skin, the freckles dusting all the fun places I crave to explore, or the smart mouth I want to devour with every inappropriate word delivered by a perfect combination of a sharp tongue and quick wit.

Then there's her eyes. I'm thirty-five years old and have never come across another pair so unique. One would think from afar they are deep brown. I know I did, but up close they are a rare combination of burnt sienna and amber. So rich one can mistake them for a desert sunset.

When did I become a fucking poet? My dick twitches. As discreetly as possible, my hand covers the crotch of my pants to shift my dick into a more comfortable position. The bartender's eyes clash with mine. She mistakes the rearrangement as my body's response to her. *Fuck. Hope she enjoys disappointment.*

The announcers' voices boom through the speakers, introducing the fighters, which pulls my focus back to the screen. Hopefully, ignoring her will draw a clear picture because it isn't happening.

Utah's been my home for five years, seven months, four days, and nine hours. But who's counting? It's pathetic. My brows twist in disgust as I take another swig of beer.

Nothing is distracting enough to remove her from my memories. Even now somehow still…my soul calls to her. She consumes every waking moment of my life. She haunts me late at night while the rest of the world is silent. Thoughts of her are so loud, every one of them revolves around her consuming me, the ember of my soul held in her palm, the very palms that held my heart before she obliterated it.

She chose him though. Of course she did. My teeth clench, locking my jaw in a painful awareness of having never been good enough for her.

Bitterness coats my tongue while the onslaught of memories attacks my consciousness. Standing there on her porch, pleading with her to stay with me. Her eyes held so much pain as she denied me. The ache in my chest is just as brutal tonight as it was all those years ago. Adhesive from the sticker on the beer bottle spirals as my thumb peels off the label, while memories churn that I beg my conscience to forget.

Out of the four of us from Arizona, she's the only one with any honor. Mistakes were made, words were spoken. They can't be taken back, much to my regret, self-induced exile isn't enough to curb my craving for her. Part of my soul is in another state with a prick who doesn't want her. He wants the idea of her. She knows it. I know it. Hell, the fucking priest who married them knows it. Her words hold more weight than ours. She said her vows and her stubborn ass is going to stick with them. So, she chose the cheating bastard over me. One wasn't enough for the son of a bitch.

That was the last straw. Phoenix wasn't large enough for all of us. They weren't leaving, so I had to. The distance between Arizona and Utah wasn't enough miles between us. That rat bastard moved them to Virginia shortly after my departure.

Even now, being across the country still doesn't provide the space I desperately need, especially with the amount of emotional baggage I drag along with me.

Now I spend as little time as possible with others. If Phoenix taught me anything, it's that you can't trust anybody. Our decisions shattered the homes of several people we once called friends, even family. I was not exonerated from the consequences of our actions. I lost it all; my job, my home, friends, the woman I loved--little Toby. All for the illusion of true friendship. He destroyed all of our lives in one selfish decision.

After five years in self-proclaimed exile, only one of them is in constant contact with me, no matter how many times I tell her to leave it be. Every few weeks, she has to confirm that I'm alive. Fucking walking contradiction. She didn't care enough to stay, so why should she care if I'm okay? As if I could ever be okay after she refused me.

While nursing the now more than lukewarm beer, I glance around the crowded bar. Everyone's eyes are glued to the match. Not even an establishment packed with like minded individuals willing to pay high dollar to see blood splatter across an octagon is enough to distract me. Revulsion rolls through me, souring my stomach. Lifting a cigarette to my mouth, I light it and take a long pull. The taste is atrocious, but the nicotine coursing through me calms my frazzled nerves, if only slightly.

"Um, sir, you can't smoke in here." The bleach blonde bartender leans over the bar, her breasts nearly popping out of her halter top. I take my time, appreciating the view. My gaze lifts to hers, the exhale of smoke filtering between us. Her green eyes spark with the same interest I've seen all night. My dick deflates, refusing to be used by anyone but the one who doesn't fucking want us. Well, it was worth a try. Useless fucking appendage.

"Apologies." The cherry of the cigarette sizzles out on the bar top.

"Hey!" she snaps at me, rushing to clean it up. "No need to be a dick, dude!" The firecracker of a woman whirls around to snatch up the cleanser. It's only as she's in front of me, fuming, that her name tag stands out. I want to feel bad but I don't, can't, won't. My absolute existence has been apathetic since my dark-haired beauty left me standing alone on that scorching front stoop in the desert. Jessica picks the discarded butt up, sliding it into a nearby beer bottle.

An emotion that's definitely not guilt, has me flicking a large bill out to lay down in front of her, those heavily lined eyes glancing at it before locking on me. She's gauging my authenticity, questioning whether I want her to keep such a large bill after pulling my dick move with the cigarette.

The sincerity in my eyes must convince her that over-tipping is the only apology I can offer. Manicured fingers snatch up the Benjamin. I take another pull of my beer. Burnt tar and ash coats my tongue, lodging in my throat. My eyes go wide as I spit out the offensive object. *Is that?* No…The little wench snuck my cigarette butt into my fucking beer bottle.

Fantastic. You can't trust anyone, I think bitterly. I grab the nearest glass, swishing the cold water in my mouth, before promptly spitting it back into the cup. Flakes of brown and black tobacco swirl in the glass. Putrid bile rises in the back of my throat. I force it back down and stand. It's time to get out of here before I choke the life from her.

You wouldn't put your hands on a woman, asshole. You were being a prick and she got payback. Get over it. A little voice resembling *hers* reminds me.

A firm grip on my shoulder brings my attention to Tommy's glassed-over eyes. "Hey man, where's my beer?" the words slur slightly.

Perfect. Now I have to be responsible for getting his ass home. "Have you tried looking up your asshole?"

He laughs as I throw my arm around him, tossing a few more twenties on the counter to cover Tommy's tab.

"Let's go, fuckface. I need to get you home to your bitch." My arm tightens around his neck, dragging him more than leading through the crowded joint. The whooshing sound of the exit opening is music to my ears as we're greeted by the night sky.

Tommy leans into me, slurring, "I'll have you know my husky is all male."

"Yeah well, I would expect nothing less from you. Regardless, let's get you home. No need for you to turn into a pumpkin at midnight." I ruffle the curls on top of his head, knowing he'll hate the reference. The humor of my only comrade in Salt Lake being a total asshole isn't lost to me. Does that speak to how the world views me? Or my personal opinion of myself? Perhaps I only deserve this level of friendship.

Tommy sidesteps, trying to break my hold on his collar. We both know he can't. A vibration in my jean pocket breaks my concentration long enough for Tommy to slip out of my grasp. He lunges for me, almost clipping me, but I swat him away, pointing at the truck. "Get. In."

He falls against the truck door instead, making an obscene gesture.

Only one person on this planet calls me instead of shooting a text. The phone vibrates again.

I don't have the energy for this tonight. Maybe ignoring it will make her go away? Here's to hopes and prayers. The voicemails in my inbox are only of her, the sweet melodic voice of an angel. I listen to them on the nights when peace eludes me. The nights when I'm desperate for a connection to her, if only through the lilting tone of her voice.

She won't let me move on. Every few months I hit the answer icon knowing it will be my utter ruin. She plagues me with questions. 'Are you alright? How's Salt Lake City? Are you seeing someone?' Her questions cause my unequivocal destruction, leaving me an obliterated shell of a man.

How am I supposed to respond when she calls asking questions? No, I'm not okay. You ripped my fucking heart out. Salt Lake's great, but its beauty doesn't compare to the ass that's wrapped in my sheets this morning! Am I seeing someone? Which one? There's a whole gang of women. Orgies. Every. Fucking. Night. But I won't say any of it. She's been hurt enough by the men in her life. And none of it is true, well the part about being not okay and my heart is. Can't even fucking lie to myself.

The exhale leaves my lips on a hiss. Like I've even considered another woman. The stars twinkle above me, mocking me with their incandescent glow. I want to scream to the heavens that this isn't fair.

The Samsung vibrates again, signaling a new voicemail. My fingers lock behind my head as I stare into the abyss envisioning her with me. How can a woman break my ever-loving fucking heart then continue to carry on as if it never happened? Like I didn't present myself at her feet just so she could fucking cut it from me with the dullest of utensils. A spoon, her weapon of choice, from *his* kitchen. If only I could be a dick to her. If only I could resent her for it. But I can't.

The phone chimes this time, signaling a text. One…two…three… I remove the offensive piece of metal and glass from my pocket. Out of my peripheral vision, I see Tommy trying to climb into the passenger side, the sound of his head hitting the frame of the door registers right before gravel crunches as he loses his footing. A string of curse words follow that would make Sunday school teachers blush. I want to check on him, but when I glance at the screen, I freeze. It's not from her. It's from *him*. One line.

1

Running Shoes

Thena

"Tobias Montgomary Sullivan! Get your shoes on please! We're running late!" My voice sounds shrill even to my ears. I'm teetering on the verge of a panic attack. My watch ticks, the sound amplified by my frayed nerves. We should have been out the door twenty minutes ago. We cannot be late today!

My freshly polished toes slip into my favorite bright red flats. The handle of my bag fits snuggly in my hand, slightly bulkier than usual. Okay, so it's a small book bag that doubles as a purse, a first aid kit, entertainment, and emergency snack dispenser. Today, it's also my briefcase. Filing for divorce is a messy business.

I check my bag for the fourth time, making sure everything is there. The papers and small hard drive arc still hidden inside the mystery dino egg, my son's collection of these things is impressive. If there's a new size on the market, he's got to have it. The plastic egg holds the key to our freedom. It may seem like an odd choice, but my son's toys are the only safe place to hide the evidence. My stomach tightens painfully, this morning's coffee threatening to make a reappearance.

You need to relax, I remind myself.

After steadying my shaking hands as much as possible, I peer into the mirror hanging on the foyer wall. Checking to make sure my makeup hasn't melted off in my haste to make it out the door in time. The natural pigmented lipstick accentuates my full lips perfectly with just a hint of gloss. "Tobias! Let's go!" I call out again.

His reply is too muffled to hear.

I check the time on my watch again. This has to work. It has too. What if I misjudged his intentions? What if I show up and he's not there? What if my husband finds out?

The husband in question has never physically abused us, but the threat has been implied numerous times, hidden between double entendre. Apprehension takes hold, forcing me to question, not for the first time, if I'm making the right choice. At this point I would almost prefer he hit me. The sigh that leaves my body is one of crippling defeat. After giving him everything, my best wasn't enough.

My husband is a serial cheater, manipulator, and his verbal abuse has left invisible scars that never will heal. It's taken a full year of careful planning and secretly recording him to get the evidence I need. After hitting roadblock after roadblock, I made a judgment call and texted someone I have no right to ask for help.

I need the backup. I just pray that he shows.

Mitchell, my husband, has manipulated our son into pleading for me to stay with him. Tobias is the one person on this planet I would sacrifice everything for, and Mitchell knows that. So, he exploits it. I clench the strap of my bag so tightly my knuckles turn white. Tobias is so young; he just doesn't know how dangerous his father is becoming. I hope he understands that this…marriage is one sacrifice I can no longer make.

I jump at the sound of a door closing. Feet slap against the floor as my eight year old runs straight at me in a full sprint. I open my arms on instinct and we wrap one another in a quick embrace. The lingering smell of chlorine and downy cling to him. He's all kid, swimming so much the fresh clothes can't hide the evidence of summertime. The smile I give him is warm as I cherish this stolen moment. He laughs, wiggling out of my arms.

"Hey sugar, are you ready to go?"

"Mom! Don't call me that!" He looks so distraught over the endearment. I laugh a little, straightening the ball cap over the blonde curls wrapping around his ears.

Will he forgive me for what I'm doing? The guilt is a constant reminder of my uncertainty. Will he blame me for this? Tears well in my eyes.

"Mom, you can call me sugar if it means that much to you." Tobias mistakes my glistening eyes as his fault. The stabbing in my chest is completely my own doing. My sweet boy.

"Honey, you didn't make me cry. You could never. I was just thinking of how grown up you look is all," I say instead of vocalizing my desperation to right a wrong. The words seem to bring him immediate relief.

"Dad says girls cry for no reason, just because they are ladies."

"You're not wrong," I agree, my heart shreds for another reason entirely.

"Can we go to the park today?" he asks, giving me the best pouty face I've ever seen.

"If we hurry, we can stop by the trampoline park on the way home," I tell him. As predicted, he takes off at a break-neck speed.

My phone rings in my back pocket, the only place my screen is safe from prying eyes, as I lock up the house. I need to make sure it's not my attorney, so I hurry to the car and throw everything in the passenger side before checking the screen.

Mitchell. Great, this should be fun. When I don't answer until the fifth ring, I know that alone will cause a battle, but I try for an even, calm tone. "Mitchell, what's up?"

"Took you long enough. Is everything alright?" His tone is unusually pleasant, so I know he must have co-workers around.

"Apologies. I was loading the car and had to find my phone. It was in the bottom of my bag." The lie rolls off my tongue with ease.

"I was worried about my wife. Although that bag of yours is unnecessary. You don't need a diaper bag anymore. Tobias is grown and carries his own supplies. He doesn't need all those toys and snacks toted around." As always, he forgets our son is only eight and not eighteen.

"Yes well, as I've said before, I don't want him hungry, hurt, or bored while out and about running errands." The words emerge more clipped than I intended. Who does this fucker think he is? What kind of parent doesn't look out for their child?

"You baby him."

"I parent him," I counter.

"We'll discuss this later. I'm calling on behalf of the company." We've been married long enough I know he isn't happy. I'll hear about it later, but for now he'll keep the professional tone.

"Yes?" I prompt him.

"It's Kye Kincaid, he's on the east coast."

This is the call I've been waiting for. I'm not surprised Kye is here. After all, I'm the one that asked him to come. "He is?" My breath hitches, but I try to convey bored curiosity.

"As inconceivable as it is, yes. His company purchased the land adjacent to ours."

"That's…" Unable to find the proper thing to say, I stumble over my response, "that's something."

Mitchell, forever wrapped up in himself, charges forward as if I hadn't spoken. "I was just informing my CEO of our long friendship with Mr. Kincaid--" he pauses, before continuing, "I've taken it upon myself to host a quaint little dinner in hopes of enriching our future relationship between our companies here in the eastern region."

I roll my eyes. By quaint he means maxing out another card for top notch catering. My fingers strum on the steering wheel. "I'm sure you're elated to have your best friend back in your life. Who would have thought the man would be joining us in Virginia?" I say with thinly veiled sarcasm. He and Kye *were* best friends before that cataclysm in Arizona.

"We will *not* be discussing the past," he snaps, his composure slipping. A ruffling on the other line alerts me that he's covering the mic before he says, "Charlotte, I'm sorry can you give me a moment? My wife changed her meds again. You know how these things go."

My blood boils. I am not on any medications other than the birth control I no longer need. It will be a cold day in hell before I sleep with him again. Playing the irrationally emotional wife card is getting old. God, I hate this man. I hear a door closing on the other end, the loving husband facade slips, his tone turning vile. There are so many sides to him. Would the real Mitchell Sullivan please stand up?

"Now you listen to me, *wife!* We left what happened in Arizona, *in* Arizona. You *will* go to the caterer and order something suitable for twenty people. You *will* have them deliver it tomorrow, where we *will* be a united front. Family is everything to this company and you *will* be grateful that you have one. Am I clear?"

My irritation flares, his intimidation routine falling short. It's the same routine we go through every time. This will be over soon, I remind myself. I won't have to deal with him anymore if my plan works. "Crystal clear, husband," I say as sweetly as possible, although chewing broken glass is more preferable to kissing his ass.

He doesn't dignify me with a response. Instead, the line goes dead. Huh. That's new.

I watch the phone screen switch to my wallpaper, a photo of Tobias and I, before it goes dark. I won't slip into hysteria in front of my son. I won't.

Setting the phone down, I dig my sunglasses out of the console while tightness pinches along my hairline. I don't have time for a headache today.

My attention is drawn to the rearview mirror, Tobias's reflection assures me that he's comfortably tucked in the backseat with his headphones on, a game beeping away at him. At least he didn't hear that. I'll take the small blessings where I can.

After putting my car in reverse, I back out of the driveway.

2

Bookstores & Schemes

Thena

My thumb nail splinters with the force of my nervous bite. The surrounding skin is red and raw with little pockets of blood. I thought it was a habit I had broken. Guess not.

I hoist my bag up on my shoulder and wipe my sweaty palms on my shorts. My body is a livewire of chaotic energy. I inhale, surrounded by stacks of books. I should be relaxed in this comforting place. Instead, my adrenaline works double-time. I fidget with the frayed hem of my jean shorts.

I look like a dumpster fire. The chopped up Ramones shirt looked edgy and cute earlier. Now? I probably look nomadic. What is wrong with me? I'm anxious to see him again, at least I can be truthful with myself.

The bookstore is never busy this time of day. Everyone is either at work or out to lunch. Choosing the safest time to meet in public is only one step to my exit strategy.

I lean against the bookshelf and watch Tobias. He's combing the children's section for new books on guppies. When my fish obsessed son's eyes find mine, I plaster a calm smile on my face, before pushing my hands in my pockets, fighting the temptation to bite them again.

The man we're meeting has always elicited this response from me. The mutual attraction we felt over the years is still very much alive today. At least for me. I remember the day he left. I was so scared I would never see him again. Our friendship is one I value, it broke my heart when my marriage caused him so much grief. Not that it bothered my husband.

Mitchell is, and has always been, in a state of oblivion to the others around him and how his actions cause harm. He's reached out to Kye on several occasions, inviting him on bro trips and offers to work at the company in the eastern region as if nothing happened. Kye only makes an appearance once a year. Mitchell usually uses it as an excuse to male bond. Although Kye is polite, their friendship is *not* salvageable.

I've asked myself a thousand times why Kye continues to show up for my birthdays. Why come in year after year only to have to revisit what we went through in Arizona? I've tried speaking to him as often as I dare via text messages, but his responses leave much to be desired: I'm fine, life's great, tell Turbo Toby hello from Uncle Kye.

Turbo Toby. Kye always says Tobias has two speeds, quick and super quick. So he dubbed my son Turbo Toby.

Shit. How is he going to react to Mitchell's treatment of Tobias? I absentmindedly chew on my nail again, but the pain is not enough to curb my growing jitters. Breathe bitch, you got this! It's just another day at the bookstore. Stop looking so fucking suspicious. Chastising myself won't work, but it's worth a try.

I glance across the aisle to my son. He's having a typical shopping day with his mom. Going to the bookstore is not something unusual for us. Reading is one of our favorite activities besides swimming, so this is nothing out of the ordinary for him.

For me? I'm waiting to see if Kye is the man I remember, the one who claimed to love me. I hope he has at least one ounce of that love left, because I need his help. He is the key to my plan working.

Mitchell doesn't mind bullying women and children, but men? He wouldn't dream of stepping up to another man. Isn't that how it usually goes though? Abusive assholes to those who are easy prey, and Mitchell is no exception.

That's why I chose to meet here. I need to make this as random as possible for Tobias. It's not in a kid's nature to keep a secret, and I wouldn't be a good mother if I asked him to keep one. This way, bumping into Uncle Kye at one of our favorite shops is merely a stroke of luck.

Mitchell can't rationalize getting mad over a chance encounter. Will he still be angry? Yes, but will I have a better footing in the upcoming argument? Also yes.

I glance at my phone to check the time. He won't be late. I desperately want my faith in Kye to be unshakeable. The tenuous belief has carried me through this last year, hoping I can count on him to get us through without harm.

Mitchell's behavior has been escalating with each passing year. He no longer tries to wear his mask when alone with us. Because of that, Tobias hides in his room whenever he's around, and the few friends I've made here won't dare grace my doorstep if he's home.

A tingling sensation travels up my body in a vivid moment of déjà vu. The feeling almost causes me to pivot, but I stop myself at the last minute.

My eyes close and I try to steady myself before facing him. I know he's behind me, watching, waiting for me to turn. *Turn around,* a tiny voice urges me. Apprehension forces me to remain still. He's going to see the desperation in my eyes, the devastation I feel every day.

Once again, I'm trapped between the man who owns me and the man I *want* to possess me. This meeting had to be face-to-face, so why do I suddenly want to flee? *Because you want to run into his arms and stay there and that terrifies you after what Mitchell has done,* that little voice whispers.

While fear holds me in place, Tobias's face lights up. His expression transforms into one of happiness and excitement, and for a moment, I'm ashamed he doesn't look at his father that way. But why should he?

"Uncle Kye!" Tobias exclaims, darting past me. Left with no choice, I summon my bravery and turn to watch the reunion.

"Turbo! Dude what are you eating? You're so tall!" Tobias is fully wrapped around Kye, burying his little head in Kye's neck. The man speaks to my son in a hushed whisper, but his eyes are locked on me. His assessment must not be to his liking, because his stare darkens, causing me a pang of self-consciousness.

The world spins slightly, my fingers reaching out to the nearest bookshelf, trying to steady myself. Kye's as gorgeous as he was the last time I saw him. Lord give me strength, I silently pray. Not that praying has ever helped me. Kye tries to set Tobias on his feet, but the boy clutches his neck harder. That's when I realize Toby's shoulders are shaking slightly and I hear him sniffle.

"Hey dude, what's all this about?" Kye asks him gently.

"I just missed you is all," Tobias tells him in a small voice. I cross the aisle, smoothing my hand over Tobias's back. I've never seen him show this much emotion toward another person other than me, the reaction confirms my concern about how the emotional abuse affects him, solidifying my resolve.

I'm making the right decision.

"Hello Thena," Kye's voice crashes over me in a wave of euphoric delight until my body hums.

"Hello Kye. We've missed you." Surprise widens his eyes slightly before he recovers. The gunmetal gray specks in them pop out beneath the fluorescent light. I don't know what came over me, I didn't mean to say that out loud.

Tobias giggles as my face heats. Kye appears skeptical at first, but his face transforms into one of relief.

I hesitate, remembering Arizona. My statement must be confusing to him after everything that happened. I nervously back up a step and the heel of my flats catches on the carpet. I stumble backward, but a large hand wraps around my waist. Kye pulls me toward him and Tobias. This close, his aftershave surrounds me, bringing with it an all new awareness.

I clear my throat, and put distance between us. When I can breathe again, I laugh nervously and glance at anything but the imposing man before me. "Thank you."

"You're welcome."

"I've become a clutz."

"As opposed to when you weren't one? When exactly was that?" I risk a glance and see Kye's dark eyebrows lift. "If I'm remembering correctly, and I am, you've always been accident prone. It's fortunate for you we ran into each other at our favorite place." He flashes a smile that makes his dimples pop.

"It is! I heard you were in town. We're obviously very happy to see you," I say.

"Hey Toby, would you like to go to the cafe and grab some treats?" Kye asks Toby, who is now calm as he is lowered to the ground.

"Heck yes!" my son shouts, fist bumping Kye. His excitement vibrates throughout the store. Who doesn't love a happy child? It's infectious really. Toby grabs both our hands and pulls us to the little shop tucked away in the corner.

"How long are you in town for Kye?" I already know the answer but ask anyway for the sake of Mitchell questioning us later.

"Oh, my company purchased land to develop for a new tech firm here in Richmond. It's remote until the building is complete, so technically I can work from anywhere, but I like the area and want to see what it has to offer," he responds casually, I read between the lines and it warms something in me.

Kye wants to see if his offer in Arizona still stands, however with Tobias here, we can't speak freely. That's why I brought the documents and hard drive. I just need to slip it to him when we leave so he has everything. One move at a time. That's the only way to get through this. I need to be cautious though. With our past, I never want him to ever feel used, not by me.

"Uncle Kye! Can I have the brownie *and* the cake pop?" Tobias interrupts with all the enthusiasm of an eight year old.

"Yes," we both respond at the same time, "no."

"Pleaseeee." Little lashes flutter while he pleads with me.

"How about we get both and you have one treat now and one for later?" Kye offers.

Tobias hops from one foot to the other with his hands in a praying gesture. My lips purse while I pretend to think for a minute. I haven't seen him behave like a happy child, unafraid to show his eagerness and wonder, in so long. I want to extend the moment for as long as possible.

Mitchell's voice echoes in my mind, ruining my blissful joy. *'Children are to be seen not heard. Make him stand still! That boy should be taught a lesson'.*

Soon, Tobias will be free to run wild, laughing and playing as a child should, free from Mitchell's constant criticism. The thought brings a smile back to my face.

"Okay, that should be fine," I finally say, Tobias spins in circles cheering. I watch as he approaches the lady behind the counter. He points to his choices, I nod to the lady confirming he has permission.

"What was that look that crossed your face?" Kye asks too quietly for Tobias to hear.

While my son is distracted, I pull out the egg and open it.

His eyes widen in thoughtful surprise, most likely at the lengths I've gone to conceal everything. He recovers quickly, instinctively grabbing the contents as I hold them out to him. With a look of protectiveness now on his face, he places them inside his jacket. "Thena, what's going on?" he asks while his fingers push a stray strand of hair behind my ear.

I shiver at the contact, unable to disguise it for anything but my attraction to him. His smile indicates he's translated what I can't verbalize. "I need your help. Everything you need to know is in what I handed you. I need a yes or no tomorrow at the dinner party. I just ask, no I beg you, if your answer is no, please don't tell Mitchell. It's too dangerous for Tobias and me if he were to find out."

Kye's eyes darken so deep I could swear the gray turned into a swirling silver universe stretched out before me. When I finish my request, he goes rigid, heat radiating off of his body as it brushes against my own. "Has that son of a bitch hit you? Or Toby?" The deadly calm in his voice sparks fear in me. Kye Kincaid is a dangerous man when provoked, I remind myself. Isn't that what I'm doing? Provoking him?

"Not yet. But…" The words are hard to form. How do I explain the thinly veiled threats hidden within his promises of what will happen if I leave him?

"But you're scared he will?" he asks.

I seek out Toby before I answer. He's at a table a few feet from us, devouring his brownie. Chocolate icing is smeared around his mouth. He looks so carefree, tears spring to my eyes. I shove down the nearly overwhelming need to cry. How do I explain that I fear Mitchell will rip what innocence is left from Tobias to punish me?

I shuffle from side to side, unsure how to proceed, but when I glance back at Kye, his eyes haven't left me. I don't want to talk about it in the open and I don't want Tobias to accidently hear something he shouldn't, so I say the only thing I can. "I fear what the day brings, when screaming at us isn't enough punishment."

As hard as I try, I can't help the single tear that falls down my cheek. I sniff, attempting to reign in my emotions. Gunmetal gray eyes track that single tear before his calloused finger wipes it away.

"Whatever you need from me. You already have it."

3

Reflections

Kye

My calloused thumb rubs across my pointer and middle finger inside my pants pocket, a concentration impulse from childhood I never truly broke. The silk lining of my pants cools the rising heat of my skin while I soak in the view of lush green mountains with native oak and pine creating a natural barrier around the place. The view is worth every fucking penny and the property gets bonus points for carrying the scent of nature inside.

My vision pauses on the James River, which cuts between the backyard of my temporary home and the mountains. The river's fierce currents have carved into the earth over the course of thousands of years to create this spectacular scenery, I can't help drawing a comparison.

Life, like the river, can cut through the hardest parts of us. Against our consent, suffering carves lessons into our souls and we carry them for the rest of our lives.

My forehead connects with the glass, swaying slowly from side to side in another failed attempt at self-soothing. Thena and Tobias carved their way into my heart against my better judgment, against my will, without my consent, from the very first moment. Now, I can't see any future without them.

The darkest parts of my soul rage for dominance, forcing a war into my heart and that not even the serene scene can temper.

How can it? When I now know how much they have suffered? My forehead slams against the window. Heat from my skin instantly warms the cool glass, stealing its cold comfort.

If I continue this way, I'm going to have a stroke. I'm too young to have blood pressure issues, no doubt a side effect of my temper. Thena and Tobias wouldn't have suffered like this had Arizona gone differently. Fucking Mitchell, he's always been a prick. The fucktwat thrives on stealing from others.

I thought I learned to control my rage while sparring in the ring as a young adult. Apparently, not. Recalling my earlier years only sends more frustration rippling through me.

The cult I was raised in viewed my high-strung emotions as the Devil's work. My parents mistakenly thought they could beat or starve him out of me. But little did they know, I didn't have any of that in me. I *am* the Devil. I had to be... I didn't realize that until high school, when my parents were forced to send me to public school. That's where I first met Mitchell. My proficient abilities with technology attracted a certain crowd. Before long, I was coding cheat apps for spoiled rich kids on campus. Mitchell was as much of a prick back then as he is today, except this time it's not my homework he's passing off as his own, it's my future family.

Between Mitchell's first betrayal, religious trauma, and unraveling the pitfalls of society, I was vulnerable. For the first time, I enjoyed fast cars while bumping to the latest rap music without a sinister voice in my head telling me I would burn in hell, but I didn't know who I was without that voice.

Basically, I was a train wreck when I first saw her. I had no real understanding of the world. I was nothing more than a young man with hate in my heart, hell bent on revenge. Fighting in the ring trained my mind and body, gave me a release, but it wasn't until I found myself celebrating holidays and birthdays with *her* that my soul began to heal.

But I was stupid. I abandoned her. Leaving her in a revolving door of hell with him.

I bang my head against the glass in frustration. The pain racking my head is nothing compared to what she and her son have suffered. Hours after reading the documents and combing over the files she sent me left me in an emotional ruin no man should face unprepared.

No woman and child should have to face that kind of shit either, I think bitterly. The desire to wrap my hands around his neck, to squeeze as I watch the life leaves his eyes is so overwhelming. I smash my fist into the glass pane.

Mitchell has put his wife and son through so much: infidelity, emotional abuse, threats of physical violence. His presence torments them daily.

If Thena had just taken me up on my offer…I would have treasured them. Tobias would have wanted for nothing. My very existence would surround them, ensuring their happiness every single day.

I hear his voice from the recording that now plays in my head every time I close my eyes. The harsh words towards a small child not big enough to defend himself boils my blood. 'You're just a big, dumb animal, aren't you? You can't even pour yourself milk without fucking it up, can you!? What is this mess? You're not smart enough to be a scientist, put it away! You're ruining my sidewalk brat!' It's always the same; Tobias doing something by himself, staying out of the way, and Mitchell finds him, seeking a target for his frustrations of failure, taking them out on the poor kid.

In the recordings, his words toward Thena are just as bad. Mitchell openly admits that he married her because she seemed desperate for a family, and he wanted to advance in his company. The fucker even went on to quote the company motto: *God first, then family, then helping others.* I feel sick to my stomach.

Hearing Mitchell taunt Thena, laughing as she cries, brings that devil back out in me. I crack my knuckles, needing something to pop.

However, the last straw was hearing Mitchell proclaim Tobias is his son in name alone. I couldn't stomach hearing that. If the asshole didn't want the kid, he shouldn't have asked for him. I *want* Tobias. Hell, any man would be lucky to call that pistol-whip a son. He's brilliant, and kind, just like his mother.

My fist clenches as their pain transforms into my own guilt. I left them alone with him.

I slam my fist against the glass.

I left them alone with him.

My fist slams the glass again and again and again, embodying my guilt for abandoning them. Then an all-consuming grief for the time lost and the pain they've endured overcomes me. The onslaught of emotions is too much to contain without an outlet.

Rage erupts as I lift the nearest object. Shards of glass ricochet off the wall as the paperweight shatters. It does nothing to curb the acidic burn in my stomach, the seething hatred for Mitchell, and my own self-loathing.

He hurt them, and you let it happen. It's a small voice but the poisonous words hurt all the same. Mitchell's vicious words repeat over and over and over until I fucking lose it.

I shove everything off my desk and curl my fingers around the edges. Lifting, I flip it into the guest chairs in front of it, crushing them. He didn't protect her. He enjoyed cheating on her. He hurt her and Toby. He never loved her…I fucking love her. Absolute hatred makes my vision hazy as I snatch a small corner table, which I obliterate with a crack.

Everything my hands touch is leveled. Bits and pieces fly through the air, dust floats through the room. Debris scatters in all directions. Small jagged pieces of wood embed themselves under my skin, but my discomfort is nothing compared to what Thena and Tobias suffered at *his* hands.

Each piece I decimate is like a stone thrown at a glass house. As much as his actions have broken them, my lack of action is just as culpable. At least my ruined office is an accurate description of the hell they endured from a man I once called my best friend.

I will stop at nothing. I will grant him the same respect he bestowed her. His family will be mine, and in the end, the bastard will live with the same humiliation and suffering he caused them.

My boots carry me to the final piece of furniture; a couch that's covered in the debris of my anger. Leather crinkles as the cushions absorb my body weight, a coppery tang coats my taste buds as I rub my busted knuckles over my lips.

His opportunity to cherish them has come to an end, I vow it. Thena will never know another day of questioning whether she deserves to be loved or not. Tobias will have anything that his young heart can imagine.

I lean back, reclining on the couch when something pokes my back. I shift my body slightly, yanking a broken picture frame from behind me. *Huh...* I toss it across the room. It clatters to the ground, the only noise left besides my heavy breathing and thundering heart.

I should call the cleaning service and have someone to replace everything. That can wait until tomorrow. Tonight I want to plan my next move. I'm playing for keeps and I don't intend to lose this time.

4

Swimming With Temptation

Thena

"Thena!" Mitchell's voice booms across the open space of the backyard, interrupting my moment of serenity. "Would you get out of the pool? Dishes need to be finished."

Our acre backyard is not enough distance between us to enjoy the day. No, that would require thousands of miles. Fucking asshole.

My eyes flip skyward as I glide across the water on my back. The pool's soothing temperature usually eases my broken soul, but it's not enough right now. I hate this man.

Is it supposed to rain tonight? If so, I'll be right back in this pool. Water is my sanctuary, the only thing that washes away the sorrow from my epic fucking failure of a marriage.

This is the man I chose? Six point two billion people on this planet and I said 'yes, I will take this one'. I can't wait for this nightmare to be over.

The sun has been down for hours. Fireflies dart across the sky, reminding me of a more innocent time when joy was common. The little blinking fairies used to make me smile, now the memories they summon bring me nothing but longing. I crave happiness, companionship, and a partner. I hunger for laughter so desperately that my body physically aches for it.

The water laps lazily over my body, my dark hair fans out, dancing around my arms as if trying to comfort me. I am a ghost of the woman I once was, used up by a selfish, prideful man who worries more about his image and what my body can provide than the soul beneath my skin. And I allowed it. I was so desperate for his love and approval. After years of suffering, all I have to show now is a loveless marriage and empty nursery.

It's been exactly one year since I lost our twins, a tragedy I can never heal from with his constant reminders. Mitchell's eyes hold such bitter disappointment even when he's not spewing judgmental and hateful words. The sad fact is, I blame myself too. I should have left sooner.

I inhale deep, letting the air expand my chest and mentally prepare to leave my sanctuary. I dread entering that fucking prison of a home. Mitchell has blissfully ignored me most of the day, with the exception of catering to his buddies when they need a beer cracked open. None of them are my friends. I'm only instructed to act like they are, playing the dutiful wife.

I flip under the water and surge back to the surface, the cool liquid caressing my face as I come up for air. Instead of swimming for the ladder, I float on my back again, letting the water lap around my body and lull me into a rare state of peace. Ahhh, fucking wonderful. If only I could just stay here, at this moment--alone.

"Thena! Are you coming?" Mitchell's brittle voice raises, his speech slightly slurring. Great, he's drunk again. He's going to be so loud and obnoxious tonight. Our neighbors must love us.

I raise a thumbs-up, hoping the idiot is wearing his contacts. It seems like he is since he acknowledges my gesture with a shake of his head before turning back to his soiree. Everyone inside laughs a second later. He must have said something funny because he's definitely not capable of being clever in his current state--or any state, if I'm being honest. The man can barely wipe his ass without instruction some days. He sure knows how to send out a dick pic though. A confusing mix of jealousy, anger, and self-loathing churn in my belly. Ugh, don't think about that disappointment.

A heavy sigh rushes past my lips. Fuck my life. I need time to relax and unwind. With Tobias staying at a friend's house tonight and Mitchell's friends occupying him, I thought I'd have more time to myself, to just...be. Planning a secret divorce is messy business and it's left me depleted.

Awareness tingles up my neck. As the air shifts around me, I already know who's approaching from behind me without bothering to look. Our souls are tethered, recognizing each other whenever they're near. Anticipation tightens my belly and my heart fractures a little more. Right one, wrong time, is forever our mantra. I wonder if he's as aware of me as I am of him? His near silent entry into the pool moments ago did nothing to hide the fact that I'm with an apex predator. Alone.

"Brat," his low voice murmurs from the water directly behind me. "He knows you aren't his servant, right?" His words rumble across my skin, eliciting a shiver.

Kye Kincaid, the man I entrusted with our future, the one that will forever hold my tragically jaded heart. With him hovering so close, my thighs tighten as a deep longing pulls low in my belly, and close my eyes, steeling myself. I don't have the self-control to deal with this man today. Against every primal instinct, I move away from him, toward the chest-deep water. I refuse to turn around. I can't look him in the eye.

Every time we're apart, I forget the effect his nearness has on me. Our encounter at the bookstore was reminder enough, and I'm vulnerable right now. If I'm not careful, I will end up splayed on the side of this pool begging him to take me any way he chooses.

He closes the distance and leans in, his full lips grazing my ear while running his calloused fingertips down my spine. Their touch leaves delicate shivers in their wake, as if even my body is afraid to believe the promise they hold. "Come on, brat."

His voice sends electric volts straight to my core. I can't help it, I fucking melt. All my pep talks of staying strong are nearly forgotten, and I'm at the mercy of his touch. My traitorous nipples harden, a deliciously painful tingle. God I should not be feeling this. I hear the water ripple, feel the heat of his skin soaking into my chilled backside, I close my eyes.

I need to focus, to project the appearance that I'm not attracted to this man. Mitchell is the cheater in this marriage, not me. I took a vow. I will stand by it no matter how much my loyalty devastates my soul.

"I know for a fact that you heard every word I said." He rubs his nose over my neck and shoulder blades, eliciting a gasp from me. "Now, answer the question, brat. Does that piece of shit know you are *not* his servant?" The words are sharp as he whispers against my ear, his hands slipping down my forearms, turning me slowly to face him.

Long wet tendrils of hair float out around us, grazing Kye and myself, the touch is erotic in its innocence. My heavy tits graze Kye's chest, their painfully taught nipples hardening more as we make eye contact. The thick tension makes me freeze. Kye is so close. His air is my air. His fucking smell, the one that has haunted me for years, suffocates me.

At this close distance, he's even more devastatingly handsome in his uniqueness. His dark hair is slicked back from the water, droplets cling to the dark eyelashes that frame his grayish blue eyes. The hue is so bright they almost take on a frosted glow when he's angry, like he is now. I soak him in. Why does he get to have beautiful lashes? It's not fair, every other person here reeks of chlorine, stale beer and brawts, but not this beautiful lunatic. No, Kye smells of cedarwood, whiskey, amber, and fucking sin.

Does this nearness mean he will help me escape the prison I have wasted away in? I knew he'd be here. Mitchell's yell of triumph at getting Kye to attend was loud enough for the neighborhood to hear.

I'd done my best to avoid him, lest I giveaway our secret rendezvous yesterday. Of course, there were worse consequences of sharing space, which are perfectly illustrated right now. Someone might have realized that we don't merely look at one another but drown in one another's gaze.

I've never believed in soulmates or true love. Life's lessons beat the fairy tales out of me long ago. But with Kye, it's different. I feel hope, a dangerous fucking thing. It's almost as if we share a dream state and the world abandons us to revel in one another's company.

Answer him. Respond. Give him something, the voice nudges me, but I can't seem to find the words. His question is too close to the truth of my existence.

I lower my gaze. Without having Tobias here as a buffer, our intensity borders on uncomfortable. Eye contact with him is difficult, and my embarrassment over how low I've allowed my life to sink heats my cheeks with shame. Of course, he sees through the facade. Kye's my best friend. He knows me better than I know myself.

My eyes well, shoulders slumping as I suck my bottom lip in between my teeth. Maybe if I stay quiet he will get the hint that this conversation is *not* happening. Not now. Not here. God, this is humiliating. I should sit at the bottom of the pool and practice not breathing.

When he breathes in deep, his chest presses against my breasts, the pang of wanton lust brings a fresh wave of guilt. Please… Please just let me get a cramp so I can drown like the miserable piece of shit that I am. No matter what is happening between Mitchell and I, feeling desire for another, even one as familiar as Kye, is a new low for me. Filing for divorce does not equate being single. I'm a miserable human. I'm no better than Mitchell.

Kye's calloused fingers lightly skim my jaw, brushing the tears off my cheeks. "Baby, please don't cry over that jackass."

How can a man built for destruction be so tender?

"I'm not crying over him." The words leave me on a ragged breath. Kye steps into me. My toes scrape the bottom of the pool as I push myself back, trying to keep distance between us. He stalks me. Of course he does.

We move to the side of the pool where the fountain is and it's not lost on me that the thing hides us from sight. If anyone looked down from the balcony, the pool would appear empty, the cascading water would drown out any sounds. Not that I'm planning anything...like stripping his trunks off and climbing him like a tree. Nope. Not me. Shutting that train of thought down now.

Kye places his hands on either side of my head, caging me in and forcing me to meet his eyes. "Then why is there water leaking from your eyeballs, babe?"

I shrug, feigning ignorance.

A knowing smile brightens his face and… Jesus Christ, please Lord, give me the strength to keep my vows, even if I did make them to a cheating, abusive, narcissistic excuse of a man.

That little voice is whispering seductively again, *well, Thena. When you put it like that…*

His fingertips lift my chin, and his penetrating gaze hardens as he takes in my pitiful expression. Desperation and heartbreak fight for dominance inside me, below all that simmers years of unchecked desire for this man.

His jaw clenches while his grip on me tightens enough to capture my attention, but not enough to hurt. He leans into me, his mouth mere inches away. Our heavy breathing mingles, mine from nervousness, his from rage. "Tell me you don't want him here. Tell me you want him out of that house. I will pack his shit tonight. If you never want him to grace your doorstep again, I will bury him somewhere light will never touch him. Just say the fucking word, princess."

Kye's declaration gives me the first ray of hope I've had since I began scheming our escape. He's going to help. Relief courses through me. I don't want Mitchell dead; I just don't want him here. Although, if things go wrong, it may come to exactly that, as much as I might try to avoid it. "I have a plan."

"How long do I have to wait to kick his ass?"

Every threat Mitchell whispered during my past attempts to leave him rushes through me and my pulse races. I know it's going to be the hardest battle of my life, but I have to do it. I set aside my fear. Remembering that I have this all planned out, I just need Kye to go along with the plan.

Kye sees the shift in my body language, the resolve in my eyes. He never misses anything.

"You will do no such thing," I say as quietly as possible.

The stern expression he wears makes my back straighten and my mouth clamp shut. He always does this, calls out what he thinks is bullshit with a single look. I know it's useless to speak until he says his piece, so I wait. "I swear to God, if you apologize or make a single excuse for that piece of shit, I will bend you over my knee right here and now."

My mouth pops open. Did he… Did he just say he would…? Do adults really get spanked? My body flushes with adrenaline and an odd curiosity.

Interest sparks in his eyes.

He obviously likes the idea, but do I? The picture his words paint has my thighs rubbing together again, but the friction is not enough to ease my burning desire. Nothing is never enough with him. I guess I have my answer. "I wasn't going to make excuses. I have a plan in place and I need to be careful."

"Well that's refreshing," he says.

"I don't follow?"

"That you're actually leaving the fucker this time."

I cringe. *This time.* Kye must have gone through everything I gave him and learned how many times I've tried. Embarrassment flashes through me, quick and spiteful. The corner of Kye's mouth quirks up, missing nothing. Ever the observant smartass. Fucker.

"Now, princess, why don't you tell me what is making you look so goddamned sad tonight?"

"I'm not." I refuse to utter a single word to him of my epic failure as a mother; as a wife. That's why I gave him the recordings. I can't voice those things.

It's humiliating that I'm not enough to keep my husband from straying or making him behave like the loving father he promised to be. I'm an epic goddamned failure, and worst of all, I traded Kye for all of this.

No thanks. I'm not uttering a word. I just want all this to be over. Marriage has always been my priority. It's just taken me several years to realize Mitchell isn't the one. Why continue to suffer?

An expression crosses his face that I can't decipher, and he leans in again to run his lips along my forehead. The feather light touch leaves me wanting more. Once again, it isn't enough. My heart cracks and my soul reaches for him in a desperate desire to entwine with him.

It's always like this with him.

But you've been wrong before. That nagging voice in my head is insistent.

"You are sad, and I want to know why." The light breeze carries his voice so faintly that it's difficult to make out his words.

My shoulders sag under the weight of too much. How do I defuse this situation and reclaim my space? He is a temptation I need to remove. My altar of sins is already overloaded without adding more shame. I try to move away, but he cages me in, forcing me to look at him again. To my disappointment, the lie easily rolls off my tongue. "I'm just tired."

"You're just miserable," he counters, his lips grazing my forehead again.

"Excuse me?" I jerk away from him, my back connecting with the cold fountain tiles which dowse my overactive libido. "What gives you the right?"

"When's the last time that asshat made you smile? Hell, has he ever made you cum?" Kye's nose grazes mine, his lips so close that I suck in his minty breath when I inhale deeply.

What. The. Fuck! Kye has never spoken to me like this. What is he doing? And why do the words resonate in my battered soul? This is too dangerous. He is too dangerous.

"I'm married, Kye! You can't say that to me!" God, I just shouted. I hope the cascading water is enough to drown out the noise. Someone overhearing us is the last thing I need. Society always blames the woman. Mitchell's numerous infidelities won't matter. Our friends and family will place the blame at my feet, and so will my husband.

"Does he know that?" Kye's sharp tone is one I don't often hear. I'm so unaccustomed to his quiet demeanor that I'm honestly shocked. "Does he know you filed for divorce?" he asks, his tone softening a bit as if he recognizes my distress.

"No, he doesn't, and he can't find out tonight. His bosses are inside."

Over the years, Mitchell's conditioned me to ignore my needs, putting his first. They always come first, I think bitterly as his demeaning and hurtful words play through my head again like a goddamned mantra. *Nothing is as important as my placement within the company. I will be Vice President before I'm forty. I need a supportive wife, not a nagging girlfriend.*

"Just drop it, Kye, please. If you went through everything I gave you and judging by your behavior tonight I'm guessing you have, then you already know I'm not the important one here. Tobias is," I plead, needing him to understand that my son's safety is my only concern.

"Who makes *you* the priority? Who keeps *you* safe?" His voice demands an answer from me that I am not ready to voice. I don't feel worthy of it.

"I'm…" I start.

"If you say you're fine again, my promise stands. Knee, ass, hand brat. Although, I think you want me to spank that delicious ass of yours." His lips are back on my forehead, beads of water dripping onto my flushed cheeks.

"Kye!" I bristle. This has to stop. Between the sexual tension and the newly filed divorce papers, I simply do not have the strength for this tonight. I want him. I want him more than the oxygen in my lungs, he fucking knows it.

"What?" The feigned innocence in his question only irritates me. At least, that's what I tell myself.

"Again, for the daft man in front of me, you can't say that!"

Kye shrugs at my response like it doesn't bother him at all that I'm still married.

"You filed for divorce, Thena. I intend to remove him from the equation. He's been holding up the line for far too long."

"Excuse--" I stammer, "excuse me?" My nerves go haywire and the anxiety this conversation summons makes my pulse drum faster and my hands shake. Oh God, please don't let me have another panic attack. What is wrong with me? My ears ring as I stare into Kye's eyes, my brain still trying to process what he's just said.

"Come on, princess. Use your words," he smirks.

I feel like a child caught with their hand in the cookie jar. My heart pounds so hard in my chest, surely he can feel it. He can't mean what I think he does. I know how I feel about him, but it's Kye. I've never seen a woman not fall at his feet. He can have any woman he wants. Why the hell would he want an absolute trainwreck like me?

"You…don't think of me like that!" I stammer as he looks at me incredulously.

"I traveled over six hundred miles to free myself of the hold you have over me, but no amount of distance could purge you from my heart. I smell you everywhere. I see you everywhere. I lay in bed at night, scrolling your social media pages, hoping to find some evidence of your unhappiness to justify coming back and taking what's mine."

A heavy sigh rushes past his lips while I continue to stare at him, startled by his sudden confession.

"At first, I told myself to stay away, that you were happy, but I no longer aspire to make memories without you in them. Baby, you are my sole reason for existing in this world. I know I can't take back the decisions I made over the years. I will never be able to adequately explain my regret for that stupid fucking mistake. Please, give me your time. I need it and you will never have to beg for mine. It's all yours. Every fucking second belongs to you, only you, and always has. I will spend the rest of my days showing you how many ways a woman can be loved by a man."

"Kye." A desperate need to make him leave washes over me. I can't accept his pretty words. I can't.

He's been my constant companion throughout my time married to Mitchell, always picking up the pieces of my broken heart and molding them back together. His unwavering devotion is my only constant over these painful years. Kye has *always* been one call away. He literally drops everything for me, time and time again. Our friendship is the foundation of my life. So, why can't I trust him with my heart? Why can't I believe his seemingly earnest confession?

Because you've been hurt too many times. There is that little voice reminding me once more.

I stand there in the pool, searching his eyes for any hint of betrayal, any sign that this sudden change in him is the result of too many drinks. His eyes are clear and show nothing but sincerity.

While I'm frozen with indecision, his hands trail over my neck, wrapping into my hair while his eyes plead for me to listen. "In all the time I've been away, what was the only day I came back to this hell house each year?" he asks gently, his eyes now filled with something like pity, as if I'm on the outside of an inside joke I should know.

"What?" I ask, my brain too scrambled to figure out what he's asking.

"Come on, baby. You and I both know you're a hell of a lot smarter than you let on. For the last few years, I have traveled here for a single day each year. What happens on that day?"

"My... My birthday," I whisper, my bottom lip wobbles. I bite down on it to hide how much his words affect me.

He arches one single dark eyebrow, his fingers swooping in small circles along my hairline that make me shiver. "Your birth is worth celebrating. I want to spend the entirety of my own life commemorating yours."

"You *can't* say those types of things to me."

"Why not? Afraid that little shit will hear?"

"Yes. I am."

"Let him. Can you imagine how sweet it would taste to give him a dose of his own medicine? Baby, there's no one for me but you."

"Kincaid this isn't appropriate. I can't do this."

"Thena you couldn't do *us* in Arizona. Now after years of suffering, you say you still can't. You can. Be brave for me. Be courageous enough to endure my love for you."

His words cause tears to slide down my cheeks, I crave nothing more in the world than my freedom so that I can love him. "Kye, you have to understand. Mitchell swore he'd make me miserable, to take everything from me. I have to stick to my plan. It's about Tobias. Mitchell said if I leave…" I swallow hard as the very thought causes me physical pain. "He'll take Toby from me and place him in a boarding school. We can't be separated. We just can't," I whisper with defeat in my voice and in my heart.

Even with my clever plan, Mitchell is too controlling, too worried about his image to ever allow me to leave him, especially if he thought it was for another man. What if it doesn't work? What if there is no escape? What if this is my life now?

"He has no plans to ever let me go. He's said so in the past. This isn't my first attempt at leaving. It's just the first you know of." I say in a voice so small it sounds foreign to my own ears.

Kye tenses, his muscles bunching up. Anger replaces the gentle look in his eyes, making them seemingly frost over. "I've changed my mind. I'm not going to move his shit out. I'm going to fucking kill him after he digs his own grave."

"You can't kill him Kye."

"I can, I will." The absolute violence in his voice summons my courage. No. My plan has to work.

"Please, Kye. Just give me time. I had a consultation with a divorce attorney. Due to Mitchell's habitual cheating and the results of his infidelity, there's a chance I won't lose everything when I leave him, and I am leaving him," I say adamantly, trying to convince myself as much as I am him.

When he doesn't respond, I softly touch his shoulder in an attempt to soothe him as much as I feel comfortable. It still feels bizarre. Kye has never needed comforting. He's always been the one to provide it. "I need to try to do it this way for Tobias's sake."

"He never deserved you," Kye scoffs.

"I'm not arguing that fact. I was young and reckless. I wanted the happily ever after and he manipulated me with pretty lies. I helped to create this mess and now, I need to right it," I state flatly. The years of tolerating Mitchell's behavior has taught me one thing, how to go numb. I compartmentalize each piece of the pain burying it deep enough that it can't hurt me.

"Of course the motherfucker did. He doesn't want you, he never did, but you're right. He won't let you go, not willingly." He searches my eyes looking for something and must have found it because his grip tightens in my hair. The sensation has the opposite effect I would have imagined. "You will be my revenge Thena. Mitchell will have to live the rest of his life watching as I love you."

Maybe because it's Kye. Maybe because I do trust him. The realization makes my pulse quicken, my breath coming out in short rasps.

Kye notices, his eyes darkening for a very different reason making the doubts in my mind fall away one by one as if he's hypnotized me somehow. His expert fingers massage my neck, relaxing me into his hold, our breaths mingling, our heartbeats matching in rhythm, working toward a perfect crescendo in a melody only our souls hear.

He drinks me in, as if he is dying and will never gaze upon my face again. The look holds so much longing, it's a declaration all on its own and suddenly, I'm standing on the precipice, hovering on the brink of something I vowed I'd never do.

He leans in, his chest connecting with mine as an electric current runs through me. My nipples harden to the point of delicious pain, aching to be touched. My bundle of nerves twines so tight that a tingling sensation fills my center and I can't breathe. I can't think. I can't fucking move as he whispers his next words. "Let me love you, princess."

I forget everything, everyone, every vow I foolishly took seven years ago in my desperate need for affection.

When his lips collide with mine, the stars go out and the world disappears around us. We're cocooned in a world of our own, built on years of friendship, years of starving for one another yet never able to quench our thirst. I lose all sense of pride, every promise I ever made to myself: honor, loyalty, dedication. Gone. I lose sight of it all in this kiss.

I lift myself up, wrap my legs around his waist, and part my lips for him, granting him access, giving him permission, succumbing to the moment. His tongue moves against mine in a dance typically reserved for long-time lovers. His lips are so fucking soft and full.

My hands tangle in his hair and I shamelessly rub myself against his hardening cock. Jesus Christ, his dick is fucking huge. But not even that scares me in the absolute delirium of the moment. The friction from the thin scraps of material between us, pulls a delicious feeling from my already throbbing pussy. I moan loudly, and he swallows it with his kiss.

Pulling away to run his tongue down my neck, nipping and sucking all the sensitive spots and driving me absolutely wild. I arch into him, tilting my head to give him better access as the water sloshes around us, not that we care. The sensation of his lips, his tongue, his teeth seem more important than anything else.

When his fingers brush over my hardened nipples, I cry out. The electricity of the moment is too much. I'm overwhelmed with a primal need for him to claim me. He grabs my ass, lifting me higher, just to lower me back down against his length.

"Fuck, princess," he groans against my tits as he moves the bikini top out of his way with his teeth. Stubble grazes my nipple, it isn't enough.

"Don't stop, Kye," I beg.

"Never." He latches on to the sensitive flesh, pulling another sinful moan from my lips. I feel him shift us, placing his knees under me to hold me up as his fingers trace up and down my slit. The gentle caress over my tight bundle of nerves has my body tensing. His thumb moves my bikini bottoms aside, and I close my eyes in anticipation. God, I haven't been touched in forever.

"Look at me, brat."

I shake my head, beads of water and sweat running down my spine, eliciting a shiver. His thumb stills while the grip of his other hand squeezes my ass cheek, *hard*, and my eyes pop open.

"Show me how pretty you are when you cum on my fingers, Thena." His voice is thick with desire when lips graze over mine. His thumb circles my clit in barely there touches. As he watches my face for reaction, deep-seated lust fills his eyes.

The sexual release he's intentionally edging me toward has my toes curling. I desperately want to cum. I just need a little more. I'm so close. So. Fucking, Close…

He inserts a finger, pumping in and out slowly as his thumb circles me still, the promise in his eyes holds me captive. I can't define it, but it's there. He leans close again to murmur against my lips, "you only cum when I tell you to, brat,"

I whimper as my core liquifies at his rumbling words. This is a game I've never played. I'm not sure I know how, but I'm willing to give this man anything if he continues to grant me this pleasure, to make me feel alive again.

He draws out his finger slowly, adding another as he pushes back in, penetrating the most private part of my body. I feel him stretching me, his fingers curling at the right time. My legs shake and my pulse thrums so loud I feel it throughout my body. My walls tighten and I clench around his fingers.

"Please…please…" I'm crying, the pleasure bordering on pain. *I need release.*

Kye grins down at me. "Good girl. Now let me see you cum for me, baby."

His words shatter any pretense of self-control and I don't feel any of the embarrassment that being on display would usually cause. The dam breaks. My release drenches his fingers, but he still slowly guides his fingers in my body, ramping me up for another orgasm before my last one ends.

My walls clench around him again, this time tighter than before. I feel his calluses against my swollen muscles, he freezes. Shock along with some emotion I can't identify flicker across his face as he peers down at me. "How the fuck are you getting even tighter?"

Those words hit me like a bucket of ice.

Immediately, I hear Mitchell's voice in my head, the scenes playing out so clearly my breath catches. '*Jesus, Thena! You're such a freak. It doesn't feel good when I have to force it in. What the hell is wrong with you?*'

Every hateful comment, every argument… I can't breathe through the humiliation, the utter fucking embarrassment. I slide down Kye's body as he removes his fingers. Kye's always been good at reading me.

"I need to go." I can't look at him, I can't bear to see the disgusted look on his face. Not him, anyone but him. I hiccup.

Gentle hands cradle my face, the heady scent of my body lingering in the air. "Thena, look at me. What did I do wrong?" he asks quietly.

I shake my head, not willing to look up.

"Baby, did I…did I hurt you? Was I too rough?" His voice is so hesitant. It breaks my heart.

I shake my head again, still refusing to even glance at him.

"What is it?" he asks yet again.

I realize he has no intention of letting this, or me, go without having this extremely uncomfortable conversation. I steel myself for the onslaught of nasty reactions I've been forced to accept over the years. Once I tell him, he'll be as disgusted as Mitchell.

"When I...ya know." I start, but my voice trembles. God this is awful. I twist my fingers together trying to find my courage.

"Orgasm," he supplies.

"Yes, when I orgasm... I get tighter each time until I, um..." I can't do this. I can't say it out loud.

"Until you what?" I glance up at Kye, the patient look on his face stops my heart and heat blooms across my chest, rising to cover my neck and cheeks. I am absolutely humiliated. How do I say this to him?

"I should just go," I say.

"Try again, princess." He chuckles and I lose my temper as my frustration and humiliation build, reaching a boiling point. I really should fall back on my anger more often. It's a useful emotion that's gotten me through plenty of tough times.

"Well, Captain Asshole, if you must know, I get tighter each time until I squirt, then my body loosens up." Aggravation floods me. I'm so sick of never being enough. Why can't I just be normal? Like having a boring normal vag? Huh, universe?

Kye chuckles again, grabbing me by my waist and positioning me back onto his hips. "Oh, I knew you were a brat, but this information is just too good," he grins while rubbing his nose against mine.

I'm so confused. "Don't you think I'm a freak?"

He stills so much I can't tell if he's still breathing. "Why the fuck would you think that?"

"Mitchell says–"

Kye cuts me off before I can finish. "Thena, baby, look at me. I want you to remember this conversation, our time together in this pool. Every time that doubt tries to invade, every time it fills your mind with the poison he instilled in you. He cannot steal your pleasure and joy anymore. Mitchell is a little bitch who couldn't handle what was his. You're *mine* now, and I look forward to your pussy holding my dick like a vice grip."

With that, he devours me again.

5

Beer Bellies & Humiliations

Thena

"Thena Sullivan! Where are you?" Mitchell whines in a whisper teetering between annoyance and anger. It's always worse when his friends are here. He thinks they won't dote on him if they witness him doing woman's work which starts a panic. He's become such a prick.

"I'm here, sorry Mitchell! Time got away from me." I swim over to the ladder using the rungs to pull myself up. The night air's chill raises bumps all over my arms and legs. I shiver, looking around for my towel or a cover up, neither where I left them. One of the other wives must have used them earlier. Shit it's fucking cold.

While continuing to tremble, I glance around and spot one of Mitchell's shirts hanging haphazardly on an Adirondack chair. I sprint over, pool water dripping from my body. Sweet baby Jesus, it's fucking cold without Kye's body heat. Mitchell gets to the shirt before me, snatching it up as I reach out for it. He looks down his nose at me, growing more annoyed by the second.

"Thena, you know I prefer you to wear your own clothes. Your perfume seeps into the fabric and ruins them," he slurs. Oh great. He's fucking toasted. Maybe if I push him in the deep end of the pool, he'll stay there.

"Mitchell, I'm freezing. Don't be silly. I'm not wearing perfume." I admonish him, reaching for the shirt. He pulls it behind him, shaking his head and laughs. He fucking laughs. *Yeah, because watching your wife, the mother of your child, freeze is just so fucking hilarious.*

"You'll clean the kitchen *before* you get dressed and not a moment sooner."

"It's cold, I'm wet. Give me your shirt or I will go find one of my own." Holding my hand out I expect him to pass it over to me.

He shakes his head, his glazed eyes burning through me. His hand shoots out, his fingers wrap around my wrist as he pulls me off balance, flush against him. The smell of pissy beer fills my nostrils, turning my stomach. "You will do as I fucking tell you. You are not to question my authority in this home. Am I clear?"

I jerk my arm out of his hold. My skin warms as my irritation grows into a surge of rage just below the surface. This fucking unappreciative asshat won't let me have one of his shirts? I wash the fucking shirts! Mitchell would confuse a toaster oven for a washing machine. I just want to cold clock him one good time. Wipe that smug grin off his face. The disrespect that I have to deal with… Every. Fucking. Day. I'll be starring in an episode of Snapped soon, if I don't get him the hell out of here.

I throw my hands up in a gesture of surrender. I'm tired and I refuse to play his game. My anger dies out, leaving a wave of disappointment, my already battered heart breaks a little bit more.

But will you get out? You've changed so much. You fell for every stupid line, gobbled those beliefs he shoveled into your mouth for years. You believed him when he said no one would ever want you. He conditioned you, trained you. Who are you without that? My ever present subconscious voice whispers in the recesses of my mind.

I pinch the bridge of my nose, a headache forming behind my eyes. It was always his way or no way. All the gaslighting, manipulation, lying… The cheating.

Now look at the mess you're in. All because you weren't strong enough to leave when you should have. Or maybe, you didn't really want to, that little voice whispers again.

I will myself to stay calm, to project the perfect vision of the dutiful housewife. I'm almost out, I have to keep reminding myself. I brush past him, still shivering as I make my way through the crowd that's loitering on the back deck now, vultures hoping for a show to spread through the company on Monday morning. I won't give them the gossip they're looking for.

I square my shoulders as I head up the inclining backyard, steading myself as I take the patio steps one at a time. After plastering a fake smile on my face, I take the last step onto the back deck. I'm met with a handful of his closest friends, who look at me in varying degrees of pity and curiosity.

These men all have traditional stay-at-home wives who care for their families. The wives and children are all seen but never heard. The difference is, these men all treasure and adore their wives.

Not him. The one time I tried to kiss Mitchell in public was at a formal company event. I was so caught up in how dashing he looked in his suit and tie that I leaned in and kissed him in front of some coworkers. My lipstick left a cute imprint on his cheek. After the event, he informed me to never *'embarrass me again, you're not a paid whore. Don't behave like one'*. I don't remember a time before that night where I have ever cried more.

I wonder, as I enter my prison, how appropriate it is to have his wife clean house wearing nothing but a bikini for all of his friends to leer at?

I scrub grease off a baking dish I had to pull out today since the small mixer turned into a rager. The caterer's food disappeared in moments. I had to rush out and grab more food. I should have known to double the amount of guests.

The scalding water burns my skin like acid, the bubbles sticking to my arms. The pain barely registers as my thoughts drift back to my thirtieth birthday. Mitchell partied too hard in the Las Vegas swimming pool and passed out in the hotel room with his buddies. Kye was the one who spent the day with me. He surprised me at the hotel room with a cupcake and candle, telling me to make a wish.

When he'd peeked into the room taking in the beer cans and takeout containers that littered every surface, disgust became evident in Kye's expression, deepening my embarrassment. He threw pillows at Mitchell and his friends who were passed out in various places around the room, but no one moved.

Kye ordered me to get dressed, and we spent the day together eating pizza, taking silly photos, and people watching on The Strip. It was a perfect day.

I scrub the baking dish harder, consumed by the thought of how many perfect days I missed out on.

"Wife! Grab us another beer, why don't ya?" he yells over his friends. One of them makes a joke, and Mitchell laughs.

If I throw this pan from here, will it hit him?

Another joke is told, and the entire group erupts into raucous laughter, their beer bellies bouncing in time.

I gag, turning around to glare at them while continuing to scrub. If they want a beer they can damn well get their asses up and walk the two steps to the fridge. I pray for dissociation so I can ignore the next terrible wife beater joke. Is this why so many women lose their shit? I get it. I really do.

The sliding glass door opens, but I don't turn around. I don't need to. The energy of the room shifts whenever Kye is near. Mitchell peacocks, a lifelong competition still very much in play between them, but one that only Mitchell participates in.

Kye seems unaware of it. He isn't bothered by men and their egos.

Mitchell's friends throw out a round of insults and backhanded compliments about the use of steroids and being grass fed, but Kye ignores them, his eyes landing on me. He appears so calm as if he's not bothered by me scrubbing dishes in nothing but a swimsuit.

I probably look like a drowned rat. I turn back to my task. The quicker I get through these the faster I can shower and go to bed. I was over this day before it began. Now, I'm wet, humiliated, ashamed, and angry. I just want to go to bed.

The air conditioner kicks on, the vent directly above me blasts cold that could compete with an Alaskan winter. I give it a nasty look as the water still clinging to my skin and hair starts to feel like ice.

I'm back to being frigidly fucking cold, I sigh. I should just go shower.

If you leave before finishing the dishes, Mitchell will just humiliate you more. That little voice nudges its way into my thoughts. It's right, so I submerge my hands in the scalding dish water in search of some small amount of relief, letting the warmth seep into me.

"You're freezing, Thena." Kye is standing beside me now. I was so caught up in morose thoughts, I didn't notice him move to my side.

"I'm okay." How many times will I say that tonight? It sounds fake even to my ears.

"Let me help you. Give me the sponge." Kye reaches for the one in my hand.

"No, no, it's fine. Really," I insist. I really don't want to go round for round with Mitchell tonight, and allowing Kye to wash our dishes will set him off. I just want to finish so I can sleep.

"Don't be a brat," he insists.

"And here I thought you liked my bratiness." I snap harshly. I didn't mean to. I'm just so fucking tired.

"I'm not your fucking husband."

My head jerks up, and I risk a glance at the table behind us. Mitchell is engrossed in a story, laughing and snorting. He didn't hear anything.

I stare at Kye in confusion. Why would he say that here? In front of Mitchell? And what the fuck is he talking about? I didn't compare him to my husband. There's zero comparison. Mitchell doesn't hold a flicker to Kye's flame. "What?"

"Give me the sponge. I will do the dishes." He takes it from me before setting it down to remove his shirt. I'm so taken aback by his abrupt behavior, I'm left speechless. Why does he need to remove his shirt to wash the dishes?

Then he holds his shirt out to me. "You're cold and since you're hell bent on being a server for the pieces of shit in this room, you're at least going to be warm while you do it."

I shake my head. That will open a whole can of worms I'm not prepared to deal with tonight. I couldn't possibly host Mitchell and his friends while wearing Kye's shirt, his smell enveloping me.

"Again, I'm not your husband. Your perfume doesn't scare me. So stop being a brat. Put the shirt on. You look better in my clothes anyway." He looks at me expectantly.

Oh my god he heard what Mitchell said outside? Could this night get any more demeaning? Looking at the shirt he offers me, I have a decision to make. Is it a petty decision? Yes. Am I petty? Not usually. Now with Kye's shirt within grasp, I find myself leaning towards it, towards him, despite the possible consequences. After all, if Mitchell loses his shit, it won't be on Kye. Maybe that's what I want, deep down.

I concede if only to stop the tension rolling off him in spades. I've never known Kye to be a patient man, especially when it comes to his protective streak over women and children--especially me.

I take the black tee shirt out of his hands. It's worn with some MMA gym logo across the chest. Go figure. Kye wears two types of shirts, MMA logos and rock band tees. He accepts the win with a shit eating grin directed at the man holding court over his drinking buddies. Mitchell doesn't seem to notice.

The soft cotton is so well worn, it slides over my frame like butter. His smell envelopes me, small hints of cedarwood, whiskey, smoke, amber, and something I can't quite place. Holy hell. Has Kye always smelled this fucking delicious or are the margaritas going to my head? Yes, yes he has.

The unique combination is reserved only for Kye. It's unique like him, and the pheromones oozing from his shirt have my thighs clenching and my delicate parts swelling with desire already.

Gods, I want to beg him to fuck me right here on the kitchen floor, the counter, the table, anywhere honestly. I don't care that my husband and his friends are ten feet from us. I have *never* reacted like this to a man. It's as if that indiscretion in the pool cracked something in me wide open.

I trace my fingers over the hem of Kye's well-worn shirt. My yearning for him clouds my mind, my actions, everything, as I bite my lip. When Kye glances down, he catches on, his eyes heating as I blush.

This is not good, surely everyone notices how flushed I am? How Kye is drinking in the sight of me in his shirt like a starved man in front of a feast? His deep brown eyes darken with a primal promise, his grin turning into a full smile. "It looks better on you, brat." Kye skims the shirt, his fingertips grazing my thigh where fabric meets skin.

I melt, clenching my thighs together.

"Thena," Mitchell's voice interrupts Kye and me, our moment stolen, the proverbially bubble busted. My small glimmer of happiness evaporates as quickly as my lust, leaving the ever constant darkness to swallow me whole. Mitchell interrupting us is the equivalent of your favorite vibrator's batteries dying right before you peak. A real fucking drag.

Kye rolls his eyes, saying something under his breath about 'decking the lazy son of a bitch'. I turn to face the pain in my ass, not bothering to hide my disdain and total contempt. He's looking between Kye and I, and I know he sees it, he's just too scared to say anything.

Is my attraction to Kye wrong? Yes, it is. But my loyalty only goes so far, and after years of suffering for a marriage where my husband does not feel the same about monogamy, I'm done. *I want to live, I deserve to live*, I say desperately to myself as I face Mitchell.

"Why don't you come over here, wife, and sit with us?" Mitchell's voice rises slightly higher, but not enough for his friends to take notice. They'll simply see it as an invitation.

However, to me... I know that tone. I've heard it plenty these last several years. It's a warning, *don't you fucking dare embarrass me in front of my friends, woman.* If I don't obey, things will only get worse. I only take a step or two, before Kye's fingertips graze me, a barely there touch right down my ass crack. I suck in a breath as Kye chuckles lightly.

I cannot believe the audacity of this man. He just doesn't give a fuck what Mitchell sees or doesn't see. That's so fucking hot to me. Irresponsible, but fucking hot.

I walk around the table and lower myself into a chair beside my husband. My skin crawls, as if there are a thousand little insects roaming all over me. Nausea rolls through me, I swallow the acidic taste in my mouth. The margaritas I had today are threatening to come up. After the pool, it feels wrong to be beside him.

Mitchell leans over, placing his hand on my thigh under the table so his friends can't witness his touch. He squeezes and I gasp. His grip is bruisingly tight, as Mitchell whispers in my ear, "if you want to behave like a whore, I will treat you like one and have every man in this room take their turn with you."

A sharp pain radiates down my leg as he squeezes down even harder. "Mitchell, you're hurting me," I whisper to him, trying to keep the fake smile plastered on my face so no one notices.

He sneers at me. "I will break you one way or another, *wife*. Now go take that fucking shirt off and fix yourself up. You look like the pathetic trash you were when I found you in that bar." When he clamps down on my thigh even harder, I can't help myself. I cry out in pain.

Mitchell lets go and joins in the conversation with his friends like nothing happened.

A fresh humiliation rolls through me. He's never put his hands on me. Threatened? Yes, but never physically hurt me until now. My body doesn't seem to know how to move. The shock of it has me glued to the chair.

"Thena, weren't you going to go do something?" A hint of malice leaks into Mitchell's tone. I nod but keep my eyes downcast, unable to look at anyone.

As I rise from the chair, I notice angry red marks on my thigh. The shirt is just long enough to hide what he's done. I start to walk away when a harsh sting accompanies the sound of a hand slapping my still damp ass in brutal fashion.

The room goes silent and the unexpected assault makes me lose my footing. I fall forward, unable to do anything but watch the floor rush up to meet my face. I squeeze my eyes shut.

Instead of whacking against the floor, two strong arms wrap around my body. For a brief moment, I'm suspended in midair.

I wince at the pain still radiating through my ass cheek and thigh. *Nothing like public degradation to get your wife in line*, I think bitterly to myself as Kye helps steady me. I don't look up, I can't meet any of their eyes, especially his. The guys at the table must be shocked because they aren't speaking. I wonder if they regret their DV jokes now?

"Are you okay?" Kye asks me quietly. His fingertips touch my chin, lifting my face to his. I am mortified as the tears I can't hold back run over my cheeks. I don't answer him. The words won't come so I shake my head.

"Forgive me, Thena?" he poses it as a question.

I'm confused. Why would I need to forgive him? He isn't the one that just manhandled me. "For what?"

He directs me to the couch, wrapping me in a blanket before he whispers, "for fucking up your plan."

"Kye, I think it's time for you to go," Mitchell declares from the table. His buddies are all looking at him in disgust. Even drunk they would never put their hands on one of their wives.

Kye strides across the room and approaches Mitchell, towering over him. "How often do you put your hands on her?" Kye asks.

Mitchell pales, his eyes widening. "I have never put my hands on her! It was a joke! I just slapped her ass a little too hard is all!" Mitchell screeches, his voice sounding far less masculine than the man glaring at him.

Kye glances around the table. "Fella's, do you hit your wives like that?"

One by one the men shake their heads, disapproval clear on their faces.

"I didn't think so," Kye states. He levels a look at Mitchell who now has his hands up, a beer still in one, I roll my eyes. The man has his priorities.

"You need to go. She's *my* wife. If I want to slap her ass I..."

Kye grabs Mitchell by the throat, dragging him out of the chair. Mitchell opens his mouth to speak, Kye cuts him off in a tone I've never heard him use. "You will not utter a fucking word."

"I was only..."

Kye draws his fist back and a crunch follows the brutal hit. Mitchell cries out as Kye tightens his grip on him, which is the only thing keeping him upright. Blood squirts down the man's face from his now crooked and swollen nose. *Holy shit!*

"I said not a fucking word. Nod, if you comprehend the words coming out of my mouth?"

Mitchell tries to nod but it ends up looking more like a grimace, blood is freely flowing now.

"Excellent. Go get your shit. You have ten minutes. One minute longer, and I break something else of yours. Got it?"

Instead of answering, Mitchell's beady eyes that I once thought were a beautiful shade of the deepest brown, dart between myself and Kye.

Kye shakes him by the collar with all the anger he's hidden, which is downright palpable. "You don't look at her anymore! You look at me now." He shakes Mitchell again with an expression that looks like he's itching to strike him again.

I find my footing. If Kye can punch Mitchell in the face, I can be brave enough to stand while my assaulter is escorted out of my home. I make eye contact with each one of the men here tonight, daring them to speak up.

No one says a word, their eyes downcast as Mitchell disappears down the hall. Typical men with no backbone. If they don't make eye contact, they can pretend what transpired here never happened. I arch my brows, drawing on the deepest parts of my inner badass, and speak my mind. "I wish I could say it's been fun, gentlemen. It hasn't. Get your shit and get out. Don't forget to wait outside for your drinking partner. He will be joining one of you tonight. I'm sure one of your accommodating wives will allow him to crash on a couch."

His friends race for the door, knowing more is at stake than friendship. If the police show up, all of them will face public intoxication charges as soon as they step off my property. Better yet, they could all lose their jobs if the company caught wind of tonight's events.

The front door closes as the last one leaves.

Mitchell returns with an overnight bag in tow. His shoulders are slumped and his face a bright red as he attempts to cry. Bullshit.

To an outsider, he would look remorseful, sorry even but we've been together too long, I've seen this all before. And the fucker put his hands on me. Years ago, I would have fallen for it. Hell, I have fallen for it…after every one of his affairs. Fucking pathetic…

I watch Mitchell take his time, waiting for me to ask him to stay. He doesn't realize yet that I'm not going to ask. I refuse. All of the toxicity that has left his mouth, the mood swings, the impulse spending, the controlling thumb he has suffocated us with these last few years. I have nothing left to give him.

Except my middle finger. I gave him all of me, he held my world in his hands and he obliterated it.

Kye rolls his eyes when Mitchell stalls in the hallway entrance, shuffling his feet while staring at our wedding photos as if they actually mean something to him.m"You have ten seconds left, before I break something else."

Mitchell snaps his attention to Kye. He must be thinking of his broken nose because I've never seen Mitchell move so fast.

The door slams, and I take my first gulp of air as a free woman.

6

Micro-cuts On The Heart

Thena

I sit on the edge of my couch, not caring if I ruin the fabric with my still damp body. I flex my toes against the lush carpet, soothing myself so I can focus on the next step. Did this really happen? Was it really that easy to make him leave?

"Thena, baby, let me see your injuries." Kye kneels down in front of me, while I continue to process tonight's events.

There's a slight ringing sound in my ears as my head begins to throb. I don't have time for a migraine. "I'm fi--" I stop midway, knowing what I'm about to say is a lie. My dignity left the same time Mitchell insulted and smacked me, so what could it hurt to be honest?

"It's all right to not be okay, princess." Kye slowly brings his hands to the hem of his shirt I'm wearing and together we lift enough of it to witness Mitchell's handiwork. I choke back a sob, my hands tighten around the hem of Kye's shirt so hard my nails nearly pierce the fabric. How could he put his hands on me after everything he's already put me through?

Something hardens inside me as I look at the angry handprint. The small half-moon-shaped cuts are lined with blood. The last bit of softness I reserved for life with Mitchell turns to stone and my heart rate only increases as anger ebbs into my nervous system entwining with my panic.

How dare he do this to me? I know I'm not innocent. I can admit to myself what Kye and I did in the pool was definitely out of line. But at least I waited until I filed for divorce to make out with someone else. Mitchell has been fucking everything with two legs for years. But, to put his hands on me? Absolutely not. I steady my breathing.

I need to pull it together. Time is of the essence now. The plan I meticulously thought out is in ruins, tonight's events moving the timeline up several weeks. Now is the time to push forward. Hesitation isn't an option, especially not when the prize is freedom for Tobias and myself.

"I'm sorry." I whisper to Kye, he flinches as if the words physically struck him.

"Don't ever apologize for what someone else does to you. You didn't do this. He did." He runs his hands through his hair, tugging at it. He's angry with himself and the situation, not with me. I can recognize that.

"You're right," I say to him as I lower the hem of the shirt, feeling too vulnerable for my comfort. He smirks at me, crossing his arms.

"When am I not?"

"Cocky much?"

"When I know I'm right..." he pretends to think about it, "which is always," he finishes.

I laugh lightly at his antics.

Kye has always been the breath of fresh air I need when the world is suffocating me. The years we've spent tiptoeing around the subject of our attraction to one another, mostly due to my obligation to Mitchell, is glaring at me now. I will always regret not walking away from my marriage sooner.

How do our actions tonight change the course of our relationship? I wonder to myself as my eyes roam over him. We've always been close, the glue that seems to hold our worlds together, but now? After giving into the temptation…

His swimming trunks ride low on his hips, a trail of dark curls spans from his navel to his groin. I forget my current state of unrest as I lick my lips, my mouth suddenly too dry. His eyes darken as he follows the motion of my tongue. The detailed black and gray tattoos covering his arms come to life when he clutches the couch, forearms flexing.

Desire becomes a tangible thing as we stare at one another. Christ he is pure unadulterated sex. My face must reflect my thoughts, because he suddenly sobers, flashing a small smile before rocking back on his heels to stand. The heat of the moment sizzles out, extinguished by his annoying ability to be rational.

"I'm going to get your first aid kit. Where do you keep it?" he asks.

"The hallway closet. You can't miss it." He leaves me there to stew in my conflicting thoughts. I don't know if I want to be incensed, dismal, or horny. It really is quite the predicament.

Kye comes back with the first aid kit and makes quick work of cleaning and bandaging my thigh.

"Do you think this is really necessary?" I ask him, a bit taken aback with the amount of little bandaids he places on me. He nods, not taking his eyes off of his handiwork.

"Stand up, let me see your backside," he insists.

"No," I say. There is no way in hell I am taking my bottoms off in the middle of my living room.

"Don't be a brat. I need to see if you're hurt," he says flatly.

"I'm not, it's just sore. The strike took me by surprise, that's why I fell." He doesn't look happy with my refusal, but he can kick rocks if he's going to try and control me, too. He must see the conviction in my eyes because he nods.

"If you're sure."

"I am. Promise." I hold up my fingers in a scouts' honor gesture, trying to lighten the mood. My attempt at humor falls flat as he stares at me seriously.

"How many times?"

His words take me by surprise but my brow wrinkles as I try to decipher what the question is. "How many times what?" I ask him.

His strange expression makes me think he's disappointed in me. Maybe he is. "Has he hit you often?"

My heart sinks. Of course he's questioning the last few years he's been gone. How can I be making jokes, while Kye is obviously struggling with the decisions I've made in my life and their repercussions? I take his hands in mine, his so much larger than my own. I always forget his mammoth size until we touch.

"I swear to you. This is a first. I didn't realize how much he'd had to drink today. I should have never put your shirt on." My words seem to anger him and I realize too late how they must sound to him, like I'm defending Mitchell's behavior and shouldering the blame, when I'm not.

He releases my hands, snatching up the first aid kit to return it to its proper place as if he just needs something to do. When he comes back he kneels down in front of me, I want to look away but I don't. I've never been on the receiving end of this determined frown from Kye, it's an expression I won't soon forget.

"There lies the problem. You're usually a firecracker, yet you always make excuses for the one person who promised to love and care for you and failed. Why defend him? He's always taken great pleasure in playing king with no true kingdom. Do you think I don't know him? Believe me, I do, all too well. We were friends for years. Did he tell you we went to school together? Or did he let you believe that we met at work? I bet my small fortune he did."

Kye stands, running his hands through his hair in frustration. I don't know what to say about this new revelation, so I say nothing, and let him continue.

"Mitchell and I grew up side by side in high school and attended the same university. Supposedly, we were bonded brothers. It was one sided though. He had no qualms about stealing for his own gain. He copied my work for years and passed it off as his own. When he got caught--it was me he blamed. I was expelled from school and had to finish my studies on my own."

Kye paces in front of me, his hand finding its way back into his unruly hair. "When a mutual friend called me a few years later, telling me there was an opening in the same tech firm Mitchell worked at, I immediately applied and got the position. Pissing him off daily was my only goal until I met you. I pretended to mend our friendship so I could be near you."

A heavy sigh sends his shoulders slumping forward. "I have had to watch from the sidelines as he broke your spirit time and time again. I am a man who learned to be in control of my every emotion. Until you, I am powerless. You are a force to be reckoned with, a tornado who swept into my life wreaking nothing but havoc. For years, I have suffered in his shadow, watching him take for granted the only person I have ever wanted."

The devastating truth of how he's suffered to stay in my life rips my heart open, tears blur my vision as I look down in shame. The years of Mitchell's destructive behavior has caused so many around us pain, it makes me physically ill. *Who had I married?*

Everything that I kept bottled up rushes to the surface, claiming me like a rogue wave. The onslaught of emotions crashes into me with so much force, the pain pierces my fucking soul. My shoulders shake as I crumple into myself, crying for all the reasons I promised myself I wouldn't.

Kye's arms wrap around me. Cradling me to his chest as my sobs soak his sun kissed skin.

The suffering we both kept hidden steals the very breath from my lungs. Nothing could prepare me for this onslaught. The sound of pure torment I expel in this moment is so animalistic I barely recognize myself as the source. Hot tears flow freely now, my grief too great. My heart aches for what's been done to Kye, Tobias, myself. Mitchell's path to success has been paved over our bleeding souls in his search for self-gratification.

No. I did this to us. He may have been the instigator, but for too long I denied myself happiness, unable to get past the shame of a failed marriage to admit my love for another. The pure devastation of it all was a truth I hadn't been strong enough to face. I have lied to my heart for so long about both men, that having to face it now is almost unbearable.

A friendship is all I ever expected to have with Kye. Keeping him in my heart and life was more important than having him in my bed. Yet, here he is, after all this time, protecting me, caring for me, still after all the years loving me.

The weight of it is suffocating. What am I doing? Why am I crying? Why am I not angry? Mitchell has finally crossed a line that I cannot defend. One that I would never try to. There is no coming back from what he's done. I'm somber, yet, I feel determination taking hold. I won't let him win.

Kye's warm hands caress up my arms and shoulders to cradle my face as he tilts my head back to meet his eyes.

"Princess, if you need to get it out, do so. Don't hold back on my account." His eyes hold such sincerity, a little piece of the ice around my heart chips away. Only Kye could bring me warmth on my coldest night.

I hiccup, giggling slightly to cover my embarrassment. "No, thank you. I believe I have behaved like a lunatic enough for one night."

"Don't do that," he says flatly.

"Don't do what?"

"Deflect. You never have to hide from me. You've been in an unhealthy relationship for years. A boy has told you what to do, instead of a man allowing you to navigate your own life, including your emotions. You wanna fight someone? Cool. Tag me in if you need. You want to burn the world to cinders? I will hand you my Zippo. You want to lay in bed watching terrible eighties action flicks and eat an entire pizza in one sitting? I'll be there with napkins to wipe cheese grease from your chin. It's your world, brat. I've just been orbiting, hoping to soak up the sun." He wipes my eyes with his calloused fingers as I cry harder. His words warm pieces of me Mitchell had left frozen for years.

"Baby girl, let me take care of you. Let me help you heal. We can take our time. There's no rush. I'm not demanding anything. As long as it takes... Promise." Kye lifts his hands, gesturing the scouts' honor, and it pulls a little laugh from me. He brings his forehead down to meet mine, his curls tickling my face, I debate what to do from here. I want to kiss him. I want him to make me feel and forget. I just...want him.

I nod my head slowly, the unmistakable smell of his minty breath fans my face. It's as if he has been holding it, waiting to hear my response to his request.

"I need to hear you say it, princess."

Kye rubs his nose across mine as I whisper, "please, take care of me. If only until morning."

His gaze holds a vow that melts me more as he tells me, "I want you to wrap your legs around my waist brat, we're gonna go get wet."

7

Showering In Sin

Thena

My ankles lock around his waist and he lifts me from the couch. Tonight's disaster is nearly forgotten already as Kye sweeps me into his arms. I have the briefest moment of doubt. What if he drops me?

"I don't know what caused that doubt in your eyes, but give me just a moment to remedy that shit." He nips my ear causing me to squeal. His fingers squeeze my ass, pulling me closer against his body, the outline of his already hardened cock presses against my stomach. Totally terrible timing to compare, but Mitchell was not a grower or shower, if you know what I mean. I wasn't with the man for the fireworks. He had stability, a plan. He offered a secure future…or so I once thought.

His dick rubs against me again. The friction is delicious in every way. I'm ready to say fuck the plan. I want to throw caution to the wind. Fuck, I want to find out if I can fit all of him in my mouth.

He lifts me higher, my core connecting with his dick and I moan as he groans. Only our bathing suits separate our bodies. While squeezing one side of my ass with enough force to show me he appreciates it, I lift my hips enough to slide back down the bulge again.

Jesus Christ, the friction isn't enough. I'm somewhere between wanting to curse, pray, or fuck him here in the hallway…perhaps all three.

"I want you in my bed and only my bed. Always. Unfortunately, the shower will have to do for tonight," he says in a guttural tone as his mouth moves down my throat.

I pause. Confused. "Shower? I thought we were, ummm…" Fuck, I'm too awkward for this shit. I haven't had sex in over a year, despite being married for over seven. How does one ask for such things? *'Hey! I thought you were going to fuck me until I couldn't walk anymore?'* Yeah, real smooth.

Kye brushes the strands of hair away from my face as he sits me down beside the tub.

"So impatient, princess. Don't worry. I'm going to have your legs wrapped around my neck restricting my airways while I taste that sweet cunt of yours. Suffocate me, drown me, or strangle me. I've been a dying man my entire life."

I stare at him completely dumbfounded, until my lust induced brain catches up to his words. The image of my legs wrapped around his head as he struggles to breathe…*damn.*

Suddenly, his arms windmill as we both lose our balance and end up a naked tangled mess against the tub wall. We both look so ridiculous in my mind. I imagine this isn't exactly the effect he planned. My shoulders shake with laughter and I double over, sliding on the floor. When I regain my composure, I gaze up at him. His arms are crossed over his expansive chest, watching me with a mixture of bemusement and desire.

"I should have known you wouldn't be able to take sex seriously, you little minx," he shakes his head at me as I pick myself up off the floor.

"I'm sorry, but what I imagined is just..." I chuckle some more. "It's just too good."

"I have no doubt that what you're about to tell me is going to be entertaining. Please Thena, share with the class?" he teases.

I chuckle again, my intrusive thoughts more ridiculous by the moment. "You meant your words to be sexy and instead I saw us looking more like a weird abstract version of an octopus flailing all over the shower floor..." I cover my face. I'm a mess. I peek through my fingers to find Kye still shaking his head laughing at me, but it doesn't feel degrading like Mitchell's. There I go, comparing them again.

Of course, Kye's demeanor changes as I pull off his shirt, his humorous expression morphing into something more primal.

The hunger there sobers me.

"I'm sorry," I say. Wait. Why am I apologizing?

Kye peers at me in confusion until it seemingly dawns on him, and he looks stricken.

"Do *not* apologize for laughter, Thena, I'm not him. One day you will realize that. Let's get you washed off." He leans past me, turning on the faucet, glancing back with one eyebrow raised, a smirk of pure evil on his too handsome face, "brat."

I try to hold back my reaction when he calls me his favorite nickname. I really do, but my cheeks heat and my belly tingles like I'm plunging downhill on an unexpected rollercoaster. My toes curl. Smitten for the first time in years, that's what I am. He makes me want to be brave, to be daring and sexy. He makes me feel desired.

I square my shoulders, pushing my bottom lip out just enough to grab his attention, closing the small distance between us until the flecks of silver in his blue eyes shine like a beacon calling me home.

I run my hands over his chest, taking my time to savor the chiseled muscles under the tips of my fingers. His quick inhale gives me the confidence to rub my breasts on his body as I stand on my tiptoes. His breathing is heavy, his chest expanding and relaxing, causing a delicious almost painful friction on my nipples.

He moves his hands around my waist, squeezing hard enough to be in control, without being painful. No, this man would never cause me physical pain solely for his pleasure. I would beg him for it though I realize.

The warmth of the tension radiating from him, knowing this man wants me, just the way I am with my curves, stretch marks, quirky sense of humor, and broken heart.

I graze his earlobe, whispering as seductively as I can muster, my voice wobbling from nerves a tiny bit. "Yes, Daddy?"

Kye's eyes sharpen with desire, and he wraps his massive hands around my waist, lifting me off the ground. His lips crash into mine and I lose myself in the velvety texture of his full lips, my head swimming, endorphins flooding my system. A loud moan escapes as his tongue brushes across my lips, demanding entry. Once I grant his silent request, stars dance behind my eyes as our tongues clash together.

My fingers sink into the hair at the nape of his neck, the curls just long enough to wrap around my fingers. While shamelessly rubbing myself against his hard body, Kye backs me up, the hot spray pulls a shocked gasp from my lips. When he breaks his sweet torture to take my face in his hands, his eyes hold such intensity I want to tear up again. My throat feels tight, soaking him in as he stands before me, looking at me like I'm the most precious thing in the world.

"Thena, what am I to do with you?" He nearly chokes on the words as his lips graze over mine. Those lips are so fucking soft. Should men have such soft lips?

"I want it all," I whisper back. Our breath mingles, drawing the tension between us tighter before our lips meet again, tongues moving in a perfectly choreographed kiss.

A soft whimper escapes him and he pulls back. "Everything, precious. I want to do everything."

My breath catches, his words sending a thrill through me, making my legs feel like jello. The desire I have always felt for him snaps my control. "If you don't stop talking and fuck me, I'm going to go get my vibrator to finish the job." He looks shocked before his expression turns downright feral. His fingers hook onto the waistband of my bikini bottoms, yanking hard.

I'm so turned on, I barely register the fabric ripping. He brings one of my legs up and thrusts his hips against me. I need more though and I'm tired of playing games. I jerk his trunks down and his cock springs forward.

I knew he was well endowed from our time in the pool, but honestly his cock is massive. How is that going to fit? The look on my face must be comical, but it doesn't deter him.

He rubs the head of his cock over my sensitive bud and I gasp. The all-consuming need racing through me makes the sensation almost painful. Hot water clashes with cool air, as another overwhelming wave of emotions washes over me. I'm too caught up in the moment, unable to wrap my mind around a single cohesive thought.

Running my hands up my stomach, I lift my breasts squeezing them as my head falls back against the shower wall. Moans of pleasure escape me every time he circles his dick around my entrance, still teasing me.

When it becomes too much I growl in frustration. He laughs, the cruel prick. I'm still not sure how this is supposed to work. I've read about shower sex, but it's not something I've ever performed.

"Umm. Kye, how does this work?" I ask. Feeling insecure and turned on at the same time is a bitch.

"Thena, make sure this is what you want. I want to hear you say it." He sounds as if he's in pain and I glance down. His dick is so hard, the veins are popping along the length of it, so maybe he is.

Desire clouds my every thought, and I can't speak. I only want to feel. Sensations run through me, the heaviness of my tits filling my hands accompanied with the head of his shaft moving around my opening. It's just too much. I shake my head in an effort to clear some of the fog. "Tell you what?" I murmur.

"Tell me I can have you in every way," he demands, moving my hands off of my body so he can grasp one hard nipple in his mouth. I arch into him, but he pops his mouth off. "Say it, Thena," he demands more forcefully.

"Yes. You can have me. You can have all of me. Just. Fuck. Me. Already." Our lips crash together, in the most soul-shattering kiss I have ever experienced. His calloused hands grip me tightly, eliciting a moan from deep within. My back collides with cold shower tiles as Kye lifts my legs wrapping them around his hips. He uses the wall to hold me in place for those wandering hands to go to work.

His fingers find my clit, his thumb rubbing small slow circles, drawing out my pleasure. His other hand wraps around my hair, tugging just tight enough to make it a mixture of pleasure and pain. I'm ready to beg this man, to give him anything he wants. I move against his hand, shamelessly wanting more, needing more. "Don't you fucking move, brat."

Stilling my hips, I whimper. The combination of emotions is almost too much for me. He slips two fingers inside, pumping while circling my clit. I toss my head back, moaning in pure ecstasy.

"Jesus Christ you're so tight. My fingers barely fit."

"Please… please don't stop," I beg him.

"Oh, princess, you're soaking my finger and I've only just begun," he whispers across my lips. He slides another finger in, curving them at an angle that sends me over the edge. I cry out and his lips capture mine. He groans into my mouth, working his fingers in and out of my sensitive pussy. I tighten around him, my walls locking around his fingers. He stills, a look of shock across his features. "Oh, you weren't exaggerating when you said this little pussy gets tight."

I still, hesitating as Mitchell's cruel words invade my thoughts yet again, forcing their way into this special moment. Shaking my head, I attempt to remain in the present moment with Kye and find our rhythm once again.

He, of course, notices everything, and shakes his head. "Whatever just happened in that pretty little head of yours, allow me to fuck it out of you. You're exquisite. Remember what I said in the pool? I want your pussy to be my cock's vice grip." My eyes go wide, and my mouth forms a small O as he shoves his cock fully into me.

We both groan loudly. Holy hell, how am I supposed to breathe? I'm so full I swear I feel him seated in my guts. My body instinctively clenches around him causing his eyes to roll in the back of his head. With a groan, he slowly pulls out as my walls tighten even more. "I would ask you if you're okay, but your pussy is doing the talking for you," he says as he thrusts back in.

His cock is so thick, he stretches my body to the point I have to break. I'm breaking right? The feel of him thrusting in and out of me does something to me that words just can't describe. Moan after moan escapes my throat as my body milks his cock, pulling a groan from him.

Suddenly he stops, a wicked grin curving his lips. "You've made my cock so wet, Thena. Let's make her drench it as well."

While my sex-addled brain is still trying to decipher the words, his thumb rubs in a circular motion around my sensitive nub: one, two, three…on the fourth, my stomach tightens, the walls of my pussy close around him and it's more than I can take.

I shake my head, wanting him to stop, but I can't find the words to plead with him. I just pant, trying to catch my breath until he runs the pad of his thumb over my clit again. This time, when I clench down on him, I feel it. A flood washes down his cock, my body sings and my juices flow until they coat my thighs as well. My legs give out as I come down from the release. Kye is the only reason I'm still vertical.

8

Therapy After Orgasms

Thena

Laying in bed next to Kye, cocooned in his warmth within tangled sheets, a cooling contrast to his body heat, is pure heaven. I sigh contentedly, more relaxed than I have ever been. I've waited forever for a moment like this. Now that it's here, with him, I want to savor every sensation. Kye massages his fingers into my scalp, I burrow closer into him.

"Was this part of your plan?" he asks.

My plan was to enlist Kye's help to escape from my husband, not to fall in bed with him. A stab of guilt attacks my already battered soul. How do I tell Kye? While I don't regret what we did here, this can't happen again. I know in my heart I haven't betrayed Mitchell, but it still feels wrong because of that now worthless piece of paper I signed? How do I articulate that despite my soon to be ex husband's multiple affairs, I still feel guilty for this indiscretion? Even after everything that's happened?

He rolls me onto my back, bracing himself above me, his dark hair falls forward. Every part of me craves to reach out and brush my fingers through his curls, but the rare softness in his eyes is what makes me still. "You're stunning when you're overthinking," he states as my hips cradle his groin, a fact I'm suddenly very aware of as my thighs tense. "How easy it is for me to distract you with innocent physical connection," he whispers, leaning down to brush his lips across mine.

"I am not distracted, *Sir*. I am simply gathering my thoughts."

"Well, by all means, *Madam*, take your time. But…I must warn you. The next time you call me Sir, I will be marking that delectable ass of yours while you beg for me." He grinds his semi-erect cock against my core again, dragging a sound from me somewhere between a plea and a moan.

I close my eyes in another weak attempt to gather my thoughts.

He's right. I'm easily distracted by him. The noise that leaves my body this time is more of a sigh. I'm trying to be annoyed at myself for my reactions, but I can't. He's hot as fuck and he's my best friend. Is it wrong to steal your husband's best friend and fuck his brains out? Surely there are rules about this?

"Have I told you lately that it's like pulling teeth to get you to talk about topics you don't want to?" Kye asks me.

"I don't want to talk about my husband while I'm naked in bed with another man." As soon as the words leave my mouth, I know they are the wrong ones.

The softness in Kye's eyes diminishes and his body goes stiff around me. An iciness fills the space that was bursting with warmth seconds ago and that loss makes me shrink into myself, wanting to become as small as possible.

My reaction doesn't go unnoticed. Kye immediately relaxes his body, looking me directly in the eye, stressing his seriousness. "He's not your husband."

"Tell the judge that after he throws the book at me in divorce court for adultery. Did you forget? We're in the south, and Southerners love to protect their men."

"I don't need the government to tell me when he is or isn't your husband. He lost that fucking privilege. What I want to talk about with you has nothing to do with *him* and everything to do with *us*." Kye rolls off of me, moving to stand by the bed, his body flexing with the movement. I lose myself for a moment, marveling at his body, which seems so perfect to me. While Kye zips up his jeans, he catches me staring and snaps his fingers at me, amused by my lack of self-control. We laugh together, and the tension eases. "I'm getting you some water and a warm cloth. I want you to lay here and rest. While you're resting though, I want you to think about something for me."

"Hmm?"

"What's it going to take for you to move forward in life?" he asks.

My eyebrows pop up in surprise. "Why?"

The question is one I wouldn't have guessed he would ask. He must understand my confusion and surprise because he stares at me with so much patience, I want to hang my head and cry. Of course, Kye notices my subtle body language when I can't seem to vocalize my thoughts. "Because, when you finally accept facts, I want you to be able to be all in. I have loved you since the first moment I saw you. I have done nothing but crave this, but if you can't move forward from the past and love yourself, you will never be able to love me…not the way I do you. So, until you can, I will love enough for both of us. We aren't responsible for the shit that happens to us. We're responsible for how we process it and move forward. So, I will ask you again, what are the triggers we need to work on?"

As I mull over his speech, emotion clogs my throat. His declaration of love leaves me too stunned to speak, and memories of that day in Arizona pop into my mind. I quickly shut them down, unable to acknowledge them.

His perception hits too close to home and my instinctual response is to throw out a sarcastic remark. But his earnest expression is too raw, too real for me to hurt him. "If I had a therapist, they would say a lot," I respond honestly, lifting my chin.

"What would your hypothetical therapist have to say about your psyche?" he asks, curiosity evident on his handsome face.

"I'm a walking contradiction with a shopping list full of triggers."

"Start at the top," he motions for me to begin.

If I roll my eyes any harder, they may never go back the same. This will consume our entire night. "Fine. Don't say I didn't warn you though. This may take a while," I tell him, my list is longer than I am tall. I have no qualms over it, I acknowledge it. Linking my fingers together I begin. "I'm sensitive to smells, but I believe you already know that, with the way I react when you're around."

He flashes a dazzling smile that screams the answer. Although I'm not surprised, I thought I was being discreet when I took deep breaths around him.

"Anything else?" he asks me so gently, the ice in the middle of my chest begins to melt. I take a moment to center myself before continuing, with growing confidence.

"The silent treatment, being ignored or excluded by proximity are all major triggers for me. Mitchell would sit next to me for hours, without uttering a single word to me, even when I begged and pleaded. He was a master at ignoring me, like he couldn't hear me despite being inches away. It's a horrible feeling." I tighten the sheet around my frame as the memories bring with them a bitter chill.

Kye's body stiffens. He may be getting the answers he asked for, but the details of Mitchell's emotional abuse clearly anger him.

After a breath, I push through, wanting to be done with this conversation. "Loud, leering men, lying, certain tones of voice, and last but not least and the most contradicting one of all…cheating." A shadow passes over Kye's face.

"That's oddly specific, Thena," He comes over. Tucking the sheets around my body. "I have an idea, although I would never want to overstep,"

"Go on."

"What if you start journaling? It can help you work through everything you're keeping up here." He taps the side of my head. "All the things you're not able to say out loud about all the fucking god awful shit that's been done to you. Journaling is also a great way to determine if it's the action or sound that is triggering you or if it's the association of a memory attached to either."

I blink up at him, perplexed. When did Kye go from sex god to therapist? "What qualifications do you have to hand out suggestions on identifying and handling trauma and triggers?" He doesn't seem put off by my terrible attitude, but my immediate remorse is bitter tasting. It is pretty sound advice.

"It's only a suggestion. I've gone to therapy and I found journaling really helped."

"Maybe I will… Journal, that is."

"You're not going to acknowledge the other part of what I said, are you?"

"Nope."

He smiles at me. "We'll see about that."

I shrug. "I guess we will."

"Just remember, only you can do the work of piecing your heart back together once someone has wronged you. Their actions are their own, but you are responsible for how you move forward. If at any time you can't move on with your life with him still walking the earth, just say the word and he's dead."

With that, he leaves the room. I curl into myself beneath the sheets, my mind spiraling out. Fuck.

9

Introducing The Ladies

Thena

"Hey hooker! We're back after a long night of partying! Where are you?"

I hear her before I see her. As always, Rita does not simply enter my home, she's a parade of one. All that's missing is the marching band accompanied by confetti falling from the sky.

"I'm in here!" I call out loudly from the bedroom.

"Mom! My Aunties are *wild*! We went to the trampoline park and Auntie Rex almost got into a fight!" Tobias yells as he runs through the house in search of me. I roll my eyes, knowing Tobias has a habit of exaggerating certain tales.

Don't freak out until you hear it from the adults, I think to myself.

"Snitches get stitches, kid." I hear Rex yell at him as they come down the hall.

Tobias laughs and loudly whispers back, "My Mom would kick your as-"

"Tobias Montgomary! You will eat soap for supper if you finish that word." My tone is impressive and I hear a muffled apology from my son.

"Hey lady, if you and Mitchell don't have plans today, we thought we could have a movie night." Blanca, the fourth and final friend in our little group, begins.

I finish folding the shirt in my hands, placing it neatly on the pile I've been building all morning. Then I plaster a smile on my face before turning to my most trusted girlfriends.

Blanca places her hand over her mouth as she takes in the sight. The twins, Rex and Rita, stare with eyes so wide it would be comical if I wasn't so concerned with the little dude standing in the middle of them.

Tobias takes his time focusing on every box stacked in the room. I stand quietly, patiently waiting for him to take it all in. I want to handle this as delicately as possible. Had the time not gotten away from me, I would have been waiting in the living room for them. I hate that he has to come home to this.

"Are… Are we moving?" Tobias asks, his eyes shift to mine, clearly afraid of my answer.

I approach him, nervous and fearful at first. How will he handle the news of his parents' separation? I take him in my arms, gently swaying like I often do to reassure him. I peek over his head at Rex, who's directly behind him. She nods, already fully understanding the situation, which gives me the confidence I need. With the silent love and support of my friends, I tell my son, "We aren't the ones moving, sweetheart."

I close my eyes, the fear of my son's reaction so strong, the panic is suffocating. *You are his mother, you must not show him anything but strength,* I remind myself. Tobias steps back from me and my anxiety ticks higher. This is it, this is the moment you lose him forever.

"Is this because he cheats on you?" He asks so innocently.

My friends share nervous glances, while I steel my resolve to be strong. I don't cry. My days of crying are over. I successfully rein in my emotions and contemplate what I want to say. I need to choose an appropriate response. Parenting a child with an IQ north of one-forty comes with its own challenges. He may be eight years old, but Tobias's level of intellect will never allow me to gloss over a conversation because it's deemed too mature for him. My best bet is to face this topic head on.

"What makes you think Dad cheats on me?" I ask.

Tobias twists his little hands together, avoiding eye contact. We are so much alike. He must make up his mind, because he stops fidgeting, squaring his little shoulders. "Dad must not remember that I can read. He lets me use his phone for homework when he doesn't want to deal with me. The woman in his phone isn't you."

I stare at my son in horror, bile creeping its way up the back of my throat until that barely checked rage I've been holding at bay comes barreling to the surface. Of all the ways I imagined this conversation could go, *this* was not one of them.

How could Mitchell be so stupid? He allowed our child to see that? How long has my son had to keep this secret? What has that done to him emotionally?

"I'm going to go make us all some lunch," Blanca announces to the room. She leaves, quickly followed by our other friends, who wear expressions that range from rage to astonishment. I hear Rex ask if it's too early for wine. I want to smile, but I can't find humor in this situation.

Once they're gone, I bend down so I'm nose to nose with Tobias. "I'm sorry. You should never have to see that. Ever. How did that make you feel?" I ask him gently.

He thinks on it for a moment and then shrugs. "Dad's a real douche canoe." When he breaks into a grin, my heart melts. I should correct his terrible language, but I won't. I'm going to let it slide this time. I'm going to have to talk to Rex about this though, as I know she is the one he heard that from.

"Are you going to be okay if I have Dad move out?" I ask him as I fight to hold in my laughter from his previous statement.

"I want to help pack his stuff, but I know you will tell me no. I just have one question," he says to me in a mature manner far beyond his years.

"Yes?" I prompt him, feeling more at ease now that I know he's going to be okay.

"Do I get to keep my aquarium?" It's the first real look of fear I've seen on his face since this conversation started, and I ease his mind at once.

"Of course. Your fish won't go anywhere."

That puts a smile on his face. "Okay. Can I play video games now?" I respond with a nod of my head.

10

A Sisterhood

Thena

The spicy aroma of seasoned chicken and vegetables waft through the house causing my stomach to grumble, the hunger finally registering. Nearly all of Mitchell's belongings are boxed and labeled. The rest will have to wait, I need food.

When I enter the kitchen, I'm not at all surprised to find my girlfriends busy. Blanca's blackened chicken paninis are legendary. Rita and Rex are both passing bottles of wine back and forth, trying to match perfectly to our meal. Do people usually pair chicken sandwiches with wine? No idea, but here at this shitshow, we do.

"Go with the red blend ladies. You won't regret it," I walk right past the twins and head for Blanca. Maybe if I grovel she'll allow me to sneak a bite. When did I eat last? Yesterday? The day before? I can't remember.

"Excellent choice!" Rita responds cheerfully.

Out of our group, she's the one who's least comfortable when one of us is in pain. Wanting to fix the source of our anguish comes naturally for her. I summon one of my best smiles for her and wink, my attempt to silently convey that I'm okay. I'm relieved when the tension slips from her face and her posture eases.

"Where did Tobias go?" Rex asks while grabbing our favorite wine glasses. The bright rainbow glasses were gifts from last year's white elephant exchange. When Rex places them on the countertop, the bold letter charms wrapped around the stems tinkle, lifting my spirits immediately. My chest warms even more as I read the words to myself - Drink Wine, Don't Whine! There's No HR Department!!

"He's playing video games." Nervousness has me adjusting my top knot, the action tugging at my roots a little too hard, the slight pain a necessary distraction. I know they have questions. I'm just not ready to give them the answers.

Rita moves to stand beside Rex filling our glasses to the rim. No prim and proper servings here. "Bitch, I have an amazing garlic press that's been passed down through generations. Rumor has it my great-great Nonna used it on her first husband when she caught him with her sister. You could borrow it." With a devious grin, Rita places the nearly overflowing wine glass in my hands.

I open my mouth to refuse her rather tempting offer, but Blanca chimes in first. "Before we use your family heirloom to cause bodily harm, let's eat."

I turn to go tell Tobias, but Blanca stops me with a hand on my shoulder. "I already asked him if he was hungry, but he's still full from our brunch date." She pushes a plate into my free hand. "Now eat."

"Thank you."

She nods before taking a sip of wine and settles into a chair at the table, but I can't bring myself to join them. The events that led to this moment are too fresh. When I look at the table I was once proud to have in my home, all I see are Mitchell's fingernails carving into my thigh and his brutal slap to my ass. I scrimped and saved for this stunning oak dining set for months, whittling my budget to almost nothing and I can barely look at it. Another thing Mitchell has stolen from me, more collateral damage.

"Let's eat in the living room, we can cuddle on the couch while we munch." I walk past the dining room table, not sparing it a second glance but I still experience a torrent of emotions I don't have time to process. Maybe I should dust off my old journals after all.

Blanca and I melt into the oversized cushions while Rex and Rita take their usual places on the connecting sectional. When I bite into my panini, the flavors burst across my tongue, and I moan.

"Will you marry me, Blanca?" I ask once I finish my first bite, we all laugh.

"Not if she marries me first!" Rex declares firmly, joining in on our friendly banter.

Blanca simply rolls her eyes at us, more than accustomed to our incorrigible ways. "You know neither of you can afford me." She wiggles her eyebrows, eliciting another round of laughter.

"Keep cooking like this and we might just try though," Rex quips back at her.

I toss my balled up napkin at Rex, but she leans out of the way and it ends up hitting Rita square in the face. Rex erupts in laughter until Rita whacks the back of her twin's head, almost causing Rex to spill her wine.

"Sorry, Rita! I meant to hit Rex!!"

Rita gives me a reassuring smile. "I assumed it was meant for her."

"Then why did you hit *me*? I didn't do anything to you." Rex sticks out her bottom lip, pretending to be hurt.

"Cut the theatrics. You won't receive an ounce of sympathy from me. It was a love tap."

I glance over to Blanca with a playful pout. "Mom, the children are fighting again."

She giggles while Rita and Rex lock eyes in a staring competition that only lasts moments before we're all laughing again.

A comfortable silence falls over the house as we finish our meal. I know they've been avoiding the subject, giving me time to process my thoughts. I appreciate the gesture. I really do, but I still don't want to talk about the events that transpired yesterday.

How do I explain Kye to them? How do I explain Mitchell? I'm in a vicious game of tug of war with my emotions, and right now…they're winning. Still, the girls are expecting me to talk eventually.

Nausea takes root in my stomach, and I slide my empty plate onto the coffee table, exchanging it for my glass. I watch the dark wine as I swirl the contents, trying to figure out where to begin. All I know for sure is that I don't want to relive Arizona.

I don't feel guilt for finally kicking Mitchell to the curb. It was long overdue and I know my friends will support my decision. I have no doubts about that. My hesitation is about Kye. How do I explain having sex with Mitchell's best friend on the same night I kicked my husband out? When I put it into simple black and white terms, it doesn't paint a pretty picture, but then nothing about Kye is simple.

I sip my wine, wondering who will bring it up first. I don't wait long.

"So are we going to talk about it?" Rita probes.

My humorless laugh has three sets of eyes turning my way, brimming with concern and confusion. Why wouldn't they be? Who laughs about boxing up their husband's belongings?

Me. I do, apparently.

I look at each one of them in return, dreading what comes next. "I don't know where to start."

"How about at the beginning?" Blanca suggests as she places her hand on my shoulder. I smile slightly at the contact, only now realizing how much I need that small amount of comfort.

Finally, I steel my resolve, face down the impending humiliation, and start at the beginning. "Mitchell only married me to fast track his career."

They all gasp, and I watch them closely, praying I don't see pity on their faces. When I only see outrage and astonishment, I tell them every dirty detail of my marriage.

11

Garlic Press Threats

Thena

"That bastard." Rexy shoots up from her place on the couch and grabs up our now empty wine glasses. Then she hesitates, muttering to herself. "This will require more than a glass or two."

I unfold my legs and stand, reaching toward the ceiling to stretch my joints. The popping sound is a guilty pleasure that brings me instant gratification. "I have Toby. I don't want to over indulge," I say as we all head into the kitchen.

"I knew I didn't like that fucker for a reason." Rita plops her glass down in the sink a little harder than necessary but, thankfully, it doesn't break.

"I'm so sorry that you've been suffering like this. Is there anything we can do to help?" Blanca asks with an almost hopeful smile.

My heart swells with gratitude as I stand there and take in my friends. No. These three have truly become so much more than friends. We're family. "You being here is enough for me. I'm grateful to have you ladies. Really."

"You know what? You need to get out of this house," Rex declares adamantly.

I shake my head slightly. My friends have already done so much for me. Listening to me detail my trainwreck of a marriage is enough. "Oh, I don't want to impose."

Rita whacks me over the head as she passes.

"Nonsense. You need a girls' night out," Blanca adds.

I open my mouth to protest, but Rita shoots me a sharp glare. "Don't make me use my garlic press on you."

We all peer at her, confused.

"How would that work?" I finally ask.

"Fingers, toes, nipples, nose." Rita counts each one off with her fingers.

Laughter fills the room, and I throw my hands up in surrender.

"Ohhhh! I'm taking you to Jasper's!" Rexy exclaims, doing a happy little dance.

"What's Jasper's?" It sounds like a nightclub. If that's the case, my answer is no. I'm far too out of practice for that.

"You'll see! It's nothing crazy. No dress code."

"If it's a club…" I start.

"It's not," she adds quickly. "I wouldn't do that to you."

"When is Mitchell coming to get his stuff?" Blanca cuts in.

"He's not. His things will be delivered to him."

"By who?" Rita asks with a raised brow.

"A…friend," I say hesitantly, focusing on my fingernails a little too hard.

"Who?" she presses with a firm tone.

"You don't know him."

Three pairs of wide eyes land on me.

"You naughty girl," Rex whispers with a mischievous grin. She pours herself another glass of wine, finishing the bottle and staring at me excitedly. "Tell me more."

"Maybe later. Right now, I'm exhausted and need to spend time with Toby."

"Okayyy… But I *will* extract every juicy detail from those lips on girls' night," she promises.

"Until then, ladies, we've worn out our welcome. Let's get out of here and give Thena some space," Blanca announces to the group.

After walking my friends out, I stand on my front stoop and watch as they head down the street toward their homes. A smile graces my lips while they laugh and carry on with one another. I'm blessed to have them.

For a moment, I lift my face skyward, breathing in the fresh air. My friends know about Mitchell. Just releasing my death-grip on those secrets almost makes me feel free or at least less…lonely. I open my eyes, feeling the first honest and pure ray of hope since he left.

With a relaxing sigh, I lean against the doorframe and enjoy the landscape around me. The sun lies low behind the trees lighting up the sky with vibrant hues of burnt orange and pinks that fade into blues, purples and then black. Its beauty is almost ethereal.

I take notice of the time. It passes so much quicker when your life is being turned upside down. Before I turn to go back inside, the stark white mailbox at the end of the drive catches my attention like a beacon. When did I last check it? The thing is probably packed full of junk mail.

Once I step off the porch and my bare toes slip into the cooling grass, I feel more grounded with each step, but the sensation doesn't last.

When I get closer to the mailbox, an irrational feeling of being watched creeps over my skin. My body shivers slightly and every tiny hair rises until I tense, scanning my surroundings. Nothing looks out of place in the quiet little neighborhood. The crickets chirp while the sun's diminishing rays cloak the sleepy houses in near darkness. Everything is still. An owl hoots ominously and I jump.

Well that's not fucking creepy or anything.

I reach for the mailbox but pause as a paranoid thought rises to the surface. What if he's tampered with it? I glance around the yard again, but everything is as it should be…except for me. I should be inside, not out here in the dark giving myself a panic attack. I'm annoyed with myself, but still have that eerie feeling when my fingers wrap around the mailbox's metallic handle. The lid jerks open with a pop and I peer inside.

Nothing sinister jumps out at me and I breathe a sigh of relief. Get a grip, you're freaking yourself out. I gather my mail, the frustration continuing to eat away at me. Why are you behaving like this? You're literally the only person outside.

Of course…there could be a ghosty behind me…standing there…creeping up on me…one I can't see.

Damn it. There goes my imagination, running rampant. No matter how much I chastise myself for being irrational, something still seems out of place. Call it intuition or human nature, but something's not right. I snatch up the mail and turn back toward the house, my strides quickly eating away the distance between me and my porch. My feet pound up the steps and then I rush inside, slamming the door behind me.

The click of the dead bolt only brings a small comfort. My heart pounds and fear escalates but I have no idea why. Come on, Thena. Calm the hell down. Damn, I need another glass of wine.

Once I have things under control, I toss the mail on the nearest table, but a crimson envelope slips from the stack and drifts to the floor. It's for me, but there's no return address. Who sends mail without a return address?

Dread prickles over my skin as I bend down and grab it. No postage, no stamp from the post office, someone hand delivered it. The ominous feeling only escalates when I flip it over to see a golden wax seal. Who the hell uses those anymore? Of course, who still writes letters?

My hands tremble slightly while tackling the wax seal and I manage to slice my finger in the process. "Fuck!"

The envelope and its contents fall, scattering across the floor. Dammit! I hate paper cuts. A coppery tang coats my tongue when I pop my finger in my mouth. This is what happens when you let your emotions get the best of you. My gaze drifts to the mess on the floor, and my brain can't seem to process the scattered photos. It's a trauma response, my mind protecting me, or at least trying to.

Everything finally sinks in. Images of pigs in varying stages of slaughter stare back at me from each and every photo: bare bones, chunks of flesh, what looks like remnants discarded by scavengers, pigs hanging from a trestle, torsos skinned and gutted.

Vomit rises in the back of my throat and I choke on reflex. I will never eat pork again.

I drop down on shaky legs to gather the photos up before Tobias sees them. *Please stay in your room child!* I thank whatever gods there may be that he wasn't the one who checked the mail this time.

What kind of human does this to someone? Why? Seriously, why? I gather the abhorrent photos one by one, trying to take in as little detail as possible, but each glossy photo scorches a new appalling memory into my mind. You have to be a sick fuck to send this to someone. To hell with this. I will not allow this monster to win. Does it piss me off? Yes. Scare me? No. I won't allow it.

When I retrieve the last one, the image stops me in my tracks. There's no butchered pig in the photo. It's a black and white of two lovers wrapped in one another's arms, and not just any two lovers...

The lurid snapshot tarnishes my intimate moment with Kye from last night. How the fuck did someone take this photo? Who would know? This happened less than twenty-four hours ago?

After removing my phone from my pocket, I clutch the slaughter collection in one hand and shoot a text to Kye with the other.

We need to talk tomorrow morning

Little dots appear on the screen as he types out a reply.

911?

What should I say? I don't feel comfortable saying it out loud. What if Mitchell or whoever sent these can read my messages? The thought is unsettling. Fuck it. Let him or whoever this psycho is see.

Window peeper who really loves his meat

Despite the horrific pictures in my hand, I chuckle. Humor is always my go to in stressful situations. Better than panicking. The bubbles appear, stop, and reappear again.

Be there soon

No wait until morning I don't want to upset Tobias

The bubbles appear again.

10-4

The CB radio term makes my eyes roll, but I slip the phone back in my pocket and eyeball the room, thinking. I need to hide these atrocities somewhere Tobias won't find them. Some place he'd never look…

After an internal debate, I hurry to my bedroom closet and stow them in an old box on the top shelf. Christmas is too far away for him to bother snooping.

Once the offensive pictures are safely tucked away, I gather myself before pacing down the hall to check on my son. The door is open, so I lean on the frame and watch him for a moment. He's sprawled out on the floor in front of his giant fish tank, the colors reflecting on the light colored carpet around him in a kaleidoscope of pinks, oranges, and blues.

Over the last year, Tobias has collected at least twenty fancy guppies. The boy is obsessed with anything that has gills. Smiling, I watch him leisurely skim the new aquatic care magazine. He must have found an interesting article, because his tongue pokes out and his brow lifts with an expression of more concentration than I've ever seen from any other child his age.

"See anything interesting in there, buddy?" I lower myself to the floor beside him. Relaxing into the lush carpet is a welcome reprieve from my tension.

Tobias flashes a small smile but doesn't break his focus. "I'm reading a study that says fish are really smart. I think I can train them." He snaps the magazine closed, jumps up, and races out of the room.

What is he up to now? I wonder with a grin. Seconds tick by while I stare down the empty hall. I'm about to get up and go after him when he runs back down the hall, cradling a few things in his hands. "Kiddo, what are you doing?" I ask him, unsure I want to know the answer.

"I'm training my fish, Mom! You know, like they do in the circus. If they swim through a hoop, they get a treat!"

"Honey, I don't think your fish can be trained."

Tobias's forehead wrinkles, his little eyebrows nearly touching one another as he concentrates on tying a string around a metal hoop. "Mom, they already come to the surface to take treats from my hand. My fish aren't boring fish. They have style and pizzazz."

I can't help but crack a grin at his enthusiasm. "Tuna with attitude. I like it."

"Mom!" he rolls his eyes with a disapproving frown.

"Okay, but bedtime is in an hour. Good luck on your endeavors." I climb to my feet and stroll toward the hall. I giggle when I hear him say 'welcome to the Sullivan circus ladies and gents'.

The rest of our home is nearly silent, I can't help reflecting on the night's events while pacing down the hall. The photos need to be addressed. I can't have something like that happening again or worse. What if photos aren't enough next time?

It could be Mitchell. I contemplate that as I wander into my bedroom. He's certainly capable of it. Maybe he thinks he can frighten me into asking him to come home.

If it is Mitchell, I don't want to confront him alone, but that last picture, the one of Kye and me... The whole reason I asked Kye to come was to act as a buffer between us, and hopefully prevent things like this. I should keep that in mind. Kye is not here to be a bed partner. Maybe writing it all down will do me some good.

When I open my nightstand drawer, I notice a few photos sitting on top of my old journal. My fingers skim across the one on top, an old wedding photo. Even now I can't bring myself to throw it away, but the couple within it are strangers to me now.

I study every detail, trying to summon the memory. It's a photograph of Mitchell and I during our first dance with stars littering the sky behind us. Mitchell beams with one arm wrapped around my waist, the other cradling my hand to his chest. My wedding gown flows around us, my head is tilted as I peer up at him with an elated smile, long tendrils of dark curls cascade down my back. Everything looks so perfect but looks can be deceiving.

How was it all fake? My heart rips open once more until anger replaces my sadness. I toss the photo aside, refusing to give it any more of my time and pick up my old black and gold journal.

I need to get it all out in a healthy manner or I'm going to kill him myself. After climbing onto the bed, I rearrange my overstuffed pillows and burrow into my mattress, but I can't get comfortable. Mitchell's pillows are packed up with his clothes, but his ghost is still here.

I need to burn this fucking bed. The thought gives me pause, my eyes watering again. This is my favorite mattress out of all the ones we'd shared. That asshole has ruined so many things for me.

After wiping my eyes, smearing eyeliner on my sleeve, I open the journal, flipping to an empty page. Where do I start? Do I write the most heartbreaking first? Pushing my thumb down on the metal cam of the pen makes the ball point drop with a click.

He exploited our son. Click.

He manipulated me. Click.

He used me as a pawn. Click.

He fucked everyone around us. Click.

He used my body. Click.

He violated my trust. Click.

He never wanted me. Click.

"Mom?" a tiny voice whispers from the doorway and I snap up, forcing a watery smile.

"Yes, honey?" My arms open for him and he approaches hesitantly.

"Are you okay, Mom?" he asks as he climbs up and his little head lands on my chest.

"Yes, sweetheart. I'm okay." I speak the words into his hair. When I breathe in his scent, a calm settles over me. How do children make even our darkest days better just by existing?

"You didn't come to tuck me in," he states in a disappointed tone.

"Well, you were working so hard to train your fish, I thought you could stay up a little later than normal." I tickle his side as I tell him, causing him to squirm and giggle. Mission accomplished. "Come on Kiddo. Let's get you tucked in."

"Mom, can I tuck myself in?" he asks me, my heart squeezes slightly. When did he start growing up?

"If you're sure?"

He rolls his eyes. "Yes, Momma, I'm sure."

"Love you, kiddo."

"Love you too, Momma." He climbs off the bed, and races toward his room. Turbo Toby.

I look down at the journal and click the pen one more time, finally knowing where to start. Pen to paper, ink flows to paint the pristine page with my pain. I start with where and when.

12

Journal Entry:
Before Worlds Collapse

Thena

Arizona, 8 years before this clusterfuck.

Cold beer sloshes over the rim of the frosted mug, running down my arm before it drips onto my knee-high, brown suede boots. The draft's staleness hits my nose. Disgusting, but at least it's cold. Summertime in Arizona fucking sucks.

'One more year of bartending...just twelve months. I've got this!' I repeat my mantra for the twentieth time today.

I'm exhausted. The tiny shorts and low cut tank look foolish on me and they do nothing for the stifling heat. I want to be home, curled up, reading a good book instead of being stuck here. I've been bartending on weekends in this dive for tips and unsolicited numbers while attending college full time. Being a new mom is not for the faint of heart.

You love it bitch. Miss Independent, my inner badass chants. I never saw myself as a single mom, but sometimes that's just how the cookie crumbles. Now that I've completely sworn off men, I'm only focusing on parenting and finishing my education. I'm pretty content, honestly there's no point in dating right now. As soon as you catch feelings they catch Ashtray Ashlee from two streets over.

Being used as a man's good time instead of being their long time is exhausting. Giving everything I have time and time again, with the broken promises of him not being like the others, yet as soon as I catch feelings. Something happens and boom, I'm left to pick up the pieces.

"Hey Thena! Where's my beer, babe?" Ronnie shouts over the music to me. Normally I would tell customers who have no patience to fuck off. But Ronnie's one of the only regulars in this joint I enjoy.

"Coming right up, Ron!" Setting down the pints in front of a biker. I run to the cooler, grabbing Ronnie's beer. I pop the top and slam it down in front of him causing the liquid to foam and spill over the sides.

"Better suck it up, Ronnie. Really deep throat it, buddy." I wink as he starts slurping his beer, causing us both to laugh. He chokes, so I tap his sweaty back and whisper yell in his ear, "What's wrong, Ronnie? You out of practice sucking shit down your throat? Me too, buddy." My Southern accent is thick with sarcasm.

He laughs harder, coughing as I swipe up his five dollar bill. Two for the bar, three for me. That's how Ronnie and I have been since the first shift. I'm sarcastic while he does his damndest not to choke on his beer as I pass our nights with raunchy jokes. I check on the cocktail servers and customers. It's relatively quiet tonight.

A few guys are teamed up in the corner playing shuffleboard. Recognizing them from the expensive suits they have loosened and discarded in pieces on the tall tops near the game. Why they slum it here, I will never understand. The tech firm they work at pays well. But, who am I to judge? They tip and never give me problems. They're all smiles when they notice me. I Ignore them for the most part. Holding up the empty bottles gesturing for another round.

Looking around, I notice the ringleader is missing tonight, if he was here, my job would be much harder. He's pretty average looking, but he has a depth to his eyes. When he's looking at you, it's hard to notice anything else. Heat hits my back as the front door opens. Moving around the bar I drop the bottles in the trash so I can greet whoever just entered.

Well fuck, its him. Mitchell…

"Hey there honey, can I get a cold one?" Mitchell's straight white teeth pop against the contrast of his tanned skin and dark hair. His brown eyes roam over me quickly before settling on my own. He does this every time. He'll come in, order, check me out, grab his beer and proceed to ignore me for the rest of the night. He's not a GQ kind of handsome, but still… Attractive in his own way. Fortunately for me, he never makes a move. With his charisma and my foolish heart. I wouldn't stand a chance.

"Of course, the usual?" I ask him, already reaching for his Bud Light.

"Yes please." His smile melts my hypothetical panties off. I don't wear them, but if I were… He slips his money on the bar top, winking as he turns to join his friends. Great, now I have to try to be a functioning independent woman with him here. Wonderful!

"Thena! Can I get a round over here for my boys?" The taller one of the group yells over the country music that's playing through the sound system. His dirty blonde hair is cut tight to his sides, his baby blues dancing with humor and a slight buzz.

"Pick your poison, Blake!" I yell back, smiling.

"Dealers choice, ma'am!" He bows to me, my heart warms as I laugh.

"I bet those manners make your momma proud!" We laugh together. Blake's charm is infectious.

His buddy pushes him in the shoulder. "Dude, she totally wants that D!" The little fucker shouts right as the music turns off. Blake whacks him on the back of the head, while Mitchell pulls the guy down to his eye level from the stool he's sitting on.

I can't hear what Mitchell's saying, but the offensive short stack of a man looks terrified. The reddish tint on his cheeks from him consuming too much alcohol drains from his face, leaving him pale. Mitchell pushes him towards me, his short legs carrying him quicker than I would give him credit for. Sigh, this is going to be a long night.

"I'm so sorry Miss. I didn't mean any harm."

He looks so uncomfortable that I decide to let it go, but I'm a curious cat so I ask, "What did Mitchell say to you that made you sweat so bad?" I grab enough shot glasses and pour the Maker's Mark in them.

"He's the boss, miss. He can have my job for poor conduct outside of the workplace. It's a Christian company, employee behavior is a direct reflection on the company as a whole."

"I thought you guys worked for a tech firm?" I push the shot glasses towards him.

"We do, but it's more than that. It's a family." He lays down eighty bucks, my eyebrows lift. "Keep the change." He grabs the shots, shuffling back to the group.

I wonder what that's like? To be a part of something so important it creates a family?

I look over to the group of men. They're all laughing with one another, slapping each other's backs, making memories. I want that, deep down in the recesses of my soul, I want to belong. Far too long I've been an outsider.

'WOAH bitch, stop that shit. You do belong. With your kid so shut the fuck up.'

I pull myself back from that train of thought, resolved to keep my expectations low so I'm never disappointed.

"Excuse me, ma'am?" His voice is smooth as velvet. I close my eyes for a moment collecting myself. I turn, already knowing it's Mitchell addressing me. He's taken a seat at the bar with one of his buddies. The look in his eyes contradicts the nonchalant mannerism he is portraying.

"I'm too young to be a ma'am. Are you being contrite purposefully or are you just a dick?" I retuck my rag in the back pocket of my shorts,

"Oh, I assure you, it's with the utmost respect that I regard my bartender in," he says winking

"Yes," I reply, "I hear you're the most upstanding gent in this place." I wink back at him before making another round for the rest of the customers at the bar.

Stopping a few feet away to refill a drink, I hear Mitchell's buddy beside him snicker, "If you aren't going to get a piece of that. I will. With a mouth like that, I bet she sucks a mean cock."

Mortification fills me as I make eye contact with Mitchell.

"I don't date my bartenders. And you will never speak about her like that again." Mitchell replies, color dusts my cheeks. Why do men think it's appropriate to say shit like that?

Mitchell shakes his bottle in my direction indicating he needs another. With the last call so close, all of the guys will pound back a few quicker than normal. Grabbing two more from the cooler I turn to see Mitchell's eyes eating up every curve I have.

My competitive streak comes to the surface. Of all the things for him to do after making a statement like that. Especially after how I notice he is always trying to not get caught looking at me. I open the next round of Buds and slam them down, causing the head of the beer to run along the neck of the bottles. Soaking the bar top, I smile. "While you're enjoying your cheap beer, soaking in every sway of my hips three nights a week, I want you to remember what you said."

Both men straighten looking rightfully contrite. Mitchell gathers himself first attempting to play it off. He says to me, "What I said?"

I lean over the counter, my lips inches from his own, in that sultry tone that seems to get me into trouble. I say in a conspiratorial whisper, "About not dating your bartenders." Fluttering my eyelashes I take my time watching him stare at my lips. My smile widens as I tell him, "I guess you'll have to marry me." Winking, I saunter off, adding more sway to my hips than necessary. Assholes.

"Wait! Thena come back!" I hear him over the music. Nope. Not this time. I will not fall for another man and his games. I will no longer be a man's notch on his bedpost. The next man will put a ring on my finger and actually follow through. Or I won't have any man at all.

Tossing the last of the bottles into the nearby trashcan I notice I quite literally have nothing that needs cleaned or stocked. Sighing, resigning myself to another round of humiliation. I start the walk around the bar to the far side corner where I left Mitchell and his buddy. His friend is gone. Mitchell sits alone, nursing his beer. Might as well rip the band-aid off. Saddling up to him I steel my resolve.

Just pretend like you didn't throw yourself at him. It's fine, everything's fine. "Last call Mitchell."

"Do you like baseball?" He asks me, those dark brown eyes never leaving mine. The jukebox clicks off, the song Are You Gonna Kiss Me or Not coming to an end.

"I love it." Leaning on my elbow, I prop my chin up with my hand. He mimics me.

"Favorite team?"

"Not really a favorite team, more like I'm a fan of the sport." The bar is empty now, I should be closing it down so I can get home and rest.

"If you had to choose?"

"New York Yankees." I say too quickly, why the hell did I choose the Yankees? Fucking pick me energy is thick tonight. He smiles and it lights up the entire dark as fuck bar. His teeth are perfect, straight, white. Insecurities start to sink in like an old friend. He won't want you for a long time, just a good time. Look at him. He's beautiful, he has a solid career, he's intelligent. You're a bartender with a baby, attending cosmetology school. Oh yeah, you're a real catch.

"Ever been to a game?"

"A major league game?"

"Yes."

"No, can't say that I have."

"Wanna go with me to this week's game? I have dugout tickets." He leans over the bar, running his fingers through my hair that's escaped my high top knot, sending shivers down my back. His earlier words come back to me, reminding me I'm just a lowly bartender. I straighten my spine

"I thought you didn't date your bartenders?" I state flatly.

"I don't." He stands, turning to leave, "I will, however, be marrying you." He lays that on me as he walks out the door of the bar, pulling the string to the open sign, causing the bright glow of the neon light to go out.

13

Croissants

Thena

After a long night of sleep eluding me. Hours spent tossing and turning, reliving the past. I pour my coffee and skip the creamer going straight for the cowboy way. With every memory came the vile threats disguised as jokes, unlocking new fears I hadn't realized I had. My frazzled nerves had me waking up checking the locks every hour. *Ugh.* So much for writing it all down. *I will not allow this man to steal my peace.* A silent promise I make to myself.

The doorbell chimes. *Damn he's prompt.* I cross the room and open the door for Kye, the morning sun burning my retinas. I crinkle my nose, disgusted with how happy the morning looks. Bright, beautiful, and fucking cheery. It's the opposite of how I'm currently feeling. He looks fresh, eyes alert and all that, his smile compliments the morning around us. *At least one of us matches the scenery.* Standing in the doorway, I lift my cup. Blowing the hot liquid, warm steam mists across my cheeks.

He goes to speak but I quickly silence him by placing my hand over his mouth. His lips are softer than I would expect. Gunmetal and frost eyes spark with some emotion I can't decipher. Raising a single dark eyebrow in warning, I take a sip of my brew. The dark amber liquid scorches the roof of my mouth, burning its way down my throat. My eyes close savoring the dark, hazelnut flavor.

I hum with pleasure as the caffeine boost is immediately felt coursing through my tired body. *Perfect*, it's the official elixir of life for any adult wanting to make it through the day without committing murder. *Glorious.* I open my eyes, finally adjusting to the bright light of the morning.

"Some things never change." Kye nips my fingers and I yelp.

"Don't do that! Toby could see!"

"He should probably get used to it, seeing as I'm not going anywhere."

"Kincaid!"

"Thena!"

"That's not funny."

"Am I laughing?"

"I change my mind. I don't need your help." I hiss as he holds up a bag.

"An olive branch for my behavior?"

Shifting my focus to the lettering on the bag in question, a bold font reads: *MOMMA'S CROISSANTS & BAGELS.* I squeal, reaching out and yanking the bag from him. The yummy aroma is already filling the room. I smirk at him. "Don't be a prick."

Deciding to be slightly petty, I slam the door in his shocked face. Serves him right for biting me. Running to the kitchen, I tear open the bag digging through it, pulling out my prize as Kye strides in shaking his head, chuckling.

"Was that really necessary?" Approaching me, he flicks the tip of my nose. I bat his hand, leaning away from him.

"One hundred fucking percent."

"Come on pretty girl, let me have a bite. Please?" he pouts, leaning into me, I hold the croissant out to him. Before he can bite down, I jerk it back, taking a massive bite. I ignore his protest, too focused on my mission to interact with him. Warm jalapeno, ham, and cheese croissants melt in my mouth.

Fuck my manners this is my all time favorite. It's been too long since I had one of these. The heated cheese and savory ham bursts on my tongue with just the right amount of spice. Sweet, sweet victory. Kye tsks at me.

"Mrs. Sullivan, where are your manners?" Rolling my eyes, I flip him the universal hand gesture for fuck off.

"Sharing is only caring when you're still small enough to fit inside a sandbox, asshole." He laughs. I stop chewing, his laugh is so alluring.

He lifts a single brow. "Something on your mind? Or should I say someone? Maybe a certain activity shared between two…" He doesn't finish his sentence as he leans into my space again, his eyes expressing exactly what he's referring to.

I smile around another bite of my heavenly delight. Taking my time to slowly lick the melted cheese from my lips, his eyes track my every movement. Hunger and anticipation build like an electrical force between us, driving us towards one another.

The sound of tiny feet racing across the floor snaps me out of the moment and back into the present. A flush dusts my chest and neck. Of course I would be embarrassed over something I started. "Not at all. I'm just curious why you didn't bring enough for yourself." At my teasing. His eyebrows raise.

"I brought six," he exclaims, back to grinning. His dimples appear. I don't let him distract me this time from being my usual snarky self.

"Yes, six for me. Where are your croissants?" I take another heaping bite, rolling my eyes and moaning dramatically.

"By all means don't stop on my account you vicious, little beast."

I ignore his jab, finishing off the first, and grabbing my second one. I take a bite and ask him around a mouth full of food, like the little beast he accused me of being. "You're here early."

He reaches over and closes my mouth with his finger, thoroughly entertained by my antics. Cheeky bastard. "Eat first. I have something out in the truck for Turbo."

"It's age appropriate right?" He feigns offense.

"As if I would give him something that isn't," He's already moving towards the door.

"You gave him a Winchester three-oh-eight for his fifth birthday!"

"Well you can't hunt buck with a pellet gun, Thena."

"A WINCHESTER! He was five!"

"I was setting the kid up for success." He dusts off my worry. Irritated, I snatch one of the unopened croissants up and chuck it at his head. He catches it midair, laughing at me as he opens it and takes a bite. Annoyed with his fast reflexes, I do the mature thing and stick my tongue out at him.

"Be right back, I'm gonna go get his bubble wrap. Gotta keep champ safe."

"Oh fuck off, I'm not *that* bad." I will never admit that I am, in fact, that mom.

"Love you too, babe," he says over his shoulder as he heads outside.

"Do I hear Uncle Kye?" Tobias screams as he comes barreling in the room at high speed. *Does he ever slow down?* I wonder, shaking my head.

"Yes, you do." I sip my coffee to have something to do with my hands. I don't know how to adequately explain how it feels to have Kye here in our space after what we shared together. Should I feel comfortable around him? Shouldn't it be weird? It feels pretty fucking normal actually, and *that* is the problem.

Tobias pokes around at the breakfast options scattered on the kitchen island, he looks put out. His shoulders deflate a bit, a look of disappointment crosses his face. I'm about to ask him what's wrong when the front door opens again.

"Hey there, Turbo! I come bearing gifts to appease the small ruler of this mighty kingdom." Kye lifts his supplies in the air for Tobias to see, earning him a squeal of delight and hug from said small ruler. Suck up.

"Donuts *and* a new guppy?!?! Bruh, that's legit! Thanks man." I watch my son do some weird dance shaking his arms back and forth.

"No problem kiddo." Kye passes the donuts to him.

"You eat, I'll dump your newest victim in the torture chamber."

"After I eat, can I show you a new trick?" Tobias asks Kye as he promptly stuffs his sugary pastry in his mouth.

"New trick? Did you learn how to escape the bubble ball your mother puts you in?" Kye quips. I flip him off behind Toby's back.

"Huh?" Tobias looks rightly confused.

"Nothing kiddo. What's the new trick?"

"My guppies can swim through hoops." Toby sticks his finger through the hole of a donut, portraying a fish swimming through a hoop. I laugh at his antics.

"I will have to see it to believe it," Kye tells him. Kye looks up to me, mouthing over Tobias's head, "Age appropriate enough."

"Smartass," I mouth back, and we both laugh.

"Tobias, what do you want to do today?" I ask as I lean over to kiss his head.

"I'm going to name my new guppy. Maybe call Nana and Tata to see when they are coming to visit," he says while standing to brush crumbs off of his pajamas. He takes off at neck breaking speed towards his room.

I follow behind him at a much more leisurely stroll, enjoying my coffee, feeling more at peace than I have in the past. Photos of slaughtered pigs excluded from said peace.

Both Tobias and Kye are laughing at something I can't hear. I stop right outside the entrance to the bedroom. Tobias's chest is puffed out proudly, his favorite ringmaster cape hanging haphazardly from one of his tiny shoulders, as he shows Kye his display of fish.

"And this one? What's its name?" Kye asks from his spot on the floor.

"He's Fynn."

"What if Fynn's a girl?"

"Look at the colors of his gills and tail, they are bright colors, that's definitely a dude." Tobias informs him like he's instructing a smaller child.

My shoulders shake with the restraint not to laugh. I can't say the same for Kye, his body reverberates from the force of his laughter. The sound warms my chest making me all gooey on the inside.

"Very clever name. Do you have a Hook and Tail in there as well?"

"Uncle Kye, are you being cheeky?" Tobias's eyebrows wiggle. Kye laughs some more.

"Is that code for calling me a smartass?"

"Uncle Kye! I can't say that!" Tobias shrieks as he runs across the room, his cape billowing out from behind him in streaks of red and blue. He launches himself on his pseudo uncle, Kye catches him, tossing him from his sitting position over his head where Tobias flips midair, aiming for a landing on the bed. Tensing, I hold the air in my lungs as I try to mentally calculate if he has the velocity, height, and speed to make it safely onto the bed.

All I see is a blur of colors twisting in the air and my child giggles as he lands safely in the center of his bed. He jumps up, his hands over his head with a look of pure joy. I don't feel anything close to joy. The urge to shit myself is still too real for me to do anything but stand there stock still and wait to see if they end up cracking my kids head open. A million different scenarios run rampant.

What if he had hit the headboard? Or went through the wall? What if he didn't flip all the way and broke his fucking neck?

I hear Toby beg Kye to throw him again. Kye glances over at me, seeing the panicked horror on my face. "Maybe later kiddo, let's keep the heart attacks for mom to a minimum."

"Hard fucking agree," I retort.

Both Kye and Tobias say, "language!" At the same time. I roll my eyes and dart back down the hall so I don't have to bear witness to my kid's future accident in the making. Now is as good a time as ever to get dressed for the day, I guess.

14

Creeping & Peeping

Thena

"Holy fucking batman balls, Jesus Christ." My bangs are in a *There's Something About Mary* pose, sticking straight up and fanning out in the most absolutely, mortifying way. Kye saw me like this and didn't say anything? No one gave me a head's up?! Like *'hey there Thena. Your hair is mimicking a wild hair monkey! You might wanna go tame that shit'*. Nope, both Kye and Toby left me out there looking like this.

I grab my hairbrush from the vanity and start yanking it through my hair a little too vigorously. The layers quickly tangle together, I stop. Frustrated with how this day has turned out already. Fuck it, I'll wash it.

Grabbing my essentials and walking to the sink, I throw my body over, placing my head in the basin and switching the water on. Not waiting for it to warm up, I quickly scour and condition my hair before wrapping it in a towel, scrubbing my face while I'm at it. The mascara from last night crusts and clumps around my eyes, it smeared down my cheeks. I look every bit like a character from a low budget horror flick.

Did I get thoroughly fucked last night and somehow miss it? No, no I did not. Instead my night was spent writing in that stupid journal, realizing how truly fucked up my failed marriage has left me.

Grasping the edge of the sink, holding on for more than just my balance, I lean precariously close to the reflection of the woman looking back at me. Disappointment oozes from my pores as I study the shell of the woman I once was.

Dark circles encompass my sullen, brown eyes. My usually tanned skin is lacking the vibrant glow it usually has. Slapping some eye patches on to hopefully clear up the dark circles I've acquired, my shoulders curl in on myself. I look so defeated. A woman shredded by broken promises and insincere vows.

Will you stop being so hard on yourself? Pull it together and fucking rock this day. You have bigger fish to fry than this, I remind myself. *Yes, I do. Don't I?* I have to show Kye the photos. One part of me wants to burn them and forget they ever happened. The rational side to my brain knows I have no choice. Kye is here for a reason and I need to show him so we can take the next steps to protecting Tobias before this escalates into something more.

I let go of the counter to rummage through my closet looking for something that will hopefully give me a confidence boost. After tossing a few items and swiping through my garments, I search for the perfect items to create my body armor. *I need to find a perfect alibi so I can just handle my problem with some good, old fashion, wild western justice.* Exasperated with my choices I dig out my favorite cut off shorts and Pac-Man shirt that's older than life itself.

So much for finding something that makes me feel confident.

I grab the box of photos from the back of my closet to take with me. I climb up on my bed and open the beat up, cardboard lid. The dents and grooves are a testament to how long it's sat forgotten in my closets. It's my catch all for memories I wish I could forget, but will follow me forever. Literally labeled the *FUCK IT* box. Its contents are old family mementos, death certificates, and the few photos I kept of Mitchell and his family for Tobias.

I gingerly finger the photo on top of the pile, lifting it for closer inspection. So many questions surface in rapid succession. How did someone get a photo of us at this angle? Was someone in my home and we didn't notice them? Did I leave the door open? Is this the only one they have? Will there be more? Who has a copy?

Looking at the angle, I back up to the area around me. It's an impressive room with a connecting bathroom and walk-in closet. Both are on one side while the other is designed as an extra seating area for me to read my books in peace. I crawl off my bed and walk around the room. There's no way someone was standing at the footboard and snapped a photo that we weren't aware of. Looking over the space again, I walk over to the headboard. The large windows on both sides of the bed are my favorite feature of the room, but they are tinted and it would be the wrong angle.

Two quick raps on my door brings my attention to the doorway. Kye is leaning into my room, one hand on top of the doorframe, his ankle crossed behind his other foot. The sight of him wipes every worry away momentarily. He's beautiful. I'm gawking, I know I am, but I can't help it. His dark shirt is riding up, showing off the muscles that cover his stomach area. Something about the way his hair falls across his forehead barely brushing the tips of his eyelids, gives him an angel of death look just does it for me, pushing all the right buttons. He grins knowingly.

"Something on your mind, brat?" he asks.

My face heats, a tightness sparks low in my belly. "Just wondering why there's a neanderthal in my doorway," I quip.

He stalks over to me, his long strides eating up the distance. "Don't pretend to not enjoy this neanderthal standing in your doorway, I brought treats." He winks, running his fingers over my eye masks. I jump, tossing the photo on the bed as I run to the bathroom to peel off the eye masks. *Well this isn't embarrassing.* I toss the patches and pull the towel from my hair. Running my brush through it. Kye comes up behind me, a look on his face I can't decipher.

"Do you know what consent is?" He looks angry now.

I scrunch my nose, confused. I turn to face him, noticing the photo in his hand.

"What...the...fuck?" I curl my fingers around the brush I'm holding. Silently pleading with myself to not chuck it at his thick skull. He moves so close to me, looming over me until our noses are a mere space away from one another.

"If you wanted some snuff films and dirty pics to rub that delicate pussy with later. All. You. Had. To. Do. WAS. ASK!"

Something deep in me snaps. I *do* whack him with the brush and once I start I can't seem to stop. I punctuate each word with a hit against his biceps.

"I didn't do it you asshole. That's why I messaged you!" I stop smacking him to continue my tirade. "I would have shown you sooner but, news flash buddy, I didn't want to scare my kid!" He jerks his head back with a stunned expression on his face. I watch him in silent glee as he rubs his arm, having the audacity to look contrite. He looks down at the photo again and glances around the room. He steps away from me, running his hand through his hair, slipping his hand into his pocket. I can see he's rubbing his fingers together in his pocket.

I will not feel bad for smacking some sense into him...I will not feel bad for smacking some sense into him. I chant to myself. I follow behind him, irritated, wanting to smack him again.

"I'm sorry, I thought you took this without my knowledge," he says. My anger ignites. I raise the brush to whack him again wishing it was a cast iron instead.

His reaction is immediate; he grabs my wrist, twisting me around. I *oomph* as my back slams into his hard body. His lips brush against my ear as he tsks at me again.

"I believe we learned at a young age not to hit others, brat." His nose tickles my ear, causing me to shiver. I want to scream in frustration. I just need to…I need to hit something.

"Then don't accuse me of something so foul as taking photos of us without your consent."

"I said I was sorry." He has a point. My shoulders slump in defeat. He's right, I shouldn't have done that. Apology flames my cheeks. For once, I'm glad he can't see my face as my vision blurs.

"I'm sorry too. Being violated. Knowing someone was watching us. It's so demeaning. I don't like…" I can't seem to find the right words to express myself.

"Someone invaded your sanctuary, your privacy. It can be very demoralizing," he responds, spinning me to face him. His eyes hold more compassion than I would expect, since I just bludgeoned him with my damn brush.

"When did you get these?"

"Yesterday, around dusk. They were in the mailbox," I state flatly.

"This isn't the only one?" He looks angrier by the minute. I shake my head and nod towards the box placed on top of the bed. I'm not sure what it is, but there's something more spine chilling, more…sinister about the box that's now opened on my bed, having the collection of photos in my place of comfort. Having the knowledge of the contents inside makes it worse. My body trembles slightly. I wrap my arms around myself, trying to protect myself from the images Kye is now laying out across the mattress top to investigate. I walk across the room, snatching up my favorite cardigan and slipping my arms in the lush, green fabric before silently closing and locking my bedroom door. Kye's attention diverts from the photos to give me a questioning look.

"I don't want Tobias to walk in while we have slaughtered pigs and porn pics on the bed."

"Good call." He goes back to studying the pictures for a minute before turning around the room, his eyes missing nothing.

"He's clever, I'll give him that," he tells the room. His eyes fall on the floating shelves on the wall across from the foot of my bed. He focuses on an item on there, something sparks in his eyes. "Thena, honey, come here."

I walk over to him and he turns me to face the shelves. "I want you to look closely at the shelves. Is there anything new there that wasn't there before?"

I look over the contents on the shelves. My most treasured books are neatly shelved together. A modest sized turquoise jewelry box with the lid propped open; displaying the meager amount of jewelry I've collected over the years as I traveled across the country sparkles. The knick knacks are items picked up at random that I couldn't say no to. A tea cup, a limited edition Carrie Bradshaw NYC snow globe, and a few small succulent plants adorn the shelves. There's not an item that doesn't belong.

"No, everything is mine. And nothing is new." I laugh a little to fill the room, hoping to cover how uncomfortable I am at my meager treasures I can't seem to part with.

Kye folds the photo of us, sliding it in his pocket. He walks to the door, opening it. Glancing back over his shoulder he informs me, "I'll be right back."

With that, I'm left standing in my room, more confused than ever. I collect the horrid photos of slaughtered pigs and place them back in the box. Closing the lid, I slide the box back to its place in the top of my closet. Moving around the room I once felt safe and secure in, doubts and questions skitter through my mind. I find myself thinking out loud. "How did he get a photo of us?"

"Hidden cameras."

I yelp, jumping a little, doing the whole Jack Sparrow dance in place. I cover my face in mortification when I see Kye smiling broadly at me. At least he finds me entertaining. Kye comes back into the room holding a remote of some kind in his hand and a large ziplock bag in the other. Correction, the remote is actually a slim black device with a circular hole at the top encompassed by little red blinking lights around it.

"You can't be serious."

"How else would that photo be taken?" He challenges me. He wants me to see reason, and I do now that I think about it. He's correct. Had someone been at the bottom of the bed, we would have seen them. The angle of the photo alone lets me know that.

"How do we find what we can't see?"

He holds his device in the air waving it side to side. "I'm not holding a vibrator brat." He arches a brow to say, 'are you not paying attention'?

I almost stomp my foot in annoyance. Almost. Instead I inhale and pray for patience. I lower my tone as I would with Tobias when he's being too rambunctious and clearly say to him, "Yes, Nostradamus, I know it's not a vibrator. What I don't know is how that thing works."

"The infrared on the device scans the area to detect RF signals either through light," he indicates to the red blinking lights on the device, "or through sound waves being emitted through the signal." He points to a small chip-like device that's plugged into the bottom of the device. He pushes a button and looks at me, he seems to be battling some inner war inside himself because he goes to speak and stops himself only to try again.

He seems to think better of it because he just shakes his head and faces the wall. Holding the device in front of him, a red laser light emits a concentrated beam out in a circular section on my shelves. The device in Kye's hand immediately begins to vibrate, giving a small beeping sound in rapid succession of one another. My stomach drops, dread fills me as Kye approaches the shelves zeroing in on a succulent plant. He picks up my smallest plant from the shelf. The sprouts are still too small to fully lay over the rim of the pot. He spins it in his hand, inspecting it.

"That slimy motherfucker." Kye plucks one single sepal off the pedicel. It's a fucking camera pushed inside to disguise it. It's so small. *Why do they make cameras this small? How many more are there? What has he seen? Where are the others? Are there others?* My breaths come out in short rapid bursts, he's watching me. My lungs begin to feel like they are being engulfed in flame, *he's watching me.* I tighten my arms around me, in an attempt to hold myself together. *He's watching me.*

The feeling of a million critters crawling on my arms, legs, stomach, chest, back. Oh my god, they are everywhere. *He's watching me.* I start swiping at my arms trying to ease the uncomfortable feeling. The panic is too much, too soon. My head begins to swim, bright little orbs of light dance in my vision.

All I can envision is Mitchell sitting behind his desk watching me make love to Kye, watching me sleep, dress, write, shower. Stalking the most intimate moments of my life without my permission. Oh gods, my hands cover my mouth, bile, thick and acidic climbs its way up my throat. I gag and, running to the toilet, I toss myself to the ground.

The pain in my knees from my hard impact barely registers with me as I regurgitate every last bit of my special breakfast up. Just one more thing that Mitchell's ruining for me. Kye's warm hand lands on my back, rubbing in small circles to soothe me. His touch does the opposite causing a chill to break out across my skin. He moves his hand from my back, the absence of it causing a hollow feeling in the pit of my stomach. I raise my hand to wipe my mouth when another reaches out, clutching my own.

"Don't, love. I've got you." Kye murmurs behind me, wiping my face and mouth with a damp cloth. I tilt my head back seeking his eyes with my own, needing that peaceful tranquility his presence brings me. Ours meet, clashing together. Mine are sad and embarrassed, his hold a look I can't possibly distinguish.

"I'm sorry." I tell him softly as I kneel before him, embarrassment flaming my cheeks.

He cups my face with his large hand, my face fitting in his palm so perfectly. The callouses littering his palm are scratchy, yet the roughness in them brings me comfort. His eyes hold mine so tenderly. "You will never again apologize in this lifetime or the next for how someone makes you feel."

"I have this overwhelming feeling deep in my chest, this has to be one of the worst violations of my life. What has he seen? How long has he been watching me? Us?" I ask my voice trembles as the truth devastates me. Kye squats in front of me, wrapping me in his arms, his natural smell envelopes me, I close my eyes and inhale. He's missing his usual smell of aftershave, however, his natural scent still soothes me. I lay my head on his chest feeling so incredibly small against him.

"With your permission, I want to do a sweep of the entire house and property. After I remove everything, I want to install cameras." I go to protest. The thought of having someone watch my every move makes my skin crawl. "I will not be a prisoner in my own home, Kye." I draw back, looking him in his eyes so he can see how serious I am. Dead serious. I will not be made to feel like a prisoner.

"Do you trust me, brat?" he asks me.

Uncertainty stays my tongue, my track record with trusting the wrong people has me second guessing myself. *This is Kye, though. He's always been there for you.* A little voice nudges me. At this moment, I have to decide if I truly trust Kye. This predicament has already become more troublesome than I had originally imagined.

I had pictured Mitchell standing on the porch late at night, drunk, issuing vile threats. I never imagined he would be fully stalking me by recording us inside of our home. Does that constitute stalking? He could argue that he too, is a victim. That he had not a clue that the cameras had been inside our home. That brings me back to Kye's question. Do I trust him? Can I trust him? Regardless, I don't have a choice. He's the only person in my life that really knows Mitchell and how cunning he really is. He's always been there for me, even when I didn't want it.

I force myself to make eye contact with him when I say, "You know that I do."

"Then let me do what I came here to do."

"And that is?" I need to know that he's here for the right reasons.

His stare pierces into mine as he cups my face with his palms. Kye's convictions do not waver when he tells me, "The safety of you and Tobias will always be my main priority. I won't go anywhere until I can guarantee it."

"No one's above death buddy. What happens when you mouth off too much and I shut your head in an oven?"

He looks at me in a challenge. "The Devil will have to come up here and try to drag me away himself. I promise you, he will not succeed." His words leave me reeling. Kye has always made his feelings towards me known, but before him coming to Virginia I had played down his commitment to me.

I've noticed today, when angered, he can be pretty scary. I was not prepared for this. In an attempt to make myself more comfortable, I pat his chest and deflect the seriousness with humor. "Good to know, caveman."

We both grin.

15

Splash

Thena

 I push the brush down more vigorously than necessary. The pool is sparkling, I just can't seem to stop. Fucking cameras, how intrusive. I've been at this for hours while Kye combs over my home. I have zero privacy now. The thought of him seeing my private stash of lingerie or flipping through the pages of my more erotic books, has my face flaming again. I hear footsteps approaching me from behind, glancing over my shoulder I see it's Kye carrying a large ziplock bag full of what

I assume are hidden devices. His eyes tell me everything I need to know. He isn't happy with his findings. *Fan-fucking-tastic.*

"Well eighteen hidden cameras have been recovered, seven mics and a very discreet yet, not as tech savvy, tracking device on your car."

"You're joking."

He jiggles the bag in front of him as if to say 'do you not see all of this'?

"It's safe to say, you didn't shit without him knowing."

I recoil. This is worse than I thought. I release my hold on the pool brush, watching it sink to the bottom of the pool. "Were you able to retrieve all of them? Or should I expect more?" I ask, lowering myself to the ground. I bring my knees to my chest and wrap my arms around them in an effort to project calmness when I'm feeling anything but.

"I've made sure to get them all, I can sweep the house daily if that's what it takes for you to feel secure again. I know this was a major violation to your privacy."

Hmph, I have nothing more to say. It is a big violation not just to me, but to my child and anyone who's been here while those were installed. I do have one question, so I ask, "Can you tell how long the house has been wired up?"

He shakes his head. "The lifespan of a camera depends on the technology used, I can give you my assumptions based on what I found but nothing concrete." He walks over to the pool opening the bag, he kneels and lowers the bag into the pool just enough to fill it with water, the equipment in it now and truly fucked.

"Hey! What are you doing? Shouldn't we give that to the police?"

He zips the bag up and tosses it onto a chair. "And say what exactly? Hey, the owner of the house had it secured with cameras and microphones. Oh and yeah, he recorded his wife and I screwing?"

I draw back offended at the audacity of the statement. "I won't give your lurid comment a response. But to the first, yes, this is his home, but it's mine as well and I didn't give consent to being spied on."

"This state is a single party consent. As long as he is using it to secure his property and *he* consents to it, there's nothing we can do."

My shoulders fall, the dissatisfaction clear on my face. "How can it be legal to do this to another human being? Everyone in the home should consent to this or it shouldn't happen at all."

"I don't disagree. Until the laws are changed, there's nothing we can do."

"Where did you find them? The cameras," I ask.

"Baby, don't ask questions I don't want to answer."

"I need to know," I urge. He clasps his hand over mine, gently squeezing.

"I will tell you this but I won't go into detail. There were at least three in each room. All of them had mics."

I gape at him in horror. I turn my face away from him, regarding the cerulean water in my pool. The enchanting color and deep depths have been my safe haven these last few years. Did I stay in the pool so much because I truly loved the comfort of being in water? Or because Mitchell hated it and very rarely intruded on my time? I knew, I think, subconsciously that Mitchell wasn't a good man.

"Thena, I can help you feel safe in your home again." I turn to him with the question on the tip of my tongue, but he cuts me off. "You will have to trust me and listen to my ideas. I know you won't like it, but I give you my word I won't betray your trust like he did."

"What is it that you want to do?" I ask. His hesitation brings me around to fully face him. I dip my leg into the pool, swirling it. He scrutinizes me for a moment before speaking.

"I want to rewire your home with my security."

I rear back, shocked that he would even suggest this. Did he not just find cameras littered across my home like fucking eggs on Easter morning? "Excuse me? I must have misheard you."

"Thena, don't be a brat. Let me explain."

I decided at that moment to just poke at him a little. I give him a hand gesture, saying, 'okay, smart ass, elaborate'. He huffs. Looking more humored than annoyed.

"I don't know if I want to squeeze you, kiss you, or toss your pretty little ass in the deep end of this pool." He states casually, now that I seem to be more open to hearing him out. "I will install cameras on the outside only and nothing on the inside at all. We won't be able to see inside your home. You and I will be the only ones with access. How do you feel about that?"

"What if he hacks them?" I inquire. Mitchell seems more resourceful than I had previously given him credit for.

"He isn't smart enough to hack my system."

My eyebrows raise at his brave statement. "Your system?" I ask.

"Yes, it's mine. I programmed it myself."

"Proud of yourself, aren't you?" I wiggle my eyebrows at him, winning me one of his megawatt smiles. I stand, dusting off my shorts. He rises with me, standing so close that if I leaned over just a smidge, we would be flush together. He flashes me another smile, leaning in to kiss the tip of my nose. I blush.

"Quite," he says.

I roll my eyes. "That was rhetorical, Einstein." Placing my hands on his chest, I lean up, giving him my lips. Our tongues dance together as I almost lose all of my senses. Before his hands can hold on to me, I promptly push his chest, hard, right into the pool.

As I prance up the yard, smiling brighter than I have in months, I yell over my shoulder. "That's what you get for calling me a brat."

16

A Boy & His Fish

Thena

I lean against the counter in my kitchen, the edge of it nipping into my skin. I wait with the back door open for Kye to make his grand appearance. I sip my wine, the rich boldness of the red leaves a heady tart, yet decadent, taste in my mouth after I swallow. I deserve this treat. Tipping my glass back to enjoy another sip, this one turns into a gulp. I'm feeling pretty smug about getting the drop on Kye and grin into my glass. It's been a long time since I felt playful. Even with this morning's disaster, it's nice to see I haven't lost my humor.

I pick up the towel that's laid out on the counter for Kye. Knowing he would need it. I laugh to myself, cracking up, envisioning his stunned face as he was pushed in. Loud steps alert me to Kye being on the back patio, the stomps accompanied with the squelching sound of his shoes on the wooden planks a dead giveaway to his arrival. I break out into a shit eating grin. I hear a clatter that sounds like he may have missed his footing, followed up by a string of curses and a 'I've never wanted to bend a woman over my knee as much as I do her'. He comes to a full stop at the door, noticing it's open.

"Are you bitter because you're all wet, or is it that I got the better of you?" I inquire.

He grins at me, showing he harbors no ill will towards me for the manipulation at the pool edge.

"Is a towel apology enough?" I lift the towel up in his direction.

"I can think of a thing or two you can do to make this transgression up to me." He gives me a sly smile.

I grin at his antics, trying so desperately to keep eye contact and composure. "So no towel?"

"Knowing how you like to misbehave at my expense, I would worry it's covered in rose hips dust." His tone is flat, accusing even.

"Rose hips?" I question. Unsure of what he's talking about. Did he hit his head?

"It's botany related. Rose hips can be made into teas, lovely really. But like all beautiful things," he looks pointedly at me, "it can cause problems. If you remove the fine hairs inside, it can be used in itching powder."

Impressed with his knowledge surrounding a rose bush, I inquire a little more. "Is botany a hobby of yours?"

"Actually, it is. I studied it in university, keeping up with it during my free time. Extremely masculine, only the toughest of men can do it."

Walking to the door, I hand him the towel. I get the faintest whiff of fresh cut grass and chlorine, a combination that is actually one of my favorites. I move back to my spot by the counter so I can observe Kye discreetly. Lifting my glass, I feign taking another drink. He's so interesting to me. To think, I've known him for seven years and, while I can acknowledge plants have come up in conversations before, I never knew he studied and enjoys botany.

"If you want a show, princess, don't hide behind that glass."

I gasp a little, forgetting that my mouth being closed was the only thing keeping the wine from spilling over. Wine fills my mouth, too much at one time, and I choke, the burning sensation in my chest causing my eyes to water.

I hear Kye say, "Needs practice swallowing, noted."

I spin around still coughing, though not nearly as much as I was. I hope my glare conveyed the message for him to shut the fuck up. I flip him the middle finger. He starts to laugh more vigorously than I would imagine the situation calls for. I bend over, sucking down large gulps of air. I force the words out, "Fuck you." My tone sounds raspy, reminding me of a chain smoker's vocals.

"Yes, please dear."

I pull myself up to a less embarrassing position. I have full intentions of dragging his ass in this kitchen and making him choke on something when my eyes land on him. I find myself sucking in another deep breath for an entirely different reason, but the air won't come. He's sucked it all out of the room, all I can think is that I may have passed out because there's no way this is happening. He's what wet dreams are made of.

Water drips from his dark hair onto his thick neck, traveling a route I ache to lick, bite, and taste. I watch in fascination as they dissolve into his shirt that's molded to his body. I flick my tongue out to dampen my lips that have gone very, very dry. He unsnaps his jeans, hooking his thumbs in his waistband. I almost whimper. I shouldn't be watching. I should give him his privacy. I should look away before he notices me. I can't, for the life of me, look away, though. The way he moves is mesmerizing. I only have myself to blame. Why did I think throwing him in the pool was a good idea?

My body tightens and loosens all at once as he moves at a glacial pace, and I find myself wanting to assist him so his stripping is faster. Inch by precious inch he reveals more of his toned, tanned skin to me causing a pool of my own desire to form in my panties. I imagine myself approaching him, pushing him down on the outdoor patio set and licking my way down his body. I want to slide myself down on his cock to relieve the tension that's building up inside me. My thighs rub together on their own accord, a sound more humiliating than the previous choking escapes me and his head snaps up. His eyes darken with his own desire as he realizes what I've been doing. He grins at me and it does nothing and everything at once. I want him. Now.

He watches me as he rips his jeans off the rest of the way, the evidence of his pleasure at my observation of him is bulging under his briefs. My chest rapidly increases in movement as I attempt to fill my lungs with much needed air. Why can't I breathe?

"Keep looking at me like that, and we're going to have a problem."

"I like having problems." My voice is as lust filled as his own.

"Hey Mom, did you know dude guppies have brighter colored scales and dudette guppies have less? Why is Uncle Kye wet?" We both watch in horror as Tobias careens into the room heading straight for the snack pantry. "Does Uncle Kye know he's supposed to wear swimming trunks?"

I'm rooted to the spot, my mind playing catch up on the newest situation I've found myself in. Kye, obviously not bothered by being caught with his pants down decides to step in and save me from my mortification. He wraps the towel around his hips, steps into the kitchen, slides the door closed, and turns to Tobias. "That is an interesting fact about guppies, Turbo, thank you for continuing my education on aquatic life."

Tobias accepts Kye's words with a simple nod of his head, popping a pretzel in his mouth, not bothering to swallow before he asks, "and you're wet and partially undressed because?"

Kye laughs a little, walking over and shaking his hair out over top of Tobias who, in return, screams.

"Not cool bro!" Tobias's swing goes wide as Kye sidesteps out of the way. He snatches the pretzels from Tobias's hand, stealing two for himself before handing them back.

"I'm wet because your mother's a bully," Kye tells Tobias in a conspiratory whisper.

I place my hands on my hips and roll my eyes dramatically at him, muttering under my breath, "Cry baby."

I watch them go back and forth with half-hearted jabs and kicks. Pretzels fly out of the container with every spin Tobias does. Neither of them care that their salty treats are being stomped into dust as they wrestle.

Mitchell would never have allowed this to happen. He would have a conniption fit if he ever saw the floor littered with snacks, water droplets by the door, and two individuals wrestling in the house. I almost ask them to stop and remind them that this is a home and not a playground. I don't, though.

Is this what home is supposed to feel like? Aside from our earlier discovery, I have longed for the day I would have a house full of laughter. I can't remember ever seeing Tobias at such ease before. Something in my chest tightens and loosens at the same time. My need to protect this moment and all the moments after this is so urgent. I vow to never allow Mitchell to steal Tobias's joy again and promise to always strive to fill our home with this much happiness.

Kye allows Toby to get him in a headlock, artfully bringing him down. The game comes to an end. Toby celebrates his victory over Kye by dancing in place and reminding Kye that he's no longer the champ. "Loser buys pizza!"

"Seems fair enough to me, but I believe I know where you get your bullying skills from." Kye climbs up from the floor, finally noticing the mess they made. He cringes, blessing me with an apologetic look. I shake my head at him, waving my glass in the air as if to silently say, 'it's not a problem. Don't worry about it. I've got it'.

Kye holds his hands up in surrender. "Looks like I need to order some pizza."

"You really don't have too," I tell him. Toby's face falls and we both notice. Kye immediately grabs him up, tickling him.

"Of course, I do. A deal is a deal." Kye sits Tobias down and gives him a serious look. "Turbo, I have some work to do around here. Do you think you're up to the task? I need an assistant." How serious Tobias becomes makes my heart melt.

"I am definitely the man for the job."

"Good. I'm going to get some dry clothes on and order our pizza. Then you and I are going to install our super secret spyware." Tobias does a fist pump, dancing in his spot, while all I can think about is how the term spyware just triggered me. Fucking Mitchell. Kye must notice the color leaching from my skin because he gently rubs my arm, giving me a look filled with such sympathy that I can't meet his eyes.

"Well if you two have it all figured out. I'm going to text Rex and solidify our plans for our girls' night out." Kye gives me a look, I just smirk as I leave the kitchen. Entering my bedroom, I have this overwhelming sense of foreboding. It's like I've been here before. *Of course you have silly, it's your bedroom.* I hear heavy footsteps behind me as Kye approaches hot on my heels.

"You cannot seriously be entertaining the idea of leaving the house for a night of *fun*? Mitchell is out there, able to stalk you, harass you, or even worse, possibly hurt you." He's furious with me and I can't find fault in his anger. It isn't the smartest plan I've ever had, but surely he doesn't expect me to hold up here like a prisoner?

"I need some fresh air," I say simply, sitting down on the edge of my bed.

"You're not going."

"The fuck I'm not. I will not be controlled by the whims of men, my friend has invited me out, and I will be going."

"Will you listen to reason just once in your life?" He looks over me, his hands on his hips like a disapproving father. It reminds me so much of Mitchell that I forget the reason he just accused me of not having. I launch up, trying my best to go nose to nose with him. I climb back on the bed, standing so I can be on the same level as him. His eyes sparkle like he's holding back a laugh and that makes me angrier.

"Imply one more time that I'm not allowed to do something that I want, and I will hit you with my cast iron, so help me God, that's a fucking promise. The days of being a constant servant to the wants of men are over." I punctuate each word with my finger poking him in his stupid, perfect chest. My own chest rises and falls in rapid succession, my skin feels heated. I become more agitated by the second. How dare he tell me what to do?

He takes in how serious I am. His attention to the detail of my body doesn't go unnoticed. His chest vibrates as he hums to himself like he's just come to some conclusion. He invades what little personal space I have left. His nose rubbing mine sends little shocks of electricity between us. His lips hover just out of reach, making me briefly forget my anger as another emotion begins to take me over. "You wouldn't really hit me brat," he murmurs against my lips.

I'm so enraptured by him it takes a moment to process what he says. I jerk back, indignant. "Say something else that concerns my freedom and you will see how serious I really am."

"You don't want to mess up my pretty face." He gives me a shit eating grin, his hands wrapping around my body, grabbing my ass cheeks. He squeezes them hard. Leaning in, he whispers in my ear, "If you destroy my face in your wrath, what will you look at while we fuck?"

I lean back, batting my eyelashes at him, wearing a look of pure innocence. I can tell by the smug look he's wearing he thinks he won. Too bad he doesn't realize how truly done I am with being bossed around. I shock him as I lean in close to him, rubbing my nose against his like he had me. I whisper above his lips in perfect imitation. "Don't suggest dumb shit like having me hide in this house, and I won't have to place a paper bag over your head while we fuck."

His shocked face is worth every threat I've made. I wink, giving him a quick peck on the cheek and launch myself off the bed.

17

Phone Calls

Thena

I stare at the blank page in my lap, trying for the life of me to decide on what to write in my journal tonight. So many negative thoughts flitter through my mind. Each one jogs one horrendous memory after another.

Buzz buzz buzz

I glance at the phone screen. Who is calling me at this hour? I pick the phone up glancing at the screen.

Unknown caller.

I hold my device feeling the little piece of metal dance in my hand with how hard it vibrates. Anxiousness begins to make my stomach queasy. Unknown caller flashes again. Curiosity getting the better of me, I hit the answer button and hold the phone to my ear. "Hello?"

Silence…

"Hello?"

Static comes over the line, a distorted song playing. It takes a moment for the lyrics to make sense but when it does, anger takes over my common sense. It's Good Charlotte's *My Bloody Valentine.*

"Hello??????" I say one more time. The song stops and I find myself holding my breath.

After a moment of no one speaking my unease begins to turn into annoyance.

"Fine, fucker. If you wanna be a weirdo, do it on your own time, I don't have it to spare." I hang up, really missing the good old days when you could slam a receiver down to intentionally hurt the other person's eardrums. I huff in irritation, tossing my phone on the nightstand.

I decide to take my frustration out in a more healthy manner. Hard, angry lines represent my feelings as I begin scribbling black circles all over the page. I rip the page out, crumbling it in my hands and tossing it into the trash bin.

Buzz buzz buzz.

I look over to my nightstand expecting the unknown caller as it rings again. I reach for it. Until the picture on my screen causes me to pause. Hell has truly frozen over. The phone vibrates, shimmying across the surface of the tabletop. The movements are a perfect announcement to the caller. Small, angry, and destructive. What could she want?

The screen flashes brightly again. My mother-in-law's picture and name are illuminated on the screen. I debate the merits of answering the call. This will only end in a fight, as it always does with her. *Buuzzzzz buuuzzzzz buzzzzz,* the little black device demands my attention.

She's probably just calling to boast about her son and I's imminent divorce. She was never in support of our union. The phone goes silent as I reach over to take hold of it, the metal as cold as our relationship. It's fitting, I think resentfully to myself.

I can't believe, at one point in time, I was actually excited to be in her good graces. *Should I call her back?* I sigh a little. She couldn't be calling this late to speak to Tobias, he's been in bed for a while now. Kye put him to bed after their anime marathon. I check the time, it's late.

I wonder if she will call back? The phone starts dancing in my hand, I guess that answers my question. With no other choice, I hit the little green button, bringing the phone to my ear, positive that I will later regret this.

"Hello? Thena are you there? Can you hear me?" Her words are curt, crisp.

I roll my eyes to the ceiling, leaning against the headboard of my bed, and get prepared for this unwanted conversation.

"Thena Sullivan?" she clips, frustration lacing her tone.

"Two calls in almost eight years, both on the same night. Who died?" I say dryly, my delusions of ever being civil with this woman long gone.

"Excuse me? Are you there?" Her tone is far from civil. Let the games begin.

"Yes, Lucia. I can hear you," I reply, praying with everything in me that this is quick and painless.

Her huff of breath travels through the phone.

I flinch, as it causes my ear to hurt. Nails to a chalkboard, that's how it feels to have her huffing and puffing, and we haven't even started the conversation. I feel a small pang begin to thrum in my head. Great, conversation with public enemy number one and a headache. I'm so lucky.

"Thena, I am in town and wish to see my grandchild," she states.

I find myself shooting up from the position I was previously lounging in. What the actual fuck?! "Why?" I exclaim. Panic at the thought of her being in my driveway. Surely she isn't?

She clicks her tongue in annoyance. "My son is in pain, where else would I be?" She tsks at me, causing me to bite my tongue.

"I'm sure he is."

"What was that?" She asks me.

"Nothing. What were you saying about visiting Tobias?" I steer the conversation to the only neutral topic.

"Well, I've traveled all this way, the least you can do is allow me to visit with my grandson."

I pause, thinking carefully over my response. I absolutely do not want Tobias around Mitchell, but at this point, I may not have a choice.

"Will Mitchell be there?" I inquire.

"It's unfortunate that your false allegations have been spread so thoroughly through the rumor mill. It has caused him some complications at work. He is, at this moment, about to catch a flight. He has a meeting with the CEO in hopes of keeping his position at the company." She snips at me.

I say my next words before I can catch myself. "Yes, well his dick being in every barely legal female across the country really isn't a rumor if it's factual."

"How dare you! You will bite your tongue when you speak to me." She's mortified and I smirk in triumph. Am I being petty? Yes. Do I care? No.

"I see you still have no respect for your elders." She accuses me.

"Elder, singular. Not plural," I reply. I want to tell her about her son's perversion with the cameras being all over my home. I rein myself in. It will do no good. She will always see him as the perfect son.

There's a rustling on the other end, and I hear some hushed tones speaking frantically to one another before a male's voice comes through the receiver.

"Thena, sweetheart. It's David." I smile at the gruff older tone. Wondering how my father-in-law was cursed enough to be stuck with that woman.

"Hello, old timer." I smile into the phone.

"May I please come scoop up Tobias tomorrow morning? I will have him back at the end of the weekend." David is the more logical one in the relationship, the only in-law I actually respect. I think over his request. If Mitchell won't be there. What can it hurt?

"I will have him ready to go in the morning, David," I say with ease. I hear my monster-in-law in the background complaining about how I enjoy making her life difficult. My smile this time shows all of my teeth.

"Thank you. See you tomorrow, kiddo." I flinch at the nickname but let it go.

"Sure thing, Pops."

I disconnect the call, replace my phone with a pen, and begin writing. Thanks to my mother-in-law's call, I'm finally inspired on what to put in this entry. The night of our wedding in Arizona plays through my head as I write it all out.

18

Journal Entry:
The Big Mistake

Thena

The woman staring back at me in the mirror shares my almond eyes. I run my fingers over her long curls, my curls. The dusting of crystals intricately placed throughout the half-up hairstyle stands out against the backdrop my dark hair provides.

Deep breaths Thena, you wanted this. This is what you want. Still do, I chide myself.

I shake my head, disgusted with myself for entertaining second thoughts on our special day. I'm so blessed to have the love of a man like Mitchell. He's a pillar of the community, everyone loves him. He loves me, he loves our son. My thoughts shame me, I bend down to pull the tulle up around my ankles, glancing at the clock while I do. Only minutes before I walk down the aisle and the back of my gown still isn't zipped.

Where the fuck is my sister? If I'm late it will throw off the entire ceremony. Mitchell likes to be punctual. It's not like I can track her down, not in this gown!

Damnit, can't she be on time for my wedding?

This is the disadvantage of not having girlfriends to be your bridesmaids.

I carefully walk over to the door, my toes gliding across the floor, amazed at how fancy the house is. The carpet feels like the softest cotton against my skin.

'I'll just peep out the door, and see if maybe someone is in the hallway that can help zip me up,' I think positively.

It's not a big deal to not have one's family here to get them in their wedding gown. Is it? I have no idea. I attend funerals, not weddings. This is a first.

I turn the knob quietly just in case Mitchell's in the hall. He told me yesterday morning it's bad luck for the groom to see the bride. It sounds silly to me, but if it makes him happy, so be it. Looking down the hall I spot one of Mitchell's aunts in the hall speaking to his Nana.

Both women are dressed for a funeral instead of a wedding. Their sequined black gowns and massive hats decorated with satin and bows intimidate me a little, but I seriously need help and can't wait for whenever my sister deems my wedding important enough for her to show up. Deciding that this will be my family in a few short moments and I need to build a relationship with these people, I prepare to call out to them. What better way than to have his elders help me into my gown? But their words have my eyebrows rising and my request left unasked.

"Poor Mijo, he doesn't realize what he's doing. Marrying this woman is a mistake! It's too soon," one says to the other in a hushed whisper.

"He has always had such a big heart, the poor boy is too good I tell you, you know it's the child. He's gotten too attached. She's using that baby to get his money." His Nana responds. Her wine is close to sluicing over the rim as she motions in my direction.

"And they say old ladies are sweet." I say under my breath.

"Did you hear my daughter had to allow them to marry here at her home? She's so gracious." Nana reports.

"I hear the check didn't clear. Mijo says it's an issue with the bank. I bet it's her. Draining him dry already." The other one confides in Nana. I roll my eyes, anger building up. I don't know anything about a check. I accepted her daughter's offer to marry here because spending obscene amounts of money on a venue is silly.

I close the door not as quietly as I opened it, the two women's conversation ending abruptly. How awful is this? Mitchell's family hates me, my sister is MIA on my wedding day, I have no one to zip my gown up, and I am supposed to be down the aisle in… Looking at the clock, I panic more. Tears brim my eyes, threatening to fall over and ruin my makeup. I'm supposed to walk down the aisle in nine minutes. What am I going to do? Just then the door swings open, and Luna bounds into the room, not a care in her world. Oh God, why is her lipstick smeared?

"HELLO, bride-to-be!" She dances across the room to me. Wine in her hand instead of her bouquet. I am absolutely not shocked at all. This is typical Luna behavior, everything is about her. Even my fucking wedding day. The tears I thought I had under control threaten to come back.

"Are you fucking kidding me?" I hiss, grabbing her perfectly tanned arm, dragging her to the mirror.

"You missed a spot!" I point an accusing finger to her lips. She leans in squinting, taking in her figure. She strikes a pose and smirks. So fucking typical.

She sashays her hips in the mirror. "I've still got it, Sis."

"Please tell me it was your husband you were sucking off before my wedding?" I plead with her.

She leans in close to me, confiding in me. Her words begin to run together slightly. "Afraid not."

Great. She's fucked someone at my wedding and is intoxicated. It has to be someone in the bridal party considering everyone on my side is Mitchell's family members and his side are his best friends. Who was it?

"All the groomsmen are either engaged or married!"

"Sucks to be their woman, then doesn't it? He's not attracted to that heifer anyway. He wasn't as exhilarating as I had hoped. Can't win them all, though. Besides, she doesn't have these." She indicates her generous cleavage forgetting her wine glass. I watch in horror, unable to stop the sequence of events as the red wine tumbles over the rim, splashing down onto my perfectly tailored white gown.

The. Room. Is. Silent.

Our matching expressions are one of holy terror, I don't breathe. I can't. This is a fucking nightmare. My sister has shown up late because she was drinking and fucking with my fiancé's best friend, who in turn is engaged to a wonderful woman that I had hoped to build a friendship with in the future. Now this. This simply cannot be my life. I just want to marry Mitchell. I want to get through this fucking horrific day so we can build our future as he and I planned. I speak so calmly to her, that you would mistake me for guiding a child.

"Luna listen very carefully if you want to fucking make it through the next few minutes of your life alive. You are going to go get some club soda and a towel. You will not stop for more wine, you will not stop for another fuck, you will move in silence and you will do it NOW!" She sets her glass down on a stand, making her escape hastily. My patience for her has snapped, as broken as our bond, we will never be the same after today.

My thoughts are too frenzied for one singular train of thought. I will not lose my shit. I reach for the cell phone on the dresser beside me with shaky hands. I scroll through my contacts until I find Mitchell's number. Resigned for the conversation we are about to have. I hit the dial. It rings several times before he answers.

"Hello future wife," he answers.

"Mitchell, honey, Luna spilled wine on my gown. I need you to stall for maybe fifteen minutes so I can get the stain out."

"How does one spill wine on a wedding gown? I gave you strict orders not to allow your sister near the alcohol. The bitch is a mess." He scolds me.

I stare at the red stain. A blight on my gown, a symbol of my life. I just wanted one day of perfection. He continues as if it's not my only family he's degrading, no matter how merited it is. "Of course she's intoxicated, she can't hold her shit together for a day, can she? How embarrassing." My humiliation knows no end where today is concerned, and the ceremony hasn't even begun.

Luna creeps into the room looking contrite with the club soda and cloth. Her cheeks are rosy, her eyes hold an apology that I am sure I've heard a million times before.

"Mitchell, honey, I promise I will meet you at the end of the aisle in fifteen minutes. My gown will be pristine. Remember that I love you and that is all that matters."

I think I hear him mutter over the line as I'm hanging up, "To you, maybe."

But, when I hold the phone back to my ear, the line is quiet.

Exactly fourteen minutes later I am standing before Mitchell in wonder of the splendor of our matrimony. The moon is full, moving across the night sky with every passing moment, all of the stars in the sky are alight; bright blinking orbs of light. The backyard is illuminated with twinkling lights everywhere. The seats are full of Mitchell's family and friends. Everything will be alright, I think to myself as the pastor begins to recite our vows.

19

Thena

Sitting at a table for two in this swank, new joint in downtown Carytown was not what I had in mind for a girls' night out. The noise is atrocious. I strain my eyes, not for the first time, to try and glimpse the other side of the cocktail bar. The joint is dimly lit by candles everywhere. It's nice, but not very practical for an establishment that caters to the public.

I'm not complaining, just observing as I lean across the table straining to hear what Rex is saying to me. The volume of noise has its perks, though, I will admit. It's nice to not have to repeatedly answer the same questions over and over again from Rex. It's a shame the other ladies couldn't join us. Blanca is usually my buffer for unwanted conversations.

Ever since I opened up about my humiliating situation between my soon-to-be ex-husband and myself, my friends have peppered me with texts and calls. *Are you okay? Do you need anything? How's Tobias?* I've never received so much support in my life. It's new to me. I'm in the adjustment period. Sort of. I sip my Roaring Bitch martini. Yes, you heard that correctly. The house martini is a Roaring Bitch. The glass arrived perfectly chilled, the lemon-tasting concoction is vibrant and bright, the frothy layer on top of the liquid has the aftertaste of toasted marshmallow.

Evidently, this place has an entire team of mixologists who work behind the dark bar. A fog machine works around the clock to push fluffy, white clouds from under the seats while the large industrial fans work to keep it low enough to not choke the patrons. How do they not set off the fire alarms? Whoever engineered this place earned every penny.

Rex sits across from me, sipping her drink. Her vibrant, red hair pops more brightly than normal against the backdrop of the deep green of the interior wall behind her. To sum it up; dark, gothic chic, loud, strong but not overly priced drinks. I'm sold. This is the perfect location to lose myself for a few hours.

"Uh-oh, someone's in their thoughts." Rex leans across the dimly lit table to yell at me.

"I promise you, I am not in my thoughts. Scouts' honor." I flip her my middle finger as I take another sip. She rolls her eyes at me, clearly not impressed with me deflecting. And I am deflecting, I know it, she knows it. She signals the mixologist over, ordering something called a Penicillin Shot. The lady's smile grows as she glances at us both, nodding.

"Sure thing dolls."

"It's totally okay if you are. I would be." And that's why Rex is my best friend. She always has that clear understanding that sometimes I won't be okay and it's okay to not be okay.

"I've had plenty of time to make amends with our decision. I'm grateful he seems to finally want to have an amicable divorce. I don't want it to get nasty. I just want it over." I don't tell her about the cameras, guilt gnaws at me for keeping that from her and the others. They can never know. They would never have a sense of safety in my home again. I'm being selfish, but I don't want to lose my friends.

"Of course, you do. Who would want to stay in such a toxic environment?" She tips her glass towards me in a salute before she takes another drink.

"Some don't have the means to leave. I'm blessed to have the support that I do."

"Your friends will always be here for you," she says, causing my heart to break a little with my deceit. I should just tell her about the cameras.

Our lovely waitress drops off our shots. I pick mine up. It's in a little pill bottle with a label on it. I twist the lid off to find a pink shimmering liquid in it. I guess we're doing this, then.

"These are too fucking cute to waste on serious conversations. Let's celebrate." We both raise our little prescription bottles to one another, tapping them lightly together as we shout, "To divorce!"

I don't know how much time has passed while Rex and I ignore all of our problems, but our little slice of heaven is littered with empty orange bottles and martini glasses. I don't remember the last time I laughed this much. I'm not even sure if we are entertaining ourselves or the other patrons as we belt out the words to *Maneater*, using our latest refills for mics. I haven't felt this free in years. The song comes to an end as the others around us start applauding. I toast them, turning back to Rex. I notice she's not looking at me, though, she's watching something intently. No, not something. Someone.

Kye Kincaid.

"Girl! I don't know who that tall, dark, and mysterious person is, but I want one. No, I changed my order. I want two of them. Can I get one on Amazon?" She pretends to open her app with her phone. We laugh.

"That's Kye," I confide in her. Her eyes go wide as her face morphs into one of surprise.

"Wait...*the* Kye? Arizona Kye?" She asks me.

"The one and only," I confirm.

"Why was I not informed that he was in town?" Her tone suggests that she's hurt that I hadn't told her.

"I just haven't had the chance. He's been in town for a little while now. Rex, you are currently starstruck by my future ex-husband's ex-best friend and ex-boyfriend to Mitchell's former mistress."

"Goddamn, say that five times fast."

"As always, my life is a joke." I set my glass down.

"I don't know. I think this is the exact time we need to joke"

"Stop staring."

"He's staring."

"Creeper."

"So you call him a creeper, but I bet you know the size of his dick!"

"No one's perfect." I shrug to hide how uncomfortable I am, that she's correct.

"Bitch, spill, or should I go ask him?"

"You wouldn't dare…" I begin, but she jumps up from the table making a beeline for Kye, who in turn had already started to make his way to our table.

"Rex! Rex, get your ass back here!" *Shit.* This cannot be happening. Maybe I can leave. Irritated at having my girls' night interrupted by a guest I most definitely did not invite; and equally curious as to how the fuck he knew where I was, I cross my arms over my chest. Now I have no choice but to wait this out until the two dipshits decide to join the table. I don't really want him to come over here! We haven't seen each other in a relaxed capacity. Our interactions since his arrival have been one dramatic disaster after another.

Why *is* he here? Shit. I swivel around in my seat, trying to not look ridiculous as I watch Rex and Kye speak. My best friend is currently leaning in towards Kye so he can say something to her. She laughs and swats his arm. Unlike myself, Rex is almost six feet tall, so she doesn't have to go on tiptoe to listen to Kye. They aren't touching each other, but they stand so close to one another. Both at ease, joking and laughing.

I have the irrational urge to go over there and stand in between them. I don't know why I want to separate them. My girl bestie meeting… I pause, not knowing what to refer to Kye as. *Is he still my best friend? Or now is he my fuck buddy bestie? Boyfriend?*

I strain to make rational thoughts, but it's way too deep to think about after the amount of alcohol Rex has plied me with. What is this that I'm feeling? Is it… Am I jealous? Over my best friends laughing together? *Of course, I am. Insecurity is a bitch.*

Your husband cheated on you, it's okay to feel this way right now. A voice says in the recess of my mind.

Fucking insecurities. I turn back in my seat reaching for the cool glass of water that must have been dropped off while I was preoccupied by the scene behind me. I can't fault Kye for being enamored by Rex. She's tall, stunning, successful, and has a style that rivals any model on a runway.

I sigh. Disappointed in myself, I never would have had these thoughts before Mitchell. Before my marriage, I would be sitting here confident and relaxed. I drop my shoulders, the weight of insecurities too much to bear right now. *Don't you dare start crying.* I silence the other voice in my head that's stirring up all kinds of problems for me that I'm not ready to handle.

I turn back once more, Rex is pulling on Kye's hand, gesturing for him to follow her over here. I watch where their hands join, my heart freezing over. There's no other way to describe how the intense jealousy that ignites in my gut burns worse than the alcohol I've had. Against my better judgment, I look up into his eyes. Gunmetal clashes with burnt sienna, he must see the pure devastation on my face because he gently removes his hand from hers.

He isn't mean or rude, I can't hear what they say to one another, but their body language is indicating they are still very much relaxed. He's looking me in the eyes while speaking to her. I read his lips plain as day when he says, "I'm here for her."

Rex smiles at Kye as he pushes past her, coming to stand in front of me. I risk a glance past Kye to Rex.

Try as I may, I giggle a little. Her eyes are the size of saucers. Her eyebrows threaten to run off in her hairline. "I'm going to give you a minute," she mouths to me before heading off towards the bathroom.

"Eyes on me princess," Kye tells me as he leans down to frame me in with his arms. This close, his aftershave hits me, and I fucking melt. As in, if I were wearing panties they would be on the floor. As it is, I am not. So now I will have to deal with my thighs being damned with my desire. *Great.*

"Wanna tell me why you looked like someone kicked your puppy?" He asks.

"Um...I don't own a puppy."

"Don't be smart. I saw every expression that passed over this beautiful face." He bends down, rubbing the tips of our noses. His hair falls forward, tickling my forehead. I lean away from him so I can concentrate, his nearness taking my every adequate thought from me. I want him, all of him. How he had me the other night.

He says something else to me, but I'm too wrapped up in my fantasy of us. I don't hear. I raise my eyebrows in question.

"What was that?" I ask him, he chuckles as my cheeks flame.

"Tell me." He demands.

"What are you talking about?" I lean into him, running my hands up his forearms. He watches me, his eyes deepening in color.

"Don't divert from our conversation." He grasps my hands to hold in his own.

"It's nothing."

His eyes flash with anger and I draw back. "We don't lie to one another. *Ever.*"

Does he the truth? Does he want to be privy to my every humiliating thought? Fine.

"I didn't like how easy it was for you two to look so perfect beside one another. She's so tall and beautiful and polished. You two looked flawless while I...well...I look like this!"

He freezes, pulling back to study my face. Open mouth, insert foot, you dumbass. He's not going to want an insecure woman. That's not attractive. Shame coats my tongue as I stare into his eyes wondering what kind of woman he sees. Does he see a broken shell of the woman I once was? Does he see the desperation that Mitchell claimed reeked from my pores? The indecisions are currently eating me alive.

I reach up and tuck a lock of my hair behind my ear, disgusted with how low I've allowed myself to go. I know I'm jaded. More so than others at my age. I can't help it. I've been hurt too many times, been naive too many times. Every time I listen to pretty words they end up slicing through me. I may have a tough exterior, but my interior is as soft as rose petals and just as easy to destroy. I clasp my hands in my lap, locking my fingers together. I can't look him in the eyes. I don't want to see the judgment there.

"You want to run that by me again?" Kye asks as his body goes rigid around me. I nibble my lip, noting the taste of my cherry lip gloss is absent. That's too bad, I like that flavor.

"Not particularly," I mutter as I raise my eyes to him.

Kye tilts his head, studying me some more. The energy between us feels like a livewire. "Are you drunk?" He asks me suddenly

"No..."

"We don't lie to one another, remember?" He reminds me, and I sit back, thinking before I speak. *Am I drunk? Are the fuzzy thoughts and wildly strong emotions a by-product of the amount of alcohol I consumed tonight?* I think it might be. I go to stand, but my equilibrium is off and I stumble into Kye's waiting arms. I glance up at him sheepishly. "I may be slightly intoxicated."

"You lie to me one more time and I will swat that delicious ass of yours so hard that sitting will no longer be an option."

"Yes. I'm a smidgen drunk, you ogre." I hold up my thumb and forefinger close to his striking face and push them as close as I can manage without them connecting. He nips at my fingers, latching onto one and sucking it slowly. The feel of his tongue wrapping around my finger brings on a torrent of need I desperately want to explore.

"Want to reevaluate your earlier statement about me belonging to another woman? Because the only one I want is standing in front of me, completely tanked."

"Just a teenie weenie bit." I pop out my lower lip, pouting a little. How this conversation went from jealousy and insecurities to being turned on is beyond me. I'm here for it, though.

"I see."

"You see what?"

"I'm going to blame your ridiculous remarks on the amount of alcohol you've consumed. I won't give you a lecture on being a responsible drinker, but I will be escorting you to the nearest restaurant to put something on your stomach."

"Mmmhmmm, food. That sounds yummy."

"I bet it does."

"What about Rex? I can't leave her here."

"Nonsense, we would never leave a friend here. No drinker left behind." His smile is so genuine that I melt against him as he wraps his arms around me again.

"Oh, and Thena?"

"Hmm?"

"Tomorrow, we're going to have a conversation about you accepting facts."

"What facts?"

"That you are my perfect future."

I have no words as he kisses the tip of my nose. I stare at him in stunned silence. He laughs as Rex walks up to the table.

"So, guys, what did I miss?"

20

Dumplings

Thena

“Open your mouth for me, brat.” Kye taunts me by waving a dumpling in front of my face. The smell of pork and soy makes my body lean forward before I can stop myself. I wrap my lips around his chopsticks, flavors burst on my tongue, and I close my eyes, humming with pleasure. God, I love these delicate treats. I swallow my bite, opening my eyes.

Kye stares at my mouth like a starving man, his pupils dilate into ice pools. My heart flutters, and my pulse picks up.

He licks his lips while watching mine. I want his tongue on my body so bad. I wink at him playfully, and he smiles at me.

Rexy snorts beside me, reminding me we aren't alone. I straighten in my seat, clearing my throat. I grab my water, suddenly feeling like my mouth is sandpaper. Kye adverts his eyes from me as I'm plagued with intrusive thoughts.

What if I have food on my face? Or vegetables in my teeth? How awful would it be to sit here making googly eyes at him with a carrot sticking to my teeth? As I watch him, a new kind of fear is unlocked. I can see the moment his eyes shift from heated to concerned. "What are you looking at, Kye?"

Rex snorts beside me. "Kye, allow me to answer this one. Thena, you don't know how you look; slightly drunk, with swollen lips while sucking down your dumplings like you're turning cocksucking into a fucking Olympic sport. I bet you can suck a golf ball through a garden hose."

I gasp! The reflection in the restaurant window shows my face turning a demeaning shade of beet red. Of all the audacious things for her to say to me! Kye bursts out laughing. I scrunch my nose, wishing that looks could cause permanent damage.

"Oh, look at those laser beams. Watch out, Rex, she's out for blood." Both of the idiots laugh at me while I snatch up the extra pair of chopsticks, stealing another delicious bite of heaven and eating it *without* turning it into a Pornhub episode.

"I can, in fact, confirm her talent." Both of them chuckle again while I want to recoil within myself. Dark, intrusive thoughts whisper through me. I no longer hear my friends laughing with me. Every nasty word Mitchell ever spoke echoes around me. Doubts cloud my judgments. *Why does he want to feed me? Does he not think I am capable of feeding myself? Are they being mean to me? Or are they...* No, they're just joking. This is your trauma. Calm your racing heart. I sigh in frustration and hopelessness, how am I supposed to move on with the seeds of doubt Mitchell has placed in me? My good mood is ruined. I place my chopsticks over the rim of my bowl as they both sober, realizing I'm no longer in a playful mood. Kye pins me with a stare. I glance out the window.

"Thena, look at me."

I obey; of course I do.

"It's okay to laugh at yourself. It's not an attack when you're in a safe place. We are that place for you."

"I know."

"That motherfucker really did a number on you," Rex says, rubbing my back in soothing circular motions. I shake my head, feeling like I ruined everyone's fun.

"I don't want to talk about him."

"I wouldn't either. Not with this stud muffin here hand-feeding you. So some chicks will stop staring at him like he's their meal ticket."

"What?"

"Oh yeah, the two blondes sitting across the way from us? They've been eyeing him up and down since we walked in. Instead of paying attention to them, he's been enjoying you and your industry-worthy sounds."

"*He* is right here," Kye states, not impressed with our conversation topic or that Rex seems to be enjoying this way too much. Seeing how quickly she became comfortable with Kye lifts my spirits a little more, giving me hope that all of my friends will like him. "And for the record," he begins, "I was feeding her because I like to watch her lips wrap around…"

"Hey! I don't need to hear this!" Rex covers her ears, shouting enough that I'm glad the restaurant is almost empty at this hour, but there are still patrons here.

The color of my face deepens more. If I change my posture, will it hide me from being on display? The men across the aisle from us look curious while I'm guessing that's disgust on their dates' faces.

"Will you two get a room?" Rex stands quickly, laughing at us; she grabs her purse. Her look is downright scandalous as she wiggles her eyebrows. "I have an Uber outside for me. I will see you two sex fiends later."

"We can take you," Kye offers.

"No, thank you. Unlike some," she stares pointedly at me, "I can read a room, and this one is on fire."

"It's not safe for you to take an Uber this late at night," he cautions her.

She just smiles at him. "No, I'm okay. You two need to…iron this tension out." She laughs as she hugs me. "Bye sweetheart, call me tomorrow. I want *all* the details. STAT," she whispers in my ear, not low enough for Kye to not hear, though. He chuckles at her antics.

"Sure thing," I say. Unable to stop the heat from creeping up my neck again.

She turns to Kye, wiggling her manicured fingers at him. "Bye, lover-boy."

She walks out, leaving both of us in an uneasy silence. I pull my glass of water closer, spinning the straw around. The restaurant seems to heat up, and it's just us two at the table. I contemplate running. If I leave now, can I catch up to Rex and share the Uber?

"Staring at the glass won't make me go away." Kye's melodic voice washes over me.

He's right, it won't. I have no idea what's wrong with me. We've known each other for years. This shouldn't be awkward. It isn't uncomfortable and *that's* the problem. It was easier having Rex here as a buffer. Now I have no choice but to focus on him. He's always had this aura of energy about him that's left me absolutely enamored with him, but now when I look at him, all I see is us the other night. Our bodies joined, my hands in his hair as his hips thrusted into me while I arched into his embrace as he ravished me. When he looks into my eyes, does he see how much I want him? Does that make me pathetic? Does that make me appear desperate?

"You have the most expressive face."

I look up so fast I feel the color draining from my face. Nooo… "I don't," I deny.

"You do and it's adorable. I bet I can tell you exactly what you are thinking."

I shake my head. My buzz is long gone, and this is a conversation I'm not ready to have. Most certainly not here in a public place. I attempt to divert the conversation away from us. "It's late…"

Kye cuts me off, "You were thinking about how you don't know how to move forward now that your friend isn't here to distract us."

"We should…" I begin again.

"You were thinking about us the other night and how I worshiped your body."

"…go."

"I couldn't agree more, we should go. I want to take you home and remind you of all the reasons you should feel confident in my devotion to you." Kye stands, coming around to pull out my chair for me.

"You don't have to do that," I tell him.

"I do, and I will; now let me grab your coat, princess."

He holds my jacket open as I twist around to slide my arms in, smiling a bit as Kye leans in to kiss the top of my head. He watches our reflection in the window before us, the tip of his nose grazes my hair as he breathes my scent in. I gasp a little. Taken aback by how attentive he is to me while standing here for others to see. It isn't something I'm used to. I close my eyes to center myself, my belly tight, my nerves on end. Something about his nearness makes me want to climb him here in the center of the restaurant.

"Open your eyes for me, princess."

I do.

Kye and I are so close the reflection could be mistaken for us touching, my back against his front. He closes the remaining inches between us, bringing his mouth down to kiss my neck. I shiver, embarrassed and turned on all at the same time. He's really doing this in front of the other diners?

"What do you see when you look at us?" He nuzzles the curve between my collar and ear lobe, cuddling me in his arms.

I find myself taking in his rich scent, his fingers graze across my hairline along the nape of my neck. My high ponytail gives him better access to the sensitive area there.

How does he make me feel this way? I take him and all his glory in, standing behind me. I see myself in the mirrored surface, not recognizing the woman staring back at me. This woman is everything I'm not: she's confident, she's beautiful, she's charismatic, and she has a man standing behind her who is out-of-this-world gorgeous. She looks stunning in her simple, black dress and off-white coat. I'm her, and she is me. That's my reflection. I just have to believe it. "I see potential for happiness."

"Then happiness is what you shall have."

As Kye breaks away from me, he takes one of my hands, leading me out. Applause breaks out with the few remaining guests. Catcalls ring out, and as we pass the tables with the model worthy women from earlier, I notice they look extremely put out. I blow them a kiss as we pass.

Stepping out on the sidewalk side by side, hand in hand. I take in the city around us with new eyes. Something about holding Kye's hand makes this night infinitely more memorable. The usual hustle and bustle of the busy city is quieter than what's typical. The late hour and unseasonably chilled air caused most to head home early. He leads me down the sidewalk towards his ride.

My neck begins to tingle, the hair on my arms rising uncomfortably as a feeling that someone is watching me, pierces my peaceful moment. I squeeze Kye's hand harder, my pace growing hasty. The air seems colder, and an eerie thought that the night wants to close around me, snuffing out my life, has me trembling. I glance around, searching the street and pathways around us. Everything looks normal, but it still doesn't *feel* normal. I spot nothing at first. All is how one would expect it to be, other couples walking together, a few people entering or exiting the little shops running along this area. The random traffic.

How strange.

I almost laugh at the absurdity of feeling so much fear for no reason. It has to be exhaustion or my imagination running wild. But as we turn a corner, I glimpse a red glow at a darkened entrance to an alley. I stop without thinking. My abrupt halt goes unnoticed by Kye, who continues walking. The momentum of his gait causes me to lose my balance. I right myself as Kye looks at me curiously.

"What's wrong?" He asks me, but I pay him no mind.

I focus my attention on the alley where I saw the light. My skin crawls as an outline of a man steps out further away from the shadows that concealed him. He's just at the cusp where light meets the dark. The outline of his body is on display, yet his face is shrouded in shadows, successfully masking him. I know that stance. I would know it anywhere. Chills run the course of my spine, I squeeze Kye's hand, my nails biting into his skin.

The orange glow from his lit cigarette illuminates his features only slightly. The blood in my veins runs cold as I take what I can see in. It can't be. He wouldn't be following us around. Would he?

"Thena, love, what is it?" Kye asks me. He comes closer so our shoulders are brushing.

I risk looking away from the mystery man to face Kye. "It's him," I whisper. I point in the direction that I just saw the man, only when I look over, he is gone. I know I didn't imagine it. Someone was right there.

Kye scans the area and looks down at me. "Honey, I don't see anyone."

"I thought I did. I guess I didn't. From this distance, it could have been anyone. I was so sure, though." I clasp my jacket lapels with my free hand and stare at the vacant spot where the mystery man had been.

"Are you sure?"

"Yes. I saw him! He was standing there smoking a cigarette in the darkened part of the sidewalk." I wave my hand in the direction, this time positive I wasn't hallucinating. Kye observes the spot, his eyes scanning the area. Not missing anything. My nerves are trash, where did he go? I turned my head for a split second. What the fuck?

"That would have put him directly in front of the restaurant window," Kye murmurs.

"Was he watching us?" I ask.

"We don't know for certain it was him."

"It was. I know it. I can feel it." My voice doesn't waver, and I'm positive about who I saw. Kye begins to tug me further down the sidewalk.

"Here, let me get you in the car, I can go check."

"No, I--I just want to go home," I tell him.

Kye let's go of my hand, placing his hands on my shoulders. "We need to know if he's following us. If he is, we need to contact the police."

It is the most reasonable course of action. I hesitate, though. "The police. What can they do?"

"Thena, honey. Mitchell is stalking you, we really need to report it. There are protective measures we should take."

"Stalking me?" Am I a fucking parrot? I can't wrap my head around this conversation, or hell, even the situation.

"That's what it's called when someone doesn't take the hint to fuck off." His sarcastic tone grates on me.

I lash out in frustration at the control I seem to be losing. I don't mean to, but the thought of anyone following me around is mind boggling. I don't like it. "I know what the definition of stalking is, smartass. I just can't fathom why he *would* stalk me. He didn't even love me."

"It's not always about love, my darling."

"Then what is it about him?" I ask him, my curiosity peaked at what his answer will be.

"Obsession."

21

Lurking

Thena

Kye parks in my driveway, turning off the truck. He leans over, gently relieving me of the house keys to open the door for me. It's so dark outside, I would have a hard time fitting them in their locks.

"Don't move," he tells me, "a lady should never have to open her door."

That makes me smile. Between the headache I have and the events after dinner, I volunteer as tribute for the chivalry he wants to offer me. I lean my head against the headrest as Kye gets out and comes around the hood. My door opens, and I turn my head to find Kye holding his hand out to me like a gentleman. We clasp hands, and he guides me out.

"Watch your step, madame," he warns as I find my footing.

"I'm sorry, I must have forgotten to turn the porch light on when I left," I apologize.

"Don't do that," he says

"Do what?"

"Feel the need to apologize over everything."

"I just…" I begin, but he cuts me off.

"You just dealt with a dick for years, making you feel like everything was some great offense. It's not."

"You're not wrong. Wait, let me give you some light at least." I pull my phone out of my purse. Smiling a bit, I softly say, "Some light is better than no light."

We climb the steps together, reaching the door at the same time. *CRUNCH.* Glass breaks under my foot. I jump back out of reflex, but I step on something again, it too breaks under my weight. *CRUNCH.* I look down, my eyes taking a moment to adjust with the limited light. Confused, I scrunch my nose in disgust. What the hell?

Glass is scattered all over the front stoop. Kye's urgency is projected in his firm hold on me as he grabs me quickly and pushes me behind him, shielding me from whatever threat he deems necessary. He scans the yard. Little good that will do, black holes are brighter than this. He must come to the same conclusion as I have because he leads me off the porch.

"Thena, go wait in the truck."

I don't respond. He should know me better than that, I will never hide behind a man. I step back to flash my cell phone light over the broken glass. The white shards stand out against the depth of the night. Squatting to get a closer look at the pieces, I look up directly under where the light bulb would be. *Fan-fucking-tastic.* I take my time studying the broken shards of glass below me, pausing to think back to exactly how it had looked earlier.

"The light had a cover on it," I say.

"You're sure?"

"It was encased in a sconce. If there was an electrical surge of some kind and the bulb shattered, it would be trapped inside and not currently littering my fucking porch." I stand back up, resolved to go in with him. I'd know if there's someone in my home. Between the both of us, we should be good. I'm not scared. No, I'm pissed. This is where my son sleeps. I'm tired of the intimidation act. If Mitchell wants to behave like a little bitch poking at me during the night, he can be treated like one. I refuse to give him the satisfaction of seeing me upset. But how do I even know it's Mitchell?

"Mitchell is supposed to be out of town this weekend," I tell Kye.

"Then who did this?" He gestures to the porch.

"I don't know, I'm not counting him out just yet, but I also don't see his father lying to me." I cross my arms over my chest, the bite of the chilled air seeping through my dress jacket.

I know there has to be an explanation. I would prefer a reasonable one. Unfortunately, I don't think that is the case here. I don't want that explanation to be who I think it is. Fucking Mitchell.

"We can check the cameras and see what happened. This is why I installed them. Let's get you inside. I don't want you out in the open. Just in case." He slides the key into the lock and ushers me inside.

"Just in case of what?" I ask.

"You know the answer already," Kye says more gently. In case Mitchell's waiting for me to be alone, these are the words Kye isn't saying out loud. I shake my head.

"He wouldn't," I deny it. Surely, he wouldn't.

"Men do it every day. Let me just make sure everything is okay in the house. Stay here in the living room until I can check."

"Oh fuck off! I'm not cowering behind a sofa while you play Superman. *We* both can check the house. *Together*." I toss my purse on the couch and kick off my shoes. I would rather not be in high heels if I have to fight someone.

Kye gives me a pointed look, shaking his head. But I'm fed up being led around by men. I cross my arms, refusing to move out of his way.

"Looks like we're at an impasse. Because you want to be a caveman and I refuse to be too frightened to check under *my own* bed. Either we stand out here and waste time arguing, or you realize how serious I am. When I asked for your help, it was to have someone to stand beside me, not someone to stand behind," I tell him in the most assertive tone I can manage.

Kye places his hands on his hips, glancing towards the heavens. I know when he looks at me like he would rather strangle me himself, that I've won. "Fine, but stay close to me. *If* someone is in here, I don't want you alone with them," he speaks to me in a tone usually reserved for children, and that pisses me off. I move up to him, going chest to chest, or as chest-to-chest as I can with my lackluster height. Ugh, how I wish it reflected my attitude.

"Before we do this, you need to know two things. First: if someone is in here, we both know who it will be. Second: if that motherfucker is in my home, *he* will need you for protection, not *me*." With that, I push past Kye, annoyed and slightly hoping Mitchell is in my closet, that would save me a lot of grief.

The broken bulb, the sulking in the shadows tonight, the weird late-night phone calls, cameras, all of it. A nice fat stack of reasonable cause for any sane judge to grant an order of protection. At least with the paper, I would be able to shoot him the next time he harassed me and not face charges. I send up a silent prayer. *Please let him be in my closet.*

22

Thena

I take the lead through the house, we haven't been loud, but still, if he or someone else is in my home, I would prefer not to give it away that I'm coming down the hall. Kye's bitching and moaning behind me about spanking my ass, and I would be lying to myself if I didn't admit that it's totally turning me on.

I move as silently as I can throughout the area and, for once, I'm thankful for the open floor plan. With a glance, we can clear three out of the eight rooms. Kye never leaves my side, he even dares to move me to the side as he looks under the beds and in the closets of the first room. After confirming no one is here other than us, I nut check him with my knuckles in reminder that I don't like when he behaves like a total caveman.

His eyes shoot daggers at me as he mouths, "I will fucking get you back for that."

I roll my eyes and pause in my search long enough to whisper, "Don't be a big baby."

He flips me off as I leave him cupping his balls.

We search the remainder of the house, not finding a soul anywhere. I huff. Am I disappointed? I don't want to dissect that too closely right now. I don't know if I like my character at this particular moment. Did I want to find my ex in my home so I could shoot him and be done with it? Yes, I did. Because now, I'm going crazy. I was so sure earlier that I saw him standing across the road from us. I know it was dark, but I would know his posture anywhere. I need to look at the camera feed for tonight, right now. I don't know if I can fix the porch bulb and pretend like tonight didn't happen.

"Who has Toby tonight?" Kye calls out as he checks the locks on the windows.

"Mitchell's mother and father are in town. He's with them for the weekend." I slip out of my coat, preparing to return it to its proper place. Mitchell's voice echoes in my mind, *"Everything has a place where it belongs"*. I stop in my tracks. The coat's fabric bunches in my hands as I stare at it.

It's a beautiful beige color, almost white in its near perfection. Not a wrinkle or missing button on it. I remember the day Mitchell got me this, it was in a storefront window and the single most fancy item I had ever wanted. When we got home, I had laid it across the back of the couch. The action set Mitchell off and I was subjected to a lecture on everything having its place.

I glance around the living room. Everything looks brand new, with no messes, and no family photos. This house could be a showroom for Better Homes & Gardens. I walk towards the kitchen, tossing my perfect jacket on the couch as I pass. This house looks like a museum, not a home. It's time to change that. Turning in Kye's direction, I tell him, "I'm going to be up late tonight. I need to check the cameras and then do a little redecorating. If you would like to join me you can do so."

"Of course."

"Great. Wine and beer are in the kitchen. I'm going to change real quick, and then we can check out the cameras together," I announce over my shoulder as I head towards my bedroom.

I quickly strip out of my dress, tossing it in the dirty clothes as I stuff my legs into the closest pair of sweatpants that I can find. Their faded as fuck and comfy as hell. The drive I have tonight to see the footage is too high for me to worry about my outfit too much. Comfort is a must when you're trying to catch your stalker. I unlatch my bra next, it joins the dress in the hamper. I slip into my tank top.

I lift my arms enough to do a quick smell test. I pause and think of the merits of body odor, knowing that I have a slim chance of doing the hanky-panky with Kye, but always wanting to. I run into the bathroom and spray some deodorant on. I run back to my room and ram my feet in my hilarious monster house shoes.

As I enter the living space, Kye finishes closing the blinds before he joins me in the living room as I pull up the system on my phone. I cast the screen to the TV for a larger picture. Kye catches my attention, when I look over, he arches a brow in question.

"I'm not a huge fan of tablets, and my phone screen is too small."

"Old age getting to you, princess?" he jokes at me, and I flip him the bird.

"Women in their thirties are in their prime. Now be a good boy and shut off the lights. I hate trying to see past a glare." He does what I ask before sitting on the sofa beside me, his body taking up more room than I would have thought. The sofa dips under his weight, cushions tilt, bringing us much closer together. Our arms brush each other, and my nipples harden; the friction of my top, and bare skin leaves me a little breathless. *You have someone messing with you, and you're focused on being horny?* A voice berates me in my head. I roll my eyes, grabbing one of my decorative pillows and placing it in front of my chest.

"Do you need some help?" The object of my desire asks me. I try really hard to keep the blush from my face, but by this time I know it's pointless. My heart flames.

"Excuse me?" I question him, as he holds my glass of wine out to me.

"With the footage. It's not playing yet, are you experiencing technical difficulties? I can also assist you with the current situation going on under your shirt as well. Just let me watch this video real quick." He has a smug look as he drinks me in. I want to hit him, but I refrain. It's not his fault my body comes to life whenever he's within eyesight of it. His reaction to it is his fault, though. I playfully nudge him as we switch my handheld for a glass of wine. I lean back, causing the pillow to fall the wayside. His eyes drop to my chest as I silently pray the couch will swallow me whole.

My dilemma is forgotten when an image appears on the screen. Kye hits something on the phone screen, and the film fast-forwards so quickly my mind has a hard time computing the scene before a new one appears. He stops the video suddenly as Rex's car appears in the driveway. You can see a clear image of me locking up my house before I leave. I prance down the porch out into the yard, giving a little twirl in my dress. Rex is whistling and cheering on my antics.

Kye leans over to me, his eyes never leaving the screen. "Allow me to introduce to you, the real Mrs. Sullivan. Although I prefer another name."

I nudge him again with my free hand, attempting to ignore the way his words affect me. We watch for another minute until I point at the corner of the frame. "Look right there! Bottom left hand corner. The sconce is still there, which means the bulb was intact." He hits another button, again with the speed of the video it makes me slightly dizzy. I hear someone speaking and I look at him sharply. "I thought you said there was no audio?"

He returns the look. "There's no audio, Thena."

"But I just heard…" I stop myself and listen again to the noise now gone. I set my wine down. I've definitely had too much to drink tonight.

Kye pauses the recording again, rewinding it and hits play. This time there's no one in the frame that I see. Or no one that I can see yet. The time stamp on the video says nine pm as I see a small figure sneak up on the lawn from the row of trees that separate my yard from an elderly couple next door.

I watch, transfixed in horror, as the lean figure approaches with a longer object in hand. The person creeps up to my porch without noticing the camera and rears the weapon back. The first swing makes me jump. By the fourth one I'm crying as I have to watch the utter destruction this assailant is wrecking on my front porch.

The assault on my damn light only takes moments but watching this unfold feels like a lifetime. I get up and walk into the kitchen needing a glass of water. I blindly move around the area, my vision not clear from crying. I can't believe this is happening to us. I take a tentative sip of water to draw this out as long as possible. So much for being brave and facing my harasser.

Kye joins me in the kitchen wrapping his arms around me to comfort me. His touch is soothing, I feel safe having him here with me. My devastation starts to subside, a new feeling begins to creep in as he strokes my back. Even with my current situation, his touch turns me into an inferno, a flame that only burns for him. Remembering the way he relished feeding me, his eagerness to protect me, the way he makes me laugh while the world burns around me makes my body go taunt with desire. He moves back just enough to gaze down at me, his eyes shine with suggestion as he takes me in. His fingers glide down my body before flexing on my ass. He leans in, brushing his lips across my forehead.

"Are you okay?" he whispers against my skin before leading me to sit on the couch again. He squats down on his hunches, taking my hands in his. I don't know how to answer that. So I stay silent. I no longer feel safe in my home. That comfort, that security ripped from me. I just don't know how to ask for what I want. My hand feels so small in his, the electricity that travels between us when we touch is so new to me, it terrifies me. But I crave more. I want to get lost in him as much as I want to wash the last half hour of my life away.

"I need to say this out loud."

"Do tell, princess. What's on that pretty little mind of yours?"

"That wasn't Mitchell in the video."

"You are correct."

"So maybe it isn't Mitchell doing this and I need to be blaming someone else. Maybe it's a coincidence." I trudge forward with my thoughts. Kye looks skeptical but pauses to hear me out. "If Mitchell is out of town and not here, maybe… No, we *know* it's someone else that's responsible for the light. So maybe it's the same person making the calls."

"What calls?" His tone is urgent, angry.

I press on knowing I have to say this out loud. "I received some calls from an unknown caller. When I answered, it was music and heavy breathing. But that's what I'm getting at. What if it's someone else and not Mitchell? The cameras could have really been him protecting his property." I try to argue my point.

"Thena, I know you are trying to explain this away. Acknowledging the man you married isn't the man you thought he was, isn't being theatrical. It shouldn't be embarrassing or anything else other than the truth. It's fucking tragic. Let's be reasonable enough to acknowledge that how he is behaving is dangerous and needs to be taken seriously." He holds his hands out in front of me in a gesture for me to wait.

I snap my mouth closed, holding my retort to myself.

Kye continues, "I don't care that the person we saw tonight wasn't him. You can't convince me he isn't involved. However, I will prove it one way or another. All that video showed was that he has wormed his way into having an accomplice."

It's a reasonable suggestion, one I will admit, I would have made as well. I know what he's saying is logical. I'm just having a difficult time accepting that the man I married, the man I thought I would spend the rest of my life with, the same man who could adopt my son and present this solid amazing image to the world, is a danger to us. How does one cope with this? I've heard of women being murdered by their spouses. It seems to be a reoccurring crime. You don't really give it too much thought until it's happening to you, though.

Kye smiles at me. "I have an idea."

"And that is?"

"Come stay with me tonight." He juts out his bottom lip in mock pouting.

"I don't know." I would love nothing else than the comfort of his embrace. I really do. But should I really leave for tonight? What if the assailant comes back? What if something else happens?

"Come with me. We can spend the weekend at my house. Treat it like a mini vacation." He grabs my hands, pulling me into him to spin me around the room. "We can order some take out, sip on wine. I have a feeling you will love to soak that delectable body of yours in my clawfoot tub. Don't be a brat, let's get you out of here for a bit."

That sounds amazing, and I honestly can't remember the last time I had a weekend away from here. Not one that was pleasant at least. I pretend to hesitate when he stops spinning me, making him think I'm going to turn him down. His smile drops and I know now's the perfect time to announce, "Okay, let me just grab a change of clothes."

His face lights up and I return it with a smile of my own. I'm happy that he's content to just spend time with me. I speed walk to my room to grab some items, tossing them in an overnight bag. I almost walk out of the room when I remember my journal, I flip the light back on and open the drawer. Pulling out my book and pen, I stuff them into my overnight bag before turning the light off again and heading out. I wonder what his house looks like?

23

Bachelor Pad Where?

Thena

Spinning in the living room, my eyes soaking up every luxurious detail, mouth agape, I stare in awe and wonder. Kye's home is breathtakingly beautiful. It's a modern cabin with a popular, new rustic vibe. It has everything! Floor-to-ceiling windows, thick wooden beams, and hardwood floors complete with a fireplace. The overstuffed leather couches and recliner are set opposite the windows, so you can take full advantage of what I'm sure is a stunning view.

I can't wait until tomorrow morning to see it. I slip my shoes off immediately, picking them up and placing them by the door, too scared to scuff the gorgeous hardwood of the floors. Man, he has really been slumming it at my place. Knowing no personal boundaries, I drop my purse in a chair as I pass, heading in the direction I last saw Kye.

The bedroom is sublime. I stand frozen in the doorway, taking in everything I can see. The room is well lit with a bed large enough to comfortably sleep a family of five. I hadn't realized beds come in that size. The mahogany wood makes the crisp, white duvet pop against the dark color. His room is massive, yet it has a cozy energy to it. The oversized furniture must be a running theme for him, but it's all accented with throws, rugs, and other comfort items.

Kye comes out of a door on the other side of the room. Removing his cufflinks, he sets them down in a little box on a stand. I raise an eyebrow in question, knowing damn well that he usually dresses like a version of Adam Sandler. He smirks, admitting, "I wanted to make a lasting impression on your friend tonight and, on the off chance that we ran into that piece of shit, Mitchell, I wanted to remind him that I can provide for you and Tobias better than he can."

"Someone's feeling acrimonious."

"It's irrelevant in the grand scheme of things, but I have a petty streak."

"You don't say," I mock.

He advances toward me, stopping only a millimeter away. His hand brushes my hair to the side, as he bends down to kiss my cheek. His nearness brings his warm scent, that is now my favorite comfort smell. As weird as it sounds, I search for the scent whenever I feel off. "It's late, and I know you're probably upset with how I just showed up tonight. I promise when this is over, we will have healthy boundaries. Until then, like it or not, I'm your shadow. Now, let's get you in the shower." His voice is low, and I know he's trying to ease my troubled mind. It may not be appropriate for a time like this, but I want nothing more than to have him with me, naked, in his shower.

Jesus, does he do anything in moderation? My bathroom is something to appreciate, but this... His is a work of art. A mixture of rustic and modern, where the shower alone can be used as a communal. I pull my shirt over my head and lay it on the double vanity. The lights dim, and I know it's Kye's attempt at making me feel comfortable. I watch his reflection through the mirror. The muscles that make up his back ripple as he turns the water on. Jets of water spray out from multiple directions. I gasp at the grandeur of it all.

"Will you join me?"

He whips around from the shower stall, the hot water emitting steam around us. The humidity sticks to my skin. A blanket of comfort in a rather ample space.

"Come here." He beckons, and I obey. He helps me slip the sweatpants off, turning to do his own. He places them neatly on the vanity beside my old tank and I can't help but grin at his ease of domestication and care. Joining me in the shower, he pulls me to him, cradling me against his chest.

Hot water runs down my body, warming the chill left from tonight's events. Kye lathers the shampoo into my scalp until my muscles loosen and I relax. Lavender-infused soap trickles down my spine and between my breasts. I close my eyes, humming a soft sound of approval in the back of my throat. His fingertips gently massage my scalp, roaming my neckline.

Senses heighten, and everything is intensified. The way his hands move against my body, leaves me breathless, The magnitude of euphoria that sweeps me up,has me feeling light, floating, and burning with need. I rub my thighs together, my body craving something I'm not confident enough to vocalize. The bittersweet throbbing between my legs is bordering on overstimulating.

I blindly reach out running my fingertips over his chest, passing through the light dusting of chest hair. My body leans into his own, my hard nipples grazing against his own soap-slicked skin. I hear Kye chuckle softly, the air around my ear shifting enough to cause goosebumps to dance across my skin.

"Tilt your head back, my love," he whispers against my skin, his lips trailing down the hollow of my neck. I'm compelled to obey, driven by my own wanton desires. My body yearns for more of him. Hot water rinses the soap away as I grant him more access to the parts of me that covet his touch.

"Hmmmm, you're eager to obey, aren't you?" He licks back up my neck, slowly. My stomach tightens. He runs his fingers back through my hair, wrapping the long tendrils around his fist. He pulls until I'm suspended in the position he wants.

My back is bowed, causing my tits to arch on display for his viewing pleasure. The position leaves me wholly at his mercy. For the briefest moments, I worry that I may slip on the wet tile. My eyes pop open, searching for Kye; at the angle I'm in, all I see is the tile on the ceiling. Kye's lips trail between my breasts, whispering against my skin. "Trust me, baby."

I try to nod my head in agreement, but with the force of his grip, movement causes my hair to tug almost painfully.

"Don't move, keep your pretty eyes closed, and just feel what I do to you, brat." He instructs me.

If he were any other man, I would panic. My fight or flight reflexes would kick in. I would take his balls. But, with Kye, I trust him so wholly with my body that I relax my posture as much as possible. Even with the shower, my wetness soaks my inner thighs. The water's not enough to wash the evidence of Kye's wreckage of my body away.

He runs a fingertip down my chest, circling one of my peaked nipples. My breathing quickens, my brain needing oxygen as much as I need him to fuck me. The sexual sensations Kye is inspiring on my nervous system make me want to drop to my knees to beg for more. He clasps my nipple in his mouth, his teeth applying enough pressure I gasp.

I want to lift my head, to stand straighter so I can watch him torture me. He tightens his fist that's locked in my hair, and I cry out. The line between pleasure and pain makes my head spin. I sink my fingers into his hair, desperate to hold onto something.

"Do you have any idea what I'm going to do to this body, Thena?" he whispers against my skin.

He expects me to talk? Now? I start to shake my head, but remember his grip on my hair. I try to speak, to find my voice. I'm unable to think of how to form words to create sentences. His hands and mouth are already too much. I'm going to explode and he wants me to talk?

Lifting my head up, the tension from my movement brings a gasp from my lips. He tugs my hair harder. It doesn't hurt; it brings me such a deep, erotic feeling that I want him to pull harder. I want him to abuse my body in ways I've never dared dream about.

"Thena, I asked you a question. Answer me."

He brings our bodies flush together, his mouth bruising my own as he crashes his lips against mine, demanding an answer. I gasp, filling my lungs with him, my head is spinning, and my legs are shaking. My body sings the sweetest melody.

Wanting to cause him to be turned on as much as he has me, I slowly open my eyes. Adjusting to the dimness of the stall, the lights casting an erotic, secretive glow throughout the room, I have to stand on my tiptoes so I can whisper against his lips, "What do you want to do to me, Daddy?"

My tongue darts out, pulling the salty sweetness from his lips as his eyes round, flashing with such intensity I smell his arousal. His dick flexes against my stomach. Gotcha, big boy.

"You are such a brat." He grinds his dick on me, our slick bodies causing the most delicious friction I have ever felt. I am so turned on. I don't care how he takes me as long as he does. I grind myself on him, reaching between us to take his cock in my hands. His size is intimidating, I would panic if I hadn't had him in me before. Now I crave that stretching of my body to fit him snugly. My body clenches in anticipation.

"Thena, use your words. What do you want?" He uses his hands to pull me closer to him, my feet almost off the ground, rubbing his dick against my folds, slowly brushing against my clit. I cry out in frustration; it's not enough. I want more. His thick shaft slips between my thighs, caressing my clit again.

I'm so caught up in the torrent of pleasure that our connection is giving me, there's no room for embarrassment as I rock my hips as much as he will allow. I moan loudly as the tension builds. His nostrils flare as he locks his jaw, watching me grind against him in wild abandonment.

His grip tightens again, more forceful this time as he demands of me, "Don't be a brat, or I won't give you what you want."

What I want is to weep. My pussy is pulsing, and my thighs tremble. I'm so so close. I need him to fuck me. I whimper, pulling myself back from the edge long enough to whisper, "Fuck me, Daddy." The only way I can describe the look in his eyes is feral.

He grabs my ass and lifts my legs. Wrapping them around his hips, he shuts the water off. I'm momentarily confused until he tells me, "For the things I'm about to do to this body, we're going to need a bed."

I close my eyes at his declaration. The promise in his voice, and the anticipation has my body humming anew. Kye waits until I open my eyes, giving him my full attention. He drops me on my back on his bed, my stomach does a little flip at the momentary free fall. That's what being loved by Kye feels like - a free fall, a whirlwind of butterflies in my belly.

"Open your legs, baby girl."

A blush warms my cheeks as I do as he demands. Cool air caresses my intimate parts, eliciting a different sensation that's not wholly unpleasant. From his vantage point, my body is on full display for him. Does he find me beautiful? My insecurities flare for a moment and I hurry to wrap my arms around me to cover my chest.

Kye shakes his head, his wet curls falling across his forehead as he spreads me farther apart. "Place your hands above your head."

I hesitate, wondering if I'm comfortable enough to be so entirely on display.

He arches a single brow at me, squeezing my knees slightly. "Do it, now."

Hesitantly, I do as he tells me. My nipples are pebbled in the cool air. Leaning down above me, he presses his forehead to mine. "You're perfect, Thena. Now hold on to the pillow and take Daddy like the good girl you are." He gives my body no mercy, no quarter, as he slams his cock into me, deep, hard. My body clenches around him. The harsh intrusion into my body is so unexpected my nails score the pillow.

I feel my body arch off the bed as I call out, "Kye, please." His grip on my hips tightens with so much force I know I will have bruises later, but I don't care. I want more. His thrusts are so deep and brutal. His wreckage of my body is so thorough. I cry out again and again.

Fire ignites in my belly as I'm being stretched to accommodate him in a manner my body may not be used to, but my pussy clenches around him as the tip of his shaft rubs against the sweet spot in my body as it yearns for more. I shatter around him as I orgasm, calling out his name once more.

"That's right baby girl, milk my cock with your sweet little pussy," he coaxes me. Running his hands down my body, slipping them underneath my ass cheeks, he rocks back on his knees to watch his dick slide in and out of me.

My eyes pop open as I feel something at my opening.

"Shhhh, relax Thena. I've got you."

I try to calm my racing heart, but I'm stretched so tightly that nothing else will fit.

He caresses my lips around his cock. The sensation is new to me; my pussy walls come into contact with him. He groans. "You're such a good girl; you work my cock so good, baby."

I feel him slip a finger into me, then two more, his eyes roll back as he feels himself pushing in me. My head lolls to the side, and I close my eyes, wanting to live in this moment forever. He spreads my body further to accommodate him more profoundly as he continues to pump in and out of me. My stomach tightens, my legs shake as beads of sweat roll down his chest. He flips his fingers in me, rubbing them against a sweet spot in my body. I start to shake my head quickly as I pant like a bitch in heat. He smiles at me; I swear it's the most devilish smile I've ever seen.

"Oh, baby you aren't finished yet. I feel you. You want to cum on my dick again, don't you?" He slows his pumps, settling all the way in my body, he grinds against my clit in slow, precise, circular motions. The tension in my stomach coils tight. I want to scream out, I want to cry, fuck, I want to pray. Pray for this feeling to stop and to never end at the same time. The pleasure borders on it being too painful. I gasp, desperate for oxygen.

"Answer me, brat." He pulls out of me long enough to flip me on my stomach. He brings my hips up, placing my ass in the air. One of his hand's tangles in my hair as he pushes my face into the pillow and plows into me, thrusting fast, deep. Ravaging my body in the most delicious ways with his carnal desires.

"ANSWER. ME. BRAT." He punctuates each word with the most brutal thrusts of my life. With one last thrust, I free fall off the cliff I've been edging since our lovemaking began. Cumming so hard lights dance behind my eyelids, I scream out in ecstasy.

Kye lies across my back, wrapping his arms around me. He pulls me to his side as he rolls us over. I feel his lips on my shoulder as he lightly kisses me.

"Be right back." He leaves me briefly in bed to reflect back to what we just did. I've never felt so alive before. My smile is genuine as he comes back in with a warm washcloth. He gently wipes between my legs, bending down to run his lips across my thigh. I should feel exhausted, but instead I feel more alive than ever.

"I'm grabbing some water for you. Do you need anything else?"

"My bag, maybe? I'm too wired to sleep. I want to write."

"Are you telling me I didn't wear you out enough? Because I can be more thorough."

I laugh at the challenge in his eyes, knowing he means every word. "I'm tapping out for the night with mind-blowing sex. I want to actually write something positive for once, not something horrendously sad. Maybe I could use some more inspiration."

"I can get behind that. Be right back."

I hesitate at his willingness to help, the past has taught me favors lead to leverage over me. I push back the covers he placed over me.

"I can get up and get it myself." He stares at my body, now on display for him. He licks his lips as the energy in the room shifts from cozy to hot.

"The fact that you can still walk tells me to try harder."

"Oh, you poor thing," I mock him.

He throws his hands over his chest. "You wound me," he cries as he walks out of the room, as naked as the day he was born.

24

Journal Entry:
Dinner With Friends

Thena

As I place the tip of my pen to paper this time, I let the dopamine still coursing through me pick a memory…

I can't explain it, but I feel almost giddy. Mitchell didn't tell me who to expect for dinner. I only know this person has had my usually composed husband up in arms today. His image of perfection shattered. I can't wait to meet this person.

I run to the door, only taking a moment to glance down at my attire. It's over a hundred degrees today so the cut-off shorts and tank top will have to be acceptable for our dinner. At least my tits aren't spilling out. Mitchell disapproves of my summer attire but fuck him. What I choose to wear on my body, will always be my decision.

I open the door for our guest. The glaring sun is annoyingly bright. It blinds my sight until whoever it is steps closer, blocking it. My smile feels frozen, as a sense of déjà vu comes over me. It's him. 'I know him.' It's the man from the bookstore. He cocks his head to the side, a smirk on his handsome face.

"Hello." God, his voice is a smoky velvet that I want to keep hearing on repeat.

I'm unable to respond, my voice gone. He probably thinks I'm an idiot. 'Say hello, you moron.'

"Sullivan residence, I presume? Unless I have the wrong house number?" He takes a step back to reference the numbers on the side of the front door.

"Nope, I mean, yes, you have the correct home. Hello, I'm Thena Sullivan." I stumble over my words. Feeling like a fool, my face flames. Fantastic. Now I can't string words together to make cohesive sentences. Step one: look like the village idiot. Step two: be the village idiot.

I clear my throat, stepping further back into the foyer, and I open the door wider so he can pass. He grins as he takes me in. Like he knows a secret. Or maybe I have something on my face? I can't help but notice his perfectly straight teeth. 'You're noticing someone's teeth now? Fucking weirdo. You're married, you fool, stop it.'

"Please come in! Welcome to our home." I say in an attempt to pull myself together. He steps inside, taking in our open floor plan, with a curious look on his face. I know what he sees. Everything in its place, not a speck of dust will be found. Just how Mitchell likes it. I think bitterly to myself.

"You have a beautiful...home" he finishes. His posture is slightly less relaxed now that he's standing in the living room.

I laugh slightly as I walk past him. Not the cheerful kind of laugh one would usually give at a compliment but more of the sarcastic version. One that would translate into 'yeah, I know it's ridiculous and we both know it,' kind of laugh. Cedarwood and an almost smokey almond smell envelopes me. I almost hesitate in my steps to the kitchen.

I remind myself that I'm married and this man is the sole reason my husband has been a prick all evening. Is it wrong that I noticed how attractive he is? I know it's frowned upon to fantasize about others while married but that isn't what I'm doing. I simply acknowledge the fact that he's a stunningly gorgeous man.

'Would he be as beautiful as he is if his scent didn't affect me like it does? What is it about a man's pheromones that affect women so significantly?' I quietly think to myself. It's what caught my attention at the bookstore. I wasn't even looking at him, I had my nose in a book when he walked past me.

A scent broke my concentration as I browsed the stacks, I had looked up to find out what it was. He was leaning against the bookshelf with his hands in his pockets. Watching me read my book. I recall not being weirded out by his attention. Only slightly confused as to why he was watching me.

I'm not in denial about my looks. I know I'm pretty, not stunning like my sister. She's tall and thin with a perfectly even tan and no blemishes. Two children later, and she doesn't look like she's been in the maternity ward at all.

My looks are far more muted than hers. The only feature I genuinely like is the slight wave to my dark hair and that our genetics are more robust in me. So if I'm outside for even a few moments, I tan dark and quick. Where my sister is tall, I'm on the shorter side of life. I'm a solid five foot three. With a yoga routine and a pair of platforms. So his attention confused me, I can't seem to get my husband's attention no matter what I do. So why would a stranger give it so freely?

I'm bitter and I know it. I've ignored all the signs this last year, but I simply cannot anymore. Something is going on with Mitchell and I have to know what it is. He's not the man I married. He's been short-tempered, controlling, and downright mean recently. Our son and I do our best to stay out of his way, but it never seems enough.

Now tall, dark, and mysterious is standing in my living room smelling like sex on a muscle stick. The universe is out to get me. It has to be. How does my husband know him? I risk a glance at him; he's tucked one of his hands into his pocket. He focuses on a family photo of Mitchell, Toby, and me at the last company picnic. He complimented my home. I should at least say thank you. I'm behaving like a fool and need to get my shit together.

"Thank you." I hold my hand out in front of me. "It's nice to formally meet you," I say. He grasps my offered hand, shaking it firmly but more gently than he would a man. We women can always tell when a man is being gentler with us. That strange sense of been there, done this is coming back.

"It's nice to formally meet you, Mrs. Sullivan. I'm Kye Kincaid."

"Please, just Thena. You say Mrs. Sullivan and I will start expecting my mother-in-law to be in the same room as us." We laugh at my attempt at humor. I guess we're both going to ignore our exchange in the bookstore. Works for me.

"It's a beautiful name, Thena. Is it short for something?" His warm hand is still locked around mine, completely enclosing it. A small jolt of electricity runs through me. That feeling of having done this before in the back of my mind, now almost overwhelming.

"Thanks, and yes, my mother was going through a phase. She wanted to name me Athena, but Dad told her no. So when they had me, they shortened it. Dad would say, 'happy wife, happy life'." Our eyes lock on our still joined hands wrapped around one another. I pull back, feeling uncomfortable.

I'm married. Married women do not behave like this when meeting a stranger. I chastise myself.

"I like it," he states, a single dark eyebrow lifting.

"You know your Greek mythology." This is a statement, not a question. He grins, answering anyway.

"I do"

It's then that I notice he's holding a bottle of red wine.

"Would you like for me to take that?" I point down to the bottle. He seems to remember that he's holding it as well.

"Yes, I hope you don't mind red?" he poses it as a question.

"Red is my favorite," I say. Pinot Noir will always be my bestie. Unlike a man, the wine will always finish you. I laugh at my silent joke as I walk into the kitchen to open the bottle and let it air before I pour us a glass.

"Wanna let me in on the joke?" he asks, leaning against the kitchen island. My kitchen looks smaller with him in it. He pushes his Ray-Bans on top of his head, showing his eyes for the first time. I freeze. This man seems so familiar to me. It has me on edge, but not in an uncomfortable way, almost like anticipation. Confusion causes me to crease my brows. I'm so comfortable.

It was not an easy feat as my husband worked for weeks to make me feel comfortable around him. This man just looks so relaxed in my kitchen. I realize that while I've been in my head he's been waiting expectantly for a response. What if he is like Mitchell and can't take a joke? I don't want to be stuck at dinner with two practical men. Ugh, this is going to suck.

"I wouldn't want to offend you," I say in a softer tone. Suddenly nervous about his reaction to my emasculating thoughts.

"Try me," he challenges me.

"I was thinking, unlike men, wine always finishes the job." I blurt it out before I can stop myself. I cover my mouth with one of my hands. Applaud with my own audacity, absently noting that now I will have to wash my hands before I serve the wine. Mitchell will be irate if my cherry lip gloss is smeared on his perfectly polished wine glasses. Embarrassed and more than a little shocked that I said that out loud to this man, my face heats. Oh my God did I just say that out loud? Kill me now. Please, please, please just take me out now. I silently chant to myself. "I'm sorry that was wildly inappropriate," I say quickly.

He hunches his shoulders, curling them in on himself. He's not making eye contact with me, and my anxiety is notched to another level. I think I'm going to pass out. My heart rate picks up. This is definitely the beginning of a panic attack. The ringing in my ears starts up again. His shoulders begin to shake from whatever effort is being exerted. His face turns slightly red, like he's holding his breath. Then he starts laughing.

I relax, okay so this dude has a sense of humor. Once he starts he can't seem to stop. My face is beet red. I'm so embarrassed. He is full on laughing, loud and unabashedly. I don't think I have ever made someone laugh this much over an inappropriate statement. Usually I'm admonished for being embarrassing. His laughter dies down. And it makes me sad; I want to hear that again. It was a sound that, even in my humiliation, I admit, is beautiful.

"What is so funny?" a voice deadpans from the patio side doors. We both swivel our heads to find Mitchell standing in the doorway, an empty beer bottle in his hands.

Toby runs around him, sliding to a complete stop in the kitchen as he looks up and up and up at…at…shit, I can't remember his name. My little guy pulls his glasses down the bridge of his small nose. "Whoa. Dude are you a giant?"

Mitchell scoffs at Toby, walking to his…friend to shake hands.

"Kye, good to see you. Welcome to my home. I see you've met the wife. This little guy is our son, Tobias. Toby for short."

"I have indeed met your wife. Special lady that one." Kye looks at me with a hint of something in his eyes. Mitchell glances between us as Kye squats down eye level with Toby. "Hello little dude, to answer your question, no, I am not a giant. I just ate all of my vegetables growing up." In true Toby fashion he gives Kye a thumbs up and takes off out the room like a bat out of hell.

"Dinner is ready. I was just going to open the bottle of wine Kye brought before I walked Toby to Vi's," I tell Mitchell as I grab the bottle opener. He takes it from me.

"Nonsense, wife, I can open the wine while you take Toby next door."

"If you're sure?" I want to make sure this doesn't turn into some failed wifely duty on my part. I can't handle another lecture on how much I embarrass him.

"I said I would, did I not?" Mitchell's words hold a trace of venom. I know it's just nerves. He doesn't like to be told what to do, and upper management has made him invite Kye over for dinner for them to resolve whatever issue is between them. After all, Kye is the reason that Mitchell's been in such a terrible mood all evening. I know he doesn't mean anything by it. I see Kye tense up behind Mitchell. Looking ready to defuse a situation that isn't necessary.

"Daddy, Daddy," Toby squeals as he runs through the house again. "I want Daddy to take me to Auntie Vi's!" Toby skids to a stop yanking on Mitchell's hand. "Daddy, Daddy you take me!" Toby pleads with him.

Toby isn't used to seeing Mitchell for more than an hour or two each day before it's past his bedtime. So this request is not a surprise. Toby adores his father, even when it leaves him disappointed or heartbroken. Unsurprisingly, Mitchell looks put out by the request. He loves our son, I know this. But Mitchell has this image that means more to him than the wellbeing of us, if he even presumes that Toby or I are doing something that will make someone look at him like he isn't in control of his family, we suffer the consequences.

Mitchell glances between Kye and me and laughs a little. "Looks like I have my orders from the boss. Kye, I apologize. Vi lives right next door. I will be back in just a few moments."

Kye only nods his head in acknowledgment as Mitchell walks past him. It's clear on Kye's face that he's irritated. I have no reason why though. He wasn't on the receiving end of Mitchell's humiliating tone. I was. When the front door closes, Kye takes a seat at the island in one of our high back barstools. He watches me closely as I work the bottle opener into the cork. He's only in his seat for a moment before he huffs, striding across the kitchen. He gently takes the bottle from me, screwing the corkscrew into the cork with ease. He looks like he wants to say something, but he's hesitating. Interesting. He sets the open bottle on the counter, looking towards the door briefly before lowering his voice. "Does he always speak to you like that?"

My eyes jump to his, and mortification colors my cheeks, Kye doesn't miss it.

"He's just had a hard day." I don't know why I defend Mitchell, but I do. He can't be that bad. He adopted a child that wasn't his and married me. I'm not an easy person to love. So he can't be that bad. Can he?

"If today was hard for him, I would hate to see what he deems a really hard day."

"What happened today?" I ask, the gray flakes in his eyes catching the lights. He's stunningly beautiful. I know I shouldn't think that. But I do.

"He didn't tell you?" Kye is grinning again. His smile is contagious, I smile back. Kye draws up to his full height, a strange look in his eyes. "Why wouldn't he tell his wife?" he finally asks.

"Well, it's his business." I shrug casually, trying to hide my hurt.

Kye sees through my indifference. "I thought husbands and wives shared what's bothering them? Isn't that one of the perks of a marriage?"

"He's private when it comes to work." I look away, unable to hide my watering eyes. At first I used to beg and plead with Mitchell to tell me what was troubling him. Sometimes he would offer small bits and pieces of his day.

It never seemed like the situations deemed his outbursts though. Something as simple as an employee showing up a few minutes late would ruin his entire day. Thus bringing that attitude home with him. I've learned over the last year that if I want to keep our home peaceful, happy, and as healthy as I can, I shouldn't ask too many questions.

"Or he just doesn't want you to know that he's been called on his shit," Kye says as he pours a glass of wine, handing it to me. The topic of conversation has my hands slightly shaking. Mitchell has never hinted at problems at work, at least not at this level.

"Called on his shit?" I inquire. My curiosity is getting the better of me.

"My dear Thena, I have been instructed by our superiors to wine and dine Mitchell in order to make him more pliable at work."

"Pliable?" I sound like a broken record.

"Easier to approach. More, shall we say…likable?" He swirls his wine, sniffing before taking a sip. He hums in appreciation. I smile in return. My nerves have settled from just the small sip I had. I am a true lightweight. It's almost embarrassing how little it takes.

"Mitchell seems very well-liked with how many 'bro dates' he has," I clap back before taking another sip.

"I can assure you, according to headquarters, he doesn't have many friends left. His behavior after being passed for the last promotion has left him bitter. Everyone sees it," Kye tells me this like he's reporting the weather. It doesn't bother him at all to be standing in a man's kitchen, talking shit about said man.

Maybe Kye isn't as warm and welcoming as I first thought. My perception could be clouded because I want to climb him like a tree. My own thoughts shock me. I sit the glass down on the counter. That's enough wine for me. My low tolerance gives me secondhand embarrassment. Here I am in our kitchen, which Mitchell provides for us, allowing some stranger to come in and disrespect him. I may need to learn more about his work. But this man sure as hell doesn't know him either. I cross my arms, leaning against the counter.

"What gives you the authority to do all of this? Hmm? To wine and dine him as you call it. And why would you tell me this?" My emotions are getting the better of me and I know it. This man shows up, gives me wine, butterflies, and insults my husband. Being Indignant is not a strong enough adjective to describe my thoughts and feelings currently.

Kye sets his wine glass on the counter. Taking his time to look me over. His eyes travel up my body; he doesn't look happy with what he sees, and I've never cared more about what someone saw when they looked at me. 'STOP IT THENA, YOU'RE MARRIED IT DOESN'T MATTER WHAT HE THINKS!'

"A few things you should know about me, Thena. I will never tolerate disrespect between my coworkers and myself. No man will ever speak to me like I'm somehow below him. So when your husband approached me today, yelling and making demands, I told him to fuck off. I meant it then and I mean it now. He can fuck all the way off. He thought he could fire me and that upper management would have his back. Unlike him, I'm an actual asset to the team. So he was told to play nice. The last thing you should know is that any man who speaks to his wife in such an aberrant way, doesn't deserve the wife he has to begin with."

I stiffen, shame and humiliation washing over me. 'Mitchell really treats his coworkers so bad that headquarters has sent a man in to tame him? He's right.' I think to myself. 'If he speaks to me the way he does here at home, how does he treat people he doesn't live with? How does he still have a job I wonder?' Too scared to vocalize the question.

"You're wondering how he still has a job?" Kye's eyebrows rise slowly.

I nod, too appalled to speak.

"He's excellent at his job when you look at the overall picture. He drives numbers and is by the book. Unfortunately, his downfall is his attitude. The air of superiority has caused him to have multiple write ups and numerous employees quit. Ten years ago, it would be fine. In today's society, though? It doesn't work anymore. The younger generations are becoming adults and are not willing to, nor should they have to, work in toxic environments." I pick up my glass as he finishes, giving me more information in a single conversation than Mitchell has the entire time we've been together.

"So you're here to what, take his job from him?" I inquire. Glad I accepted the position at the salon.

"Not if I don't have to. I'm here to watch, evaluate, and report back to the higher-ups." He doesn't mince words, does he?

"What happens if you find that Mitchell can't be…I don't know, reformed?"

"If Mitchell cannot respectfully handle the stress of everyday operations, he will be demoted." Kye picks up the bottle to refill our glasses.

"Speaking of Mitchell, does he always take this long to drop your kid off at the babysitter?" Kye glances at the door curiously.

"Vi is a good friend, I'm sure she's talking his head off," I repeat the same words I have spoken to myself countless times before.

"A good friend to you both or…" Kye takes another sip, leaning his hip on the counter. His eyes hold a deeper meaning. One I refuse to acknowledge.

"Our children are close in age, Lily and Tobias play well together." An excuse I use every time I become too paranoid. My husband spends more time alone with Vi than even I do. This stranger doesn't need to know that though, he seems to know more in the hour he's been here than I do after living here for over a year. A stranger in my home, a ghost. I am invisible here. The ringing in my head starts again. I shake my head slightly, wincing. Tension headaches are the worst. The front door opens, and Mitchell rushes inside.

"Sorry guys, it took longer than I expected. The real reason I wanted my wife to drop Toby off. Vi will talk my head off every time." Mitchell's face is flushed, and neither of us misses the barely-there nude shade of lipstick smeared on his neckline.

Kye's posture becomes rigid as he stares at the lipstick smear. "I'm sure."

25

Surprise!

Thena

 I wake to a slow trail of damp kisses down my spine, the contact causes me to shiver slightly. Rolling over, my eyes open briefly to find Kye above me. A glimmer of light breaks through the curtains, casting him in an angelic glow. His lips brush against mine, coaxing a moan from me. He growls low in his throat. "For all the life left in my soul, I wish we had the time for me to do all the naughty things I want to do to this body of yours." His words are strangled, leaving my body floating this morning.

"Five more minutes," I plead, not known for enjoying mornings. I often don't find sleep until the wee hours of the morning.

"Sorry, no can do." The bed dips as he lifts himself up. Rustling alerts me to cover my eyes right before the glaring sun assaults the room. I squint up at him, trying to shield the offensive light with one of my hands. Fuck, I hate anything that bright before nine. Kye's fully dressed. Finding myself more than a little annoyed that he seems to have the jump on me, I groan into my pillow. "You're going to want to get up and get dressed."

I sink lower in the bed, lifting the warm covers over my head. "If you're not waking me up for some morning nookie, I'm not interested." I close my eyes, loving how comfortable the bed is, I'm enveloped in the smell of freshly laundered sheets. I huddle under my pillow, ready to go back to bed. *WHOOSH!* Covers are yanked from my body, coldness seeps into my skin, leaving me shivering. I jump up, grabbing a pillow to cover my very naked body. Angry and irritated at his rudeness, I shoot daggers out of my eyes at the mammoth of a man who's currently dangling the blanket over his head.

"If you fall asleep, we will be behind schedule. That can't happen."

"Did you have to yank the fucking covers off of me?"

"If that's what it takes." He shrugs. He. Fucking. Shrugs.

I throw the fucking pillow at him. "Here, have the complete set asshole!" My voice is shrill, but I don't care what I sound like. I'm fucking cold.

"You really aren't a morning person, are you?"

"What gave you that idea?" I'm bordering on hysterics. He has left me naked, cold, and in a blazingly bright room with not an ounce of caffeine in sight.

Seeing how upset I really am over his behavior he lays the stolen items down, walking across the room to grab me an oversized robe from his closet. He approaches me like you would approach a wounded animal. I scoff, crossing my arms over my chest. Like that's going to do anything for him? He stops before he gets to me looking like we're about to have a battle of the wills. "If you can have some manners, I will give you the robe, and I will go a step further and bring you some coffee."

I huff, too pissed to speak to him, knowing my sentences will be nothing but a string of insults. I nod, turning my nose up at him. He laughs but doesn't hand the robe over. A static sound cuts through the room as we face one other, caught in a battle of the wills. I squeal on reflex, dropping to the floor to cover my naked body. Peeking over the top of the mattress, I'm greeted by Kye bent over, clutching his side, as I'm once again his entertainment. Dropping the robe at my kneeling body he collects himself enough to stab a button on a little box by his bedroom door, speaking into it. "Yes?"

"Mr. Kincaid?" A Southern accent filters through.

"Bingo you found me." My ears perk up. *Why would a woman be looking for Kye? Does he have a girlfriend I don't know about? Please don't let him have a girlfriend,* I pray.

"It's Summer, I'm here for the boudoir shoot." That melodic Southern accent comes through the box again. Something I don't want to avoid dissecting too closely takes hold in my gut. I want to go over there and take charge of the conversation. I want her to know he's mine, she can kick fucking rocks.

With that thought I begin searching the floor for my clothes, looking under the bed. We left them in the bathroom last night. Ah ha! I go to retrieve my clothes so I can face this Summer person and let her know she can leave the same way she came, when Kye's next words freeze me in my tracks.

"Perfect, Summer, I will buzz you in. You and your team can begin immediately. My wife and I will join you momentarily." My jaw must be lying on the floor with Kye's response. He called me his wife? Why did he do that? She can't mean anything to him if he's claiming me as his wife to her. Try as I might, I can't stop the butterflies in my stomach at the thought of having Kye's last name. Growing old with my best friend. He finally turns to me, a look of excitement on his face.

I don't share in it though, I have no clue what's happening, so I ask as I don the robe. "Who is Summer, and what is a boudoir?"

"Your surprise, cranky pants." He crosses the room to stand before me. "With everything that's happened between what Mitchell did and the photos, I thought this could help you regain your power back." Kye's words make me weepy, and I blame it on the fact that he woke me up without coffee, because I am not moved by such a beautiful gesture.

"Kye... that's so incredibly thoughtful. Thank you." I walk into his waiting arms. He cocoons me in his warmth, speaking into my hair, his hot breath causing my body to shiver.

"Go get fresh, stay in the robe. They have a new wardrobe for you and don't bother with your hair and makeup. Summer's team will do that, but if I can make a recommendation?" I draw back to look at him. Delight evident on his face, he gives me a mischievous grin. "I would brush your teeth." I feel my eyes widen in mortification. I lift my hand to my mouth giving it the one two check. *Sweet Jesus.*

With that he leaves me standing in the middle of his room in his robe, horrified that I was kissing him so freely with morning breath.

26

Take A Snapshot,
It Lasts Longer

Kye

"This is an amazing location, Mr. Kincaid." The photographer waves her hand around the open space of my living room. "I'm excited to capture this moment for you," she continues.

I'm only half listening, I could give a fuck if she likes it. I wasn't having Thena photographed anywhere else. Her 'team' hustles around us, my furniture being rearranged for a massive bed to replace where the usual couch sits. My eagerness to see

Thena in one of the barely-there pieces I hand-picked for her has made my patience so thin that I want to sneak into the guest room to take a peek.

"Mr. Kincaid?" Summer drawls. I realize I haven't paid attention as closely as I should, my focus solely revolving around my woman.

"My apologies, what were you saying?" I fiddle with the cuffs of my dress shirt. I know the importance of a well-dressed man in today's society, doesn't mean I have to like it.

Summer giggles nervously tugging on her curly locks, they're wild but styled to suit her. I decide right there that I like this chick. She pushes her glasses up her nose. "I was asking if you would mind being in a few shots with Mrs. Kincaid?" I pause, it's not something I thought to do, my intentions were to help her feel confident again after what that prick put her through. Being in highly intimate poses, half naked with the woman of my dreams, doesn't sound like such a bad thing though.

"Consider me at your service, Summer." We share a conspiratorial smile just as the clicking of heels reaches my ears. A reflection in our photographer's glasses catches my eye and I find myself turning to find the most stunning creature I have ever beheld. Thena does a little spin, wobbling slightly. Compliments, I should be giving her compliments. Awed by her beauty, no words form.

Summer's makeup team painted my siren's lips a shade of red that I will forever compare to the fire in my soul that burns for her. My petite vixen is wrapped in black lace with straps that crisscross under her breasts. The leather weaves together meeting in the back wrapping around her neck in a choker. My cock's hard already. I am convinced she is my damnation for the sins I have and will continue to commit to keep her. A sentence I shall serve happily. If it means I get to continue basking in the glory that is Thena.

"Do you like it?" Thena asks me, a faint coloring to her cheeks. I gulp, stumbling over my words. It feels like the first time I spoke to her all those years ago.

"I like you." The words tumble out. Sounding weird to my own ears. Am I choking on my tongue? Thena giggles, something I rarely hear. A sound so beautiful I vow to myself to spend the rest of my life pulling more from those lips.

"Mrs. Kincaid, you are radiant! I love this piece on you!" Summer rushes forward to save my ass, taking Thena by the hand as she leads her to the area in front of the large windows. Thena hesitates in her steps when the view catches her eye. Then I watch as she falls in love with it as much as I have.

"Okay, Mrs. Kincaid, I need you to lay on your back here." Thena does as she says and Summer walks her through the poses. I lean against the couch soaking in a much better view than my windows boast. She's on her back, one hand buried in her hair, another stretched above her. I hear Summer faintly say, "Now arch your back. Point your toes. Yes! Perfect! Now freeze!."

I hear the camera *click click click*. "You're a natural, these are going to be G-O-R-G-E-O-U-S!!!!" My dick leaks in my briefs. Disgusted with my lack of control in regards to this woman, I cross the room to the fully stocked bar. I pour a bourbon, downing it in one gulp. I sneak a look over my shoulder. Summer has Thena on her stomach in the bed with the river and mountains as her backdrop. Foolish to believe the view would compare to the perfection of Thena. "Mr. Kincaid, would you join us over here please? Bring the bourbon, too."

Thena's eyes spark with interest as I approach; the glass and bottle in my hands. "Okay, Mr. Kincaid. Stand behind the bed in front of the window. Yes, like that. Mrs. Kincaid, I want you to put your back against his front, now pull one leg up towards your chest. Yes! Now Mr. Kincaid, if you would prop the bottle against her thigh and bring the glass close to your lips. Fuck yes."

My head swims being this close to Thena. Whatever they spritzed on her soft skin smells heavenly. I'm not able to control myself, so I run my hand through her hair while I take a drink. It burns my gut as much as my need for her does. Summer clicks her camera as my skin heats.

I sit the glass between Thena's legs, the ice inside frosts the outside against her skin, and she gasps, her back arching against me. My dick twitches as our eyes burn for one another. *Click*. I unbutton my cuffs first, *click click*. I untie my tie, allowing it to hang. Thena's eyes miss nothing as my first button pops open, then the next, until I'm left with my shirt completely open. *Click.* Reaching between Thena's legs, I pick the glass of amber liquid back up, slowly bringing it to my lips, her eyes track every movement.

I hear someone clear their throat. "Mrs. Kincaid, can you please turn around to face your husband fully? I would like for you to kneel. Can you unbuckle his belt, please? Maybe his pants, as well. Yes, like that." *Click.* "Perfect." The photographer coaches us, it's unnecessary, though I allow her a few more moments before I drop the glass. It shatters on the hardwood. Ice skitter across the floor, I don't give a fuck.

I seize Thena's ass, her cheeks more than filling my hands, I lift her off the bed completely. Her little shriek brings a shit eating grin to my face. I slam her a little rougher than I had intended into the window, successfully pinning her against the glass. Her mouth forms a little O as she automatically wraps those delicious thighs around my waist.

"Hello, kitten," I whisper against her lips, my tone gruff. My hips grind into her as one of my hands travels the length of her thigh. "So perfect."

Off in the distance somewhere a *click* sounds with slight chuckling.

Thena looks wicked as she juts out her chest, her movements causing her heated middle to rub against my stomach. My eyes roll back as I try to regain control of my own situation. Her lips brush mine as we stare at one another. Flecks of gold and red hues dance in her eyes and I melt against her more.

"Mr. Kincaid, I do believe you want to fuck me."

"That is on a very long list of things I crave to do to you, Mrs. Kincaid."

Click. Click. "Okay Kincaids, that's an awesome way to take the initiative. Let's get Mrs. Kincaid on the bed on her knees, face down, with Mr. Kincaid behind her." Summer's voice breaks through the trance Thena has me in. We jerk our heads apart laughing. Our bodies shake with the force of our laughter, causing a whole new wave of turned on as Thena's breasts bounce in my face, begging for my kiss.

We obey Summer's demands, and the anticipation grows within me as Thena gets in position. Her hair tumbles on the bed; long, dark, and slightly curled. The curvature of her spine taunts me. My feet carry me forward to the bed on their own accord. Summer told me to stand but my body demands to be near her. I crawl into position behind her on my knees, running my hands over the round curve of her ass. The lace covers very little, I gulp in the oxygen I need to stay sane. I want this woman like this every day for the rest of my life. Her arousal fills me with a heady sensation. *Click.*

I climb over her, jokingly thrusting my hips into her ass. A guttural sound cuts through the silence of the room and makes my control snap. *Click.*

"Summer."

"Yes, Mr. Kincaid?"

"Out. Now," I demand of her, the urge to bury myself in my woman so great, my arms shake from the exertion of holding my urges back.

"Did I do something wrong?" she panics.

"No, but if you stay you're going to see me fuck my wife. I think we would all like privacy right now." Thena's outraged laugh bounces her ass against my dick, so I thrust my hips forward to silence her.

"Consider me gone," Summer squeaks as she rounds up the other members of her crew from the other room where they were waiting in case hair and makeup touches were needed.

"Be good or I won't wait for them to leave." That gets Thena's attention. She bucks against me, her ass slamming into my painfully hard erection. I grunt as the uncomfortable sensation stings my balls, the pain radiating in my spine. Furious with the little minx's audacity, I snatch her hair in my hand, pushing her face into the mattress. A string of muffled curses fall from her filthy little lips as the team scuttles out the front door. "Oh brat, you're gonna pay for that."

She pushes her head up high enough to scold me through clenched teeth. "You wouldn't fucking dare." She bucks against me again, this time I'm looking for it, though. As she thrust her ass towards my crown jewels, I smack my hand on her ass, my thumb pushing against her back hole. She freezes as her ass clenches around my digit.

"Are you going to be a good girl for me? Or am I fucking this tight hole back here?" I ask against her ear, yanking her head back closer to my chest.

Her chest rises and falls in rapid succession. Her pupils are blown.

"Oh, you like that idea, don't you, you naughty girl?" I lick her ear and she rewards me with a shiver. I pull her head back further, wrapping my other arm around her to keep her where I want her. From my vantage point, I see her supple breasts. I run my finger over each one, feeling her nipples pebble. I search for the reason I chose this outfit for her. *Ah-Ha!* Wallah. I tug at the outfit with enough force the velcro bursts open releasing her nipple to me. I repeat the action on the other. Her rosy buds mine for the taking. Fucking perfect.

I push her head back in the bed, grinding my hard cock against her again, pinching her nipple at the same time. She rewards me by crying out.

"Do you trust me?" I ask her. Immediately, she gives me a muffled yes. Something squeezes my heart hearing her say it. I release her to move off the bed. "Don't move, princess, or you will regret it." I instruct her as I walk to the window. Bending over, I pick up my dress jacket, rummaging through the inside pockets until I find what I'm looking for. I turn to look at my beautiful bounty wrapped in lace and leather. My chest heaves with the force of my restraint. I stalk over to the head of the mattress.

"Crawl to me, Thena." Seconds tick past, feeling like an eternity for me before she raises her eyes to meet mine, she slowly lifts her body, crawling toward me with so much intention I know she's pleased with our little game.

"You were a brat today, you know that right? Throwing fits this morning, only to taunt me all day in this." I indicate to her outfit, she is truly a vision with her peaked nipples poking through.

"When am I ever a brat?" She's closer now.

"When are you not?" Reaching for her, I drag her the rest of the way to me. Our chests collide.

"What are you going to do about it, Mr. Kincaid?"

"You're about to find out, Mrs. Kincaid."

"That's not my last name and you know it."

"I know it will be. So you better get used to it," I say against her lips. I drop my present on the bed beside her. Too distracted, she hasn't noticed it yet.

"Your makeup is too perfect. Let's mess it up." I free my pulsating cock from my pants. The appendage is painful, and hard. I take it in my hand while wrapping my other back in her long hair. "Ruin that lipstick."

I brace her head where I want her as I slide my dick in her mouth, not giving her time to adjust to my size. I shove it in the back of her throat. Her eyes roll in the back of her head as I tell her, "You may be my delicate little flower out there for the world to see. But when we're in here, you're what I tell you to be. Right now, I want you to be my filthy little whore."

Her hot wet heat encompasses my cock as she bobs her head down on it. She moans around it, vibrating my dick until my balls tighten. I yank her hair, she comes away with a little *pop*. She's stunning. Her lips glistening, cheeks flushed. Such a look of innocence on that perfect face. I'm going to be its ruin.

"Your lipstick isn't smeared enough for my tastes." My tone is strained with the pleasure she's brought me. I force her head down on my dick again, I hold her as her lips mold around the base of me. I feel the back of her throat on my tip, only pulling out as she starts to gag. Taking the base of my cock, I watch as my pre-cum coats her lips, successfully smearing her lipstick.

"What a pretty, good girl you are on your knees before me. Do you like sucking my cock?" I ask her, cradling her face gently, my thumb rubbing at the eyeliner under her eye, watching as it leaves a dark trail across her cheek.

The raw hoarseness of her voice, cracking as she gives me the answer I want informs me that I thoroughly fucked her throat. Male pride swells in me as I take note of how eager she is to please me.

"I want you to be a good girl and roll over on your stomach, princess. I'm going to do something new to you and I want to watch you cum undone beneath me." Thena doesn't waste any time turning over for me and I place a nearby pillow under her hips. Her hair tumbles to the side, revealing the choker. My pulse quickens at the sight.

"Bring your arms back, baby." I climb behind her, running my hands over her thighs and ass. I unbuckle the interconnected straps in the back, and weave them around her wrists, securing them. I see her begin to tense. With firm strokes, I calm her. "That's a good girl," I praise. "Relax honey, it's just us. I'm right here," I soothe her. Once she relaxes again, I slip my fingers over the lace running down her crack until I find the small silk tag. I pull and watch in rapt fascination as it falls open to bare her to me. My woman is drenched, I lean in to inhale her. The heady scent of her arousal is goddamned *perfect*. "You're so wet for me, baby," I tell her in a gentle tone.

She bucks her hips, I knew she wouldn't be able to listen to my orders. She such a brat.

"Do you want to please me?" I taunt her as my finger dips in her sweet little cunt. Her moan filling the room is the highest form of aphrodisiac I have ever had.

"That's all I want to do. Forever."

I dangle the toy in my hand to the side where she can see it. Her eyes widen as she stares at it.

"What's that?" She breathes, a mixture of curiosity and fear on her face.

"It's your future. I'm going to place this in your tight little hole and stick my cock in that cunt of yours until that pretty little pussy squirts on my cock. You will thank me and ask me to do it again." She whimpers and something about the broken cry makes my dick jump, leaking more pre-cum. I capture her lips with mine. This woman is my perfection, she is the symbol of everything I need and want in my miserable life.

I squeeze her hips, yanking her ass higher in the air. Her heady scent clings to me and I can't help it. I lean forward, darting my tongue out for a taste. Her saltiness slides down my throat and I groan in pleasure. I replace my fingers where my tongue was, beginning to pump in and out in slow strokes, painfully aware that this is torturing me as much as her. Her hips buck and she pants and moans. I drag her juices to her asshole, circling it with slow precision before pushing my thumb in. Her ass tightens, clenching down on me, her breathing changes, I rub her ass while working my thumb around.

"That's right, baby. That's my girl. Relax your body. Just like that." Her body relaxes, and as it does, I reward her with my other fingers sliding into her dripping cunt, she clenches around them as she cries out squirming. She's ready for me. I pull my thumb out as she whimpers, lifting her hips searching for more of what only I can give her.

I take the buttplug in my hand, bathing it in her pussy, I tap the little button on the top of the jewel. The toy begins to vibrate and immediately my hungry girl begins to moan loudly, I watch as her folds convulse around the machine, the bindings cutting into her skin as she writhes beneath my power over her. Her back begins to arch and I know she's coming.

I pull the plug out before she can finish and she cries out. "Please…*please* don't stop! I need more."

I grin against her thigh as I trail my tongue over her silky smooth skin. I brace myself on my knees with the head of my cock at her entrance. She pushes her ass on me, trying to fill herself with my cock. I laugh with the pleasure I feel knowing I have done this to her. "Do you want me to fuck you baby?"

Her cries carry across the room.

"Hmm? Do you?" I taunt her

"Yes! For fucks sake I want you to fuck me like you mean it," she screams.

"Your wish is my command." I grin in anticipation.

Lining up the plug and my cock at her holes I ram both in at the same time. She screams out in pleasure bordering the amount of pain I know she sometimes likes. Her body goes taunt around me before she relaxes, whimpering, beseeching me for more.

I grab her hips, thrusting deeply inside her, grinding my cock into the deepest parts of her. Her pussy squeezes down on my cock and I know she's close again. I drag my dick out slowly watching it come away soaked in us. I take my tip and sit it at her entrance, I grasp her collar in my hand, pulling her back to me, our bodies flush together as my cock fills her completely, so tightly, so close together I feel the vibrations on my thighs.

Groaning together, sweat beading on my forehead as I hold back the urge to spill my seed in her. I hear her raspy intakes as she tries to breathe. She pants my name over and over again, her sexy little voice going straight to my balls. I direct her by her collar, ramming her down on my dick over and over until we both shatter in pleasure screaming out one another's names.

I gently remove the plug from her body after I untie her arms. She buries her face in the pillows quietly weeping. I snag the soft sheet to cover her body, giving her back her modesty. Sometimes after intimacy, emotions can run high and it becomes overwhelming. I cradle her to my chest as she hiccups, her tears seeping into my skin. We both tumble sideways on the bed. I run my hand over her back in circular motions, while I gently rock her back and forth. "Honey, did I hurt you?" I ask, holding my breath, scared that I got too carried away. She calms down to sniffles as I wait patiently for her response. I won't budge on this. I have to know if I hurt her.

"No, I just didn't know it could be like that," she whispers against my skin.

She didn't understand what could be like that? Sex? I need her to clarify her meaning, when it comes to sexual partners there can be no room for error. Giving one's body to another is something special, a treasure. I've wanted all of my sexual partners to feel cared for. Even if it's only for a night.

"I don't understand Thena."

"I've never been able to trust someone enough for them to have power over me like that."

Something in my chest fractures.

27

Here Fishy Fishy

Mitchell

Nobody's home at the residence. It's blanketed in the darkest depths of shadows. The thick foliage on this side of the property is perfect for obscuring me from prying eyes. The ease in which I am able to hide here, standing in the shadows, on a property that I am now unwelcome at, makes my blood boil. This selfish bitch and her bastard child are so ungrateful for the life I have provided them. I worked diligently over the years to cultivate the perfect projection to those around me, one of near perfection.

She did this…she did this…she did this…she did this…

I would have left her unbothered, forgotten, discarded. A used-up toy, her purpose served, one easily replaced. Except the morning after I was wrongfully fucking removed from my own home, I was put on leave pending an investigation at work. I would have kept my career had she not sent those photos of slaughtered pigs to the CEO of my company. She has taken everything from me. She set me up, she sabotaged me. And for what? For getting some side pussy?

My once shining life is now desolate. Those around me I once thought loyal showed their true colors. All turning their backs on me, pinning to climb that ladder to take my spot. Dogs fighting for scraps. All of them. I spit at my feet, wishing it were one of their faces. The wind blows, causing the branches before me to sway. A breeze carrying the faintest traces of lilacs and rhododendrons encompasses me and for a moment my nose tingles. I hold my breath for a quick moment, waiting for the urge to sneeze to pass. I hate those fucking flowers. My eyes stop watering and I am able to once more resume my surveillance.

Our home, my home, a beacon in the dark calling to me. The voice that's plagued me since losing my life says the same words viciously in my mind. *She did this...she did this...she did this...* I slap myself on my head trying to beat the voices into submission. I need them to stop. *She did this…she did this…she did this…* I hit myself again and again until the near constant chant subsides.

The time has come for some payback. I approach with silent steps. Blades of grass, flowers that dot the land lay down under my boots in surrender, the branches scattered throughout the yard are strong under my weight. Complete silence as I slowly make my way to the porch. Mother Nature knows Thena's time is up. The ground, like myself, craves to swallow her up and leave her decaying and forgotten in the dirt.

Thena only has herself to blame. She did this to me, to us. She wanted a war, she's got one. I won't end her life quickly. No. I want her to suffer. I will ensure she loses her comfort, her friends, her confidence, her goddamn lover, her security, her son. She will lose it all before I take her heart from her body. I'm going to rip her sanity from her, like she has done to my own.

I take note of the subtle changes made. By the door are brightly colored flower pots, one would assume painted by her brat judging from the quality. New flowers and herbs litter the stoop: poppies, asters, lavender, rosemary, and more I can't name. The bouquet makes my nose itch immediately. I lift my foot and bring it down on top of each of them. By the time I'm finished only spilled soil, broken ceramic, and the remnants of flower petals are left. Decimated, as I am.

I tilt my head back looking directly into the lens. I want them to know who it is. Who is bringing their reckoning down upon them. I reach in my jacket for my newly modified straps, releasing one of them. I slowly show the camera my pry bar, grinning gleefully and turn my attention to the door. The traces of fresh paint linger in the air, the new coat of bright blue gnaws at me. Memories of a previous conversation so long ago wrap around me like a vice. How dare she go against my wishes, I seethe.

"Honey, I want to paint the door a shade of blue," she had asked me.

"Absolutely not, we will not devalue our property," I had told her.

"What could a little color around here harm?" she had asked.

"I said no Thena." My order had left no room for argument and now that she has alienated me from my home the bitch has added color everywhere.

My prybar's cold metal warms with my touch as I slide it between the door panels with ease. I glance once more into the camera as I apply very little pressure, taunting whoever may be watching. A *popping* sound accompanied by a *crack* fractures the silence. I watch in glee as the front door swings open, welcoming me home.

My feet carry me across the threshold of a home I no longer recognize. I lose my grip on the pry bar as anger pulsates so loudly in my ears. I don't hear the sound it makes as it crashes to the floor. I'm overwhelmed by the onslaught of warm raspberries and freshly baked bread. Photos of her with her spawn clutter my once pristine walls, children's artwork framed and placed throughout the living room. Every clean surface I once took pride in is now ruined with mismatched colors and badly crayon colored portraits in the place I once called mine.

I make my way through the horrid display, curious if the entire home has been wrecked or just the front room. I walk around, my fingertip brushing over the newly framed shit. "Whoops!" my fingers graze the framed fish photo too hard. It tumbles off the tabletop. I watch its descent as it hits the floor. The webs of shattered glass are the perfect replica of how life will be for her when I'm through with her. The sounds of destruction are music to my ears. I go through the common area of the house, breaking and shattering.

As I enter the kitchen my eyes are drawn to the front of the fridge where a child's family portrait is held in place with a magnetic strip. I stop, observing it. It's clearly the main star of the little artist's show. The vibrant hues that overlap one another mix and mold together to create a form of a mother in a swimming pool, clearly it's meant to be Thena, I disregard her all together. Focusing on the man the little boy is perched on, balancing himself on the man's shoulders while holding a baggy containing a brightly colored fish. His hair is longer than mine, though almost the same shade. His stomach has little boxes on it. Is that supposed to be abs? I wonder. I rub my own slightly protruding stomach, realization dawns on me the moment my eyes land in the shade of his eyes.

This isn't my child drawing a portrait out of one of longing, missing his father as he should. No, of course not. The little brat has always been ungrateful. He would never allow me to put him on my shoulders. He would snivel and whine until Thena would interject herself. That's not me, because it's Kye.

I shake with my fury, freeing my hammer from within my jacket. I hold the rubber handle so hard one of my knuckles pop. I run the head of the hammer over the drawing. I. See. Red. *BANG!* I swing at the fucking thing so hard, the hammer bounces back almost colliding with my face. The impact causes my arms to vibrate with the force of it. Stepping back, looking at the large dent in the fridge, smiling as I watch the drawing flutter to the floor. Ripped in two from my wrath. I turn towards the little shit's room. Hell bent on teaching him some respect.

The door is open as I approach it, the picturesque room is so different from what I had as a child. A soft light from his night light illuminates all in a gentle glow. I did this for him. I gave him this and he still chose another over me. Well if he wants Kye as a father… So be it.

I pound my weapon of revenge against anything it connects with, so lost in my fury, I pay no mind to the splinters flying from the bed as I rage against it, over and over until my palms are slick with sweat. I lose my grip on the tool, absentmindedly watching it as it free falls from my hands. Landing on a hot wheel car, breaking the small plastic toy. I relish the sound of shattered plastic. I bend at the waist dragging in large gulps of air, spent from the uncommon excursion.

She did this…to me, she did this…to us. She turned the little brat against me. He chose Kye over me. The words on repeat in my head won't stop and with every word uttered, I become more enraged.. I pick up the shark plushie I got him from our aquarium trip, I wrap my hands around it and tug. Stuffing bursts out, sprinkling the air in fluff.

A rainbow of muted colors dances across the carpet in an almost hypnotic way, a soothing wave cascading over me for a moment. I don't want to be soothed. I want to be pissed. The immense amount of disappointment I feel for a child I helped raise with a woman I gave my name catches me by surprise. I crush a nerf gun between my hands. Stepping over the broken pieces, my focus solely on the aquarium.

I stand before the massive tank, full of vibrant fish. They have thrived under Tobias's care. I was so impressed as I watched him from the cameras as he trained his guppies. A feat that even I could admit was admirable. *He chose Kye over you.* I flinch at the thought remembering why I am here. He must be taught a valuable lesson. He really only has himself to blame. I grasp the edges ready to pull it over and watch the little fuckers flop around until their little bodies give out when a streak of yellow, blue, and silver races by, swimming in and out of some hoops. I stop.

What the fuck is that? Why does it look familiar? The epiphany happens, thinking back to the stupid picture on the fridge. Kye dare put a fish in my tank? I huff loudly shaking the tank, water splashes over, soaking my feet. I leap back, disgusted. I leave the room for a moment, running down the hall into the kitchen. I open the cabinet, tossing items over my shoulder as I go. Everything has been moved around. Can that insufferable bitch just leave well enough alone? Ah ha! I found it! Jerking up the appliance, I dart back into the room. The whisper of Tobias's door closing is the only noise in the home. The soft click shuts me in with the collection of little pets. I approach on near silent feet.

"Here fishy, fishy," I taunt as I plop my accessory down on the nightstand, I have no hesitation as I take the little green net in my hand. The boy will be taught a lesson. I juggle the net in my hand as I open the top, tossing the lid to the side. I'm met with the cheerful colors darting back and forth, one of them comes to the surface of the water, used to the treats the boy gives them.

"Hello Fynn."

I scoop the little fish up, momentarily watching it as it flips that way and this way in the net. Knowing this little guy is Toby's favorite… Or is the new one Kye brought over his favorite now?

"I know the feeling, little friend. To fight for all your worth and not be good enough. I know what it's like to crave something just out of reach. I too, find myself fighting for my life," I confess to him, as I lead him to his doom.

"Next up in the swimmers best dive competition we have Fynn Sullivan! Fynn is an expert forward free driver with all the aquatic knowledge of a guppy!" I shimmy causing the net to shake.

The little guppy convulses in terror. His little mouth gasps, opening and closing.

"Fynn, are you ready to show the crowd what you can do?" I lean in close to inspect the little guy. "Why Fynn, you're so good at diving! You're a real fish out of water!"

His round eyes bore into mine.

I laugh at my own jokes, enjoying this tremendously. "Okay Fynn, no more stalling! Give the people what they want! DIVE! DIVE! DIVE!"

I tip the net, Fynn flips out sailing through the air and into his final resting place. I watch in rapt fascination as the blade at the bottom slices through his tiny blue and yellow gills. His tail flops, dancing to its own tune as his insides slide to rest at the bottom of the glass. "Oh no! Sorry folks! Looks like Fynn's nose dive flopped. That's too bad, oh well onto our next contestant."

One after another participants in the diving contest follow Fynn. Flipping, flopping, one of them misses the makeshift pool all together, his little head exploded on the side of the table, leaving a dark little stain. I repeat this until the last one remains. It's the newest addition, bright yellow, orange, red, and blue. The tail is a splattered rainbow of happy colors. "I shall leave you behind to tell the story of how our actions have repercussions little fishy."

I drop some treats in as an apology for his fishy trauma, laughing at myself. *Fish have trauma?* My shoulders shake with my laughter, the sound booming, bouncing off the walls around me. I regain my composure. "Alexa, set a timer for ten minutes."

The female voice blares over the little round speaker in the corner. "Alright, ten minutes, starting now."

I rest on the edge of the bed, my shadow cast on the wall is as menacing as my actions in this darkened room. Leaning over I snatch up the black rubber cord dangling from the bedside table. I plug it in and wait. Tobias used to recite 'fun facts' about his guppies throughout the house.

'Hey Dad! Guess what? Did you know guppies can live outside of water for over ten minutes? Guppies are like the superheroes of the sea!' Moisture runs down my face in a lonely trail. I focus on my little rainbow collection, making sure to watch each one parish, to suffocate all of them because they belong to him, and if I hurt him, I hurt her and when she hurts, that motherfucker will too.

The sound of rain echoes in the room and I know it's time. "Alexa, turn the timer off."

"Timer now off."

I tap the side of the glass tomb. *Ping, ping, ping.* There's no apparent movement from within, no fins to flop, no little mouths moving, gasping in futile attempts to save them from what I'm stealing from them. Their lives. Snickering, my finger only hesitates over the button momentarily.

I want them to pay. With that final thought, I push down on the blend button, small crunching sounds accompany the loud whirring sound of the blender. All the vibrant colors are sucked into a tornado of blades. Small scales float, small white bones break, I watch until they merge and melt into a murky brownish burgundy. I remove my finger from the button with one last glance. I turn to leave as one small eyeball twirls in my direction.

28

The Johnson Hotel

Thena

Kye jerks his truck door open harshly, jolting the metal frame causing it to briefly bounce, my stomach flips.

"Was that really necessary, caveman?" He pauses momentarily before winking at me.

"Not my fault Ol' Betty can't handle me." He slides in, causing the pickup to drop enough for my stomach to roll. This is what I get for trying to go for a drink with Kye yesterday after the shoot. I push my cheap glasses up, blocking as much light as possible.

Betty? Who would that be? I scrunch my nose, irritated to be up and moving around. "Who's Betty?"

Kye gives me an odd look before informing me, as he sits his cup and baggie down, smacking the wheel, finishing it off with a rub, "This masterpiece is Betty, my first love." He croons at the dashboard. Frowning I glance over. Who names their fucking vehicle? Apparently this one. Must be a guy thing.

Kye dangles the foam cup and greasy paper bag in my face, my mouth salivates as I catch a whiff of the warm bread. "Coffee and croissants for the small demon in the passenger seat who, for the record, is very clearly not enjoying waking up to another glorious day." I glare at him over the rim of my glasses, reaching out to snatch my breakfast. He jerks them back. "Magic words first."

I scowl. "Please and thank you," I tell him between clenched teeth. He smiles, his dimples popping. My stomach spins for a different reason than my aching head.

"Who's a grumpy gus this morning?" He teases me, he puckers his lips at me and I can't help wondering if he will make the same face with my hands around his thick neck?

"I don't care how amazing yesterday was, if you continue to fuck with me before my caffeine jump starts my battery enough to deal with your ass, I'm going to throttle you."

He picks a cup up, ignoring my threat as he blows across the top, causing the steam and smell of what I so desperately want to float in my direction. I punctuate each word. "Give. Me. My. Coffee." I lean across the seat, trying to snatch my cup from his hands. A sudden and sharp twinge of discomfort in my bottom has me straightening again, leaning back in my seat. I glance over to see Kye grinning with male pride, he winks. Finally handing me my food and drink. He puts the classic truck in gear, heading towards the highway.

I tip the coffee back, not waiting for it to cool. Kye barks at me, "I wouldn't do that if…" It's too late, I take a long pull of coffee. He mumbles under his breath, "unbelievable." Not able to help myself. I smile, filling my tone with sarcasm. "What a glorious day." And it is, the sun is shining and the birds are chirping. Disgusting… I roll my window down wondering if

Kye will step on the gas pedal or if we are going to coast there the whole way.

"Smartass." He pushes my shoulder, knocking me off balance for a moment.

"Geriatric driver."

"You wound me."

"Keep it up and I'll take your balls." I bat my eyelashes at him, knowing he can't see through the tint of my glasses. He cups his family jewels with a hand.

"Baby, my balls have always been in those dainty hands of yours."

"Did you just call my hands dainty? Dainty can still injure or maim."

"If I call them delicate will you act like a pretty flower and blossom for me?" He blows me kisses.

"More like wilt," I scoff. He looks momentarily hurt, though I know it's just a ploy to get me to agree to whatever he's selling me. "There's something wrong with you."

"How about we stop sparing and rescue Toby instead," he supplies.

I quickly agree, leaning my head against the seat rest. I've missed my son so much. I pass the time taking in the buildings on the horizon, as we cross the James River, knots form in my stomach. What will they think of Kye being with me today? I know my mother-in-law will have something to say, she always does. I sigh, unable to keep it in, my nail pulls at the sticker on the side of my now empty cup. I should have requested two.

"What's going on over there?" Kye asks me, my head tilts to the side so I can peer at him as we talk.

"Why did they have to stay at the most expensive place in the city?" I ask.

"Mitchell's parents?"

"Yes."

He chews over this for a moment before responding. "Money makes you uncomfortable. Doesn't it?" The look on his face as he takes me in briefly while still driving safely is knowing.

I shrug to hide how this conversation is making me feel. "Hard to feel uncomfortable with something you've never had."

He reaches over, giving my leg a quick squeeze. "You can't bullshit a bullshitter." I feel my brow arch as I give him my best lopsided grin.

"Watch me."

We pull into The Jefferson Hotel valet parking area, a lanky kid with shaggy red curls swiftly approaches. I look at Kye. "Do you think he's old enough to drive this thing?" Kye chuckles at me as I open the door right before the kid in question can. He straightens as the door comes close to whacking him.

His face colors slightly, he grabs the handle as he greets us, "Welcome to The Jefferson Hotel."

I stand there momentarily trying to figure out what I'm supposed to do. "Uh, hi, thank you."

I step onto the walkway waiting for Kye, while he chats the kid up like old friends. I hear him say something along the lines of, 'she was talking shit about you'. Appalled, I lean over, my face in the window, fixing Kye in my line of vision. Kye smacks the kid on his back, both of them laughing at something I can't hear. They exchange the keys for a tag before Mr. Shitstarter heads around to join me on the curb. As soon as he's within reaching distance, I clip him in the shoulder, he pretends to be hurt as we start up the unbelievably tall staircase.

"You didn't have to tell him what I said!"

"Your face was worth it though, Kenny and I had a good laugh at your expense."

"Two seconds and you already have a new friend in the sandbox. Your mother must be so proud," I say.

His bark of laughter is sarcastic, uncomfortable. He ruffles my hair. "You know my mother hates me."

I flush, feeling ashamed for not thinking before I spoke. After years of friendship, I should have known not to cross that line. I stay silent as we enter The Jeffersons grand entrance. If the name and valet didn't give the hotels grandeur away, the extremely large ivory pillars and hand-woven oriental rugs would. Are those oil paintings of dead presidents?

"What do you think, brat? Could you see yourself staying here?" Kye's question is a joke, meant to tease me. I take in the expensive drapes and robotic staff.

"It's exquisite, absolutely enchanting…"

"Yes, you are."

I startle, noticing Kye's eyes tracking me as I take in all the hotel's features. The grandeur of the place makes me feel inadequate. It's not that I want to, it's just. *Wow.* The meals must be amazing in a place like this, you know? Stained ivory pillars are placed throughout, with a stunning shade of deep red that covers the walls. Are those portraits of dead presidents? How does one feel comfortable in a room that swallows you up?

"Mommy!" Tobias's shriek has me spinning, I search the spacious area, spotting him as we run for one another. He leaps, trusting I will catch him. *OOMPH!* His little body knocks the wind from me.

"You are never allowed to leave me again! Two days is way too long to go without your snuggles!"

"I missed you, Mommy." Tobias giggles in between his words. He hangs from me like a little monkey, clinging to me. One day soon, he will be too tall to do this. What will I do when that day comes?

"Did you have fun with Nana and Tata?" His shoulders sag, my pulse picks up. Were they mean to my baby?

"They made me eat my vegetables." I ease my stance, smiling as I put him on the ground. I notice he keeps one of his little hands in mine and I melt a little somewhere in my chest. He's such a good kid.

"Young man, Lemaire serves delicious vegetables, and it's important for a boy's body to have them." I look toward the speaker. Lucia and David are standing a few feet away from us, frowning at Kye and me in disapproval.

"Hello, Lucia. David, thank you both for visiting with Tobias this weekend. I'm sure your visit means a lot to him." My words are rushed, I struggle to get them all out while Lucia sniffs, looking down her nose at me. Here we go…

"Yes well…" she sniffs again, "Just because you're not willing to be a part of our family any longer doesn't mean that he's not." She clasps her hands together, a gesture meant to be regal before she continues, in a nasal tone.

"One would think a wife would be at home, fixing her marriage." Voicing her opinion has never been an issue for my mother-in-law, I'm just slightly taken aback that she would pull a stunt in front of my child.

"One would think a grandmother wouldn't be so self-centered in her righteousness to make the child pay for the sins of the parents. Watch your step while my child is present," I retort, causing her lips to purse, she looks around to ensure we aren't being overheard.

"Come on kiddo, take it down a notch. We are obviously very worried about you and Tobias. A boy needs his father." David steps closer to me, Kye matching the distance, places himself a foot ahead of me in a clear message of, if you want to get closer to her, you will go through me first. David halts his approach, looking from Kye to me.

Tobias squeezes my hand, the tiny fragile softness of his own captures my heart, forcing me to rational thought.

"We're leaving, thank you for spending time with Tobias."

David steps forward again with his hands in a placating manner, Kye's hand lands on his chest. Halting his steps. "Thena, take Tobias outside. I need to have a conversation with the in-laws on how to shut the fuck up." I feel like the air is sucked out of the room as Kye's cold tone breaks through our dispute.

Lucia and David pull back affronted, unaccustomed to being spoken to this way.

Tobias tightens down on my hand. He squeezes down on my fingers, I cast my eyes down to him. His face is stricken, his little feet moving in a pattern, the constant movement alerting me to him being overstimulated. I hunker down, lowering myself as much as possible to be face to face. I stroke his small hand on my own.

"Tobias, let's tell Nana and Tata goodbye," I coax him in a manner I haven't had to do in a while. He bites his lip, his little feet shuffling. My anger for allowing him to witness us behaving so poorly has me standing, leading him out before anyone can say another word.

As I guide Tobias through the foyer out the front, he whispers, "I'm sorry Momma."

"What are you apologizing for?" Gentle brown eyes look away, bouncing around the area around us. He settles on staring at a fountain with a stone statue of an alligator crawling out.

"Nana was asking questions and accusing you of lying about Dad. I told Nana and Tata about how I saw the lady on Dads phone and I saw the messages to someone and when I looked it wasnt Mom. Now Dad doesn't live with us, It's all my fault." He sobs into my side, as I stand there feeling helpless. I wrap him in my arms, comforting him. My God, has he felt this way this entire time and I had no idea? Am I really that out of tune with my own child?

"No honey, listen to me. None of this is your fault. I knew, I've always known. You didn't cause anything. This is not on you, my sweet boy."

A clusterfuck of a mess follows Kye out of the front door. I hear Lucia crying out, indignant as ever. "How dare you put such thoughts in the boy's head, who are you to accuse our son of such horrendous acts?"

Kye walks calmly down the stairs, directed straight for us. His hands are in his pockets. He looks cool, calm. How is he so collected? David places his hand on Lucia's shoulder keeping her at the top of the stairs near the hotel's impressive entrance. If looks could kill, I'd be a dead woman.

Tobias hiccups beside me, so I turn my focus back to him. "Tobias none of this is your fault."

Kye saddles up beside us, instantly Tobias sobers, waiting for guidance. Kye slides a hand out of his pocket holding it out to Tobias. "I'm thinking a few scoops of ice cream can fix all of my problems. How about yours?"

Tobias surveys the adults, settling on Kye's outstretched hand as he takes it. Sniffling, my little man shakes his head. "I'm going to need at least three."

Kye's smile is warm as he looks down at Toby. "Done."

With that the boys head toward Kenny to collect the truck. Kye whistling a tune I'm unfamiliar with as Toby's little legs briskly keep pace beside the tall man, I hear him mimic the same tune as Kye.

Maybe today isn't so shitty after all?

29

Ice Cream & Heartache

Thena

The streets pass by in a blur from where I sit, glancing over to the two other passengers to watch them rush to eat their ice cream cones before they melt. Both Kye and Toby chose three flavors. Luckily for me, the ice cream has no smell. I don't particularly think rocky road, pistachio, with cookies and cream combined would smell or taste great. However, both ice cream connoisseurs have reassured me that they chose the perfect combination and that I needed to get my head examined if I disagreed with them.

The frozen treat lifted Tobias's spirits, his smile is more at ease now.

"Tobias, did you really need three scoops?" I ask him as green drizzles down the cone.

He leans in quickly to slurp the running frozen treat down before it splatters on his pants, humming as he does so.

"Tobias, tell your mother that respectfully, when it comes to ice cream, a variety is always mandatory." Kye winks over Tobias's head towards me.

Tobias, finished saving his clothes from the melting cone, snickering with the confidence every little boy has at this age has. Or at least I hope it's every kid and not just mine. "I would have to look at the numbers to know the exact probabilities, but I feel extremely confident that I could have easily handled four scoops."

I roll my eyes to the roof of the cab, have smart kids they say, it's a blessing they say. Yeah, until you try to have an argument or draw parental boundaries. I need an attorney to negotiate a proper bedtime with this kid. Luckily, Kye takes mercy on me with the preverbal mental tag team tag in. "The nice lady at the shop said four wouldn't fit with the cone you chose buddy."

"She's wrong. It would have fit just fine, she was just too scared after seeing Mom's eyes bug out of her head like an alien to say yes."

I swear I hear the ding of bells of a wrestling match go off. *Round two,* I think to myself looking over Toby's head at Kye to mouth, "told you."

Kye mouths back, "challenge accepted."

"Tobias if you had gotten the fourth scoop where would that giant as- I mean astronomically large marshmallow that you had placed on top have gone?" I watch, curious to what Tobias would say to Kye's question.

He thinks about it, spinning his cone between his hands, viewing the world differently than the adults around him. I know the moment his *ah-ha* moment happens, when a spark of an idea takes root. "I would have chosen the mini marshmallows instead of the big one and I would have had them sprinkled on the top."

"Huh." And just like that I watch Kye tap out of his mental sparring with an eight year old. My body shimmies with the effort to conceal my laughter at Kye's expense.

"I don't need four. I'm just saying I could have *had* four. Either way, today is a perfect day." Tobias's words tug at my heartstrings, and pride swells in my chest at having such a wonderful child.

Kye leans closer to Tobias and softly tells him, "today *is* a perfect day kiddo."

Geeze at this rate I'm going to melt before the ice cream does with how sweet they are.

The truck pulls into the driveway and I sigh, not wanting our day to end and Kye and I to part ways. This weekend meant more to me than I could ever express to him. He will never know how much I appreciate him for our time together. The sex wasn't that bad either. What am I saying? I've never had sex that amazing, I didn't know it existed in real life.

I tug on the handle to the door to hop out first so I can help Tobias exit without smearing ice cream all over the leather seat. I have to admit the blacked out ride is pretty cool. Gravel crunches beneath my shoes as the smell of fresh cut grass hits me. *My favorite.*

"You two can go inside, I'll get the overnight bags," Kye calls out as he slams his own door, rattling the thing. Better he have this massive thing, a mini cooper wouldn't stand a chance.

"Okay, thank you. I'm going to grab the mail." Gratitude sparks inside me. Not used to having someone to carry our luggage, it really is the little things in life that I appreciate more than fancy dinners and expensive material things.

I'm smiling as I help Tobias out, his smooth hand leaves a sticky layer of melted ice cream on the arm he held on to. I feel Kye's eyes on me as I smile wide at the small chocolate handprint now decorating my shirt sleeve. Happy to be able to enjoy these little moments with my son and not have a man around that yells for innocent acts such as this one. In true Turbo Toby fashion, Tobias takes off the minute he's regained his balance from hopping out. The GMC isn't really all that high, but it's an older model, one of the classics. There's no step up on it. So for a child, it would take some time to get used to it. I find myself enjoying the evening sun, warm on my face as I stroll to the mailbox to collect the items I've missed from being away this weekend.

The small stack consists of bills that are due or subscriptions. Thank God I didn't have to deal with photos on such a pretty day. The ear-splitting shriek followed by loud wails that comes from inside the house has my heart pounding out of my chest, I take off at a neck breaking speed, sprinting for my house. The mail I dropped forgotten on the ground behind me.

Kye makes it to the house before me, by mere moments. He barrels through the front door passing over the threshold as I launch myself on the steps. I hear him shout angrily, "what the fuck is this?"

As I enter the house, the sight before me almost causes me to stop, almost. I've never seen devastation like this, there's not an inch of space that hasn't been vandalized in one fashion or another. I can't think about that now though. Where's my son? My only purpose is to find Tobias. I race through the house towards his bedroom shouting at the top of my lungs. "Tobias? Tobias Montgomery, where are you?"

I barrel around the corner of the darkened hallway that Kye had just moments before. Halting my sprint so abruptly, I slide on the carpet colliding into Kye. My body ricochets off his back so forcefully that I have to catch myself against the wall, the contact with both is jarring. Pain lances up my elbow, but nothing is going to keep me from my son.

Regaining my composure enough to stand, I move to step around Kye, he's standing outside Toby's room, in the hall that I now notice is saturated in something long dried but dark and clumpy. My brain can't compute what it is, nor do I want to. The most repulsive swamp smell is permeating the air and I clamp my hand over my nose and mouth in a feeble attempt to block out that god-awful putrid scent. Kye hasn't moved, his eyes still fixated on something in Tobias's room, I step around him, searching for my baby. The smell is worse here, I can't help it as bile rises in my throat. I swallow it, holding my breath the best I can.

The most heartbreaking of keen whining sounds have me spinning around the dimly lit room searching until my eyes land on him. Tobias is in a fetal position half tucked under his bed, his arms are bent around his head, hiding his eyes from the scene before him. His little body quivers with the force of his fear. The desperate whimpering sounds like a wounded animal fracture something in my chest. I race across the room to him.

"Tobias? Honey, come here," I coax him gently, keeping my voice calm so as to not scare him more, hoping it's not conveying the fear that I feel.

His teeth chatter as he says something too softly for me to hear.

Jesus Christ what is that fucking smell? I feel Kye enter the room, coming to stand behind me, he crouches down as I try to pull Tobias out from his little hiding spot. The exact one he used to hide as a toddler, now it's too tight and I'm not sure how he wedged himself there or how I'm supposed to get him out without causing him any physical harm.

"We need to leave Thena, we shouldn't stay here," Kye whispers in my ear and it's not lost to me that he used the term we.

I tug on Tobias again, grunting with the exertion. He shrieks, his body near convulsions in his panic. Kye crawls on the floor, the sound of plastic breaking under the weight of his body combined with Tobias's panic crying sends me near the edge. I look around trying to think, but unable to with the chaos and destruction surrounding us.

A gentle hand resting on my shoulder brings me around. Kye leans in closer to talk to me where Tobias can't hear, not wanting us to cause him any more discomfort. "I'm going to lift the bed, I want you to grab him and run. We don't know if someone else is still in here. But with this kind of damage, this is personal."

I look at him questioning.

He quickly explains. "Personal means dangerous. We need to be quick. Don't stop for anything. No bags, no toys. Nothing. We can replace everything. When you get him in your arms, you run and don't stop until we get inside the truck."

A coldness settles in my bones at his words. An eerie feeling of once again being watched unnerves me.. I hope my face isn't revealing how I truly feel. It's like a million tiny spiders are crawling all over my skin with no way to get them off. The hair along my arms rises, my pulse picks up. I try to tamp it down, to focus on the here and now, but in between the mewling sounds coming from my sweet boy and the rising fear that someone else is in here with us, my mind starts to race.

What if someone's wedged under the bed with Toby and that's why he's behaving like this? What if the person is out in the hall waiting for us to exit and bash us over the head? What if this was a trap to distract us while they cut the brakes to the car?

"Thena. Tobias needs you. I need you to pull it together." Kye's words have his desired impact, I glance around the room to make sure before I pull my baby out that we are well and truly alone, that's when I see it. What has Tobias in a horror stricken panic.

There on his nightstand sits a blender. I know what happened with the smell more strongly in this direction, and from the vile chunks in the glass pitcher matching the dark streaks on the wall. I'm going to murder that asshole. I'm going to grind his fucking bones myself. I will turn him into a chum and feed his ass to the goddamned sharks. That sick fuck blended my baby's fish into sludge and left it for him to find. Fuck this. "Kye, lift the bed."

He nods at me. "It's okay Turbo, Uncle Kye is here. Your Mom and I are going to get you out." Kye counts. "One, two, THREE!"

The metal squeaks as Kye pushes the bedframe in the air, I snatch Tobias by his shirt lifting him enough to get my arms around him. I heave him against my chest and I run. I run like the hounds of hell are chasing us. My feet reverberate against the floor, blood pumping through my ears. I don't take any time to risk looking anywhere but straight ahead, getting my baby out of here so we can get him to safety is my only mission. I'm almost to the door when Kye shouts at me to run around something. I give it a moment's notice as I pass over it, my heart exploding into a million pieces and fire raging in my belly as I process the significance of Tobias's ice cream cone, melted on the floor. His perfect day was ruined.

30

A Little Ray Of Sunshine

Thena

The tips of my fingers tingle, the circulation is long cut off from the rubber band. Leaning against the wall opposite my child, I observe him quietly playing on the tablet I ordered as soon as we arrived here after the nightmare Mitchell exposed us to.

I twist the band again, making another loop around my fingers. The discoloration goes from cherry-red to deep purple. I put us here. I made the decision to marry him. I was so fucking desperate to have a family. Fucking blinded to the control. Ignored the condescension in his tone. So many goddamn red flags.

Now my baby sits by a window every day, too scared to leave the protection of a home that's not ours. Because I was fucking desperate. This shit's on me. I twist the small black band around my fingers. *SNAP!* Pain floods my appendages as the blood begins to circulate again. The broken band rockets across the room, my head snaps up.

Tobias looks at me alarmed by the unexpected *POP* of the band and with my sudden movements, for the briefest of moments his eyes glass over. I watch entirely frozen waiting to see if he will relax again or if I need to intervene. Pride swells in my chest as I watch my child regulate his emotions before returning to his program. My shoulders shake with tension as the gouges on my heart fester, white, hot, boiling rage has planted roots deep down inside me.

For four weeks Tobias and I have been locked inside Kye's property. The first two weeks of our stay here will be permanently seared into my brain forever. Along with the inside of our old home. That's another hurdle I will have to face soon as well. I can't take him back there. Reaching in the back pocket of my jeans I fish out… No, not fish. I will never use that word again. I pull out another hair tie, wrapping my tousled hair in it, my top knot fully secured, my hands move to adjust my t-shirt. There's nothing wrong with my outfit, the clothes are fine.

Kye and I made sure that everything Tobias and I needed was ordered the same night we arrived. He had to pay, of course, because we're both in agreement that cards are a big no-no right now. Too easy to track. I crushed the SIM card in my phone. So that had to be replaced as well. My car was searched for tracking devices, but I don't trust the results enough, so it's parked at the old house for now.

I yank on my topknot again. My nerves are fucking shot and in the time I've fidgeted, At a loss with how to get my kid out of the house. I see he's finished coding another program. I check my wristwatch. That one only lasted seven minutes. I'm going to have to pay for a more advanced subscription.

"You don't have to stand over there and watch me, Mom. I'm okay today." His eyes find mine and I can tell he's lying. His face is still leeched of color from the sudden noise of the band snapping.

My heart melts as I realize he's trying to comfort me, the parent. Shame burns through me as hot as the ever present rage that accompanies me daily. I clamp down on how I feel knowing he needs more support than myself. "You're a terrible liar Turbo."

The crooked smile on my face in hopes of easing his worries was not completely forced. Guess I might as well join the party instead of creeping in the hallway. I'm probably freaking him out. Crossing the room, I haphazardly plop myself onto one of the oversized chairs, the leather folding around me. My placement brings me closer to Tobias but not enough to crowd him.

Clouds begin to roll in on the horizon. The tall windows behind him provide us both a backdrop of a spectacular view. The lush greenery thick with orange-red leaves from the maple trees, dotted with white oak spread across the river bank. I feel my body melt into the cushions, feeling safe for a moment.

Squinting, I try to peer through the trees curious to what's on the other side. Impenetrable foliage surrounds us, the security in this moment. The decorum of privacy the landscape provides us brings a slight reprieve from the heaviness in my heart. Lightning strikes across the sky in the distance. One… Two… Three… *BOOM!* Tobias's body jackknives from the lounged position he had just moved himself into as I crossed the room.

"Just a storm baby," I soothe him.

"I…I…kn-know…" Stuttering over his words, his body begins to tremble slightly. His fear of the sudden loud and thunderous applause from the sky as the storm begins to make its way towards us has me cringing inward, knowing tonight will be as tough one as the previous nights have been. We're all exhausted, the only one of us who doesn't show signs of slowing down is Kye.

He often makes it to Tobias before I do after screams penetrate the silence of the night while we're asleep. More often than not, tantrums ensue if I leave his side. I would be the same if I were a child and my father slaughtered my pets and coated the walls of my home in their guts. My eyelids feel heavy. The weeks of little to no sleep are starting to catch up to me. My body is a live-wire these days. I feel completely hopeless as an undercurrent of electricity runs just under my skin. An itch I'm unable to scratch.

I want to kill Mitchell for all he's done to us.

"Would you like to play a game?" I ask him hoping to distract him.

"No thank you. I'm okay." His words are low, his shoulders curved in on himself.

Beep beep, the door's security system sounds out over the room. Tobias jumps to his feet, the first real smile he's worn all day flashes across his face as the door swings open, bringing Kye, Blanca, Rita, and Rex through the entrance. The matching shrieks from both sides of the room erupt from all of us.

As Tobias and I race to get to our friends, Kye steps to the side, avoiding being trampled. I mouth a thank you to him as I pass him to wrap my arms around my best friends. Weeks of not having them with me, after becoming so close with one another, has made me sick at heart. I practically knock Rita off her feet as I sling my body into her.

"*OOMPH!* And to think I thought it was Tobias that would knock the wind from me." Rita chuckles as we cling to one another. I feel my other friends step to my back.

"Move over hooker, I want to see my nephew." Rita's voice rings out above my head, I have to tilt my head back to look at her. Her big doe eyes sparkle as she wiggles her brows at me. "I think you made the other two jealous, now that they know I'm your favorite."

The laugh I bark is so joyous, so real, I want to cry all over again. I spin to find Blanca and Rex waiting, arms already open. I squeal and wrap them both in a fierce hug. The lilac and jasmine fragrance Blanca favors envelopes me as Rex gives a conspiratorial whisper. "We know who your real favorites are. She just doesn't know that."

"Ignorance is bliss." Blanca giggles as she releases me.

"What are you guys doing here?" I ask them. Tobias darts across the foyer to launch himself at Kye. His bags drop to the floor with a thump as Kye lifts him, flipping Tobias over to secure the little boy to his back.

Kye spins him in the center of the room, keeping him occupied so my friends and I can get reacquainted. It doesn't go unnoticed as we speak, my friends' eyes periodically track Tobias and Kye playing. Looks of approval are directed toward me and I can't help myself. I smile a bit.

"A little birdie told us you and Turbo were having a difficult time with the change of scenery. So we decided to come to derail the espresso depresso train, turning this weekend into a party," Rex finishes as Rita puts two fingers in her mouth, whistling loud enough for all of us to slap our hands over our ears.

She finishes her attempt at bursting our eardrums to call out to Kye, "Hey, pretty boy! Do you have a manservant or do we carry our luggage ourselves? Oh, and I refuse to bunk with Rex. Her snores raise the dead."

I look around for Kye and Tobias to see their reactions to Rita's antics. The space is empty. Huh, they were just here. I mentally shrug, knowing they're probably preparing rooms for my friends. Rex huffs, looking appropriately affronted at Rita.

My eyes dart between the ladies. I can't help but compare the two, both are taller than I am. Where Rex's skin is alabaster, Rita's has the slightest touch of sun to it. One has short, bright red hair, and the other has long, light brown hair with highlights blended in. While Rex rocks the more mature grunge look, Rita is all sunflowers and dressed to impress. Twins, yet they are two completely different individuals on the outside. Yet, their personalities are identical. Which leads us to many of these stand offs. Rex scoffs, pushing her wire rimmed eyeglasses up the bridge of her nose.

"I do *not* snore," Rex argues, crossing her arms over her chest.

"Fine, you dream you're a motorcycle. Whatever. Either way, I'm not in a biker club, so I room alone." Rita puts her hands on her hips, arching a brow as to say it doesn't fucking matter what you think, you snore so fight me on this.

Blanca and I take in the scene before us, I lean in to whisper to Blanca, "I've got twenty on this coming to blows."

Blanca cracks a smile that lights up her face. She sticks her hand out for me to shake. "Fifty dollars says I can stop this before it escalates."

"Challenge accepted."

I hear a cork pop from somewhere in the house, just loud enough to echo in the massive room. Kye's voice booms over the intercom. "Ladies, as entertaining as a cat fight sounds, I just opened a bottle of our finest champagne, and Tobias is constructing a very impressive charcuterie board. Would you like to join us in the kitchen?"

Rita and Rex both jump at the sudden intrusion into their spat, Rita's hands fly to her chest. The looks of shock on both of their faces have me holding my side as I wheeze, "If you could see your faces!" I try for the life of me to catch my breath. "You both look ridiculous!"

Blanca agrees with me. "You would think you two would be so overcome with joy at seeing our best friend after weeks away you could both behave." She chastises them, trying hard not to laugh with us. Blanca focuses her attention on me and says in her melodic voice, "And you, Missy, did not tell us you were holed up in a mansion."

I stop laughing, her words forcing the reminder of why I'm here to the forefront of my mind.

My friends must not pick up on the change in my energy because Rita walks past Rex slapping her purse across the other woman's chest, leaving her with no choice but to take it so it doesn't fall. Rex's eyebrows rise to her hairline, and her lips purse. Looking at the bright yellow bag she flicks her eyes at her sister. Rita only shrugs. "Don't look at me like that. You're closer to the pile of luggage. Just set it on top. I want to have champagne with my bitches." Rita takes off in the wrong direction.

I exchange a quick look with Blanca, both of us trying to hold back our matching grins.

"Does that hooker know where she's going?" Rex pipes up. I take the bag from her and place it on their luggage.

"She's going in the wrong direction," I inform them.

"Should you tell her that?" Blanca asks me.

"Not a chance in hell. We'll let her wander around for a bit," I say as I start leading the girls in the right direction. Rex snickers and I say over my shoulder as we head down the hallway, "Karma." I throw the girls a wink over my shoulder and we have another round of laughter.

31

Paint & Sip

Thena

We all enter the kitchen, minus Rita. Who's probably lost in a closet right about now. I chuckle a little, feeling lighter than I have in weeks. I hear my friends gasp as they get a view of the kitchen.

This is a culinary dream for a professional. The stainless steel appliances are top of the line. Like the rest of the house, it's a very well blended modern and rustic room. With high wooden beams across the ceiling and industrial Edison bulbs running on a tight wire over the island, the craftsmanship is unique, yet beautiful.

I smile brightly at Tobias and Kye as we join them, sitting at the island in the center of the room. It's a massive marble top the size of my dining room table at home. A kitchen like this makes me want to spend my days attempting to bake. Kye gives me a knowing look, like he sees what I'm thinking. His answering smile lets me know that he would like that too. To have me here, in his kitchen.

"You have a beautiful home, Kye," Blanca compliments him.

He joins us at the island, pouring glasses of champagne for us. "Thank you, Blanca. I'm thinking about buying it."

"So, you want to stay in the area?" she responds to him.

He sits a glass down in front of me, a mischievous look in his eyes. "If the brat will have me, then yes. I wouldn't mind staying in the area."

Both of my girlfriends eyes light up at his response to Blanca's question. Before the ladies continue commenting on the home and how unique and lovely the floor-to- ceiling windows in the living room and kitchen are, he informs them that every common room of the house has them, along with the master bedroom and bath. Rex makes a snarky remark about window peepers, and I half hear him informing her that the double paned panels are not only tinted to allow us to see out, and others can't see in, but they are also bulletproof. This home was owned by an arms dealer with government contracts in the nineties. The information would usually have me asking a million questions, but I can't concentrate on anything but how Kye's words affect me.

It feels like someone is squeezing the air from my lungs. My heart rate speeds up rapidly, and my entire body lights up in awareness. He is willing to stay here if I want him to. I chew my lip, tugging at the sensitive skin there. Not knowing if I want to hightail it and run or melt on the spot.

I save myself from any kind of response by quickly picking up the flute of champagne and taking a long pull, the carbon dioxide tickles my sinuses and before I know what's happening I'm sneezing and coughing into my arm. Humiliation fills me as my friends laugh and continue on with their conversation with Kye, like their best friend isn't currently choking to death beside them.

"Reach for Jesus, sweetheart," Kye mocks, using my favorite phrase for Tobias against me. Once my coughing has subsided enough, I lift a one finger salute to him, earning me one of my favorite smiles from him. He props his hip against the island, tipping his glass towards me in a mock toast.

"I think what you're doing for them is the sweetest. Not many men would put himself between a single mother and danger," Rex observes. Her eyes track Kye as he processes what she's said. I know this moment is a pivotal one. She's going to form her conclusion on him by his answer.

He seems to think the same because he thinks about his response for so long my anxiety starts to spike. His eyes meet each of my friends and he earnestly says "Thena has never needed me or any other man to stand between her and someone foolish enough to make her their enemy. I will always be beside her in any dispute." He turns to Tobias, who hasn't left Kye's side since he arrived. "Should we show them the surprise?" he asks.

Tobias bobs his head, leaping from the island chair. "Hang tight! I have to grab the chutto-er-to board!" Laughter fills the space as he darts to the fridge.

"I believe what you were trying to say is, Charcuterie board."

Tobias's little head pops out from behind the fridge door. "My dude, that's what I said," he says before he goes back to digging around. He comes away with a massive board with a variety of aged cheese, meats, fruits, and some bread with oils to dip them in. My eyebrows raise. Did they do all of this? In that short period of time?

Kye must see the question on my face because he leans over the island beckoning me to get close. I lean as far as I can before he speaks low enough for only the adults to hear. "He couldn't sleep last night, so we prepped everything for today and stashed it all out of the way."

I hope the gratitude I'm feeling is written plainly across my face. Kye's support for Tobias, by encouraging him to focus his time and emotions in such a healthy manner, has me in the feels. I mouth a thank you to him, my eyes misting with appreciation and adoration.

His love for us is evident in the look he gives me, when he mouths a you're welcome brat back to me.

Why am I so hesitant to give him my heart? It's not like he doesn't already know that he has it. I just won't admit it. I do love him, I've always loved him. His dedication to this potential family is proof of his intentions. *There was another who showed this level of devotion and dedication too, and you know how that turned out.* Why does that little voice have to pipe up now?

Kye sets his glass down, gives me a once over, and then claps his hands together and announces to the room, "I can see you doing combat against yourself over there. I'm on kiddo duty tonight, so please drink up and relax a little, and for the love of all that's holy, have some fun. It's okay to smile, even during the dark times."

"Oh, you are a darling!" both Blanca and Rex exclaim simultaneously.

Kye shakes his head slowly raising his hands in a surrendering position. "I'm no saint, ladies. For seven years, I've known what or who I want, and I've had to wait for my time to prove I'm the one she needs. She just needs a little convincing"

He turns to Tobias, standing in the doorway, his tray of yummies delivered to wherever this surprise is happening in the house. He's been listening intently to the entire exchange. The adults freeze when we notice him, he rolls his eyes, scrunching his nose. "Can we move past the gross stuff and get to the fun part?"

"You know what's not fun?" a booming voice belts across the space, we all turn to see Rita entering the room.

"Walking in fucking circles trying to find another human. I was ready to call the Coast Guard. Why the hell do you need a security code to use the intercom? Also," she continues, not appearing to be winded in the slightest, "nice fucking pool." She comes to a halt at the island, picking up my glass of champagne, she sniffs it, shrugs her shoulders before tossing it back. Unlike myself, she doesn't seem to have an issue swallowing it.

"You have a pool?" Blanca asks Kye, trying to prevent the conversation from deviating into another tense moment between Rita and Rex.

Kye confirms telling Blanca, "you ladies will have to enjoy a swim tomorrow. It's temperature controlled and indoors."

"Did you have a nice stroll Rita?" Rex asks her, and I immediately intervene, not wanting another epic battle between them. Their bickering is notorious and frankly I do not have the mental capacity to deal with it today.

"Shouldn't we follow Tobias?"

"And I'm going to bring a new bottle," Kye adds.

Rita looks like she will say something to Rex as she passes her. I catch her attention and silence her with a look. I point to the open doorway with my son standing there and she has the sense to look ashamed. I'm not sure what's going on between them, but this is an all new level of petty from the twins. *What drama did I miss?*

I don't say anything to Tobias while he leads them out of the room. Kye walks up behind me, his mouth trailing along my ear. "I've missed feeling this body beneath me." He wraps an arm around my waist, pulling me against him. A chill from the champagne bottle seeps through the thin material of my t-shirt combining with the warmth of his breath the mixture of the two does scrumptious things to me.

I shimmy against him, little sparks of desire run through me as I'm immediately turned on. Gods it's been weeks since we've had time together alone. I would be lying if I said I haven't missed the physical connection. I settle my weight against him, relaxing into his touch. In a whisper I confess, "I've missed you too."

"You have no idea how much I want to sink myself into you and feel your body respond to the things I do to you," he growls low in his chest as his arm tightens momentarily. "Come on brat, we don't want to keep the gang waiting."

Kye leads me into the large dining room and I stop, moved beyond emotions. In the center of the room, a long table is covered in a white drop cloth. Art supplies, canvases, brushes, and everything needed are neatly placed on the table. They did this for me?

I take in my friends seated at the table with their drinks and supplies. Tobias clicks the projector on and a YouTube video image replaces the white wall on the far side of the room.

Step-by-step paint and sip home tutorial. A smile breaks across my face at this beautiful surprise.

"I hope you don't mind. I ordered the fruity scented acrylics, but just in case those weren't what you wanted, I also got the turpentine ones as well. I know you're sensitive to harsh smells, but I also know you love to paint, so I had to make a judgment call," Kye tells me as he gestures to the table.

I raise my hands to cover my face. The chill from my glass cools my heated cheek. I'm flushed, and I know it. Slightly embarrassed and overwhelmed by the kindness Kye has shown me, and knowing Tobias was included, I'm not sure how to react.

Do I say thank you? Those two words don't seem adequate to show my gratitude.

"A simple thank you *will* suffice brat." His words imply that, not for the first time, he's been able to read my body language. I dazzle him with a smile that I know is as radiant as I feel now. His eyes glaze over as he looks into mine. "I only ever want to make you smile like that one."

"Okay you two! Stop making googly eyes at one another and get over here," Rex calls out. We laugh and approach the table, taking our seats next to one another.

"Are the old people ready? Can you see the screen? Should I make it larger? I probably should enlarge it more." Tobias inquires. Protests ring out across the room.

"Hey! I'm not old!" Blanca's cry of outrage is trumped by Rex and Rita's simultaneously yelling. "You *used* to be my favorite child!" and "Pipsqueak! You just canceled your Christmas."

Tobias doesn't look worried in the slightest. He taps a button on the phone and we all settle in to paint our cactus.

We work in silence for the first half hour. When it comes time to paint the glochids, the little barbed thistles, Rex decides to break the silence. "I can't believe you are holding up in this stunning home with an even more stunning man and you are sad. Girl have you seen this place?" Rex speaks over her canvas.

"I hate to agree with my sister..." Rita chimes in but doesn't finish the second half of her statement.

"Adults are disgusting," Tobias announces. He looks around at our paintings then proudly back at his. "I don't want to embarrass you old timers, but I'm finished. Looks like youth wins again. It was bound to happen with the geriatric pace you five have going for ya." He bounds from his chair, barely missing Rita's hands as she tries to whack him for his joke. He runs to me and throws himself at me.

Kye chuckles beside me, muttering. "The kid is going places."

I nod, humming my agreement. I lean back enough to catch him without ruining my own painting. We look at mine together. It's slightly lopsided but it's perfect in its imperfection.

"Nice. Can I play on my tablet?" he asks. I nod, my ponytail bobbing.

"Of course. Just clean up your area."

"Actually, I'll clean up the mess later. After all, he did do the set up," Kye says, earning himself a fist bump from Tobias.

"My dude."

"I got your back, kid," Kye offers him as Tobias darts out of the room.

The three women to my side watch him go. As soon as he turns the corner out of sight, they pounce. "So guys, how long has this friendship been a situation?" Rita inquires, lifting her drink to her mouth to sip it.

"Oh my God, you just can't mind your own business can you?" Rex's tone is chastising, and I feel bad for Rita, so I look to Kye, who in turn just shrugs, responding for the both of us.

"I've been in love with Thena since the first moment I saw her."

"And when exactly was that? When her husband introduced her?" Rita claps back, my spine stiffens, offended by her tone.

"Actually, we met in a bookstore. Well, we didn't meet. We saw each other. I didn't know at the time she was married to Mitchell."

"And did she tell you she was married?" she asks.

Kye shakes his head. "No, because we didn't speak to one another," he tells her. He's being way more patient than I would be. His hand clasps my thigh, his thumb rubs small comforting circles to show me support. I have to be honest, my friend's accusations are hurting my feelings.

"I'm confused," Rita begins to speak but Kye interrupts her.

"I saw Thena for the first time in a bookstore in Arizona. It's an encounter in my life I will never forget. She had this ridiculously bright mustard yellow skirt on. Pretty sure it's called Bohemian style. When she would turn to check on Tobias, who was just a little guy then, her skirt would spin out around her." Kye leans back in his chair, a small smile on his lips. "Her dark hair was curled and pinned high on her head. She had these gold bangles on both wrists with a form fitting white tank top. I remember leaning against a shelf, feeling like a total fucking stalker, but I couldn't look away. I was mesmerized by her. Her smile, the tone that she used while soothing her baby. She was absolutely incandescent, I wanted to approach her. And almost did. I wanted to get on my knees right there in the middle of this random store and beg her for a moment of her time in hopes that…that a moment would become something more."

I lift my eyes to my friends to gauge their reactions. Rex and Blanca look to be wiping their eyes, but Rita looks unconvinced. What has gotten into her?

"So what did you do?" Blanca asks in wonder and amazement at his story.

Kye's smile is sad. He tugs on my ponytail playfully as he regards me. "My cell phone rang, distracting me. Believe it or not. It was actually Mitchell calling. When I looked up, she was gone. And along with her, my heart."

"But that's not the end of your story is it? Because we're currently all sitting here," Rita snaps. My eyes go wide with surprise. It isn't like Rita to behave in such a rude manner. I open my mouth to remind her that she's in his home when Kye chuckles lightly.

"No, it wasn't the end. A few weeks later, I was invited, well ordered, to Mitchell's home for dinner to see if we could have a more civilized relationship at work. Thena answered the door. To say I was surprised is an understatement. I thought to myself, how could this be? How could this stunningly breathtaking creature belong to this piece of shit? But, she did. Upon meeting her, I knew that Thena was a woman with integrity. She would never step out on her husband. But, she wasn't the one doing the stepping out. It was Mitchell. Still, she stayed. So I stayed. I gave her my friendship, knowing that that would be all I could give her, all that she would accept from me."

"Until the day she did accept," Rita bites out angrily. Everyone, including our softest companion Blanca, stares at Rita with disappointment.

"What are you implying Rita?" I ask her. She knows from my tone it's not a request so much as a what the fuck? Rita glares at Kye, then rolls her eyes and looks at me with pity.

"Do you not find it a little suspicious that you and Mitchell seemed to be working through everything and moving on with your lives. Not that I believe you should have stayed with him. I'm just saying this is too much for me to wrap my head around. None of us were informed there were issues until we showed up and boxes were packed." She does the last bit in quotation marks, I feel the energy in the room begin to shift. My frustrations rising with each word. I want her to stop speaking, but in typical Rita fashion she pushes on.

"Miraculously this guy arrives and now. All of a sudden, your child and you are going through hell and he's conveniently here to save the day? Sweeping you both up and whisking you off to his mini mansion in the woods! Hasn't that thought even crossed your mind? Or is the dick so good you lose all common sense?"

Audible gasps from my other friends combine with the knowledge that Kye has to sit here and bear witness to this level of disrespect. Not only to him, but to call my judgment in question is out of line.

"That's enough Rita." My tone is colder than I have ever used toward one of my friends. Maybe I would feel bad, a smidgen guilty about how I just spoke to her, but Kye has done nothing but be here for Tobias and I and I won't allow any of my friends to question his integrity. "I asked him to come."

"Wh-What? Why would you do that?" She stumbles over her words.

My next words will hurt her, but they deserve the truth. So I tell them. "I trust him."

"Pardon me? You don't trust me? Or us?"

I stay cool as she rises from her chair. "It's not like that."

"Well, excuse the fuck out of me, if I'm just a little taken aback by the fact that you didn't trust us enough to fill us in on all the shit going on with you."

"You're overreacting."

"It's not about you," Blanca and Rex chime in at the same time.

Rita scoffs looking at all of us in astonishment. *It's not like we have been insulting her in her own home*, I think to myself. She grabs the bottle of champagne and storms out of the room calling over her shoulder, "I'm going to find Tobias, he's better company than my current one is."

I shake my head, rising from my seat as well. I am disappointed in my friend for her poor behavior. "What has gotten into her?" I ask them.

Rex looks away, her shoulders curling in on herself. Blanca puts a comforting hand on Rex's shoulder, who she nods to her. "Our mother was murdered by her abusive husband when we were teenagers. Rita witnessed it and now she's reliving those memories. She'll be alright. It's just a lot."

I gasp, that's fucking god awful. "I'm so sorry Rex."

Rex walks to the windows, sipping her drink. "She'll come around. She is just stubborn."

"Kye, Thena. I'm so sorry. Kye, you opened your home to us, and Rita's behavior is unacceptable. Honestly, she's just worried about Thena and Tobias. We were in the dark for so long about everything, it just caught us off guard is all." Blanca pauses looking back to Rex before she continues, "I would like to take Tobias night swimming in the pool if that's okay. You two should have some time alone."

"Blanca, my home is your home. Enjoy it for all it has to offer. As for your friend, she has every right to question me regarding those she loves. So, no hard feelings. Go enjoy the house, it has a lot to offer. There's a fridge of snacks and a mini bar by the pool. You can't miss it."

"Okay, you two have fun."

"Don't do anything I wouldn't do." Rex wiggles her eyebrows at me.

"That's not a long list," I tell her, she laughs.

"My point exactly."

32

Pantries & Bananas

Thena

"Here, let me help you." Kye takes the serving tray from my hands and leans down to kiss my forehead. His masculine scent, which I love, draws me in, and I can't help but be slightly embarrassed when I lean into him after he pulls back. I'm not able to fight the effect he has on me. He smirks. Oh, it's just not fair.

"Grab the stack of cups and follow me, brat," he tells me.

I pick up the stack, tickled that I still have a free hand to carry my glass. I've quite literally never had champagne this good before. Kye juggles the charcuterie board and the extra supplies as he opens the pantry door. It never ceases to amaze me the sheer size of this place. This pantry is almost the size of my bedroom back home. I follow him to the back of the pantry, not surprised that the beginning is only a hallway that turns into a larger room in the back.

"Here, we can sit all of this on the top shelf, out of the way," he tells me over his shoulder.

Placing my champagne flute on one of the shelves, I pull one of the extra chairs from the corner to reach the top shelf. I stretch up and place my items beside Kye's.

I feel him, more than I see him, as he runs his fingers over the bare skin where my tank top has risen, sending little jolts of electricity through me.

"Thena…"

"Hm?" I look down, meeting his heated stare.

"Don't move, princess." Anticipation courses through me at his order. It's been weeks since I've had his hands on my body, and I've longed for his touch. But, we're in a pantry…

"What if someone walks in?" I croak. He can't mean to do what I think he wants to do here? Can he?

"Everyone's on the other side of the house." He unbuckles his belt, and pulls it free of his pants.

"Give me your wrists." His eyes captivate me, and his words leave no room for me to argue. I lift my wrists as ordered. The belt is cool to the touch as it meets skin when he methodically wraps it around my wrist. I watch, unable to find words. His imposing form looms over me as he loops it to a utility hook above me. I gasp in surprise, not knowing what to expect.

Well…that's convenient, I think as I inspect my bindings. He crossed them together and latched the belt to the hook where I can lift my arms up and get down at any time.

He leans in, his lips fusing to mine in a scorching kiss that leaves me panting and wanting more. Then he steps back, taking the chair with him.

"Umph." The air whooshes from my lungs as my feet drop to the floor, securing me more tightly. My weight is held up by the belt and the tips of my toes. His lips find mine again, merging together as he devours me.

"Be right back," he murmurs against my skin as I lean back against the shelves, dazed.

"Mmhm." I hear his footsteps as he leaves me momentarily. Shuffling feet makes me open my eyes, focusing on him. Kye's studying the shelves and I'm about to ask him what exactly he's doing but he picks up a tub of coconut oil, coming back over to where I impatiently wait. He sits it down and moves to the other side of me.

"What are you doing?" I ask him, my voice meek. My binds bite into my skin as I tug them, testing them.

"I had dinner. I didn't get dessert." His words send heat through my pussy, my core wet with need. He stalks over to me, pulling an extra linen napkin from the shelf. "I think this will be more…stimulating for you, if you close your eyes and feel what I'm going to do to you."

My breathing hitches as he blindfolds me, unable to see anything through the linen. My body responds quickly to the mystery of it all. The air shifts around me as he moves around selecting his toys for our time together. A few more moments go by until I can hear his stealthy approach. My muscles tense as he nears.

"Don't move," he orders and I feel cool metal slide up my stomach, the sound of cloth being cut fills the space. I hold my breath, scared if I move I'll get sliced. The cold air hits my midriff, the sensation more so with my vision impaired. My bra is cut next, the cups falling to the side, my nipples harden, my pussy throbs. The combination is intoxicating. He hasn't even touched me yet and I'm drenched from the intensity of his brand of foreplay.

"These right here," he growls, his hands lifting my breasts, his thumbs stroking underneath, "will be the death of me."

I moan with pleasure, encouraging him to do more.

I feel his lips run down my throat, caressing my skin as he makes his way to my nipples. His lips leave mine for the briefest of moments. A clunking sound interrupts the silence of the room. His lips latch onto my nipple and I gasp.

A burst of iciness is sharp, bordering on painful, blending into a beautiful melody of pleasure as his mouth warms my body. I writhe against him, silently begging for more. He chuckles against my nipple as his hands find the waistband of my jeans. In between one moment and the next my pants are off, his hands running up my legs to the inside of my thighs. The hot air leaving his mouth against my core, he nips at my bud, latching on through the thin fabric of my panties. His lips come away with a small pop.

"Goddamnit Kye! I can't take it!" I cry out, drunk sensations staggering to my equilibrium.

"Say thank you," he demands of me.

My head lolls to the side. I don't understand what he wants of me? I thrust my hips trying to feel that sweet friction again.

His hands grip my hips pushing me back against the shelves. "You'll take whatever I give to you and you will thank me for it," he commands me. "So, tell me thank you."

My skin's dewy, my panties wet. Emotion pricks my eyes with the ferocity of my arousal. I pant, my breasts lift and fall with how deep I'm gulping down oxygen, the way they jiggle a new form of torture. My fear of passing out is genuine The way he dominates me in the most thorough way. My head swims. I want more, I need more.

"Thank–thank you," I whimper. I feel his hand cradle my cheek, his thumb forces its way into my mouth. I don't hesitate as I suck on it greedily.

"I want you to splay your legs for me, Thena." I obey immediately. The chill from the floor on my toes is a welcoming refresher from the heat of my body. The cold metal connects with my hip bone, the fabric cut away from my body. My panties fall away, replaced by his tongue as Kye laps at my pussy. His fingers massage my asscheeks as he feasts on me. He groans against my body in approval at my wild abandonment. My moans grow louder with each flick of his tongue. My back arches as my body tightens ready to detonate. I rock my hips shamelessly, I'm so close… I pant, I cry out as his mouth leaves my body right before I career over the ledge of sweet abyss.

I throw my body against the shelves, and something crashes to the floor, Kye is there with his hands in my hair as he shushes me.

"Not yet, brat," he tells me hotly as he spins me, pulling my ass in the air by my hips. His fingers tangle in my hair as he carefully lowers my head against one of the shelves. "I fucking love edging this sweet pussy of yours. She's so tight, so ready for me." He plunges two fingers in from behind.

"Kye!" I call out his name.

"You want me in you so bad, don't you baby?"

"Ye–YES!" I cry as he pumps his fingers, pulling them out to rub around my opening. I squirm against him remembering how it felt last time he dominated my ass. His fingers leave my body pulling a whimper from me. I hear the whoosh of air before something rubbery hits my ass, I jolt as pain radiates over my rear. Unable to move with his other hand still wrapped in my hair. I'm pinned at his mercy.

"Did I tell you to fucking move, princess?"

I shake my head as much as his grip will allow, small bites of pain radiate from my scalp. The overwhelming sensations have my folds convulsing. *Whack!* I cry out as another lick of heat lands on my ass.

"You move when I say you move. Understand?"

"I under–stand."

"Good. Stay there until I'm ready to fuck you."

"Fuuccckkkkk yessss."

He lets me go and I stay where I am, still unable to see. I try to pinpoint where he is or what he's doing. I hear a sound I can't place, like the hissing sound of a lid opening, moments before the smell of coconut is heavy in the air.

"Do you remember what I told you not to do?" he asks me, smearing oil all over my rear, running his soaked fingers between my legs.

"Are you using coconut oil on me, Kincaid?" He drags his tongue up my spine. I shiver. Fuck this is too good for him to stop.

"Maybe…"

"Oh."

"Do you want to know why I'm covering you in oil?" he taunts me, the sound of a zipper whispers through the room, and I have to remind myself at the last minute not to move. I don't remember ever wanting anything as much as I wanted this man.

"Well brat, do you want to know what I'm about to stick in you?"

"Hopefully your cock," I say into the void. We should use blindfolds more often. I'm ordering some from the 'Zon' when we're finished here.

"Oh, sweetheart. I'm about to edge you with something so much better before I sink my cock into this tight little ass of yours," he promises me before something connects with my crack, moving slowly through my folds, connecting with my clit. It's cold, coated in oil, Kye pushes it back and forth. The friction makes me cry out.

He uses his secret toy to manipulate my body, the binds on my wrist bruise me as I pull against them needing more. He pulls his accessory back before plunging his cock and the foreign object in both holes. I gasp, my body tightens up with the unexpected intrusion. He stays buried in my body.

"That's right, brat. Take it like I know you can." His words are forced, like he's clenching his teeth.

My walls convulse around whatever's inside me, my body satisfied to finally be full. The moan he pulls from my lips as he pulls out of my ass is a guttural cry. His touch scorches me as he sinks back in. My body soars with pleasure.

"If I were you, I would hold onto that hook. Tight." It's the only warning I get before his thick cock pounds into me over and over again. His finger finds my sensitive bud. He wreaks absolute havoc on my body. My back bows, my hair sticks to my neck as he milks my body for everything it offers.

"Please…please don't stop!" I beg, tears leaking from my eyes as I revel in every inch of the pleasure and pain. His hips buck against me he growls out my name.

"Thena, I want you to cum now!" And I do. I freefall into a delicious avalanche of pleasure as he slams into me one more time, groaning my name as he empties inside me.

"Thena…"

I hum in wonderment and awe, moved by how passionate our carnal lovemaking is. He pulls himself and whatever he inserted in me out. The chair squeaks as he slides it back under me so I can half lay, half sit across his upper body. He holds onto me protectively as he undoes the leather and removes my blindfold. Lights dance across my vision as my eyes adjust to the light. He cradles me to him as he sits us down in the chair. His hands massage my body.

"Can I carry you to bed, my love?" he asks me as he gently kisses my brow.

I nod, too moved by my emotions to speak at this moment.

His chest rises and falls under me and I snuggle deeper into him. I'm almost asleep when he lifts me and carries us to his room. I hear the rustling of sheets before he places me between them. I crack my eyes open. Kye is tucking the blankets around me with a banana in his mouth. My grin is lazy as I mumble.

"Goodnight."

33

Thena

"You are positively incandescent this morning." Blanca's smile is so genuine I can't help but smile back. There's no way I can hide the glow. Three rounds of mind blowing sex and the best sleep of my life.

"I have no idea what you're talking about, ma'am."

"Don't play coy with us! We want the deets!" Rita chimes in. She's in better spirits this morning, though I can't help but glare at her. She was so rude to Kye and me last night and still hasn't apologized. Now she wants intimate details?

I rest my head on the pillow attached to the side of the sauna wall, envisioning the negative energy leaking from my pores. I should be more understanding. What the twins went through was horrific, yet I can't seem to help myself. I'm irritated, and if I'm honest with myself, my feelings are hurt.

"Thank you for taking care of Toby last night."

"Don't change the subject, woman! I want to know what happened!" Rex yells. I barely have time to dodge the water bottle that flies through the steam at my head. My hands lift up, snatching it at the last second, and I twist the top off to guzzle it. I sit it down beside me, smirking at them. I give the ladies a one finger salute.

"I'm almost positive he fucked me with a banana last night."

Blanca chokes, spraying water across the sauna.

"*UGH!* Don't spray your spit on me, hooker!" Rita's disgusted voice cries out as she swipes her towel over her arms. Blanca mumbles an apology.

"Although, I can't be sure." Three sets of eyes land on me. I pause, loving the suspense. "I was blindfolded so I can't be sure. But after he carried me to bed I saw him eating a banana." I shrug as if being blindfolded, tied up, and fucked with fruit was a typical Friday night.

"WAIT BITCH STOP! You were blindfolded?? He fucked you with a banana?? And I thought getting bent over a counter was adventurous." Rex slides down the wall, looking put out. My shoulders bounce with laughter, and by the time we're done, my side cramps.

"I forgot to tell you, it was in the pantry while we were cleaning up from our sip and paint. He tied me up with his belt, covered me in coconut oil and had his way with me."

"Positively scandalized," Blanca whispers.

"Absolutely not! I have never felt more desired in my life. He takes such good care of me after our *harder* sessions."

"Does he know how to have vanilla sex?" Rita deadpans.

I hesitate. Is she being rude again?

She flushes. "I'm not being an asshole. If I'm being honest, I'm jealous as fuck right now. I need to schedule a dick appointment that's *that* interesting."

"We have vanilla sex too. Just not that often. He enjoys–being in control."

"And how about you? Do you enjoy him being in control?"

There's not an ounce of hesitation in me when I answer Blanca. "Absolutely. I trust him irrevocably with my body."

"Do you trust him with your heart?" Blanca asks me.

A stillness falls over me as I give her question the attention it deserves.

Do I trust Kye with my heart? I love him. I know that I love him. Trust and love are not the same. One would think they go hand in hand, but I've loved people I couldn't trust and trusted people I can't love. Kye told me once that he loved me. He last told me in Arizona, though. Does he still love me? Is he as hesitant as I am to admit how we feel to one another? How do I give her an honest response without showing my own insecurities?

"Trusting him with my heart isn't the problem. It's just not the right time." I shrug. "Who knows? After everything settles down and Mitchell leaves us alone, Kye may not want to stick around."

"Look," Rita begins, "I'm sorry for being a cunt. It isn't fair to you or Kye to have to deal with my shit."

I cut her off before she can finish. "It's okay."

Rita throws her hand up to stop me from shrugging off her actions. "My behavior was not okay. This whole scenario has me on edge. I guess I never really dealt with my shit." Her hand reaches up to swipe something under her eye. "Watching you and Tobias go through this–is heartbreaking, and I feel helpless. Regardless, it wasn't cool of me to treat Kye like that. I will make sure to apologize to him today as well."

No one should have to go through watching the horror of their mother being murdered. An adult would be affected, but a kid? The lifelong effects of that trauma… I can't imagine it. "We're solid."

"Fuck yes, we are," Rex says, giving us a small fist pump.

"May I ask an intrusive question?" Blanca's phrasing alerts me to the fact that I'm not going to like the question. But if my friends can be honest with me about their shit, I guess I can do the same. I nod, causing my top knot to fall to the side. I gather my hair as she collects her thoughts, resecuring it to the top of my head. "This won't be phrased correctly, just know I don't mean it the way it sounds. But, why did you stay with Mitchell?"

I deliberate on what to tell them as steam collects on my skin. I consider my friends to be beautiful, successful, and strong women. As much as I adore them, I've always felt self-conscious around them. The twins are both tall and elegant, confident with themselves. Blanca's beauty is something you read about.

Me? I'm average on my best days. My ability to blend into the background anywhere I go has always helped me skate through life. However, It has also hindered me too, sometimes making me feel lonely. Mitchell was the first to give me the attention and time my other girlfriends always received.

How do I explain that without looking like a pathetic fool? They deserve the truth, and I should be able to tell them. It's hard though, admitting out loud that no matter my achievements, I've never felt good enough for that once in a lifetime, all shattering love that I read about.

My inhale is long as I mentally prepare to hash my truth.

"I was a young single mother who had written men off altogether. Being the only breadwinner for Tobias, I worked and attended school full time. It was a struggle. Gods, I can't tell you how many mornings I cried from sleep deprivation. The books tell you that being a mom is the best thing a woman can do in their lifetime. They don't tell you how incredibly lonely it can be, especially for a single one so young. I felt like I would never find someone to grow old with. With what time? Keeping a roof over our heads and gas in the tank took up all of my time. Until one day, I was hired as a bartender, making enough pay to work just a few nights a week. For the first time in my life, I had food, clothes, a cell phone, and when Tobias needed something or I wanted to buy him something, I could.

"When I met Mitchell, it hit me just how much I wanted Tobias to have a dad and not just a father figure. I wanted him to have someone to look up to, and to guide him through life. I was mistaken in believing that person was Mitchell. It turns out that he only wanted to look like he had a family. On our wedding night, I met the first of a long line of women that he was in a relationship with. At first, I stayed because I wanted Tobias to have someone stable. By this time, Mitchell had adopted Toby and it was too late to change it. Then, it was my pride, and if I stayed out of spite, none of the others could have him full time. But after a while, it was the vows that I took on my wedding day. I thought I had married for life, and could love both of us enough for our marriage to work.

"I tried, oh how I tried. I thought maybe if I worked out more, made myself more available to him in the bedroom, and changed how I looked or behaved it would make him love me again. Then, the night I had dreaded came to fruition. Tobias asked to use Mitchell's phone for a school project. Tobias only recently admitted to me what he saw on the phone, and even then. He doesn't go into detail about it. I should have seen the signs. For weeks, he couldn't look or speak to Mitchell." I hear a collective gasp from my friends and someone sniffles. I can't look up to see who it is, my embarrassment is too great. I continue so I can get this over with. " I knew–I knew my baby had seen something awful and that I couldn't stay any longer." I stop needing a moment to collect myself.

Rex must think I'm done because she asks, "How did Kye get involved?"

"Kye was best friends with Mitchell growing up. They had a falling out during college, and when Kye was transferred to Arizona for work, he and Mitchell had it out in the office. Someone thought that having Kye over for dinner would smooth things out. Kye met me, and we formed a quick friendship. I didn't know he remembered me from the bookstore until months later. He has always respected my marriage until we literally bumped into one another on a trip to Flagstaff. We were with separate groups of acquaintances. He seemed really upset to find me on a trip without Mitchell. He asked me to blow my friends off so we could talk. That's when he told me Mitchell was having an affair. I remember asking him how he knew, and he said, it was because Mitchell told him the reason he couldn't be there. It was because he was taking me away for a romantic holiday. I, of course, didn't believe him. I left and went home, only to find my husband in bed with our neighbor. Our children were only months apart in age. I suspected something was happening, but I wasn't brave enough to confront them. I mean, Mitchell barely parented our child, but if his friend from next door called, he would jump to help. I felt like such a fool." I prop my head in my hand, the weight of my past almost too suffocating for me to relive. I now know why Rita wasn't quick to share her past. This fucking sucks.

"That slimy motherfucker."

"The mosquito dick, viagra popping, son of a bitch." The twins yell together. I flash a smile as Blanca steps in to keep us on track.

"Ladies, let her finish."

"Kye confessed that he loved me and wanted to take Tobias and I away after I found out about the affairs. I was so naive. I wanted my marriage to work so I turned Kye away. I told him that I was married to Mitchell and that's where I would stay. I believe I broke something in Kye that day, the way he looked at me, he was…devastated. I never forgave myself for causing him that kind of pain. He was always so kind to Tobias and me. When company trips would happen, he was the only person to pay us any attention. He always remembered the important stuff, like birthdays and special occasions." I go quiet, thinking fondly about the memories I share with Kye. I measure my friends' reactions to what I've told them before I begin anew. "Kye and I had a plan in place. If I wanted out, I had to text him from Mitchell's phone. The words *she needs you* and he would know it was me. We would meet two weeks after his arrival at our favorite chain bookstore at a certain time. So that's what I did. He came for me. Years later, he still came."

"Goddamn."

"Holy Shit."

"That's devotion."

"So, let me get this straight. You two had it planned this whole time? After all these years?" Rex's question doesn't surprise me.

"We made a pact in Arizona, and we kept it," I say.

"One more question from me, and I promise we can put this conversation to bed and go paint our toes," Blanca promises.

"Hmm?"

"Would you have stayed with Mitchell had Tobias not learned about the cheating?" Blanca asks.

"Until my dying day."

With the emotional shit out of the way, we all lay back, giving a collective sigh, allowing the steam of the sauna to cleanse us until we're ready to get out and finish our home spa day.

Rita asks, "where is Tobias now?"

"Kye walked him down to the boat dock to toss a line in."

"Well that's something."

We all laugh together, the heaviness of the conversation forgotten.

34

Shark Bait & Tranquilizers

Kye

"Are there sharks in the water?" Tobias asks me from his camping chair I ordered him last week. His eagerness to use it makes me feel like I ordered the right one. I've never ordered a chair for a kid before. I was sure that I fucked that up.

"Sometimes bull sharks can be found here," I tell him. His head swivels around to stare at me. Pretty sure that is shock on his face. I'm not sure though. I smirk at him. The fishing hat looks ridiculous on him, but his mom made me swear I would make him wear it. Something about getting sunburned. I'm ordering him a cooler one. Not this… God, I can barely look at him. A hat that orange belongs on a runway. Air traffic control would pay top dollar for the thing.

"Are they in there right now?" he asks me.

"I hope not, they'll eat our fish. Should I hook you and toss ya in to test that theory? You're about the right size for shark bait," I tease him.

He resembles a tarsier. His hazel eyes bulge from his head, and his little knuckles are white as they clutch the fishing pole.

Huh…I think I actually scared the kid. Fuck me, this parent shit isn't easy. I approach him, smiling. I bend down to get at eye level with him. Those big eyes never leave my own. Something in my chest constricts. I want to ensure this little dude never looks at me like this again. Well, this makes me feel like shit. "I was joking, Turbo. There's no need to panic."

He studies me, evaluating not only me but the joke itself. Jesus what did Mitchell do to this kid to make him behave this way? When he finally nods, I breathe a sigh of relief.

"Can I sit here too? I think you stole the best spot." He nods his head again, looking out at the river. "Do you see the heron flying over there?"

"Herons can be found on every continent *except* Antarctica." His wrist snaps out, the line on his rod arching through the sky perfectly. This kid is too fucking cool.

"Is that a fact?" I ask him.

"It is." His words are so earnest, that I stop speaking to him momentarily. Tobias has always been a dictionary of fun facts about random things, stats, sports, animals, states, that sort of thing. But I don't remember my little buddy ever being as serious as he has been since that motherfucker hurt his fish. My knuckles crack from holding my rod and reel too tightly. I notice Turbo watching me intently, so I make an effort to relax. The last thing the kid needs is for me to scare him more.

"So Turbo, any tips on making your mom fall in love with me?"

He leans in close to me, so I do the same. Wondering what kind of secrets he's going to share with me. "Dude, you're so toast!" His roar of laughter cracks me up, and soon, I find myself bent at the waist trying to calm down.

"Well, thanks for the vote of confidence, man." My knuckles tap his and I start feeling better about today.

He grins broadly at me, shaking his head before looking at the river. "I'm only half confident because I'm only half a man."

"What makes you believe you're only half of a man?" Assure him.

"Dude, I'm like eight."

"Well, you're infinitely smarter than most of the adults I know."

His pole bends, the line jerking hard. We both jump up, my own pole forgotten.

"Okay, here we go! Here we go! Go slow, pull on the pole, jerk it just a tad. Yup! Just like that, kiddo. Okay, now reel it in–nice and slow. Steady… Keep it steady… Do you have it? Do you need any help?"

"I've got it! I think I've got it! Do I look like I've got it?!" he screams. All I can seem to do is stand here, watching in amazement as this kid who's spent the last eight years worming his way into my heart catches a fucking fish. Hmpt. I think I like this more than I thought I would. I watch him tug the line, jerking the pole back and forth as he slowly reels it in.

"Yeah, Turbo. I think you've got it, buddy."

A sharp, stinging pain stabs me in the neck. I raise my hand and rub the spot on my neck. Fucking bees. Something cold and metal in a tube shape is sticking out of my neck. I yank it out to bring it around to see. My vision swims, the dart coming in and out of focus as I stare at it. No no no, this is not happening. I made sure no one knew where I was. How did she find me? The kid, I have to warn the kid. I have to… My lips move but no sound comes out. Thena will never forgive me for this, is the last thought I have before everything goes black. I'm out before my body hits the dock with a hard thud.

35

Intuition

Thena

"It's getting late, do you think they're alright?" I pace a trail in the rug in the living room, looking out the window that faces the water. Kye said he was taking Tobias to the docks but you can't see them from here. Why are they not back yet?

"Thena, Kye seems very capable. Maybe they decided to see what can be caught in the dark."

I spin towards Blanca. "Kye would have called me. He knows how important communication is with me where Tobias is concerned. I'm telling you, something's not right."

"How about we walk down to the docks and check for ourselves?" I agree with Blanca. We'll get a good laugh out of this once we see how much fun they're having.

My gut is never wrong. Something's not right. "Okay, everyone grab your shoes and a coat. I want to check on them."

"Before we all charge down there and interrupt the whole male bonding thing, have you tried calling or texting?" Rex suggests from her spot by the fireplace.

"No, not all, Rex. I'm just over here panicking for no reason at all." I toss the small mobile device on the table beside Rita. It slides across the table, stopping when it collides with an empty margarita glass.

"Well, there's no reason to be a bitch about it." She sits her glass down and moves with the others to slip on their shoes and jackets. I bite my nail, tasting blood. I would wince over the pain if my nerves weren't currently lit up like a fucking landing strip. Where are you Kincaid?

"Sorry," I mumble to her as I approach.

She wraps me in her arms. "No need to apologize. I get it. I really do."

And she does after what happened to her mother and sister. My phone chimes as the front door swings open, the alarm not fast enough to keep up with the intruder. Kye stands in the doorway, his face ghostly pale. His hands shake as he comes into the room. Relief washes through me for a moment before terror gripes me. Where is Tobias? "Kye, where's Toby?"

He tries to stride past me, heading for his room. His clothes are dirty, his hair disheveled. Is that *blood* on his neck?

"Kincaid, where is Tobias?"

No one moves as four pairs of eyes land on the phone ringing from the table.

I run and jerk it up so I can see the screen. UNKNOWN CALLER.

My eyes clash with Kye's, his hold such anguish that I know… Mitchell has my baby. "You said he was safe with you."

"Answer it."

"YOU SAID HE WAS SAFE WITH YOU!"

"Thena, pick up the phone."

"WHAT DID YOU DO? WHAT DID YOU DO? KYE, YOU SAID HE WAS SAFE WITH YOU!!!! WHAT HAVE YOU DONE???" I scream at him. The phone continues to chime, the rings bouncing off the walls around us. Kye's chest heaves, sweat beading on his forehead, looking like he's in pain. I. Don't. Care. "WHERE'S MY BABY?!?!?!"

He grabs me roughly, the sudden pain bringing my anger down a notch as he does something he's never done before. He yells in my face. "THENA! ANSWER THE GODDAMNED PHONE SO I CAN FIND HIM."

My voice is a broken, hoarse whisper as I plead with him. "What have you done?"

His eyebrows pinch together, his eyes sear into mine as he tells me more firmly and controlled, "I need you to answer that phone and keep whoever is on the other end of that line talking for as long as you can. Do you understand me?"

Paralyzing fear grips me. Who did I trust my child with?

The chiming stops, and the room goes quiet. I hear shuffling behind me, my friends approaching us to lend support. Rita's arms find me first. She lays my head against her chest as she addresses Kye. "Do what you have to, but know this, if something happens to that baby, I will do the same to you tenfold."

He gives a single nod before he stalks off to his room. He comes back holding a laptop and some gear. I'm still trying to determine what it is that he has. Why would he need a laptop? Why are we not calling the police? He has a black box and some cords. He plugs the cords into the box first, before connecting the computer. I stare at him, not knowing the stranger before me.

Blanca's words cut through the room like a knife. "Kincaid, I assume we can expect another call any minute?"

He confirms with another nod.

"I'll start the car, mine is four-wheel drive." She looks around at each of us, we all agree as she adds, "just in case."

"Good idea," he says.

She moves quickly across the room, grabbing her keys. The front door is left open, and I hear the thunder rolling in, as the cold metal in my hands begins to vibrate, and the steady ringing of my phone demolishes the silence of the space. I lift the small device to my ear as I hit the green button on the screen. "He–" I croak and clear my throat. "Hello?"

Static breaks out over the line, the sound of the storm in the background, the weather ramping up to match our dire situation.

"If you want him back, come and get him." A computerized voice tells me.

Chills race down my spine. My stomach tightens as I'm filled with trepidation as the line goes dead. I panic, my eyes finding Kye's as he watches so intently. I know he's hiding something from me. He seems…off. I jump as my phone buzzes again, announcing an incoming text. I try really fucking hard to keep my phone steady as I put the password in. Eight eight two six…

My screen saver appears first. Tobias and I in the pool last month. My vision is obscured by my tears, and blood rushes in my ears until my body feels hot. The blues and greens of the image blur as one. My shirt sleeve is scratchy as I blot both eyes to see clearly. With trembling fingers, I press down on the link in the text, and my world stops spinning.

The photo is grainy, and the flash of the phone is not enough to capture a clear picture of the scene before me. A shadow on half the image makes it hard to decipher, but just enough for me to notice other markers, like the city trash cans and bright white stone bricks that build the retaining walls. There's only one place in Richmond that looks like that.

The small rusted shopping cart sits alone under one of the many bridges down there. A dark box placed inside the cart alerts me to the space my child's body probably occupies. Everything clicks into place. I know where he is, and I trust no one to get to him before me. The dingy yellow light surrounding the box casts a sinister glow on the photo, with the dark murky water taking up the side of the left side of the photo. The canal…

"I know where he is!"

"Let's roll." Rita claps her hands together, bounding from her chair.

"Wait. I want you to ride with me," Kye tells me.

I don't give him the time of day as I yell over my shoulder, already darting out the door, "I think he's under the one-way bridge on Fourteenth Street. Meet me there if you want to be of help."

"I'll drive," Blanca tells me as we all race to the door.

36

The Canal

Thena

"Park here beside the handicap access. There are four of these access ramps along the canal walk, Mitchell would have had to have used one of them to get Tobias down there," I tell Blanca as I hold onto the oh shit handle as she runs up on the curb, her tires squeal as she takes the turn too fast.

Rita complains, "Jesus Christ in an Easter basket."

"Thena, what do we do when we find Toby? Shouldn't we call the cops and wait for them?" Rex's hand finds my shoulder, but I'm already unbuckling my seat belt and prepared to jump out when Blanca stops the car.

"What would I tell them? That my husband damaged his own home? That the father of Tobias took him after I hid him without a custody order? The cops can't help us."

"Thena, Mitchell could be down there with a gun, waiting for you. This is a trap, and we all know it. Even you can't deny the facts," Rex argues.

"Fine, you call the cops and tell them Toby was kidnapped. Tell them where we are. I'm going to go find my child."

"Honey, that isn't fair, we are here with you. Just tell us what you need."

Blanca's honesty causes me a moment's pause. My friends are here with me, but I don't have time for campfire promises right now. Their feelings come last in this situation. I point across the cobblestone street to the canal access point.

"I'm going down there to search between Ninth and Fourteenth. Blanca, you take Rita and Rex with you. Search Eighth down to East Byrd." It goes unsaid that Tobias may not have time to wait for the police to arrive. I don't wait for their responses as I dart across the street.

I run as fast as I can manage on the wet pavement down the handicap ramp that leads to this part of the canal. My eyes dart around everywhere, searching through the dark. The murky water is choppy and green, so deep it resembles obsidian. Its levels are rising from the storms we've had all week. A fear so intense it consumes me and glitches my brain. *What if he's been pushed into the dark water? What if the cart tipped over into the canal? Were his clothes bright enough to reflect in the water or were they neutral colors that would make it hard to see him? What was he wearing tonight?* I can't think as I jog under one of the main walking bridges. It never made sense to me why the city put a walkway beside the canal in the first place. Is it beautiful? Yes, kind of–okay, at certain times throughout the year. Right now, it looks exactly how it's being used–as a place to hold and transport kidnapped victims. Every dark passageway screams *come here if you want to get murdered*. I don't know any humans that would exercise here at night.

The bridges and by-passes crisscross overhead, blocking out the moonlight, not that there is any tonight. Rain clouds lay heavy and thick in the sky. My shoes splash through another deep mud puddle I didn't see, soaking my socks. Mud splatters against my skin and the smell of dirt and filthy water hits me. The smell is repugnant. Gods, there's not a soul down here. I've never felt more alone than I am at this moment, racing to get to my son. I pick up my pace. It's dark and dank in this part. I gag. The smell of fish is overwhelming.

Unaccustomed to cities that aren't packed with people around no matter the time or weather, the empty canal paths surprise me. Shouldn't a city have some people milling around? *WOAH!* I duck below a low-hanging branch on a maple a second before it would have smacked me in the face. My pulse pounding in my ears, I reach up, grab it, and hold on for dear life as I pray for balance, not wanting to lose my footing on the soaked ground. My hand catches on something sticking out from the branch. Ouch.

I look down, and a small trickle of blood drips down my hand. The stinging barely registers as I take off again as soon as my eyes adjust to the near blackout. The antique lamp posts are excellent during the day, when you don't need them. They fucking suck at night time. The orange glow casts an unhelpful halo around them. For all of, I don't know, six goddamned inches. Absolutely fucking useless.

Up ahead, the canal pools in a large circular shape. A significant turning spot in the water for the tourist boats. The cobblestone smooths out here, being a newly added addition. I push myself, my legs pounding harder as I pass the ticket booth and around the bend. Slap, slap, slap, I run as fast as I can, the soles of my shoes giving sound to the quiet. My heart pounds in my chest. Denial rushes through me. This isn't happening. Please, let this be a bad joke. My baby is not out here. Alone in the dark. Scared.

Under an archway of the ancient stone bridge is a lone object. Large enough that I have no doubts. I've found him–my Tobias. I'm closer now, the image forever seared into my brain. *No... No... No...*

The dimly lit walkway casts an ominous glow on top of the box as I approach it. Dread and denial fill me as my body trembles to stay upright. My baby was not put in this box to be discarded as trash. I refuse to believe it. I stop running, and my wet converses are so slippery that I have to catch myself on the side of the cart. Every nightmare a mother has comes to fruition. My body begins to shake as my eyes adjust, my brain catching up to what I'm seeing, and my mind is trying to protect me from what my neurons are processing.

I gasp, choking on sobs that rip from me as if God has placed his hands in my chest and is pulling the sounds from me himself. My baby… My little baby… He can't be inside this… He's home…safe…in his bed…

My fingers thread through the metal squares that twine together to make the basket of the cart, the rusty cold material biting into my flesh. Snot runs from my nose, and I wipe it away, concentrating on formulating a plan. I need to get my son out of this fucking box. I yank out my phone and hit the unlock button while I lay my hands on the box. It's not as wet as it should be. It's been raining all day and the box is barely damp in places. Mitchell must have just put him here before sending the photo. If this box had been here during the storm, it wouldn't have been in this good of shape. He could still be here. I don't care.

I turn on the flashlight to get a better visual. The small amount of light shows more detail. I hit the call icon, tapping the speakerphone button. The ringing over the line is faint yet sounds loud simultaneously. My heart rate picks up as Kye's voicemail kicks in. Where is he? I place my phone in my shirt, facing out to the box so the light illuminates it.

My fingers search for anything on the smooth edges of the tape, looking for a place to tear into it. It's not lost on me that this is a set up and could have been the plan all along. To have me here, distracted. I glance around quickly. I seem to be alone. I begin to tear into the box. Rows and rows of thick black duct tape encompass the box. My nails are digging anywhere I find purchase.

My thoughts become a whirlwind of chaotic mental pictures of my child being tortured, beaten, and left for dead. My desperation skyrockets as I try to pry into the goddamned box. My nail scrapes against some sort of resin, the piece breaking off, piercing the skin between my nail and the hyponychium. I won't stop. I can't stop. I won't stop. I have to get to my child. It's the last obstacle between me and opening this fucking box. Tobias doesn't have this kind of time.

"Tob-Tobias ca-can you hear me, baby?" I sob as I yank, scratch, pull, and dig my nails, trying to scorn the lacquer that coats the thick tape; my nails begin to break. Nothing is stopping me from getting to my baby. Finally! I catch a piece sticking out through the resin on the side of the box. I begin tearing at it with all of my might. My muscles strain, and I place one foot on the cart, the other on the bottom. Pulling with all I've got.

The resin cracks, then splinters giving way. But as it does, so does my leverage on the cart. My hands are still clutching the tape, and I watch as I fall, the tape ripping. And even though this is the oddest time, I hear a voice repeat a line from a movie I once heard. *Miles and miles of tape.* The cart tips over, crashing on top of me. Pinning me to the wet concrete. The sound reverberates, disturbing the silence of the night. *OOMPH!* Blistering pain erupts in my ribs and down my leg. My ankle's tangled in the lower tray of the cart. My hands slide over the box to the cart, I push and kick at the metal until it's off of me. I flip over to my stomach, catching my breath after having the wind knocked out of me.

I crawl to the box, done with the boobytrapped contraction. If Mitchell wants me to bleed for my child, so be it. My hands, soaked in sweat and little pinpricks of blood, rip at the tape. I unfold the origami box flaps, lifting them. I hesitate for a moment, too scared to look. "Toby, baby… Mommy's here." My voice cracks on a raw whisper as my son's dirty blonde head is revealed. Buried under a blanket, pristine in its baby blue material. "Toby… TOBY… TOBYYYYYY… My bab-baby… Nooo… Not my boy. Not my boy." The atrocity of it all, to stuff my baby here.

I gingerly wrap my trembling hands around him, pulling him into my arms so I can remove him from this nightmarish place. Little by little, I'm able to gather him in my arms, his skin smells of the wet mildewed prison, dirt, and wet cardboard. Underneath it is the smell of fresh laundry. Why wrap my baby in a clean blanket just to leave him in this filth? My warmth seeps into him as I bundle him in the blanket I found him with. Relief floods me as I feel his chest rise and fall in short spurts.

I cover my mouth with a bloody hand, clamping it tightly to my lips to hold the sounds of my wails of relief in. His survival is the only thing that matters. I need to get him to a hospital. I search the ground for my phone. I'm unable to locate it, but I remember I'm literally downtown. If I can get him to the top of the street, it's booming with businesses and apartments. Surely there has to be another human in the vicinity. Where the fuck are Kye and the others? Where are the cops?

I stand, my muscles in my legs spasm. I swear when we get out of this, I'll never miss leg day again. Looking down at my child, now covered the best I can, I make one last vow. I will walk through the gates of hell holding Mitchell's decapitated head in my hand with a smile on my face to receive my judgments before he gets the chance to cause my son any more harm.

37

A Crossroads

Thena

My shoes slap against the wet pavement, squelching underneath me. A train crosses the bridge above me, it's too dark to see but I hear the metals grind against each other. My hold tightens around Tobias. The booming sound echoes off the stone retaining wall running the length of the canal. I strain my eyes trying to see ahead. The street lamp overhead flickers, the ominous glow adds another layer of unearthly feelings to my predicament. There are steps somewhere around here. I just need to find them.

Water in the canal splashes behind me, like something has been thrown in. I turn quickly, my ankle throbs from the sudden movement.. Small pants of air leave my mouth as I try to quiet my racing heart. Surely whoever is out there can hear it. This area of the canal is so dark I squint to see. The underlights on the bridge that cross over the pass above me, cast a sinister yellow glow on the water but does nothing to illuminate the walkway. I spin back, knowing we'll be okay if I can get us to the top street or find my friends.

My heart pounds in my chest and my ribs burn. If I get out of this, I swear I'm working out every day. Being a swimmer has given me an edge with stamina, but I need to lift weights. If my son was any heavier or taller, would I be able to carry him to safety?

The smell of rain brushes against me right before the sky opens up, Mother Nature conveying the hopelessness of my very existence in the form of a storm. I clutch my son tighter. His chest rises and falls, against my own, yet his too-still form doesn't bring me any small amount of comfort. He could be dying and I wouldn't know it. I need help.

There! Rounding the bend in the pathway, An area opens up to a staircase that wraps around the hill side. Our way out of this hell hole is just ahead of us.. If I can get to the street at the top, hopefully, a cop or someone will be up there. Limping to the flight of steps I take in the amount before me, murmuring a small prayer for strength before I begin my ascent. My ankle throbs, but I have no choice but to put my body weight on it. I want to cry out even knowing how dangerous that can be for us. I need to be as quiet and as quick as possible. My teeth sink into my lip to stifle the cry I bury so deep in my throat, that it begins to burn. Taking the stairs one at a time, I shuffle Tobias higher on my chest and grit my teeth.

The more I climb, the more rationally I begin to process everything. Why leave my kid in a box if they weren't waiting to take me out? Why go through all the trouble of kidnapping my son if they were just going to let me find him and take him?

None of this makes sense to me. Where's the logic? A loud rumble interrupts my contemplations. Tires squeal on the road above me like someone slammed on the brakes hard and fast. Kye!

"Thena!" Kye's shouts from above. I look back over my shoulder at the bridge that's just above us. I don't see him, but his headlights are shining through a tree at the beginning of the bridge.

"Kye! We're down here!" I yell over the storm. Rain pelts me, weighing down my already soaked clothes and heavy load. I renew my efforts, ignoring the pain in my ankle as the sky rattles above me in a crescendo of thunder. As I crest the top of the landing with Tobias held tightly to my chest, I get an uncomfortable wave of dizziness. My hair plasters itself to my face as I shake my head from side to side to clear my mind. My head swims as the forlorn sense of dread settles in the pit of my stomach. Something isn't right.

As I find my center, I sprint as much as I can with my limp to the left, where the side street connects with the bridge. Kye's truck will be faster than an ambulance. Tobias needs medical attention and fast. "Hang on, baby. Mommy's getting help." I call up ahead for Kye. I should be able to see him now, but all I see are headlights bouncing off the stone archway at the beginning of the bridge.

Was I hallucinating? Fuck me, did I hit my head? I pause under the archway, shielding Tobias from the rain. It's easing up some, but the branches of the trees over the sidewalk sway with the force of the wind. Thunder claps, and I jump back. "If you're going, then fucking move," I say to myself out loud, and Tobias begins to move in my arms. "Hang tight, Son. I'm getting you to Kye. You're gonna be alright." I step out from the shelter the arch provided moving onto the bridge.

Up ahead, Kye's headlights are a beacon of hope plowing forward, I double-time it, gaining ground quickly. The storm is forgotten as we reach the passenger side door. "Hey man, what the fuck…" I stop speaking. The cab's empty, keys in the ignition. It's still running. My spine shivers as my stomach clenches in fear. Where is he? I shift Toby over my shoulder in a fireman's carry, gripping him with one arm. I open the side door to lay him on the seat.

"Mom?" Tobias's weak voice says in warning before the cold barrel of a gun is pressed to the side of my head.

"Hello, love." His voice is as cold as the rain pelting against my skin.

I don't turn as I address him. My tolerance for his behavior is long gone. "Don't put words in your vocabulary you don't understand the meaning of," I deadpan.

The barrel of his gun pushes into my skull with enough force. My head tilts forward some, giving me a clear view of the floorboard. Where I see a pistol, it's compact, concealable. That'll do. "I don't know what you gave my son, or what you thought you accomplished. But whatever you dosed him with is making him sick. He needs medical attention."

There's a slight pause. "I knew that motherfucker had his claws in you, I didn't realize how bad it was until tonight," he accuses, confusion wrinkling my brows.

"What are you talking about?" I ask.

"Is there nothing you two won't do to make me miserable? Huh? Have you not taken enough from me?" The barrel of the gun pushes in harder. I wince.

"Taken from you? You? You're the one suffering? Are you the one drugged and thrown in a fucking box during one of the worst storms in this city's history? Have you noticed we're in the beginning stages of a fucking hurricane?" I yell. Running on adrenaline alone, my arms aching, my head throbbing, and Mitchell's making no sense. I can't do this.

"Is it not bad enough that you're fucking my best friend, but now you want to frame me for kidnapping!" he seethes.

I pause. Tilting my head to the side to contemplate what he's saying. Is he really going to try to get out of this? "You must be delusional if you think you're getting away with this. No matter our problems, my kid is off limits." I step closer to the truck. "Mitchell, I'm putting Tobias in the cab now. Shoot me if you must, but my son's been through enough." I try to see him over my shoulder, but can't see anything. I feel him though, that motherfucker really has a gun to my head. *The nerve of this man.*

"Funny how quickly things change," he muses. "Thena honey, I thought he was *our* son," he mocks me, and my sanity starts to unravel.

"You lost that privilege the moment you hurt him." I lay my son inside, tucking the blanket around him. His eyes are cracked, his pupils dilated.

"Hold on, baby. Mom will be right back." I slide my hand down the front of the seat. My fingers graze the grip just as a hand grabs my hair tight. "Ahh!" I scream at the shock of the pain as I'm pulled back away from the only source of defense I currently have. He forces me to the tailgate, to the opposite side of the bridge. *Well at least he's courteous enough to not shoot me in front of my child,* I think sarcastically.

"Did you think I would let you shoot me, bitch?" I hear the click of the hammer of his gun, it echoes in the silence of the night. I close my eyes, resigned to my fate. My only prayer is that he gets Toby the help he needs. I want to be strong, strong enough to do this. But I can't help the quivering of my bottom lip or the involuntary tremble of my hands as I lift them above my head.

"Turn around. Now." He orders me. I obey. My shoes scuff against the wet asphalt. Our eyes clash and my heart rips out of my chest all over. After everything he's done to us. His dark eyes meet my own with such devastation. I can't breathe as I gasp on a sob. The revolver shakes in his hand as he points it at me.

"So this is it? This is the ending to our story?" I choke.

"I don't see any other way, do you?" his voice is lower than moments before.

I shake my head refusing to believe that he's actually doing this to me, to us. Even after everything he's already done to us. "I loved you, I loved you with every fiber of my being, my soul soared for you. And you plucked my wings." Bawling, unable to keep myself in check, I scream, "YOU DON'T CARE! YOU'RE NOT CAPABLE OF CARING!"

"I didn't mean to."

"You watched as I fell from grace only to hold me in the fire as I burned from the pain. You did that. You did that to me!"

"I didn't mean for you to hurt."

My laugh is humorless as I look at the man I thought was my forever. I search for any sign of the man I married, the man who held our son on sleepless nights, the man who danced with me and loved me well into the night. His eyes have some emotion I'm too bitter to decipher. "You didn't mean to what? Rip the final shreds of my heart apart? You didn't mean to crush me under your demands for perfection? What part did you not mean? Was it the destruction you levied to our home or just the devastation to my heart that you wrecked that you didn't mean? Or was it my… was it my love you didn't mean to take from me? Because I was there! Goddamnit Mitchell, I WAS THERE!!!! You took it freely! And you took it well… TELL ME, MITCHELL! What did you not mean to do???"

"I never meant for it to get this far." The first sign of some emotion shows on his face.

"Well that's fucking great, Mitchell. That's just real great. You probably should have thought about that before you fucking broke our home apart by your own fucking selfishness."

"I thought…"

"You thought what?"

"I don't know…"

"Don't know what?"

"I don't know how to tell you that I'm sorry!"

"Sorry?! Years of pain, years of suffering! Two miscarriages, multiple affairs, stalking, harassment, abuse and now… Now you want to say that you're sorry??? Fuck your sorry! You're sorry won't fix the damage you've done to me or to my child! You put my kid's fish in a fucking blender!" My hands clutch my chest, the pain I've buried rising to the surface. My vision blurs.

"Be quiet," he shushes me. My eye ticks. This fucking man. I want to take the gun from him and shoot him. Multiple times. In the knees, the elbows, the balls. Everywhere.

"Excuse the fuck out of me."

"Be quiet, Thena! Someone's coming."

It's only then that I hear footsteps. I try to see over the bed of the GMC to see who it is. Has Kye found us? I hope so. I could use a fucking hail mary right about now. Vapor rises in the air from someone's heavy breathing. No not, someone. Two people. There are two vapor trails. God, please let this be the cops.

"Thena, go to the driver's side and grab Tobias. I want you to run, don't ask questions. Just fucking do it."

I pivot from my spot but freeze, unable to move. The one person I thought I could trust is stepping out of the dark and coming to stand by the bed of his black ride. *No no no.* The one

I've been wondering where he went tonight instead of rushing to our aid and now I know. Kye Kincaid is shoulder to shoulder with someone I thought I would never see again.

My heart shattering into fragments more than once in a single night is not something I prepared for, nor is it what I expected. My heart is left in ruins as I put the puzzle pieces together. Mitchell had seemed confused and accusatory tonight. Like, I had been harassing him. Absentmindedly, I note the storm has seemed to settle and the wind has died down. Like the world has stopped to see what's going to happen next. A chill seeps deep into my bones, piercing the very foundation of my existence. Kye betrayed me, betrayed Tobias. He was never here to protect us. He never loved us at all. I've been played the fool.

"Well, isn't this sweet?" A cruel female voice cuts through the space. I gasp. Her voice ringing out into the night pulls me back to the day I rushed inside only to find Violet and my husband wrapped in one another's arms. The picture of something more than love. The same lick of jealousy burns through me. Angry, sharp, and molten. He had loved her, and now she will be our doom. And *he's* the one to fucking blame.

38

Consequences

Thena

"Violet," Mitchell starts. She lifts a gun with a silencer. A hissing pop sounds around us, and Mitchell drops to the ground. He lays there, holding his leg screaming. His pain echoes against the night. She fucking shot him. No hello, no fuck you. I mean, I can't say I haven't wanted to do that all night.

"Jesus Christ, Violet! What do you think you're doing?!" Mitchell snivels.

She exhales like a weight has been lifted off her frail shoulders. "That's better."

She approaches us, as gracefully as ever. I notice the subtle changes in her though. She's thinner, her hair pulled tight on top, it doesn't look as full as it once did. She looks older somehow, sadder. I mean, she would have to be something. She just shot a man.

Confused and hurt, I look over her shoulder to Kye. He's still standing beside her, refusing to look at me. His face is drawn tight, movement in the cab over Kye's shoulder draws my attention. Tobias's little head is just over the rim of the back window, his eyes wide, watching everything unfold.

With Violet solely focused on Mitchell's bleeding form on the ground, I zero my attention on Toby. His eyes find mine gradually, almost imperceivable. I shake my head back and forth. Kye notices, of course he does. He glances over, looking stunned as it registers to him that Tobias is here. Like he didn't fucking know this lunatic is the one that took my baby. Bastard. He slowly backs up one step after another until he's by the door.

My heart thunders in my ears, terror takes hold of my heart. Not my baby! Kye takes two fingers and motions for Tobias to lie down quietly. Tobias nods his head, doing as instructed. I have an uncomfortable feeling in my gut, that I won't like what happens next as Violet stands over Mitchell. Only a few feet from me, up close I can see my first impression of her was accurate. She looks like shit.

I step away from Mitchell, my hip brushing the side of the bridge.

"Don't move, princess," Violet warns, swinging the gun towards me before aiming it back at Mitchell.

"I feel like there was an insult implied there," I tell her, fed up with tonight's theatrics. Pissed that my child was dragged into their lover's quarrel. Kye shakes his head, motioning for me to be quiet. Fuck him. No one walks up with Violet and gets a free pass. He can get fucked, too. I never see the butt of the gun until it's too late and pain explodes under my eye. My head snaps back, and I fall against the side of the guardrail. I grip the edges, dragging myself back up, what I assume is blood runs down my face. The warmth of it is in stark contrast to the chill of my body.

"Violet," I hear Kye say in a lethal tone.

I can't help but take note of the rushing water below the bridge. Terror sinks its claws in me as I realize they want to kill us and have the storm dispose of our bodies for them.

"I won't be disrespected by you, you filthy whore," Violet seethes.

"Violet, do anything else to her and my part of the bargain is over," Kye deadpans. I look at him in astonishment.

"Yes, Kincaid," Violet says, looking over to where Kye stands. "You have made this arrangement exorbitantly more difficult."

"It couldn't be avoided."

"What part of fuck her did you confuse with falling in love with her?"

Kye lifts a single shoulder. "The fact that I accomplished both is a feat all on its own, she's stubborn as a mule." His words strike a chord in me, my temper flares. How dare he imply that he loves me after participating in this. *I wonder if Violet will let me borrow her gun?*

"And yet the fool doesn't even realize how deep you are into all of this, does she? Hmm... Does she know you're the one who concocted the very tranquilizer I used on you and the boy?"

I watch on in horror as Kye's body stiffens. His lack of defense tells me all I need to know. He's just like Mitchell, only so much worse. "Violet shut the fuck up right now."

Violet waves the gun my way. "Kye did make an amazing heroic effort to keep you and your kid out of this." She leers between the two of us. "Can it be? Have I finally found Kye Kincaid's kryptonite?"

"We had a deal," he reminds her. Fuck if I know what they are talking about.

"Yes– I suppose you're right. Although the deal was made before I lost–everything. So no, Kincaid our deal is off the table."

"Vi, she and Tobias are innocent in all of this. Please." His voice cracks. This man is great at acting, someone should give him an Oscar.

"Don't act like you care about me now, Kye. At least Mitchell was honest about his betrayal."

"All I have ever done is care about you, Thena. Even when you couldn't care about yourself."

"Oh, that's rich coming from the man standing in the enemy's camp. And while we're on the subject," I turn to Violet, her eyes are holding so much hatred I'm not sure who she's directing it toward, Mitchell or me. I charge forward, wanting to get off this bridge. Preferably alive. If I'm going to live, I need to know what's happening. "What the fuck is going on here?" I demand.

Kye responds before Violet can utter a word. "Brat, if you ever listen to me, let it be now. Shut the fuck up. *Please.*" His tone holds no room for argument, the urgency in it causes me to pause for a moment. I'm missing something here, much larger than a jaded lover. I just don't know what.

Her eyes void of all emotion. I watch in horror as her gloved hand holding the gun lifts to my chest. I watch Kye begin to slowly creep up closer to Violet. He looks terrified.

This is more than a breakup. This is something else. Something…more.

"Violet, don't do it. Think of Lily." I watch the shift in her that's instantaneous. Kye flinches like he's been struck. But Violet's demeanor morphs into unadulterated rage. Her body seems to tremble as she swings the gun back on him screaming in his face.

"Lily…IS…DEAD!" A single tear slips from the corner of her eye, an anguish only a parent could know.

I gasp, covering my mouth with my hands. Sorrow for mother and child rips through me. Oh no. Lily was such a bright little girl. I focus on where my child is hidden, knowing there's nothing I wouldn't do for him. This will crush him. He and Lily were thick as thieves, spending their infant and toddler years together, they rode the same bus to preschool. Everyone used to say they were like brother and…brother and sister…no… No… I refuse to believe it.

It makes sense and it was right under my nose. The nights Vi would come over upset because Lily wouldn't fall asleep so Mitchell would rock her and feed her until she did. All the time he chaperoned at the preschool and offered to give Lily a ride. The zoo trips and slumber parties disguised as Violet needing a break. Violet didn't need a break. Mitchell was helping raise their child and I never suspected… I knew they slept together. It's kind of hard no to know that after walking in on them. But this?

He fathered a child with her. My God, Tobias, and Lily were only months apart in age. I feel faint. My demands for us to move… Right before I caught them, I remember Violet upset, telling us Lily was sick. I never expected it to be that serious though. How could I? Oh God, I forced her hand when I took Lily's father away from her.

Bile rises in my throat, hot and acidic, faster than I can force it back down. I launch my top half over the barrier and vomit in the river, retching until there's nothing left. I dry heave. Disgusted with Mitchell and with myself. I can't look at her. I can't look at any of them.

"It would appear she finally figured it out," Violet sneers.

I ask the question plaguing me, not wanting to know, but knowing that I have to. "You deliberately withheld this from me?"

Mitchell begins to speak, but Kye answers knowing my question was posed to him. "Yes." His voice is hoarse.

Mitchell huffs, offended I'm not addressing him.

I'm well and truly finished with him. This–this is wrong on so many levels. "How long have you known?"

"Almost immediately."

"Be. More. Specific."

"Oh, this is too good. He didn't tell you, did he?" Violet interjects. Her laugh is maniacal as she blurts, "his working with Mitchell wasn't by chance." Mitchell and I both stare at her in shock. "The only thing that happened by chance was him falling in love with you." She rolls her eyes, giving me an unimpressed once over. "You can't seriously think he came over for dinner and never wanted to leave right?"

"Shut the fuck up, Violet." I've never heard that tone from him before and it makes me think there's a lot I don't know.

"By all means, Violet, tonight seems to be one for educating. Tell me."

She glances between the three of us, deciding to lower her gun. She walks a few steps to the opposite side of the bridge. It isn't a large one by any means, in fact, it's a oneway bridge. You know, one of those historical ones that look good for the city but could be more practical.

She leans against it, gazing at us wearily. "I guess I should start at the beginning."

"Violet, please…" Mitchell whines.

Blood has pooled under his leg. I gag a little, hating the sight of it. Yet, I don't feel bad for him. Watching in rapt fascination as his face leeches of color, I nod towards him, not in pity, but because I notice our son watching from the window. I don't want to give his presence away to Violet, so I need to do what I can to make sure he sees as little as possible. "Can I apply pressure to that for him?"

She deliberates and eventually nods.

Squatting down, I have to slide my fingers in the hole of his pants to rip the fabric away, wanting to evaluate the wound. A puncture wound from the bullet, jagged around the edges but it appears to be a clean shot. I untie my sweater from my waist to wrap it around his thigh. He hisses in pain and I make sure to convey how pathetic he is with my stare. I stand back up, wiping the blood on my pants, flinching from my own micro-tears.

Kye's eyes flash. "Are you hurt?" Again, he gets the same droll stare that Mitchell got.

"Please don't pretend to care now. You helped her take my child! I bet she didn't so much kidnap Toby, as you handed him over to her."

He steps forward. A pleading look on his face. Violet laughs. "I am living for this drama. Kincaid, stay where you are. I don't trust you to not play hero. Thena, it's really quite the opposite. He refused to give me the kid. And is only here because he thinks he can stop me from what I'm going to do to you all."

Then why have him here at all? She answers me as if I spoke out loud and I guess I did because she says, "I have a soft spot for Kincaid. However, that only goes to a certain extent. He's on his last chance with me after refusing to give me Tobias."

Kye pierces Violet with a menacing glare. "The boy is off limits."

Violets scoff. "Speaking of the boy… I saw you carry him up the stairs. I thought you would be faster at it seeing how you spend all of your time swimming. Where did he run off too?" She whips her head around to Kye. "Since someone distracted me. I had planned on putting a bullet in Mitchell and you down beside the canal." She shrugs, her raincoat slipping on her frail shoulders. "I guess here will work just as well."

I measure my words before speaking. "I understand your hostility towards Mitchell. I do, but why are my son and I involved in this?"

A tingling sensation begins in the back of my skull running down my spine as she informs me, "My daughter would be alive if it weren't for you. He was going to leave you, you know. We were going to be free to raise our precious baby girl together. But then you got pregnant and he told me…" Agony tears through me at the mention of my own babies I lost. She sniffs, twin rivulets streaming down her face. "He told me no one knew about Lily and me. And that a baby was his chance to make it right with you. Before I knew it, I was pulling into the driveway from the cardiologist after receiving the most devastating news for Lily to find the movers boxing up all of your things. While I watched my baby girl wither and die, *your* child flourished! Your BASTARD LIVED WHILE MINE DIDN'T!!!! IT ISN'T FAIR, IT ISN'T RIGHT!" She bounds up from her perch on the bridge. Coming towards us, pointing the handgun directly at my chest.

POP!

"Violet! NO!!!!" I hear Kye's shout.

It all happens so fast. A shadow falls over me, Mitchell's face inches from my own, his face contorting in pain. The whites of his eyes stand out in the night, I reach out to steady him as he falls on me, his crushing weight threatens to pull me over the side of the bridge. Warm liquid splatters across my face as he coughs. I grab onto him, trying to ignore the blood leaking from his lips onto his chin. "Hang on, Mitchell! Hang on! Kye!" Someone's yelling and some far-off thought, I think for a moment that I need to stop screaming. It's not me… It's Kye.

POP! POP!

Mitchell and I hang suspended in the air as if an angel of death is holding us, gifting us with this moment.

"I'm–" Mitchell coughs, choking again. "I'm so sorry…" Blood is pouring from the wound in his chest, dark wet liquid coats my hands and arms as I try to hold us both up.

"Stop! Mitchell! You're going to be okay," I sob. The skyline lights behind us blur. More popping echoes around us. Mitchell's body jerks again against me. His arms wrap around me tightly. It's only then I realize he's protecting me–from Violet. A scream of rage breaks out against the night. A high shrill of rage as she too realizes that in the end, Mitchell is protecting me from her once again.

"Kye!" I shout.

Mitchell's body slumps against me, pulling me further over the side of the bridge. My feet slip on the gravel, the concrete digs into my hip and lower back. I shake with the raw violence of tonight. I grunt, pushing back against his body. He's too big.

His body shifts, giving me a glimpse of what's happening behind Mitchell's bleeding and still form. My heart stops. Every fear I've ever known comes full circle. Kye is face down on the ground, dark liquid oozing from his shoulder. His groans of pain render the night air. Violet is closer now, standing beside Kye. A look of determination on her face. She raises the gun once more just as I notice a flash of blonde behind her…

My son, Tobias… Tobias is on the bridge and not in the truck where he's supposed to be hiding. The small gun I saw earlier on the floorboard is in his tiny hands. Time slows, the sense of déjà vu almost hypnotic. Screams, loud and agonizing, reach my ears, but I don't feel the movement of my lips. Two things spontaneously happen at once. Tobias pulls the trigger, Violet's body jerks, eyes wide in shock, but he's a moment too late. The blast from the gun had muffled her own as she pulled the trigger. The bullet rips through Mitchell's still body…

As the bullet's trajectory rips through my chest, the force of the kinetic projectile tugs me backward, and gravel grates across the asphalt as my feet shift. My body tilts slowly, as my precarious footing and Mitchell's body weight pull me over the side and we tumble into the open night. The swooshing sound registers briefly as the air rushes up to greet me, tangling my long locks around my neck. My arms windmill for a moment before coming to the same conclusion that my mind has already formed– I'm going to die.

Gravity sucks me down toward the raging river below, I peer up as lightning illuminates everything around me. For the briefest of moments, I observe the little boy, being held back by the dark haired devil beside him. Both wear twin masks of shock and horror. Tiny hands reach out as if he can pluck me from my fate. I lift my hands out to him in the only comfort I can provide. Shouts ring out across the large expanse just before my body breaks against the icy water. Razor blades slice into my body as I shatter into a million pieces as the dark water swallows me. Its swift current wraps its freezing clutches around me as it drags me under to my death. Everything goes black…

39

Origins
Arizona - 5 years before

Thena

The house is quiet as I enter. The heavy wooden door gives a soft click as I close it, greeted only by the cool air of the AC vent running at full blast. I walk into the open floor plan, noting the Chinese cartons on the counter across the way. Children's toys are scattered across the floor, a half empty bottle of wine sits on the table with two glasses.

Mitchell's car is parked in the drive, so he should be here. Usually, while he's at home music booms over the surround sound throughout the house. Where's my family? I set my bags down and look for Toby. He's probably in his room napping. *You're overreacting*, I chastise myself. *Something isn't right*, a voice whispers in my ear. *You're not overreacting, you just don't want to face the facts*. A malicious voice sneers, cutting through my rational thoughts.

I open Tobias's door wide, it bounces off the wall. The two toddlers in the bed react to the sound, but thankfully don't wake up. I tiptoe over to the crib to watch them for a moment. It isn't unusual to see both toddlers together. Mitchell must be helping Violet with Lily again.

"Mitchell, where are you babe?" I search in his places. The back deck, the garage. I come up empty. *HUH?* I walk back into the house, slipping down the hall. I hear a shower turn on. Mitchell, of course. I roll my eyes, breathing a sigh of relief. My overactive imagination is getting the better of me. I laugh a little, finding humor in the fact that men get to shower and relax while on baby duty. If it were me, I would scrub the floors while the babies sleep.

I'm annoyed by my conversation with Kye, which reminds me. I need to speak with Mitchell about Kye and everything he said. It's not healthy for our marriage if we have outsiders trying to work themselves between us. My marriage isn't perfect, but Mitchell loves us. Kye has me fucking second-guessing my husband. In actuality, he's trying to tear my marriage apart.

My anxiety spikes as I approach our bedroom door. I wipe my sweaty palms off on my jean shorts before I open the door. I hate that I have to admit to Mitchell that his best friend accused him of having an affair and that he was in love with me. I've never given the man any reason to pursue me, this is going to tear Mitchell apart.

I have never thought about stepping out of our marriage. I have to be honest. I will tell him what happened today. The god-awful accusations Kye made. The closer to the door I get, the more nauseous I feel. We took a vow to one another, for better or worse. I stiffen, praying this won't turn into an argument.

What I actually fear the most is that my husband won't believe me. I stop, my hand on the door handle questioning if confronting him with Kye's accusations, and declaration is the right thing to do?.. He's been acting so strange lately, it must be work related and I've just been paranoid. *I really should work on my self-esteem.*

His recent behavior aside, I am his wife. I should be more supportive. I should be more considerate of his feelings. I should have more respect for our union. I utterly failed him, us. I allowed another man to cause me to doubt him. I'm sure once I tell him the lies Kye told me, this will all sort itself out. Straightening my spine I wrap my fingers around the ornate handle and turn the knob.

"Honey I'm so happy to be hom-" My feet slide slightly against the plush carpet. I stop moving so fast that my body's reaction time is behind. I catch myself. *This isn't happening.* There's some explanation here, I'm just not seeing it. Denial buries itself deep in my bones. This isn't right. This is not happening. I take a step back, and another, until my back is against our bedroom wall. I stand there. Unmoving, unblinking, not a thought to be had other than... *This isn't right... This isn't right... This isn't right...*

Clasping my hand over my throat in an attempt to hold back the bile rising. Desperate for air, the acrid taste of this morning's breakfast coating my taste buds, I try to stop it from happening. I can't help it. I vomit all over my white carpet that I'm always so proud of keeping pristine. Funny what runs through your mind in moments of shock. Only a fleeting moment of shame courses through me, quickly followed by many more so fast I can't keep up with my emotions. Anger, shock, betrayal, humiliation, denial. This can't be happening. IT IS! IT'S RIGHT IN FRONT OF YOU!

Oh, my gods, Kye wasn't lying. He was trying to tell me, the only person to stand up and admit to it in a room full of people that knew. And no one wanted to tell me a thing. This is worse than a public humiliation; this is a quiet betrayal of everyone around us. They all watched me fall and none reached out to catch me—save one. Thoughts of this morning as Kye confronted me flash by. I slapped him and spit on him for defaming my husband and our marriage.

Vi has the decency to pull the sheet up over her very naked body. Although, I'm not sure decency is the appropriate term to describe anything about her. Ironic that those sheets were purchased for me last Christmas. A late wedding gift from the very woman wrapped in them.

I choke out, "I guess what they say is true."

"I can…" I don't let her finish. I stop her by raising my hand, trying to fend off what I'm having to witness. Her bare ass lying in my bed speaks plenty loud enough.

"Some women only want what they can't have." The joke goes over her head. Of course, it does, because really how fucking cliché can one family be? Mitchell chooses this very moment to walk out of our bathroom wrapped in a towel. A trail of steam and the smell of his cedarwood aftershave follows. I cover my face with my hands, not able to witness anymore. It's like a trainwreck that you can't stop watching, I splay my fingers watching in disgust.

"Babe, I'm good for another round before I have to head to work." The fucktwat doesn't notice me yet. So I take this opportunity to get one more zinger in. Why not? This is funny as fuck.

"I don't know what I'm more upset over," I speak through my fingers, my wedding ring standing out against my tanned skin.

His eyes damn near pop out of his head as he turns to face me. He glances down, noticing the pile of vomit on the floor. His face scrunches up in repulsion. This asshole cheats on me and *he* has the audacity to look revolted by my reaction. My hands drop to my sides.

"The fact that my life has turned into a fucking joke or how she and god knows who else is now aware of how small your dick is." With every word, my voice begins to sound like its own again.

"Baby, I can…" He takes a step toward me but thinks better of it after seeing how cold my eyes are. He moves closer to the bed. To her. My body heats with the intensity of my blood pressure rising. A whooshing sound tunnels through my ears. Their need to steal moments of intimacy is greater than the vows we took to one another.

Mitchell looks between me and his little girlfriend. "Listen, we can talk this out. Our life doesn't have to be a lifetime movie."

"You're absolutely correct. Our life isn't a lifetime movie. Just a really bad B-rated porn flick. We should title it 'The One Pump Chump: A Quick Race To The Finish Line'."

I slide my phone out of my back pocket, turning on the record button. "I will be livestreaming in sixty seconds if you both don't get the fuck out of my house." My focus on them is expressionless. As I push the little red circular icon, the whole world may not know, but *my* entire world did know and they said nothing. The blood in my veins runs cold, and small beads of sweat from the desert heat lay on my skin as the AC kicks on again, I shiver. How could I be so naive? Disgust seeps into me. I do the only thing I can. I point to the door with my free hand. Both jump to grab their belongings.

Pettiness fills my soul; black and oily, past the brink of sanity. Emotions of anger wrap her broken arms around me, holding on tight, pulsating the desire for revenge through me. I should fucking end them both. Tie them to the bed and let this motherfucker burn. But I won't. My own morality trickling into my conscience reminds me of my humanity. I take a deep intake of air. Holding it in for a long moment before exhaling. How should I proceed from here?

Let the world see what they have done to me, to us, to our family. I won't give them the chance to cover their betrayal. This is one secret they won't get to keep.

"You exit this house the same way I found you," I say in a barely audible whisper. The hair on my arms rises, and the chill I felt a moment ago comes back with a vengeance. Both look at me in shock. Did I look that ridiculous when I first came in? Mitchell begins to stammer his face turning red. Oh, he gets to be angry? Funny. We can share our wrath.

"You can't be serious?" He stands to his full, not impressive height. I remember him being taller. More desirable. More…just more. Now all I see is a boy in place of where a man used to be.

"Are you posing that as a question?" I tilt my head to the side, and snap a few photos of them.

"Thena Sullivan!" he squeaks. Weird how men sound when their hands are caught in the cookie jar. My smile is spiteful but I don't care. Fuck. Them.

"Mitchell Sullivan!" I mock him. My disdain is evident. He draws back, a ripple of skepticism on his face like he's never seen me before.

That makes two of us. I don't give a fuck.

Him having a lover, a partner in our bed, this is an act of treachery we will never come back from. He places his hands on his hips. Resigned to having this conversation with me, while both of them are still barely covered. The smell of sex and vomit lingers in the air. "Be reasonable," he tries to placate me.

"The alternative is that… I shoot you." I say flatly. Gods, how did I find him attractive? I ask myself. They do say love is blind.

"What? You would do that over us loving one another?" Vi finally finds her voice.

If I roll my eyes any harder, I'll be looking behind me. Am I serious? No, I'm not. But, they don't have to know that. "I'm dead serious," I bite out between clenched teeth. Taking this opportunity I snap a few more pictures of them. Maybe I should send them out in this year's Christmas cards.

"Mitchell, let's go! We can jump the back gate if need be. I do not want to stay another minute inside with this crazy bitch." She latches onto Mitchell's arm to pull him across the room. I slip in front of them before they can make their exit. Vi and I come precariously close to our chests touching. The hue of her blue eyes dance with barely contained fury.

"You will go out the front. And don't forget Lily." A real smile tugs at my lips. I want them to be as humiliated as I am at this very moment. We can make this an emotional threesome and go through it together.

Her jaw drops open, the color leeches from her perfectly tanned face. "Please! Thena! My kid! She's just a baby, she's innocent in all of this." Of course, she only thinks of her child and not mine. They didn't think about how this would affect my child.

My hair sways around me with the force of my movements as I deny her her request. It should be me wrapped in those sheets, it should have been me he was happy to be with. I gave him everything. I gave him my hopes, my dreams of our future, my body, my child, I took his last name. Unable to keep the swirling thoughts at bay. One after another rushes through me as I stand before Vi and Mitchell.

I gave up everything I cherished about myself for him. He held the moon and the stars, my waves danced on his happiness and crashed upon his shores. Breaking like my fucking heart. My arms begin to involuntarily shake, my body following. Surely one's heart cannot be expected to hold this much pain. I watch in absolute disbelief as Mitchell pulls Vi to his side, holding her, and comforting her.

Hot.

Burning.

Rage.

Consumes me.

I explode.

"You break us, say it can be worked out, and now you comfort her? Your only thoughts are of her and her child? What about our child? We have a kid too! Or did you forget *that* innocent child while you two played house in our home? What do I tell him? How do I tell him that a second man has chosen to abandon us? Hmmm? How could you NOT CARE ABOUT THE BOY YOU CHOSE AS YOUR SON????!!!!" My voice is a deafening plea of pain and disappointment. The two of them swim as tears fill my eyes, flowing over to wet my cheeks. As I break in front of them I realize that neither of them cares. The affair is a glaring reminder of how little Tobias and I are thought of by the two of them. So let them see what they have caused. Mitchell steps forward, his eyes pleading with my own.

"I did not abandon him, this is a minor setback," he says in such a backhanded way I see red. He really called his affair a setback?

"FOR WHO?" I shout. Unable to hide my rising anger. *He does not get to write the narrative here. This will not be swept under the rug. This betrayal ends our marriage and it rewrites our futures. Forever.* I think to myself in astonishment.

"For us, of course." His tone is one I've heard him use countless times before, when he's explaining something to Toby. When he believes the answer should be obvious. It's condescending, it's a manipulation tactic. My already teetering grasp on control snaps.

I launch myself at him. My fist connects with his jaw, giving me a satisfying *crunch*. He yelps jumping away from me, he's not fast enough though and my foot makes a solid impact to his dick. He howls! Dropping to the floor, clutching his disappointing cock and balls. It's music to my ears. I fall down on him, using my body to pin him to the floor. I draw back to hit him again. My baby boy cries from his room. I can't stop though.

My vision is red and I want blood. I don't care where my fist lands. I just want to strike him. Hit him for breaking my heart. Pummel him for his lying, cheating, for ruining our marriage. I can't stop. I won't. Someone is crying, begging for me to get off of him, but I can't. All of my rage and anger from a lifetime of disappointment boils over into a thirst for revenge. I keep swinging and kicking anywhere I can. With every punch I land I hear us, reciting our vows. For better or worse. *Thump!* Till death do we part. *Whack!* I love you Thena Sullivan. *Crunch!* Blood sprays from his nose.

Tears stream down my face, snot hangs from my nose as I rage against the man who promised me forever. My knuckles burst open, someone's crying. Large hands grab me from behind, lifting me clear into the air. My legs kick out, trying to make contact with whoever dared pull me from that motherfucker.

"THENA!" Someone shouts over...is that music? Why is there music playing?

"She's going to kill him!" Vi is shouting over the noise. The panic in her voice is opposite the tone of whoever has hold of me.

"He deserves it for what you two have done." A man's voice breaks through my rage from somewhere behind me. I ignore them, I can't because all of my focus is on the man lying on the ground before me. The one who promised me forever only to throw it back in my face. The scream of agony that tears from my lips as blinding white pain seers in the back of my skull. I feel like I'm drowning and there's nothing to pull me from these depths.

I traded my life for forever to only get a year. One year of borderline happiness. I will fucking kill him. Broad arms wrap around my torso lifting me up. "LET ME GO!" I scream, throwing my head back, not connecting to anything but air. Whoever has me, has me restrained, suspended in midair. I fight for purchase only to find air. I wiggle my body, slamming my head repeatedly into nothing.

"No." A familiar calm voice says in my ear. My body tightens, and tingles race along my skin. I know that voice, someone whispers through my mind.

"Yes," I demand, no one will distract me from this. He deserves so much more than I gave him. I want to castrate him.

"You'll kill him, love." The voice murmurs against my ear, too low for the others to hear. I twist my head to the side so I can look Kye Kincaid in the eyes. I want him to see the truth in them.

"I hope so," I seethe, kicking out again. He lifts me higher as he regards me, his eye tracking my tears. He looks– sad for me. That doesn't make sense. Why would he be sad?

"As much as I would enjoy that. I must decline your request for me to allow you to murder him. Both Tobias and Lily need their mothers." His sobering words have the effect of a tranquilizer. Suddenly too exhausted to fight. Too drained to feel anything but this overwhelming pain in my chest. My body relaxes against his as he slides me down his own, my feet touch the floor and I turn my head hiccupping into his shoulder.

"I know my love. Shhh… It will all be alright soon." His words soothe me as he whispers to me, running his hands through my hair. "Come back to me, my love."

I whimper, devastated for what this will do to Toby.

"She's insane!" Vi screams, running to Mitchell's side now that I seem firmly handled.

Kye never takes his eyes off me as he replies to the duo, "No, she's angry and rightfully so." He glances at Mitchell and Violet. "Count your blessings that I care far more for her and Tobias than you do. Or else I would sit back and enjoy her ending you both."

Mitchell stands, now that he's sure he won't lose a testicle. He grabs a discarded pair of pants from the floor. Probably left from a hasty undressing. *Don't go there Thena.* He yanks them on, not bothering to button or zip them, before storming to the closet. A few moments later he exits holding an overnight bag and a pair of shoes.

"Thank you for this Kye, she's clearly overreacting to this…unfortunate misunderstanding."

"I'm not here for you. I'm here for her."

"Well in any case, if we've learned something from today, it's that Thena obviously has some issues to sort out before I will feel comfortable around her again." He looks down his nose at me in condensation before walking past us, I hear his footsteps pause before he gets to the door. I glance over Kye's shoulder to find Mitchell looking at Vi.

I can't tell if it's longing or just his greed to feel important. She's standing there in my room, wrapped in my sheet, her makeup from last night running down her face like she's the one that's been victimized. Mitchell pins her with a stare. Sweeping his arm out, beckoning her towards the door. She looks mortified, like she has her own form of devastation as her epiphany erupts inside of her. *He doesn't love you.* I think bitterly.

Transfixed on the scene playing out before me, I watch in disgust as she holds the sheet tightly to her body while she races down the hall. A moment later she comes out carrying little Lily in her arms. She pauses one last time in front of Mitchell. "What we spoke about last night…"

"Enough!" He cuts her off. Panic flashes on her face before she covers it, looking resigned. She leaves. Mitchell peers back at me, a flash of something in his eyes. Remorse maybe? Who knows? He takes a step closer to me. Kye stiffens as Mitchell tells me gently, "The firm is sending me out east for a tour of the new location. I wanted to take you with me, but seeing your state of…unrest, it may be best for you and Toby to stay here. After my return, we need to discuss our future."

"You ruined our future." I step closer to Mitchell, Kye's only choice is to release me or move with me. He lets me go. "You ruined any chance of our marriage working the moment you decided to fuck her."

"Nonsense wife. We'll work through this. It's a speed bump. You'll come around." With that Mitchell leaves, walking out of our home with his head held high like he didn't just leave an ocean of devastation in his wake.

My heart aches, a vibration in my chest overwhelming my senses. My knees buckle. Only Kye's arms keep me from collapsing on the floor. We sway from side to side as he murmurs in my ear, "Just one more time, Thena. You can give us just one more time."

My eyebrows pucker in confusion, trying to figure out what he means by his words.

A searing pain rips through me. My gut turns again as electricity runs through me causing every inch of my body to burn. A ringing in my head begins like a taunt. The entirety of my body is on fire. I believe this is death by heartache. I clasp my clammy fingers around Kye's jacket lapels. Realizing that his jacket is wet, I look up, shocked. The room begins to fade as white, hot, blinding... pain cuts through my chest again.

I need to vocalize my pain to Kye. I open my mouth, but no sounds emerge. My head feels like a million shards of glass are ripping through my body. Every nerve is on fire. My shoulder and chest are burning with such intensity I fall to the ground. Finally the screams erupt from me while I jackknife on the floor. My vision dims, darkening around the edges. Kye's standing there, dripping water from his hair, down his lashes onto his cheeks. I hear the drip, drip, drip...drip.

I try again to speak but the words are too hard to form through the pain. Kye's mouth opens to talk to me, his lips rush over and over. Whatever he's trying to say to me is urgent. I squint trying to focus on his lips. His voice is drowned out by water leaking from his mouth. Slowly at first the rivulets trinkle until the liquid quickly becomes a stream of murky dark river water. It begins to gush across the floor. Panic consumes me as I look down wanting to move away from the pool forming below his feet, I have an unnatural fear of the water touching me. I can't move though. I'm stuck. An unseen force is holding me in place. Kye's mouth moves quickly over and over, but I can't understand what he's saying. I can't hear him. I don't hear anything over the roar reverberating through my ears. A blinding bright light burst from our chests and then nothing. Everything goes black...

To be Continued...

Acknowledgement

First and foremost I need to thank every author before me, your words have crafted and molded me into the reader and author that I am today, so thank you.

The words that take up the space in this book would not be possible without my inner circle of loyal and dedicated team members that have pushed me out of my comfort zone and into a new realm of possibilities. Those names, not in any particular order are as follows.

Avanne Michaels- You told me to write, and so here we are. Every hour on the phone, every time I asked you the same question a million times and you having to hold my hand through each meltdown. Thank you sweet woman, the publication of this book is entirely your fault.

Desiree Rodriguez- You big booty bitch of a bestie, you are the definition of perfection and I love you more than my wine. (That's A LOT!)

Jenny Allen- Our friendship is something I will never take for granted. You are a treasure and I, the dragon.

Jennifer Saviano- Trust and believe I value you and the work you put into our friendship. We are the 1%'ers of the author world.

To the entire Books and Beer crew. Angela Rita, Blanca Frappier and Rexy Reads. Thank you for being patient with me as I have gone MIA to finish this book. I look forward to many more years of slumber parties, spilt wine, interviews and shenanigans with each of you.

Luna Laurier any amount of words I put on this paper will never be enough to convey how much our morning chats have kept me going during my time on social media. I don't even mind the rooster in the background. Thank you Luna for caring about some random human enough to pick up the phone to check if she's okay after the vicious cycle of social media got to be too much. I am grateful for the bullies because now I have you to call friend. (Also- feel free to name the baby after me.)

Holly Strakenburg & Kiah McDaniel- Thank you for taking time out of your lives to ALPHA read for me. All 1 million times. You ladies have been amazing.

Sandra the editor, you have been amazing and I can't thank you enough for all the time and support you have given me.

My ARC readers, all 508 of you. Thank you for giving my story a chance. I am truly sorry for the pain you endured while reading my book, just know that without suffering we can never truly appreciate the rainbow at the end of the storm. I hope to see you all with book two.

To my first 68 on tiktok, the OG's of Buttercups. I would love to name each and everyone one of you individually but I feel that would be a breach in privacy, so I will say thank you and leave it there.

To my family you guys have been my rock and have never told me to NOT do this. Mom, I know parts of this story mortified you, just know. You made me so really it's your fault my genetic makeup makes me behave like this. I love you.

Gideon and Jameson, you two kids have been so fun to talk to about certain aspects of this book.I fear for your futures. You do not fear readers' reactions like I do and so some of the ideas you inspired had to be cut from the book, but I will forever keep them as a reminder of the late night conversations with my fellow night owl children. Your imaginations are limitless my sons, I want you both to reach for the stars.

Hayden and Alanna, I hope seeing your Mother fight so hard for her dreams, inspires you to do the same. I love you both and am so proud of the young adults you have turned out to be.

Last but not least. (Children cover your eyes.)

To every man that broke my heart….. Thank you for the inspiration.

About the Author

Nik Robbins is the Mother to 4 beautifully feral and untamable children. When she's not building kingdoms out of legos or being absolutely demolished by her kids in mario kart. She loves traveling and getting swept up in new stories. Nik can be found hosting interviews on Books and Beer every Thursday night at 7:30 P.M EST on Tiktok. Where she and her friends provide a bridge between readers and indie authors while pleasing the masses with live narrations and mediocre jokes.

You can find all of Nik's socials through the link below:

https://linktr.ee/nikrobbins

Thank you readers for taking a chance on my book. If you would like to support my book please leave a review.